CHAPTER 1

Wednesday

My stomach was in knots. I couldn't eat. I couldn't sleep. I couldn't seem to focus in class. Every day that I saw Professor Hunter I had this pathetic hope that things would somehow be the way they were before. But it never happened. He wouldn't even look at me. It was like I didn't exist. This class was becoming unbearable. He didn't have to watch me and take notes on my every word. How was I supposed to do this anymore? I'd rather just stop showing up and fail the class than sit here one more second. The room felt stifling. I was finding it hard to breathe.

"Penny?"

It took me a moment to even realize that someone was addressing me. I looked up at Tyler. He had placed his backpack on the seat in front of the one he used to always sit in. I blinked at him. Why was he talking to me? The last time we spoke he had made it clear we weren't friends. I didn't know what to say to him. I had already tried apologizing. Having everyone mad at me was exhausting. Apparently I was so used to being ignored that I had forgotten how to speak because I just stared at him.

"You okay?" he asked.

I cleared my throat. "I'm fine."

"You don't look fine."

"What?" I didn't need to be insulted right now. If I didn't feel so numb I'd probably burst into tears. But instead I just stared at him.

"Have you been eating?"

"Oh. No. I mean yes, I've been eating."

"When was the last time you ate?"

I thought about it for a minute. I wasn't eating. Everything tasted bland and I felt sick to my stomach. "I went to dinner the other night with Melissa." The other night was a few nights ago. And I barely touched my food. Tyler didn't need to know that.

Tyler grabbed his backpack, placed it on the floor beside my desk, and sat down next to me. He leaned toward me. "You know what, I actually forgot to eat breakfast this morning. Do you want to go get something to eat?"

I looked over at him. "You mean, like, now?"

Tyler shrugged. "Yeah. Let's go."

Professor Hunter walked into the classroom and put his satchel on the desk. *Look at me.* He was wearing a sweater identical to the one he had given me the first time we met. Had he replaced it? Had he replaced me? He looked calm and composed. He looked fine. He always looked completely fine. I missed him so much. But he didn't miss me back. I could feel myself falling apart. *Please look at me. Professor Hunter, look at me!* He didn't glance in my direction. I felt like I was going to throw up. "Okay," I whispered.

Tyler stood up and put his backpack over one shoulder. I quickly grabbed my bag and followed him out of the classroom. Maybe Professor Hunter would notice me now. I looked over my shoulder as I exited out the back door. He was busy writing something on the chalkboard. When had he become just another one of my teachers? The thought was chilling.

"Where are we going?" I asked as I caught up to Tyler.

"There's an IHOP on Main Street. How does that sound?"

"Really good, actually." Him talking to me meant more than he could possibly know. I felt so guilty about what

THE HUNTED SERIES - BOOK 2

THE HUNTED SERIES

Addiction

IVY SMOAK

This book is a work of fiction. Names, characters, places, and incidents are fictitious. Any resemblance to actual persons, living or dead, events, or locales is purely coincidental.

ISBN: 978-1-942381-31-0

2020 Paperback Edition

To reality dating shows, my true addiction.

PART 1

had happened between us. And if he could forgive me, maybe Professor Hunter could too. We walked toward Main Street in silence. The campus was so pretty in the fall. The leaves were bright yellow, orange, and red. The crispness in the air was refreshing. I took a deep breath.

We entered the restaurant and followed the hostess to a booth. I slid in across from Tyler and looked down at the menu. I hoped I had some cash in my backpack. Regardless, I searched for something cheap just in case Tyler insisted on paying.

"I didn't know you were one for playing hooky," Tyler said. He was smiling at me.

"I've been doing a lot of that lately." And I had. I had missed so many Stat classes that I would surely fail my next test. I actually needed to hire a tutor if I didn't want to have to retake it next semester. I looked back down at my menu. I couldn't help but wonder why Tyler was being nice. *He knows. Of course he knows.* Melissa would have told him that Professor Hunter and I were fighting. I refused to think that we were broken up. Needing time didn't mean we had broken up. We were still together. But every time I insisted on the fact that we were still together, it felt more and more like I was lying to myself. It had been two weeks since our fight. And it had been two weeks since he had spoken to me. I wasn't sure how much longer I could lie to myself.

The waitress came over and I ordered some pancakes with scrambled eggs. The delicious aromas in the air made my stomach growl. When the waitress left I looked up at Tyler. He looked genuinely concerned for me.

"Why are you looking at me like that?" I asked. It was making me uncomfortable. I didn't deserve his sympathy.

"Like what?"

"Like I'm a pathetic loser that you pity."

"You're definitely not a pathetic loser." He gave me an encouraging smile.

Then stop looking at me like that! I stared back at him.

"Melissa told me what happened," Tyler said gently.

"Right." Of course she did. She probably still wanted Tyler and me to be together.

"Did you want to talk about it?"

I looked up at him. "I thought you didn't want to be friends with me."

"Penny, I'm sorry I was such a jerk. I was pissed. But I still care about you." He paused for a moment. "Clearly more than he does."

"Tyler..."

"Does he even realize how upset you are?"

"I don't know. I haven't spoken to him."

"Penny. Come on. You deserve better than this. You deserve better than him."

"You don't even know him." I suddenly felt cold. I wrapped my arms around myself.

"I know enough."

He didn't say it, but what he meant was that Professor Hunter was dating a student. And that made Professor Hunter a creepy asshole. But Tyler couldn't be more wrong. I loved Professor Hunter. I loved him more than I even realized I could love someone. And I needed him back. "He's a good guy, Tyler. This whole thing is my fault. I deserve this."

"You deserve to be happy. And he's not making you happy."

"I really don't want to talk about this." I bit my lip. I didn't want to start crying in the middle of the restaurant.

Tyler was quiet for a moment. I could feel his eyes on me. "I think you should report what happened to the dean."

I winced at his words. I should have known that's why he wanted to talk to me. "Tyler, you don't even know the whole story."

"The whole story doesn't matter. All that matters is that he broke the rules."

"I broke the rules too." I pushed him every chance I got. Blatantly flirting with him in class, texting him, not leaving him alone when he had asked me to. "I wanted this. Probably more than he did." Clearly more than he did. *If he wanted this, wouldn't he have forgiven me by now?* The thought made my stomach churn.

The waitress put our food down in front of us. I was no longer hungry. The realization that Professor Hunter didn't want me suddenly felt like a fresh wound. I slowly cut into my pancakes and took a bite. It didn't taste like anything.

"Just think about it, okay?" Tyler continued.

No! "Okay."

We ate in silence. I chewed and swallowed and tried not to make a disgusted face.

"Are you excited for your birthday?" Tyler asked as he pushed his plate to the side.

My birthday. There was nothing I wanted more than to spend my birthday with Professor Hunter. But it was tomorrow. And he still wasn't talking to me. I didn't have any plans for my actual birthday. Melissa had planned our joint birthday party for Friday. It was still costume themed. And it was being held at Tyler and Josh's frat house. I wasn't looking forward to it at all. Whenever Melissa asked me about any of the details I'd just mumble yes to all her plans. I figured I just wouldn't go. I realized I hadn't answered Tyler's question. "I guess."

Tyler laughed. "You don't sound excited."

A month ago I was thrilled that I would be turning 20 soon. I didn't want to be a teenager. I wanted to be more mature and for Professor Hunter to want me. But now I was just sad. Turning 20 seemed like a big deal. I had been so wrapped up in the idea of what Professor Hunter thought about my age that I hadn't taken into account how I really felt about turning 20. "I feel old."

"That's because you haven't been eating."

I laughed. It sounded strange in my throat. "You know what I mean. I won't be a teenager anymore. I'm an old lady."

Tyler laughed. "Coming from a 21 year old, 20 isn't so bad. And you aren't an old lady. You only have a few wrinkles."

"What?"

"I'm just kidding," Tyler laughed. "You don't have any wrinkles. You're perfect."

Perfect. I looked down at my half eaten pancakes. He still liked me. *How could he still like me?* I had an affair with our professor. I had lied to him. I was far from perfect. His compliment was off-putting and I could feel my face flush.

"Do you have any plans for tomorrow night?" he asked.

"Just hanging out with Melissa."

"Then we'll celebrate Friday I guess." Tyler pulled his cell phone out of his jeans and looked at the screen. "I have to get to my next class because I have a test." He put a twenty dollar bill on the table.

"I can pay this time," I said. I opened up my backpack to grab some money.

"Happy early birthday, Penny. I'll see you on Friday." He gave me one last smile and walked away.

CHAPTER 2

Thursday

I had never understood what Professor Hunter saw in me. Had he fallen for me because I was so bold? If that was it, no wonder he was ignoring me now. I felt like a small fragment of the person that I was just a few weeks ago. I had to shake this feeling. My birthday was flying by in a blur. Tons of people had wished me a happy birthday, but none of them had been Professor Hunter. I needed to accept the fact that we were done. It was a tryst. It was only for a month. I had taken everything too seriously. He was my professor. He was older than me. He was married for Christ's sake. It wasn't going anywhere.

I opened up my text that I had gotten from Tyler that morning: "Penny, I hope you have a fantastic birthday. I can't wait to see you tomorrow and celebrate. Even though you're old now, to me you'll always be perfect. Wrinkles and all."

I smiled as I looked down at the words. Tyler was the sweetest guy I had ever known. But I didn't think I could date him. I couldn't take being hurt anymore. Being an old cat lady was sounding better and better every day.

Melissa came into the room with a package in her hands. "Penny!"

"Hey," I said with as much enthusiasm as I could muster. I eyed the package in her hands. She had already given me a birthday gift. It was a dress that was far too short and cupcakes that I had already eaten way too many of. At least I had gotten my appetite back for birthday cupcakes.

She walked over to my bed and placed the box down on my bed. "This is for you."

"But you already got me enough."

"It's not from me."

"Who is it from?"

Melissa sat down on my bed. "It doesn't say. It's just addressed to you. Open it, Penny!"

For a moment I let myself believe it was from Professor Hunter. My heart rate accelerated. *He actually remembered.* I grabbed scissors off my desk, cut through the tape, and ripped open the box. I opened the card and looked down at the familiar handwriting. My mom's writing.

Enjoy your day, sweetie. I can't believe our little Penny is 20! Call us when you get a chance. We love you!
-Mom & Dad

My heart fell. *What is wrong with me?* "It's from my parents."

"Oh." Melissa had been hoping for the same thing as me.

I looked through the package. It was all my favorite snack foods. Cheez-Its, white cheddar popcorn, gummy bears, Starbursts, Pringles, and a bunch of other delicious cheesy or sweet treats. And there was a check with a note saying I had to spend it on myself. I had a habit of always putting any money I got in the bank. But if they specifically said I needed to spend it, it was usually enough of a guilt trip to make me. I smiled up at Melissa.

"I'm sorry," she said.

"I don't know how to accept that it's over." I could feel the tears welling in my eyes. I didn't want to think about this on my birthday.

Melissa jumped off my bed. "Let's go out."

"I don't want to." I wiped my eyes.

"Penny. The best way to get over someone is to get under someone else."

"Don't be gross."

"Come on. Get dressed."

"It's my birthday, I want to stay in. Besides, we're having a party tomorrow."

"Yeah. Which doesn't mean tonight has to be lame." Melissa pulled out an outfit from her closet and tossed it at me.

"Melissa..."

"You need to stop moping around. It's James' loss."

It didn't feel that way. I felt like I was the one losing everything. I looked down at my phone. I had been checking it constantly all day, waiting for a text from Professor Hunter. Just a simple birthday wish. That's all I wanted. But my screen was blank. I slid off the bed and started to get dressed. Maybe Melissa was right.

***

I sat in the bathroom stall and pulled out my phone. I could hear the music from the bar. *Please. Please have texted me.* It was past midnight. My birthday was over. I slid my finger across the screen on my phone. Nothing. Professor Hunter hadn't even sent me a generic happy birthday text. The whole day I had been waiting. I couldn't enjoy myself. I had been in so much pain for weeks. And he didn't care. That's what it came down to. He no longer cared about me.

I quickly typed out a message to him. "I had a great birthday. Thanks for remembering, Professor Hunter. I assume you had something super fancy and prestigious to do tonight. Sorry I wasted so much of your precious time. I hope you have a great life." I pressed send before I could change my mind. He was such an asshole. I had made one mistake. And it was only because I knew he'd freak out. Which he did. *It really is over.*

I found myself wishing that I had never met him. That I had never gotten tied up in this awful, painful relationship, or lack thereof. I had been so consumed in him that I had completely lost myself. I was addicted to the way he had made me feel. But I wasn't addicted to feeling invisible. If he didn't want me, then why was I waiting for him? I put my phone back into my jacket pocket and put my face in my hands. I had never had a boyfriend to spend my birthday with. After a week had passed without hearing from Professor Hunter, a small part of me thought he'd surprise me on my birthday. He'd show up and kiss me and sweep me off my feet. What kind of fairytale was I living in? I thought about when I had told him I felt like a Disney princess. I lifted my face out of my hands. Professor Hunter wasn't my prince. I needed him tonight. I needed him and he hadn't shown up. I stood up and left the stall. I washed my hands without looking in the mirror.

I went back into the bar and glanced around for Melissa. I reached her on the dance floor. "Come on, let's go," I said to her.

"Boo!"

I couldn't help but laugh. I grabbed her arm and we began to walk out of the bar and back onto Main Street.

"I can't believe you didn't talk to anyone," Melissa said.

"The last thing I need is another guy in my life."

"Yeah...I don't think you know how to get over someone at all."

"I just want to be single for awhile." *Single.* I swallowed hard.

Melissa rolled her eyes at me. Melissa suddenly stopped walking, almost causing me to fall over. "Shit, is that him?" Melissa asked.

I followed Melissa's gaze. There was a man sitting on a bench up ahead. His elbows were on his knees and his hands were in his hair. He was staring at the ground. He was wearing shorts, a hoodie, and sneakers. It looked like he had just been on a run. It was undoubtedly Professor Hunter.

"Holy crap." I pushed Melissa into a side street between two buildings and ducked in behind her.

"Is it him?" she asked.

"Yes." I peered out from behind the wall. He looked distraught. I thought about the text I had sent him a few minutes ago. *Is that why he's upset?* He wasn't looking at his cell phone. He was just staring at the ground.

"So why are we hiding? Go talk to him. Obviously you want to."

"I can't." Professor Hunter always looked so poised in class. Was he actually falling apart too? Did he miss me as much as I missed him? I wanted to run over to him and kiss him. I didn't want him to be in pain. But it wasn't necessarily me that was causing him pain. The thought was numbing. "I can't," I repeated.

I watched as he pulled an envelope out of his pocket. He put his hands in the middle of it and was about to rip in half but stopped. He tossed it on the bench beside him, put his elbows back on his knees, and his face in his hands.

I stopped looking and leaned against the brick wall. Whatever was in that envelope was why he was upset. He wasn't missing me. "Melissa." It was so hard to swallow reality. "Please, I can't."

"Okay, this way," Melissa said and grabbed my hand.

I looked at Professor Hunter one more time before following Melissa down the alley. Seeing him like that made it feel like he had only just left me. The wound was still fresh. And I was beginning to think it would never heal.

But for the first time since he had left me in his apartment, I felt a glimmer of hope. There was no basis for it. He was clearly upset about the contents of the envelope. But I hadn't been eating. And I hadn't been sleeping. All I wanted to see was that he was upset too. Maybe he wanted me back as much as I wanted him.

CHAPTER 3

Friday

I woke up to the sound of my phone buzzing. My head was pounding. Melissa was a terrible influence. I grabbed my aching forehead in one hand and my cell phone in my other. I slid my finger across the screen.

It was a text from Tyler: "Class is canceled! See you tonight, Penny!"

I quickly opened up my email. There was one waiting from Professor Hunter. I clicked on it and read the message.

Comm 212 is canceled this morning. Please spend the weekend thinking about your next speech - describing how something works. Everyone with last names beginning with A through M will be going Wednesday, and everyone else will go on Friday. I'm looking forward to hearing your speeches.
- Professor J. Hunter

Why had he canceled class? I needed to see him. I needed to talk to him. I bit my lip. He never answered my calls, emails, or texts. What was I doing? I was being a stalker. Enough was enough. His problems were no longer mine.

I typed out a text to Tyler. "Can't wait!"

But I could wait. I didn't want to go to the party tonight. I didn't want to dress up in a stupid costume. All I wanted was to see Professor Hunter.

***

I walked down Main Street toward Professor Hunter's apartment building. I should have been going to the dining hall to grab lunch, but I couldn't resist. Besides, it was almost on the way. Actually it wasn't. It was in the complete opposite direction. My stalker tendencies were out of control. I stopped outside of his building. If I could just see him through his window to see if he was okay.

"So who is it that you're looking for exactly?"

I looked over and saw a man staring down at me. He was wearing jeans and a t-shirt, and was already sporting a five o'clock shadow. He looked familiar but it took me a second to place him. It was the man from the elevator; the one who had seen me flee from the building wearing just one of Professor Hunter's t-shirts. And who had probably seen even more of me when I had fallen.

Oh God. "Oh, umm...I'm not looking for anyone."

"No?"

"No. I'm just...admiring the architecture."

The man laughed. "You're a bad liar."

I looked back up toward Professor Hunter's window. He wasn't there. "Yeah, you caught me."

"So you were running away before, and now you can no longer get in?"

"Something like that."

"Sounds dramatic."

I couldn't help but laugh. "I guess it is."

"Isn't that rather exhausting?"

I turned toward him. "Yes." That's exactly how I felt. I was completely and utterly exhausted.

He put his hand out. "I'm Brendan, by the way."

"Penny." I shook his hand.

"It's nice to meet you, Penny."

I smiled at him, but only half heartedly. If Professor Hunter had canceled class and wasn't in his apartment, then where was he? My stomach churned. I couldn't help but let my mind wander to his soon-to-be ex wife. Maybe our fight had led him back to her. I felt like I was going to be sick.

"Is there a message you'd like me to relay to this person that you're stalking?"

"I'm not stalking him."

"Mhm."

I looked over at Brendan. He was eyeing me curiously. He looked older than me, possibly older than Professor Hunter. He was handsome in a rugged way. For some reason he didn't look like he belonged in such an extravagant apartment. I shook my head. There was no reason to assess this stranger. I had enough going on right now. Besides, he clearly thought I was nuts. "I should probably go."

"Penny?" he said before I started to walk away.

I looked back up at him.

"If you ever decide you're done being exhausted, how about you give me a call." He handed me his business card.

I grabbed it but didn't read it. "What, are you a therapist or something?"

Brendan laughed. "No." He gave me a funny look.

I just stared back at him.

"No." He smiled at me. "I'd like to take you to dinner."

"Are you seriously hitting on me? Even though you know I'm a crazy stalker?" I swallowed hard. I don't know why I had said that. Now he really would think I was crazy. Not that it mattered, because I was.

"Actually, I think your behavior is endearing."

"Endearing?"

Brendan shrugged.

"I'm sorry, but I'm seeing someone."

"How about I pick you up at eight?"

"What? I can't, I just told you."

"Are you referring to the man you're stalking? Even though I'm not a therapist, I do have some advice for you."

Normally I'd be horrified at someone saying these things to me. But I needed advice. An outside perspective could be just what I needed. "And what is your advice?"

"Trying this hard to make something work sometimes means it's not meant to."

I looked back up at Professor Hunter's window. "That's what I'm afraid of."

"So maybe you can give me a call when you figure things out."

"Assuming that I'll follow your advice."

"It's good advice."

It was. But it wasn't advice that I wanted to hear. "How old are you?"

Brendan smiled. "Does that matter?"

"Yes, it does."

"I'm 29."

"So you're not a student here?"

"No, I'm not."

"I am."

"I figured that." He nodded at my backpack.

"And I only just turned 20 yesterday."

"Well, happy belated birthday, Penny."

"That doesn't horrify you?"

"That you're 20? Why would that horrify me?"

I shrugged. *Because it horrified him.*

"I have to say though, you do look older than 20."

Maybe that was the problem. If I looked older than my age it could have led Professor Hunter astray.

"Have you had lunch?" Brendan pressed.

"No. I was actually just on my way to the dining hall. I should get going."

"Come with me." Brendan turned and started to walk down Main Street.

I stood frozen. I looked down the road toward the dining hall and then back toward Brendan. He stopped and turned around.

"You coming?"

I took a deep breath and followed him. I wasn't sure what I was doing. Brendan was a stranger. And for some reason it seemed easy to talk to him. Maybe he wasn't a therapist, but talking to him might help me work out my problems.

We walked up to a small stand outside of the Five and Dime. He ordered two hotdogs with the works and handed one to me. We walked to a nearby bench and sat down.

"This is delicious," I said after taking a bite. The only thing I really had an appetite for recently was cupcakes. It was a nice surprise to want something savory.

"It's good to know that you like meat in your mouth."

I choked on my bite. Had I imagined him saying that? I looked up at him and cleared my throat. "What did you say?"

He was smiling down at me. "You've never had one of these?" he asked, ignoring my question. "You've lived on campus for awhile, how could you pass by here and not try a hotdog? What is wrong with you?"

I laughed. "I never knew hotdogs could be this good. Thanks for this."

"No problem. See, eating with me isn't so bad. I'm not sure why you turned down my dinner invitation so vehemently."

"I'm sorry. I'm kind of going through some stuff right now. I'm really not in any place to start dating someone."

"Dating? That's rather forward of you. I asked you on one date. No strings attached."

"What, do you only do one night stands or something?" Melissa's advice came back to me. The best way to get over someone is by getting under someone else. I shook my head. *Ridiculous.*

"No, not always."

"So you're kind of a slut." I quickly took another bite of the hotdog. *Why had I just said that?*

Brendan laughed. "I like to live in the moment is all. Sometimes it's best to move on to better things." He raised his eyebrow. He was referring to him being better than Professor Hunter. He was rather full of himself.

"So you've never been heartbroken?"

"Is that what you are?"

I looked at the traffic passing through Main Street. "Yes."

"You're young. You'll get over him."

I wasn't sure how those two things necessarily went together. But maybe he was right. I just needed time. "If you're not a student or a therapist, what do you do?"

"You mean, how can I afford to live in that apartment building?"

"No, that's not..."

"It's fine." He smiled. "Actually, I wouldn't be able to. But I designed it. They comped me a small apartment."

"Oh. So you should have been flattered when I said I was admiring the architecture."

"I would have been if you weren't lying."

"I wasn't really. It is a nice building." My phone buzzed. I grabbed it and looked at the alarm. "I have to get to class."

Brendan stood up and put his hand out for me. I grabbed it and he pulled me into him. I gulped. His hands slid down my cheeks to my neck. His palms were rough.

He pulled my face toward his and kissed me. I immediately kissed him back. His experienced tongue made me completely forget that we were making out in the middle of Main Street. He placed one last hard kiss against my lips before moving his face away from mine.

"Thank you for the kiss," I said weakly. "I mean lunch. Thank you for lunch. Well, and the kiss."

Brendan was smiling at me. It looked like he was holding back from laughing. "I look forward to your call, Penny." He let go of my face and walked back toward his apartment building.

CHAPTER 4

Friday

"God that's hot," Melissa said.

"It was." I had relayed the story of running into the handsome stranger outside Professor Hunter's apartment building. My skin still tingled where he had touched my cheek.

"Now *he* completely understands how to get over someone. You should have just followed him right into his apartment."

"Melissa!"

"Penny!" she said sarcastically.

I actually had wanted to. But I liked the idea of it more than actually doing it. It was comforting to know just because Professor Hunter had rejected me, it didn't mean that I wasn't still desirable. I was starting to think that Melissa's advice had some merit. I didn't want to go sleep around with a bunch of strangers, but maybe kissing a few wouldn't hurt. Besides, I had already slept with my professor. Anything I did from here on out couldn't possibly be worse than that. So what did it matter.

And now I was actually looking forward to the party. Normally I'd be horrified to be wearing a costume like this, but tonight I felt sexy and confident. I had let Melissa talk me into buying it when I was still with Professor Hunter. I stood back from the mirror and examined my outfit. The dress was so short that it was basically a green bathing suit. Ivy encircled my arms and legs. I had applied green eye shadow and matching lipstick. And to make my hair crazier than usual, I had diffused it.

"I can't believe you've never dressed up as Poison Ivy before," Melissa said and turned to me. "It's the perfect Halloween costume for you. You look amazing."

"Thanks, Catwoman."

Melissa laughed. She was wearing a tight leather onesie and matching black cat ears. "Pretty sexy, huh?"

"Mhm." I looked back in the mirror. The old Penny would never wear something like this. But she was gone. I wasn't innocent anymore. This was the new me. I was going to let go and have fun tonight if it was the last thing I did. I was going to take Brendan's advice and live in the moment. I was done being upset about Professor Hunter. Fuck him. Yes I was young. And it was time to start acting like it. I strapped on the green, platform stilettos that matched my costume.

Melissa poured us each a shot. I downed it. We each had a second one too.

"Can I have one more?" I asked. I was ready to let loose. Alcohol helped.

"Absolutely." She poured us each another and I downed that one too.

I took a deep breath and glanced in the mirror one last time. "Let's go," I said. I grabbed her arm and we made our way out of our dorm. "It's so cold."

"We'll be there soon. Definitely not worth bringing coats. We'd probably just lose them."

"Definitely." I was trying to be less like myself, but I still wished that I had a jacket.

When we arrived at the frat house, the music was already blaring. It almost felt like the ground was shaking. Or maybe it just felt like that because I had already had three shots. We walked in the front door and looked around.

"Hey, birthday girl." Tyler smiled at me and walked over to us. He was wearing all black with a mask that covered just around his eyes. And a sword was strapped to his belt.

"Tyler!" I threw my arms around him.

"Whoa. Did you pregame or something?" Tyler kept his hand on my waist when I let go of his neck.

"We had a few shots before coming here," Melissa said. "Where's Josh?"

"Setting up the keg in the basement."

"I will see you two later. Remember that advice I gave you, Penny." Melissa gave me a not so subtle wink and left to find Josh.

"Tyler." I traced my finger along his sword. "Your sword is huge." I giggled to myself.

"You are so drunk," he laughed.

"No. No, I'm not. I'm just happy. It's my birthday party!"

"Well I'm glad you're happy."

"Are you?" I looked into his blue eyes. It was easy to get lost in them.

"Look, Penny, I'm sorry about the other day. It's none of my business whether you report Professor Hunter..."

"No, I am. I'm so sorry about everything. I've been such an idiot."

"Yes, you have." He was smiling at me.

"Tyler," I said teasingly and shoved his shoulder. "What are you supposed to be anyway?"

Tyler let go of my waist and stepped back. "You don't know?"

"Zorro?"

"What? No, I'm not Zorro. I can't believe you don't recognize me from your favorite movie."

"Oh my God, you're Westley?!"

"Technically the Dread Pirate Roberts, but yes."

"You're Westley! Tyler that's so sweet. God, you're like the sweetest guy ever. I can't believe you dressed up for me."

"Well it is your birthday party."

I stepped toward him and leaned in close. "Is your mustache real?"

"Does it look fake?"

I rubbed my index finger along his upper lip.

"What's the verdict?"

I kept my hand on his face. I gulped. I wanted him to kiss me. I wanted to get over Professor Hunter. "You're my Westley."

"As you wish." Tyler grabbed my waist and pulled me against him.

For weeks I had felt empty. I didn't want to feel empty anymore. I grabbed both sides of his face and kissed him. His kisses were familiar now. Soft and loving, yet enticing. I didn't flinch when his hands drifted to my ass. I liked his hands on me. There had been so many almosts with him. Tonight wouldn't be an almost. I was finally going to have him. I grabbed his collar and pulled him down so that I wouldn't have to stand on my tiptoes. I wanted him to pick me up and take me to his room. I wanted all of him.

"Oh my God." I released his collar. "I'm so sorry." I took a step back but Tyler grabbed my wrist.

"Penny, what's wrong?"

"Natalie. You're still going out with Natalie. How do I keep forgetting about her? Geez, is she here?" I looked around the room. There weren't any girls staring at us. Maybe she wasn't here yet. I needed to get out of here.

Tyler sighed. "I'm not going out with her anymore."

I took a step back toward him. "Why?"

"I stopped seeing her after you and I almost...after we...well, after you and I almost had sex."

"Why?" I asked again.

Tyler took a deep breath. He let go of my wrist and leaned back against the wall behind him. He rubbed the side of his neck. He finally looked back at me. "Because I realized that I couldn't stop thinking about you."

It felt like my heart was beating out of my chest. "Are you still thinking about me?"

"Always." He said it without hesitation. He was so sure of what he wanted. I wanted to be sure for him.

"Penny! Tyler!" Melissa came up to us.

I reluctantly broke my eye contact with Tyler. He hadn't said it, but it felt like he loved me. How could he love me? I had been so awful to him. But I liked him. I really liked him. It still felt like my heart was broken though. A part of it was still with Professor Hunter. Would I ever get that part back? Would being with Tyler help? Or would it just make everything worse?

Melissa shoved cups of beer into both of our hands. "Come on! Let's dance!"

"But..." I tried to say. Melissa grabbed my arm and pulled me toward the basement. I looked back at Tyler.

He shook his head and started to follow us.

We made our way down the steps. The room was dark except for a strobe light. I drank a few sips of beer so that it wouldn't spill while I was dancing. Melissa pulled me into the middle of the dance floor. I let my body move to the beat of the music. Before I knew it, two hands were at my waist. Tyler pulled my waist into him. I began to grind against him.

"I thought you didn't like to dance like this?" he yelled over the music.

"That's before I knew that I wanted you."

Tyler pushed my hair to one side and kissed the back of my neck. I felt chills sweep down my spine. I did want him. I had never stopped thinking about him either.

"You never guessed what I am," I said to him.

Tyler spun me around. "Sexy as hell."

I laughed. "I meant my costume."

"Hmmm...a plant?"

"Tyler! You really don't know?"

Tyler laughed. "Of course I know. You're the sexiest Poison Ivy I've ever seen."

I finished the rest of my beer. I grabbed his hand and pulled him off the dance floor and toward the stairs.

"Where are we going?" Tyler asked.

"I still haven't seen your room." With every step I was more and more sure of what I was doing.

"And why do you want to see my room? That's rather forward of you."

He was teasing me about the first time I had ever come here. I smiled at him. "Actually I just want to talk to you."

He looked slightly disappointed. "Okay." He squeezed my hand and led me up the stairs, around the corner, and up the other set of stairs. This time there wasn't a tie on his doorknob. He opened it, let me in, and locked it behind him.

I looked around his room. There were posters of half naked women on the walls and there were several bottles of vodka on his bureau. I picked one up. "What, do you bring girls up here and get them drunk?" I opened it up and took a sip.

"Just you apparently." He sat down on the edge of his bed.

"I'm not drunk." Maybe I was a little drunk. The way he was looking at me made me nervous. I took another sip and put the cap back on. "Oh my God, is this you?" I picked up a picture frame that was next to the bottles. It was a young boy with bright blue eyes and blonde hair next to an older woman that looked a lot like him. It must be his mother. "You were so cute."

Tyler stood up, took the frame out of my hands, and set it back down on the bureau. "What, you don't think I'm cute anymore?" He pretended to look hurt.

"No," I laughed. "You sir," I poked him in the middle of the chest, "are a stud."

Tyler's Adam's apple rose and then fell.

Does he want the same thing that I do?

"What did you want to talk about?" he said softly.

"So is this what you like?" I gestured to the posters on his walls.

"No. I like you. Actually, that reminds me. I have a present for you, Penny."

He turned away from me but I grabbed his arm. His biceps were so muscular. I swallowed hard. I wanted him. I wanted to forget about Professor Hunter and the pain. I wanted to be with someone who wanted me back.

"There's only one thing I want for my birthday that I haven't gotten yet," I said.

"And what is that?"

I untied his mask and let it fall to the ground. He was staring at me so intensely that it made my knees weak. Tyler was the birthday gift I wanted. And I couldn't wait to unwrap him. "You."

"I was hoping you'd say that." He grabbed both sides of my face and kissed me hard.

I put my hands in his hair and kissed him deeper. His hands fell from my face and found the zipper to my costume. There was no hesitation, just desire. He continued to kiss me as he pulled the straps on the dress off my shoulders. I pushed it the rest of the way off. I fumbled with the buttons on his shirt and pushed it off his arms, feeling his biceps as I removed the fabric. I pulled his belt from the loops of his pants. His sword clattered to the ground. I quickly unbuttoned and unzipped his pants. He took a step back from me. He was my Tyler again. Just in his boxers. He stood there examining me.

My heart was beating so fast. Why had he stopped touching me? "Tyler?"

"I'm sorry." He traced his fingers along my clavicle, down past my bra to my stomach. "It just suddenly feels a lot more like it's my birthday than yours." His fingers ran down the front of my thighs, overtop of the ivy encircling my legs, and then back up my inner thighs.

My body trembled in anticipation. Part of me had always wanted Tyler. Professor Hunter had successfully distracted me from that for awhile, but the want was still there. My thoughts quickly turned back to Tyler as he pushed my thong to the side and sunk his finger inside of me.

"Tyler," I moaned.

"You don't know how long I've been waiting for you to say my name like that." He pushed his finger even deeper inside of me as his lips met mine again. I gasped when his finger curved, hitting my G-spot.

"Tyler," I moaned again.

He slid his finger out of me and took a step back, pulling me to my knees. "I want your lips around my cock."

He pushed his boxers to the ground, letting his erection free. I didn't hesitate to oblige. I wanted this as much as he did. I wrapped my lips around his tip. I could already taste his salty pre cum. I was getting wet with just the thought of his thick cock inside of me. My lips slid down his shaft.

"Penny," he said breathlessly.

I tightened my lips and moved up and down his length. He groaned in response. I liked seeing him this way. I took his cock as deep as I could and heard him groan again. I wanted him so badly. I wanted him deep inside of me. I pulled back and looked up into his eyes.

"Tyler."

He opened up a drawer in his bureau and pulled out a condom. I stood up, unhinged my bra, and slid my thong down my thighs. Tyler walked over to me. I had never seen him completely naked before. He was so sexy. His abs, his happy trail, the way he was looking at me. He had never seen me naked before either. The only thing I was wearing were my green high heels and the ivy that was wrapped around my arms and legs.

"You're even sexier than in my dreams," he said as he pulled on the condom.

"You've dreamt of this?"

"I always dream of you." He grabbed my breasts, my waist, my ass. He lightly pushed me onto his bed. The sheets smelled like him. Tyler spread my thighs and leaned down over top of me. His biceps were on either side of my face.

"I've dreamt of you too," I whispered. The image of him fucking me against the chalkboard flittered into my head. The whole class watching us. Just the thought of it made me want him even more.

"This will be better than our dreams." He thrust his cock inside of me.

"Tyler!" I gasped.

He gyrated his hips, hitting all my walls.

Oh my God. I grabbed the back of his head and brought his lips to mine. I wanted to taste him. I wanted to remember every second of this.

He began to move slowly in and out of me. I wanted more. I wanted every inch of him. I let my hands wander down the muscles in his back. I grabbed his ass and pulled him deeper.

"Fuck, Penny," he moaned.

He began to thrust faster and harder than before, stretching me, possessing me.

"Harder!" I groaned.

"You're not as innocent as you look." He grabbed my hands and held them down on either side of my face. His hips moved faster and faster. The feeling of him sliding in and out of me was taking me to the edge.

He pulled me to his chest and rolled over so that I was on top of him. He was staring up at me, waiting to see what I would do to him. I moved my hips. He kept his blue eyes locked on me as I slowly slid up and down his shaft.

"God you're sexy," he said. He grabbed my hips and began to guide me, faster and faster. He stared at my tits as they bounced up and down with every thrust.

I leaned down and grabbed his shoulders to steady myself. He felt so good inside of me. I never wanted it to end.

His hands slid to my breasts. He squeezed them hard. "Every inch of you is perfect," he whispered. He pulled me to his chest again and rolled over so that he was on top of me. He put his hands on either side of my face again and dove deeper still.

"Yes!" I watched his biceps tense as he moved faster and faster.

"Come for me, Penny."

It felt so good. I seemed to have lost control of my body. My orgasm washed over me. "Oh, James," I mumbled. *James? What the fuck.* "Tyler," I panted. "Tyler."

I felt his cock pulse inside of me. *Had he not noticed?*

"Penny," he groaned when he finished. He rolled onto his side, pulling me with him. "Penny, Penny, Penny. What am I going to do with you?" He pushed my bangs out of my face.

"Tyler, that was amazing." I tried to catch my breath.

He studied my face for a moment. "You're not over him, are you?" He looked hurt. Had he heard me say

James? *What is wrong with me?* Maybe he was just worried that I hadn't had long enough to get over James.

"I am over him." I wanted to be. I needed to be. I suddenly felt like I wanted to cry.

Tyler stood up and began to get dressed. He looked back at me as he buttoned up his pants. Being with Tyler was wonderful, but was he right? Tyler walked over and sat down on the edge of the bed. He hadn't put his shirt back on yet and his abs were rather distracting.

"I want you to be happy," he said. He had told me that before. I knew that he meant it. His sincerity made me feel guilty.

"You make me happy, Tyler."

Tyler smiled at me. "I hope so."

"Tyler." I sat up and straddled him. "I'm so happy right now." I ran my hands down his pecks and abs. "I wish we had done that the first night I came here. It would have changed everything."

"But we didn't."

"Tyler..."

"Penny, I want you to be my girlfriend. You know that. It's what I've always wanted. And I'm pretty sure I've made that clear. But I want you to be all in. I don't want to have to worry about you running off with Professor Hunter."

"I am all in." Professor Hunter wanted nothing to do with me. There was no chance I'd run off with him.

"You fucking said his name when you came." He pushed me off of him and stood up. He quickly grabbed his shirt off the ground.

Shit, he did hear. He looked mad.

"I want to be your girlfriend."

"What?"

"You heard me. Tyler, I'm all in."

Tyler stared at me.

"I'm all in."

"Penny." He pulled his shirt on.

"What?"

"You two only just broke up. You're not over him"

"I am." *I'm not.* But I wanted to be. There was nothing left between Professor Hunter and me. He had made that clear. He was over me. I needed to be over him too. Tyler could help me do that.

He leaned down and kissed me. "I want to believe you, I do."

"If you didn't think I was over him then why did you have sex with me?"

"Because you asked me to for your birthday. And I was in no place to argue with you. You don't know how badly I've wanted this."

I suddenly felt cheap. Like I had begged him for sex. "Oh." I quickly grabbed my costume and started to get dressed. I finished zippering up my dress and turned to him.

"Why are you mad?" he asked.

"Because you don't want to be with me. You just wanted to fuck me."

"That's not true, Penny. I just told you I wanted you to be my girlfriend."

"And when I said yes you told me I wasn't ready."

"Because you're not. You haven't even told me what happened between you and Professor Hunter. I don't...I don't trust you."

Trust. It was the same reason why Professor Hunter had left me. My mind was fuzzy and my stomach churned at the memory. "You don't trust me?" *Because I've lied to him too. He shouldn't trust me.* Him saying the same words that Professor Hunter had said to me stung, though. When had I become so untrustworthy? I felt like I couldn't breathe.

"No, I don't trust you. We almost did this before and you went back to him. Do you have any idea how that made me feel?"

"Bad."

"Yeah. Bad." He rubbed the back of his neck with his hand.

"Well that's why he broke up with me. Since you wanted to know."

"Because we almost had sex?"

"No, because he didn't trust me either." I didn't realize how much I had jeopardized my character. I had slept with my professor. I had almost slept with Tyler. I had slept with my professor some more. I had kissed a mere stranger in the afternoon. And then I had fucked Tyler at night. I had lied to everyone, including my best friend, to hide all the terrible things I had done. *What is wrong with me?*

I felt so numb. I thought sleeping with Tyler would make me feel better, but I only felt worse. I felt sleazy.

"I'm sorry," Tyler said. "I didn't know that's why you guys broke up."

"Yeah, well." I shrugged. "Apparently I'm not very trustworthy. So, if you'll excuse me."

"That's not what I meant."

"Then what did you mean?!"

"Damn it, Penny, I don't want to get hurt again."

That was it. That was why Professor Hunter wasn't talking to me. I had hurt him. I had hurt him and I had hurt Tyler. "I don't want to hurt you."

"I know. But you have. Over and over again."

"I'm sorry." I had hurt so many people. I was horrible.

Tyler took a step toward me. He put his hands on my shoulders. "Penny, tonight was amazing. You're worth waiting for. And I'll be waiting when you're ready." He grabbed his mask off the floor and put it back on. "Let's go back to the party." He intertwined his fingers with mine.

"Tyler?"

"Yeah?"

"Do you think it's possible to be in love with two people at the same time?"

"I don't know. All I know is that I don't want to be one of two. Put yourself in my shoes. How would that make you feel?"

My mind flashed to Professor Hunter's wife. "It sucks."

"What do you mean?"

"It *would* suck is what I meant."

"Penny?"

"Really. I just meant it would suck."

"Okay. Sorry, I thought you were saying that that asshole was cheating on you. If that was true I'd..."

"Tyler." I touched his chest. "I don't want to talk about him. It's you. I want to be with you. And I'll prove it to you. I don't know how long it will take, but I'll earn your trust back. Thank you for my birthday gift."

Tyler leaned down and kissed me. It was soft and gentle. It felt a lot more like a goodbye kiss than a we-just-had-sex kiss.

"Come on, let's get back," he said. "There's a cake somewhere with your name on it."

CHAPTER 5

Friday

Melissa and I blew out the candles on our cake. The house was full of people. I barely knew any of them but they all cheered for us.

"Best. Birthday. Ever!" Melissa yelled as she cut us each a slice of cake.

"Yeah." I smiled over at Tyler.

He was leaning against the wall with his arms folded. He still had sex hair. A few buttons at the top of his shirt had been left undone. He looked sexy and he was staring back at me. He nodded his head to the side, gesturing for me to come over. I grabbed two slices of cake and wound my way through the other people. I handed him a plate.

"Thanks for all this," I said.

"Josh and Melissa planned most of it. And of course, there was Melissa's dad, James." He laughed as he took a bite of cake.

My lies had spilled over so quickly about Professor Hunter. "I told you that I was sorry." I lightly nudged his shoulder.

"I know, I'm just messing with you."

"Oh, I almost forgot. I really do have a present for you. Let me go get it."

I grabbed the back of his neck, stood up on my tip-toes, and kissed him. It was tempting to go with him back to his room. "Are you sure you don't want me to come up and try to convince you again that I want to be your girl-friend?" I whispered in his ear.

Tyler laughed. "Your offer is very tempting. I need a few minutes to recover, though. I'll be right back." He kissed my cheek and disappeared into the crowd on the dance floor. I leaned back against the wall. I spotted Melissa and Josh dancing. She looked happy. She had been right, as usual. This party had been a lot of fun. And getting under someone else had helped too. I cringed at myself for thinking it.

"Have a great life?"

My blood turned cold. *Oh God.* I'd know his voice anywhere. I turned and saw Professor Hunter leaning casually on the wall beside me. He was dressed in a plaid button up shirt with a white t-shirt peeping out from underneath. He was wearing slightly baggy jeans, pushed into dirty brown boots. His sleeves were rolled up and he was wearing a knit hat. It looked like he hadn't shaved in a few days. He was carrying an axe. Fake. Hopefully. My heart was beating out of my chest. God he looked good as a lumberjack. And young. He blended in perfectly with college students even though he wasn't wearing a mask.

It seemed like I was imagining him. He hadn't looked at me, let alone talk to me, in weeks. I closed my eyes for a second and opened them again. He was still standing there, staring at me intently. It took me a second to register his words. *Have a great life.* I had said that to him in the text from my birthday. I took a deep breath. All the happiness I had felt tonight seemed to get sucked out of me. I thought whenever he decided to talk to me again I'd be happy. But I wasn't. I had been so sad for so long that I hadn't realized how angry I was with him. I had never been so angry with someone in my life. How dare he just show up here? "Yeah. Have a great life." I turned my attention back to the dance floor. I wanted him to walk away. I wanted him to let me have this one good night after so many bad ones. But he remained where he was.

"Are you done?" His voice sounded cold.

I looked back at him. I wanted to slap his stupid, beautiful face. "Done what?"

"Done here? Let's go."

He reached out and brushed his fingers along my wrist. His touch still gave me that warm tingly feeling. I hated that it gave me that feeling. I took a step back from him. "No, I'm not done. This is my birthday party. I'm not leaving. And I'm definitely not leaving with you."

"You're drunk."

"I'm not drunk!" *Shit.* I always had a hard time controlling my temper. It was probably even worse since I had been drinking. But I wasn't drunk. I took a deep breath.

"Penny, we need to talk. And I don't want to do it here."

"You've had weeks to talk to me. You don't just get to show up tonight and ruin my birthday party. Why tonight of all nights?"

"I thought you'd be happy to see me."

The way he said it made my throat catch. He sounded like he genuinely thought that was true. As if this surprise appearance suddenly erased all the pain. "I'm not. Please just go."

"I'm not leaving here unless it's with you."

"You forgot my birthday." I bit my lip. I wish this still didn't hurt so much.

"I didn't forget."

I shook my head. What an asshole. "Fine. You ignored my birthday then. I feel like that's even worse."

"Please just let me explain."

"There's nothing to explain. You're my boyfriend, you should have at least wished me a happy birthday. Sorry, ex boyfriend." I crossed my arms in front of my chest.

"Well that explains a lot."

I looked up at him. "What are you talking about?"

"You and Mr. Stevens don't seem to be acting like just friends anymore."

I glared at him. "That's really none of your business."

"Everything you do is my business."

"Nothing I do is your business. We're done. You've made that very clear."

"We are not done."

"Yes we are. You ignored me for weeks. And now you finally show up. Apparently just to make me feel like shit because I don't hear you offering an apology."

"I told you that I wanted to talk."

"Then talk. Tell me why you acted like I didn't exist. Do you have any idea how hard it was to go to class and feel invisible?" The room felt stifling.

"Yes, I do."

"No, you don't." I looked down at the ground. I didn't want to cry. "It's too late to talk. You waited too long. I can't. I don't want to. Not anymore."

"Penny, come on, let's go." He reached out for my hand.

"Stop." I pulled away. I didn't want him to touch me. I didn't want him here. I could feel tears beginning to well in my eyes. *Why is he here? Just to torture me?*

"Penny." He put his hand on my elbow.

"Don't touch me." I took another step back.

"Penny." He closed the gap between us.

"She said stop." Tyler put his hand on Professor Hunter's chest and lightly shoved him back. I wasn't sure when he had appeared. I wondered how much of our conversation he had heard.

Professor Hunter looked stunned that Tyler had shoved him. "Tyler," he said coolly and nodded his head.

"James, is it?" Tyler said sarcastically.

"Look, she's drunk. I'm just going to take her home."

"Jesus, I'm not drunk." *Why does everyone keep saying that?*

"She can spend the night if she wants to. Don't worry about it," Tyler said.

"That's exactly what I'm worried about. Penny, let's go. Now." He had talked to me sternly before, but never like this. I swallowed hard. Why was it so hard to resist his authority? It took every ounce of my resolve not to go to him.

Tyler put his arm out in front of me even though I didn't move. "She's not going anywhere with you. Why are you even here?"

"Because my girlfriend invited me."

"She's definitely not your girlfriend. Get the fuck out of my house."

"What is that supposed to mean?" Professor Hunter looked at me. His expression turned icy.

"You know what it means," Tyler said.

Shit.

"Tyler. Get out of my way." Professor Hunter seemed calm, but I could tell he was on the edge.

"Or what?"

Professor Hunter took another step toward me, but Tyler shoved him in the chest again. Harder this time. Professor Hunter took a few steps back to steady himself. He shook his head back and forth.

"Tyler," I said quietly. I reached out and touched his shoulder. I didn't want them to fight. They both looked so angry now.

Professor Hunter looked down at my hand on Tyler. He balled his hand into a fist and cocked his arm.

"James!" I screamed.

But he didn't listen to me. He punched Tyler square in the nose.

Tyler cursed as he stumbled backwards.

"Oh my God, are you okay?" I touched the side of Tyler's face. His nose started gushing blood. "Oh my God, Tyler."

He wiped his nose with the back of his hand. "Hold this for me," he said and handed me a small wrapped box. My present. I looked back up and saw him charging at Professor Hunter.

"What the hell are you doing?!" I yelled after him.

Tyler dropped his shoulder at the last second, slamming into Professor Hunter's stomach. They knocked into a few couples dancing as the two of them fell to the floor. They were yelling at each other, but their words were drowned out by the music.

A girl screamed as they rolled over and almost knocked into her. Professor Hunter had blood on his face, and I wasn't sure if it was because Tyler had hurt him or if Tyler's bloody nose had just dripped onto Professor Hunter's face. I looked around for a fire alarm. It was the only thing I could think of to do. But we were in a frat house. There were no fire alarms.

The dance music suddenly stopped.

"I'll fuck whoever I want to fuck," Tyler snarled as he landed a punch across Professor Hunter's face.

Oh my God.

The room was quiet for another second and then people started yelling, "Fight, fight, fight!"

I ran over to them. "Stop it! Both of you, stop!"

I tried to grab Tyler's arm before he landed another punch on Professor Hunter, but I wasn't strong enough to hold him back. Professor Hunter grabbed his axe from the floor beside him and whacked Tyler on the side of the head with it.

He grabbed Tyler's collar and pulled him close to his face. "If you know what's good for you, you'll stay the hell away from her."

"I can end you."

"Then do it." He let go of Tyler's collar and pushed him back down to the floor.

Professor Hunter stood up. He was starting to get a black eye and there was a cut on his lip. There was blood on his face, but I wasn't sure where it was coming from. He gave me a pleading look.

I looked over Professor Hunter's shoulder as Tyler stood up. "Please stop fighting. James, please just go. We can talk tomorrow, okay? Please."

"Penny, do not make me carry you out of here," he said.

"Hey, asshole! She asked you to leave." Tyler pulled his sword from his belt and chucked it at the back of Professor Hunter's head.

Professor Hunter stumbled to the side. He rubbed the back of his head. He gave me one last pleading look.

I didn't know what to do.

"Okay," Professor Hunter said. "Okay." He turned away from me and walked toward the stairs.

Melissa came running up to me. She started talking really fast but I couldn't seem to focus on her words. When Professor Hunter passed by Tyler, Tyler said something to him, but I couldn't make it out. Professor Hunter's head snapped to the side and he rammed into Tyler. The two of them fell onto the table that they were using as a bar.

I ran toward them again. "What is wrong with you?!" I screamed, directing it at both of them. I grabbed Professor Hunter's arm and tried to pull him off. I wasn't strong enough. I let go of his arm and stood back, screaming at them to stop. Professor Hunter punched Tyler one last time and stood up. I couldn't see Tyler. Professor Hunter was blocking my view. *Is he okay?*

Suddenly Professor Hunter stepped to the side. Tyler's fist landed on my stomach. I tried to breathe but couldn't.

I stepped backwards and slipped on some of the spilled alcohol. I put my hands out to catch myself but my reaction was too slow. My head slammed against the concrete floor.

CHAPTER 6

Saturday

"Penny," a familiar voice said. "Penny? God, Penny open your eyes."

I gasped and sat up. The room was so bright. It felt like I was dreaming. I blinked hard as the room came into focus. My head was pounding. I reached up and felt something damp. When I brought my hand down my fingers were covered in blood.

"Penny?"

My eyes focused on Professor Hunter's face. "I thought you weren't talking to me?" I mumbled. I reached up and touched my forehead. "What happened?"

"You fell. Don't you remember?"

"What?" I looked down at Professor Hunter's hand. He was holding a cloth that was covered in blood. *Is all that blood from my head?*

"Penny, what is the last thing you remember?" He was standing next to me by the bed I was on. He looked concerned.

"I don't know." I felt like I wanted to cry. "You weren't talking to me." I looked around at Professor Hunter's bedroom. "Why am I here? How did I get here?" It had been so long since I had been here. The last time I was in his apartment he had told me to leave.

"I carried you." Professor Hunter looked concerned. "Penny, tell me the last thing you remember."

"I don't know." I started to cry. I felt confused. "I don't know why I'm here. I can't remember. Am I okay?" *What is happening to me?*

"You're going to be fine. The doctor is on the way." He said it calmly, but he didn't look calm. He lightly pressed the cloth in his hand against my forehead.

I put my hand over my mouth. I was going to throw up. I tried to climb out of bed, but the sudden movement made me dizzy. I started to fall, but Professor Hunter caught me. He kept his arms around me as he set me back down on the bed.

"Penny, stay still. The doctor will be here any second. You're going to be fine," he repeated. He sat down on the bed next to me and rubbed my back.

I immediately threw up down the front of him. He patted my back as I finished vomiting all over his shirt. The taste was horrible. The sight was even worse. "I'm so sorry," I groaned.

"It's okay." He rubbed my back. "It's okay. Stay right there. I'll be right back." Professor Hunter quickly stood up and walked out of the room. When he came back a minute later, he was no longer wearing a shirt and was carrying a bottle of ginger ale. He handed me the bottle.

"Drink this," he instructed. He sat down next to me.

"I'm so sorry," I repeated.

"Please stop apologizing. All of this is my fault." He suddenly looked angry. "Where the hell is he? He should have been here by now."

I reached up and grabbed Professor Hunter's chin. I turned his face to me. "You're hurt."

"I'm fine, baby. I'm fine." He took my hand and kissed my palm. He stroked his thumb against my palm as he brought it to his lap.

"No." His lip was cut and there was a bruise forming around his eye. Tears started to stream down my cheeks again. He was hurt, yet here he was taking care of me.

"You should see the other guy." Professor Hunter gave me a weak smile.

"Was this my fault?"

Professor Hunter continued to rub his thumb against my palm. "No. It's mine."

A buzz sounded through the apartment. "Finally." Professor Hunter stood up. "Don't move." He disappeared from the room.

I heard the elevator doors ding open and then hushed voices. I tried to concentrate on their words.

"She just threw up," Professor Hunter said.

"Has she been drinking?" said the stranger.

"Yes. But that's not why I'm worried."

"How much?"

"I don't know."

"Let me see her."

"Steven, she fell. She hit her head hard. She's disoriented. She doesn't even remember what happened."

The stranger walked into the room. "Miss Taylor, I'm Doctor Ridge."

"Hello," I said weakly. I couldn't help but realize how much trouble I was in. Doctors had to report underage drinking to the college, didn't they?

"Can you tell me what happened tonight?"

I shook my head.

"How did you hit your head?"

I looked up at Professor Hunter. "I fell?" That's what he had said.

"Do you remember falling?"

"No."

"Have you been drinking?"

"I don't...I don't know." I swallowed hard. My head was fuzzy like I was buzzed. "Yes. I think so."

"How much alcohol have you consumed?"

"I don't know. I don't remember." My eyes were growing watery again. His tone was so accusatory.

He walked around the bed and put down a bag on the floor. He unzipped it and held up some sort of small flash light to my eyes. "Follow the light with your eyes," he instructed.

I did as best I could.

"Please stand for me."

I slid off the bed and onto my feet. But my legs were wobbly. I felt dizzy. Doctor Ridge put his hands on my arms and helped me back onto the bed.

"You have a concussion. Sit back for me."

I leaned against the pillows behind me. He grabbed something else from his bag and blotted my forehead. It stung.

"You need stitches."

"Shouldn't I go to a hospital?"

"I'll fix you up better than any emergency room doctor at this hour. Close your eyes. This is going to sting, but then you won't be able to feel anything."

Professor Hunter climbed on the bed beside me and grabbed my hand.

Before I closed my eyes I saw Dr. Ridge pull a syringe out of his bag. *Holy shit.* I squeezed Professor Hunter's hand. I felt the pinch of the needle in my forehead and a few moments later the pain was gone.

"Keep your eyes closed, Penny," Professor Hunter said. He stroked my palm with his thumb. I squeezed my eyes shut. Professor Hunter's voice was soothing. And his fingers rubbing against my palm made me relax. I kept my eyes shut until the doctor told me he was done.

"Take it easy for a few days," he instructed.

"Thank you," I murmured.

Dr. Ridge nodded and gave me a small smile. Professor Hunter walked him out of the room.

"What about her memory?" James asked as soon as they were out of the room. I closed my eyes and listened.

"She's just in shock. She should be fine in the morning. Call me if she's still having trouble with her memory."

"Thank you for coming out, Steven."

"Did you want to tell me what happened tonight?"

"A sequence of unfortunate events is all."

"I see. How old is she?"

"Old enough." Professor Hunter sounded defensive.

"Does Isabella know?"

Professor Hunter didn't answer. Or at least, I couldn't hear his answer. I bit my lip.

"Put some ice on that eye, James."

I heard the elevator ding. A moment later James walked back into the room. He walked to my side of the bed and sat down on the edge. "Stay still," he said. He dotted some salve onto my forehead. It felt good to be taken care of after so many weeks of feeling completely alone.

"Why are you crying? Does it hurt?" he asked.

I shook my head. He placed a white bandage over the stitches. I watched his face as he applied the medical tape to keep it in place. I suddenly felt homesick.

"I want to go home."

"Penny, you are home." He cupped my chin in his hand.

"Please, Professor Hunter."

"I'm not letting you out of my sight." He sat down next to me and pulled my head onto his chest. His tantalizing scent made me feel numb.

"I need to go home." Tears began to well in my eyes. I missed my parents. I needed to talk to my mom. "Please."

He kissed my forehead. "You need rest."

His cologne had completely engulfed me. I looked down at my lap. "Why am I wearing one of your shirts?"

"I didn't want Dr. Ridge to see you in the outfit you were wearing earlier."

"You undressed me?"

"Yes."

How long had I been passed out? "You shouldn't have done that."

"Penny, I've seen you naked plenty of times."

I looked up at him. "You're not allowed to see people naked that you've ignored for two weeks. That's not how things work. You've got everything backwards." I was rambling. I wasn't even sure what I was saying.

"In that case, I'm sorry."

"Good."

He kissed my forehead next to my bandage. A rumble of thunder sounded outside. A moment later I could hear the patter of rain against the window. I breathed in Professor Hunter's cologne.

"It's raining," I mumbled.

He kissed my forehead again.

"Whenever it rains I think about you. It's when I missed you the most. You promised you wouldn't be mad at me. You promised."

Instead of answering me, he kissed my forehead again.

I looked up at him. "You should put ice on your eye."

"Don't worry about me, Penny."

"You're very worrisome," I sighed into his chest. "You never talk to me. You won't let me in."

Professor Hunter ran his hands through my hair. "I'm trying."

I yawned. "It's normal to worry about the people you love." I tried to keep my eyes open but my eyelids felt heavy. Before I knew it, I had fallen asleep.

CHAPTER 7

Saturday

I slowly opened my eyes. Professor Hunter was laying next to me in bed. His eyes were closed and his breathing was slow and steady. There was a dark bruise around his eye. I sat up. My head hurt. I reached up and felt the bandage. I climbed out of bed and went to the bathroom. I flipped on the light switch and stared at my reflection in the mirror. A bruise was peeping out from under the bandage. Everything came back in a rush. I gulped, remembering the feeling of getting the wind knocked out of me. *Shit. Tyler.*

I ran back into the bedroom. I needed to call Tyler. I needed to see if he was okay. My Poison Ivy costume was in a heap on the floor. But my phone wasn't there. I looked around the bedroom. Professor Hunter stirred in his bed. I went back into the bathroom and locked the door. I put my back against the door and sighed. *What had I done?* I swallowed hard. My mouth still tasted like vomit. I looked over at the sink. There was a toothbrush still in its plastic wrapping. I walked over, opened it up, and brushed my teeth. When I was done I held the brush in my hand and stared at the toothbrush holder. Professor Hunter's toothbrush sat there alone. I thought about Tyler's hands on my waist. I gulped and tossed the toothbrush into the trash. I leaned down and put my face in my hands.

I had turned into a slut in one day. I kissed a stranger. I fucked Tyler. And I slept over at Professor Hunter's apartment all within a day. I slid my hands down and looked at my reflection in the mirror. I pulled my hair up into a messy bun and pulled Professor Hunter's t-shirt off.

There was a large bruise on my stomach and a small one on my elbow. I moved away from the mirror and turned on the shower. I felt disgusting. I needed to wash yesterday off of me.

The water only took a second to get warm. I stepped in, trying carefully not to get my bandage wet. I put my hands on the wall and let the water fall on my back. The image of Professor Hunter in here with me popped into my head. I tried to shake it away. I poured some of his body wash onto my hands, trying to ignore the intoxicating smell. I imagined his hands on me, washing me. *Fuck.* I quickly rinsed and turned the water off. I needed to get a grip. My stomach was in knots. How had things escalated so quickly last night? Tyler and Professor Hunter had had a fist fight over me, or because of me. This whole situation seemed surreal. I needed to get back to my dorm room. Melissa would know what to do. She always knew what to do.

I wrapped my towel around myself and opened up the bathroom door. Professor Hunter was no longer in bed. There was a pile of clothes by the bathroom door. I picked them up and quickly dressed. A pair of yoga pants and a tank top. No underwear. I didn't dwell on it. I walked into the main room and over toward Professor Hunter. He was in the kitchen. He was wearing a pair of sweatpants and no shirt. *Stop being so sexy.* I took a deep breath and walked toward him. When I reached the counter he turned toward me.

"How are you feeling?"

"I'm fine," I lied. My head pounded, either from the concussion, or too much to drink, or a combination of the two. And I felt guilty for being here. "I'm going to get going."

He pushed a plate of waffles in front of me. Instead of responding to me, he just arched his eyebrow.

"I thought you didn't cook."

"I don't. They were frozen."

I looked down at my plate. It felt like I was going to throw up again. "I'm not hungry."

"You've lost weight. You need to eat."

"So now you suddenly care about me again?"

"I never stopped caring about you." His eyebrows lowered slightly. "I see that you have your memory back."

I pushed the plate away.

Professor Hunter walked over and placed two pills down on the counter. "You need to eat with these." He pushed the plate back toward me.

"I'm not taking those."

"Dr. Ridge left them for you. They're for the pain."

"I'm okay. Actually, I'm used to dealing with pain now." I took a deep breath. "Where is my phone?"

"Penny, take the pills. Eat the waffles. I'll give you your phone when you're done."

"I need to tell Melissa where I am."

"Your friends know where you are." He emphasized the word friends. *Is he referring to Tyler too?*

He had no right to boss me around. But if this was the only way he'd let me leave, then so be it. I took the two pills and downed them with water. "How do you know Dr. Ridge?" I cut up the waffles and poured syrup over them.

"He's an old friend."

"A friend of Isabella's too?" I took a bite and swallowed. *Why was he doing this to me?*

"No." He put his elbows on the counter and ran his hands through his hair.

I took another bite of the waffles and then pushed them away. "I can't eat anymore."

Professor Hunter walked over and sat down on the stool beside mine.

"Look, thank you for taking care of me last night. You didn't need to do that..."

"I did need to." He put his hand on my thigh. I swiveled my chair to remove it. I didn't need his tantalizing touch clouding my judgment. I was still so mad at him. Taking care of me for one night didn't erase how he had made me feel for weeks.

"You didn't. But I do appreciate it. I'm fine now, though. And I need to go. Please give me my phone."

"I can't let you leave. You have a concussion."

"I can take care of myself."

"You certainly didn't take care of yourself last night."

"I was fine before you showed up," I snapped. I was starting to lose my temper.

"You haven't been taking care of yourself these past few weeks either."

I stood up from my stool. "How dare you throw that in my face?" I took a deep breath. "I tried. How can you sit there and judge me for feeling? I loved you. I loved you so much. And it meant nothing to you. I meant nothing to you. You're completely fine. It's so hard to see you that way when I'm falling apart."

"Penny..." he reached out for me.

"Don't touch me. Don't you dare touch me." I felt so weak. "I couldn't eat. I couldn't sleep. Because of you! Because you left me!"

The words seem to echo in his apartment. "That's not fair, Penny. You can't put all the blame on me."

"Yes I can. You're the one that left. You're the one that refused to talk to me. You shut me out. You didn't even give me a chance. I made one mistake and you left. You left me."

"Only because you lied to me!"

"Yes. Because I wanted to be with you. I didn't think you'd want me if you knew how young I was. And I hate that I lied to you."

"I know."

"No. Not because it made you leave me. But because it made us get together in the first place."

"You wish we had never started fucking?"

His words were chilling. I had told him I loved him. "And that's it, isn't it? Just fucking? See, that's the problem. I thought it was more than that. I want someone to love me. Unconditionally."

"And that's what Tyler does? Because last time I checked, taking advantage of someone when they're drunk isn't love."

"And what do you know about love? You're fucking married to a woman that you don't love. You didn't even love her when you got married. And instead of facing it and getting divorced, you just go around screwing students like it means nothing."

"I don't go around screwing students. You're the exception. You know that."

"Do I? Because I don't think I know you at all."

"You know me." He stood up. His fingers were gripping the side of the counter. "You'll never forget what it feels like to have my rock hard cock deep inside of you. You'll never be able to stop screaming my name."

I swallowed hard. Why was I suddenly aroused? *Fuck him.* "I was already forgetting you. Tyler didn't take advantage of me. I told him that I wanted him. I asked him to fuck me."

"Because you were drunk."

"No! It was because you left me! Because I was numb! You ruined me." My voice cracked. I turned around. I didn't want to look at him. "You ruined me."

He grabbed my arm and pulled me toward him. "So it's my fault that you're loose?"

"I'm not loose." I shoved his chest so he'd let go of me. "You broke up with me. I was trying to get over you."

"I never broke up with you. I said I needed time."

"I gave you time. Weeks! In order to work things out, normal people usually talk. What was I supposed to think?"

"That's not how I work through things."

"That's not an excuse. Keep my phone. I'm leaving. I don't want to hear anything else you have to say." I stormed off toward the elevator doors.

"What is wrong with you?" He sounded so angry.

I turned back around. "What is wrong with me? What is wrong with you?!" He had no right to be angry with me. He was the one that had left me. Why did he even care that I was leaving? We were done.

"Stop acting like a child." He walked toward me.

"I'm not acting like a child. Get over yourself."

"I'm trying to talk to you now. Which is exactly what you wanted. You're being immature."

"And you're being an asshole!"

We both stood still, staring at each other. He lowered his eyebrows. He was looking at me in that hungry way. I gulped.

"You're infuriating, Penny."

Everything below my waistline clenched. He had said the same thing to me in his office the first time we had ever had sex. I was so mad at him. But somehow that made me want him even more. "Then punish me, Professor Hunter." I repeated the words that had started our tryst in the first place.

He took a step toward me, pressing my back against the wall. He pushed my tank top up my sides. It had been so long since he had looked at me like that. It was like a drug. And I needed more. I lifted my arms in the air and let him pull my shirt the rest of the way off. He grabbed my jaw and turned my face toward him. His fingers dug into my skin. "I will never share you again. Do you understand me?"

"Yes." My voice was shaky. *How could I want him so badly right now?* I had never been angrier with anyone in my life.

He shoved my yoga pants off my hips and down my thighs. I stepped out of them. He put his hands on the wall on either side of my face. "I want to fuck you. Hard. Is that what you want?"

"Yes," I gasped. He wasn't touching me, but I had never felt so aroused.

He pushed his sweatpants down, grabbed my ass, and lifted me up. I wrapped my legs around him as he sunk his cock deep inside of me.

Oh God. I closed my eyes and let the sensation fill me. He moved his hips fast, knocking my ass against the wall. I buried my hands in his hair, pulling his head down to my neck. He placed a kiss against my collarbone. He squeezed my ass as his length went in and out of me. I could feel his hot, ragged breath against my neck. I groaned.

"You think I ruined you?" he whispered into my ear. He thrust his cock even deeper.

I gasped.

He bit my earlobe. "I'll show you what it's like to be ruined."

I whimpered at his naughty words.

He kept his hands on my ass but pulled out of me. I felt empty without him. He set me on my feet and turned me around. My whole body felt alive, like only he could do to me. He leaned forward so that his erection was on the small of my back. He grabbed my hands and put them on the wall.

I was breathing fast, waiting to see what he did.

"You asked me to punish you." He grabbed my hips and pulled them back so that I was arching my back with my hands still pressed against the wall. "And I intend to." His voice sounded tight. "Don't move out of this position." He slapped my ass hard with his palm.

I gasped in surprise.

"When I tell you it's time to go, you will not make me ask twice. Do you understand?"

"Yes," I said breathlessly.

He spanked me again.

Fuck. Why is this turning me on?

"You will not jeopardize your safety on purpose."

"I didn't..."

He slapped my ass harder. "Do you understand?"

"Yes."

He cradled my ass in his hand, caressing it gently. His other hand slipped between my thighs. My body trembled with anticipation. One of his fingers slid inside my wetness.

"Professor Hunter," I panted.

And then he spanked me harder still. "And you will not lie to me." Another one of his fingers joined in.

"Never." My cheek stung. But his fingers were driving me crazy. All I could feel was the sensation of him inside of me, teasing me.

He slapped my ass again. "Tell me that you need me as much as I need you."

"I need you. I need you, Professor Hunter." And it was true. I needed him. I had never stopped needing him.

He grabbed my hips and thrust himself back inside of me. *Fuck yes.* He was angry with me. I loved when he was angry with me. His fingernails dug into my skin. There was nothing better than the feeling of him inside of me. He grabbed my hair and pulled my head back. His dick was so deep inside of me that it hurt. He was fucking me harder than he ever had before. He gyrated his hips.

"Professor Hunter," I moaned.

"Come for me, Penny." He pulled my hair again.

I was close. Every time he thrust, it felt like he was slapping my raw cheek again. The combination of pain and pleasure was too much to bear. "Professor Hunter," I groaned. As soon as I said his name I felt his hot liquid shoot through me. There was no feeling better than him coming inside of me. He knelt down behind me and placed a kiss where he had slapped me.

"The thought of you screaming his name haunts me. Never again. You're mine." He kissed my cheek again.

I turned to face him. He was still on his knees. It looked like he was in actual pain. He leaned forward and kissed the bruise on my stomach.

I knelt down in front of him. "I didn't scream his name. Actually, I screamed yours." I shrugged my shoulders.

For the first time this morning there was a glint of humor in his eyes. "I'm not as easy to forget as you implied?"

"No. I've tried."

"I wanted you to."

I looked into his eyes. He looked so vulnerable. I could tell we were about to have the conversation that I had so badly wanted these past few weeks. And now that it was here, I was scared to have it. "What? What do you mean?"

"I wanted you to forget about me. That's why I haven't been talking to you."

"Why? I told you that I loved you."

"I know. But I'm no good for you. You deserve someone without so much...without so many issues."

"What issues?"

"You were right. You don't know me as well as you should."

"I do."

"You don't."

His words haunted me. I thought I had found out all his secrets. *What else is he hiding from me?*

"So if you wanted me to forget about you, why did you come to the party last night?"

"When you sent me that text about having a nice life it made me realize that I couldn't. Not unless you were in it."

"That's a selfish reason." I repeated the words back to him that he had used when I told him my excuse for lying to him.

"It is. But I've seen you disappearing these past few weeks. Not eating. Drinking too much. Not focusing in class. I may be bad for you, but I'm better than the alternative."

"So I get to be with you by default?"

"I need you, Penny. I'm addicted to you. I want what's best for you. And I'm going to try hard to be that for you."

"You know that I'm addicted to you too. Or else our argument wouldn't have just turned into sex. But you left me. I've never felt so broken before. Tyler was there to help try and pick up the pieces. And if I'm being honest, I didn't just sleep with him because I was drunk."

"I know." Professor Hunter gritted his teeth.

"I have feelings for him too."

Professor Hunter sighed. "Here is where I should tell you to go to him. Where I should be unselfish. Please don't make me do that."

"I know you said you needed time, but you waited so long. You made it seem like you wanted nothing to do with me. You wouldn't even look at me in class. I thought...I thought..." I put my face in my hands. "I made a mess of everything."

"No, I did." Professor Hunter grabbed my face in his hands. "I never should have walked out on you that night. I understand why you lied. And I did exactly what you feared. But I need you to know that the age difference means nothing to me."

"When you were in high school, I was in elementary school."

Professor Hunter laughed. "It doesn't matter."

"You're my professor."

"It doesn't matter." He leaned forward and kissed me. I could feel the cut on his lip. But that didn't stop him. He grabbed the back of my head and leaned into me until my back was against the cool tile. "I'm sorry." He kissed the top of my bandage, then the side of my neck. He left a trail of kisses between my breasts and down my stomach.

"Mmm."

He kissed the inside of my thigh. "I missed you."

"I missed you too."

He kissed the inside of my other thigh. "I want you again," he whispered against my skin. He lightly brushed his fingers against my clit. I was still aroused. I had been without him for so long. And now that I was in his presence again, I couldn't get enough of him.

I grabbed the bottom of his chin and tilted his head toward me. "I want you too."

He leaned between my thighs again and kissed me gently. I wrapped my legs around him as he slowly entered me. He was being gentle and loving this time. I let my hands wander down his muscular back.

The contrast between him fucking me and him making love to me was unimaginable. Hard and raw versus gentle and intimate. He continued to kiss me as his thick cock stretched me wide. He reached down and touched my clit again, making me moan with pleasure.

He tilted his hips, thrusting his cock deeper.

"Professor Hunter," I gasped.

He ran his hand up the side of my torso. His touch made my whole body tingle with pleasure. He intertwined his fingers with mine and moved them to either side of my face. His hips moved faster. "Promise that you'll remember that you're mine."

"I promise," I moaned as my orgasm washed over me. He squeezed my hands as he found his release.

He rubbed the tip of his nose against mine. He placed one last kiss on my lips and pulled out of me. He stood up, grabbed his sweatpants off the floor, and pulled them on. I had never seen the look he was giving me now.

I was about to ask him what was wrong, when he said, "I have a present for you."

I sat up. "So you did remember my birthday?" I wasn't fuming anymore. I wanted to talk. I wanted to hear him out.

"I told you I remembered." He gave me a small smile and walked through the kitchen. He disappeared into a room I hadn't been in yet. I grabbed my clothes and went into his bedroom. I flipped the switch on in his closet. All the clothes he had bought for me were still hanging there. I opened up a drawer and pulled out a lacy thong and matching bra. I put them on and then finished getting dressed in my pants and tank top. There were sneakers at the bottom of the closet. I grabbed a pair of socks and laced up the sneakers. Everything fit me so perfectly. I crossed my arms. It was chilly in his apartment. I grabbed a light jacket and pulled it on.

When I walked back into the living room, Professor Hunter was sitting on the couch. I sat down next to him. He was holding a sealed envelope in his hand. My name was written in his familiar scrawl.

"What is it?" I couldn't help the excitement coursing through me. I had waited my whole birthday for a present from him to arrive.

"I wanted you to get over me." He wasn't looking at me. He was looking down at the envelope.

"You already told me that."

"Before you open this I need to tell you something."

"Okay." My heart was racing.

"I did something I regret. But I can't take it back."

I didn't know what to say, so I stayed silent.

"I thought I needed to get over you. I thought it was best for you."

"And for you?"

"No." Professor Hunter shook his head. "I always knew it wasn't best for me." He looked over at me. "You said that it didn't look like I was in pain. But I was. I felt numb. My days dragged on. Without you there's nothing for me here. It sounds like I'm trying to make excuses but I'm not. I can own up to my mistakes. I just needed you to know that I was in pain too. I need you to understand the place I was in."

"I don't want to know what you did."

"Penny..."

"Please don't tell me."

"I want you to be honest with me. How can I expect you to be if I'm not honest with you?"

"Is it going to hurt me?"

Professor Hunter ran his hand through his hair. "Yes."

I bit my lip. "You kept my clothes in your closet. Why?"

"I felt like if I got rid of them then what we had really would be dead."

"So this thing that you did didn't make it feel like what we had was over?"

"No. I thought it would, but it didn't."

"I wish you would have talked to me. I wish you would have told me that you thought you weren't good for me. I would have convinced you otherwise."

"You've convinced me otherwise the whole time we were together."

"You still should have talked to me."

"I can't take that back either."

I nodded my head. "I kissed some guy that lives in your apartment."

Professor Hunter lowered his eyebrows. "Who?"

"Does it matter?"

"Yes."

"His name is Brendan."

"Okay. Just one kiss?"

"Yes. And he gave me some advice. About how if things are so hard between us maybe we're not meant to work things out."

"It's not bad advice."

"Clearly I didn't take it."

"I know." We were both silent for a moment.

"Is what you did worse than that?"

"Yes."

"Is it worse than the fact that I slept with Tyler?"

Professor Hunter closed his eyes. "I left you. You thought I had broken up with you. You weren't in the wrong."

"Is it worse?"

"By default, yes."

"So you had sex with someone else?"

Professor Hunter leaned forward and put his elbows on his knees. "I did."

I stood up from the couch. "A stranger?" My heart was racing.

"No."

His words made my body feel cold. He didn't have to say it. I knew what he had done. He had sex with Isabella. He had sex with his wife. That's what married men did. They had sex with their wives. What should I have expected? He ran back to his wife when things went sour between us.

"Did you enjoy it?"

"It was just sex. It didn't mean anything. It wasn't like it is with you."

"So you did enjoy it?"

"Penny..."

"When we were arguing earlier you said all we were doing was fucking."

"I didn't mean it. I was upset."

I took a deep breath. "I shouldn't be upset with you. I slept with someone else too. But I am. I don't know what you want me to say." It was hard to picture his hands on someone else.

"You're allowed to be upset with me."

"It was her, wasn't it?"

He looked up at me.

"Isabella? Your wife?"

"Yes," he sighed.

"Okay."

"Penny, I didn't go to New York with the intention of sleeping with her."

"Okay."

"It just happened."

"Okay."

"Please stop saying okay. It's not okay. And I'm sorry. I'm so, so sorry, Penny."

"You don't have to explain it to me. She's your wife."

"I needed you to know."

I took a deep breath. "I need some air."

"Okay. Let's take a walk."

"I want to be alone."

"Penny, you have a concussion..."

"I'm okay. Please. I just need some air."

"Take this." He lifted up the envelope.

I shook my head.

He folded the envelope and stood up. He slipped it into my pocket. Then he grabbed my phone out of his pocket and slipped it next to the envelope. "Please be careful."

"I promised you I would be." I went over to the elevator and pressed the button.

"Please stay."

"I can't."

"I'm begging you, please."

"I can't look at you right now." The elevator dinged as the doors slid open. I stepped on.

"Penny."

"Professor Hunter."

The doors closed.

CHAPTER 8

Saturday

I hugged my arms around myself. I needed to be alone. I knew that I could forgive him for not talking to me for weeks. Hell, I already had. But sleeping with Isabella? He was supposed to be getting a divorce, not fucking her. I shook my head and looked down at my sneakers. I hated that I was wearing clothes that he had bought for me.

The elevator doors dinged. I kept my eyes on the ground.

"I apologize in advance for what I'm about to ask you."

I looked up. Brendan had just stepped onto the elevator. He hit the button to close the doors.

"So, the dramatic guy. Did he do that to you?"

"No. It's not like that." *He just spanks me when he thinks I've misbehaved.* "I fell. That's all."

"Okay." He moved closer to me and leaned against the wall. "Are you alright?"

"I'm fine."

"Then why does it look like you're about to cry?"

"I just found something out that I'm not happy about."

"Did you want to talk about it?"

"Not really."

Brendan sighed. "You seem to be having a bad day. And I don't want to make anything worse. But I do need to tell you something. And just so we're clear, it's not because I want to get into your pants. I mean, I do want to get in your pants. But I'm not telling you because of that."

I couldn't help but laugh. I looked up at him. "What do you need to tell me?"

"I'm not 100 percent sure. Closer to 85 percent. But I'm pretty sure that both of the men that have penthouse suites are married."

I looked back down at my shoes. I could feel his eyes on me. He thought I was a monster. "I didn't know that when I started seeing him."

"But you do already know?"

"Yes." I felt ashamed. "He's getting divorced."

"That's what they all say."

"I believed him." I sighed. "I believed him until about five minutes ago."

The doors opened. We both stepped out into the parking garage.

"It was nice seeing you again," I said.

"Where are you going?" he asked.

"For a walk. I need to clear my head."

"I was actually going to go for a walk too. Do you mind if I join you?"

"I find that hard to believe." He was so easy to talk to. And he seemed to like offering me free advice. "But no, I don't mind."

Together we walked out of the parking garage. The sun was bright and the autumn leaves crunched under my feet. My head pounded. I was glad Professor Hunter had made me take those pills. We walked in silence for a few minutes. "Do you mind if we sit down for a second?" I suddenly felt dizzy.

Brendan grabbed my arm and escorted me to a bench. He sat down next to me and put his arm behind me on the bench, but he didn't touch me. I rubbed my forehead.

"Do you need to see a doctor about that?"

"I already have."

"And?"

"I have a concussion. I needed stitches. Because I'm an idiot."

"Should you be walking around like that?"

"Probably not," I laughed.

"I'm curious to know how you ended up with a concussion. I'm even more curious to know how you ended up dating a married man. Girls like you don't need to date married men."

"Girls like me?" I laughed.

"Yes, girls like you." He put his hand on my knee. "Tell me your story."

I crossed my legs on the bench and turned to him. "It's a long story."

"Luckily I'm free all afternoon."

"It kind of started last semester. I was dating this asshole. He made me feel small. But when things didn't work out it still hurt. He was my first boyfriend. My first kiss. My first...well, you know."

"The first person you'd ever had sex with?"

"Yes." I looked down at my lap. I launched into the story about running into Professor Hunter before I knew he was a professor. I told him about meeting Tyler. I told him about my obsession with wanting Professor Hunter to want me. And how my feelings for Tyler had always skirted away from the friend zone. How I led him on. How I lied to both of them. I told him about when I found out that Professor Hunter was married. About my awkward speeches in class and my almost hookup with Tyler. I told him about lying about my age and my fight with Professor Hunter. I told him about not hearing from him for weeks, which led me to being a stalker and running into Brendan in the first place. I told him about taking his advice and having sex with Tyler.

"Let me stop you right there." He hadn't said anything the whole time. He was just listening. "I never told you to have sex with anyone. I just wanted you to let me take you on a date. If I had known there was a Tyler in the equation, my advice probably would have been different."

I laughed. "It was good advice. Until the professor showed up." I had referred to Professor Hunter as the professor since the beginning. I didn't want to run his name through the mud. "We got in a huge fight. And then he and Tyler got in a fist fight. Tyler accidentally hit me and knocked the wind out of me. I slipped on some spilled beer and hit my head."

"End of story?"

"Almost. The professor carried me back to his apartment and took care of me. It was sweet. We got in another fight. We made up. A couple of times." I could feel my face blushing. "And then he told me that while he wasn't talking to me he had sex with his wife."

"You're kind of adorable."

"What?" That's not the reaction I had expected from my horrific story. If anything, I expected a 'See you later, you idiot.' "

"I don't know. You look at the world in this really naive way. And no matter how many times something goes wrong, you always see the best in people. Like I said before, I find you endearing."

"I think I'm a mess."

"And that's why you keep doing messy things."

I laughed. "I guess so."

"So, who's better in bed?"

"Excuse me?"

"You heard me, Penny."

"That can't possibly be your advice."

"A sweet guy is nice. A mysterious guy is great. But a good lay? I'm sorry, but it always goes back to that."

"I don't believe that. There's so much more to a relationship than sex."

"Well, I'm assuming you're great in bed. Especially if you have two men fighting over you."

"I don't think that's why they like me. I mean, Tyler's liked me this whole time and we only just had sex for the first time yesterday."

"Then it was the idea of fucking you that kept him around. He liked the chase."

I shook my head.

"And you said you fucked the professor twice this morning. And fought the rest of the time. It sounds like sex is the only thing working in your relationship."

I lowered my eyebrows. *Maybe he's right.*

"So I'll ask you again. Who's the better lay?"

I sighed. "The professor."

"By the way, there's only one professor at your school that's rich enough to live in my building. James is a lucky guy."

"Oh my God." I put my hand over my eyes. "If you knew this whole time why didn't you say anything?"

"I thought you reaction would be funny." He grabbed my hand and removed it from my face. "I guess he's not that lucky, though. Because you're out here talking to me instead of him." He kept his hand on top of mine.

"You're easy to talk to."

"Because I'm an unassuming acquaintance."

"I don't know why." I looked down at his hand. "Do you have any other advice for me?"

"I'm sorry, what?"

I raised my eyebrow.

"I just got distracted. The bandage on your forehead makes it look like you were in a fight. You're tiny. It just put a comical image in my head."

I laughed. "I asked if you had any other advice for me?"

"I think you need to tell Tyler that James is better in bed."

I rolled my eyes.

"Did you want me to walk you to wherever he is?"

"It's not that easy."

"I thought everything was settled?"

"James is married."

"And he doesn't love her."

"But he's still married. You said yourself that all cheaters say they're getting divorced."

"Maybe he'll be the exception."

"Do you really believe that?"

Brendan shrugged. "I'd be lying if I didn't say I had my own agenda. Because if it doesn't work, I'll probably run into you on the elevator. And then you'll know what a good lay is."

I gulped. He was so forward. "So I shouldn't trust your advice?"

"I think it's pretty good advice."

I stood up and Brendan stood up next to me. "Thank you for letting me talk so much."

"Like I said, I find you endearing. I do wish you the best of luck."

"You're a really nice guy, Brendan."

"I'm actually not. I only listened to half of what you said. I was mostly just staring at your breasts."

For some reason I couldn't tell if he was serious or not. "Do you think that maybe we could be just friends?"

"Isn't that what we already are?" He smiled at me.

"I guess." I stepped forward and hugged him. He seemed taken aback, but he wrapped his arms around me. I let go of him and stepped back. "See you around, Brendan."

"See you around, Penny."

CHAPTER 9

Saturday

I wished Professor Hunter was as easy to talk to as Brendan. I walked up the steps to the front door of Tyler's frat. I took a deep breath and knocked on the door. I didn't know if Brendan was right about the sex. But it was Professor Hunter that had my heart. I had never stopped loving him. I needed Tyler to know. And then I needed to tell Professor Hunter that I wanted to be with him. But not until he divorced his wife.

The door squeaked open. A guy who I had never seen before opened it.

"Sup?"

"Hi, is Tyler here?"

"Yeah, he's upstairs." The boy walked away from the door.

Okay. Such a gentleman. I couldn't help but think he would have been nicer if I didn't have a huge bandage on my forehead. I stepped in and closed the door. The whole house seemed trashed from last night. There were empty red cups on the floor and it smelled like stale alcohol. I stepped over the mess and made my way up the stairs.

I wasn't sure how I'd feel once I saw him. He had an effect on me. I was just about to knock on his bedroom door when I heard something. I put my ear against his door. He was playing guitar. Softly. I closed my eyes and listened. I didn't recognize the song, but it sounded sad. I couldn't help the tears welling in my eyes. *Could I do this? Did I even want to?*

I listened to the rest of the song. It was beautiful. I had never heard him play before. When it ended I quickly knocked on the door before I had time to chicken out.

The guitar made a weird noise and then everything was quiet. "Umm, just a sec," I heard Tyler say. A moment later he opened his door a crack. "Shit, Penny." He came out and closed his door quietly behind him. He was wearing just his boxers. He still had sex hair. But the inside corners of both his eyes were bruised and his nose looked swollen. Professor Hunter must have broken his nose.

"Penny." He touched the side of my face. "Penny, I'm so sorry."

"It's not your fault."

"God." He put his hand over his mouth. "I called you a million times. Didn't you get any of my messages?"

I hadn't checked my phone. I shook my head.

"Penny." He wrapped his arms around me. "I was so worried."

I still liked how comfortable I felt in his arms. "Tyler can we sit down?"

Tyler glanced at his door. He suddenly looked nervous. "Yeah, let's go downstairs." He grabbed my hand and led me down the stairs. We sat down on the couch in his living room.

"Are you okay?" He eyed my bandage.

"It's nothing."

"Penny." He pushed my bangs out of my face.

"I have a concussion. I needed a few stitches. It's not a big deal. I feel okay now."

"I'm so sorry. I don't know what came over me. I just got so angry when I saw him yelling at you."

"It's okay."

"It's not okay." He put his hand over his mouth again. "I punched you. I'm so sorry. I can't believe I punched you."

"It was an accident."

"I'm so sorry," he repeated. His fingers traced the hem of my tank top. I could tell he wanted to see where he had hit me. But I didn't want him to see the bruise. I didn't want him to feel bad.

"I'm okay."

He shook his head. He pushed my tank top up.

I grabbed his hand. "Don't, Tyler."

"I need to see." There was so much pain in his eyes. I let go of his hand. He pushed my tank top up to my rib-cage. "Fuck." He put his hands over his face. "Fuck. Penny, I can't apologize enough. I'm so sorry."

"Tyler, I'm fine. Really, I'm okay." I pushed my tank top back down.

"It really doesn't hurt?"

"Not as much as my head." I tried to laugh. It came out forced.

"Which is also my fault."

"I slipped. It wasn't your fault."

"You slipped because I knocked the wind out of you."

"Tyler." I put my hand on top of his. "Are you okay?"

"You mean my busted up nose? Yeah I'm fine. I kind of deserved it, didn't I? I provoked him enough."

"You both acted stupid. But it was my fault for putting you in that situation."

Tyler shook his head. "I don't regret being with you. Not for a second."

"I don't either."

Tyler sighed. "When you fell I didn't know what to do. I let him take you. I didn't know how to take care of you."

"It's okay."

"I was scared. I was so scared that you wouldn't be okay."

"I'm okay, Tyler."

"He knew exactly what to do. I just stood there like an idiot and watched."

"I wouldn't have known what to do either."

"I'll never forgive myself for what I did to you."

"I've forgiven you. Actually, scratch that, because there's nothing to forgive. It was an accident. You're being too hard on yourself."

"You wouldn't open your eyes. I was yelling your name and you just laid there. Penny so many thoughts went through my head."

"It's over. Please stop, I don't want to hear about it." I let go of his hand and touched my forehead. It was hurting more and more as I sat there.

"I'm sorry." He looked distraught.

"It's just a headache. I'm okay." I took a deep breath. I needed to tell him that I wanted to be with Professor Hunter. But he looked so upset. And he was barely wearing any clothes. I closed my eyes. "I heard you playing your guitar."

"Oh. Yeah."

I opened my eyes. "What was the song? I didn't recognize it. But it was beautiful."

"I wrote it."

"It sounded sad." I wanted to cry. I swallowed hard. This was so painful.

"Does he know you're here? I'm pretty sure he'd come back and break my nose again if he knew you were talking to me." Tyler gave me a small smile. I could tell that smiling hurt his nose.

"He doesn't know."

"Did you walk here? I feel like you shouldn't be walking around by yourself."

"Tyler, I'm fine. I needed to come talk to you."

"I guess you and Professor Hunter had some time to talk then?"

"Time to argue, yes."

"I want you to be happy."

I shifted in my seat. "He told me that he stopped talking to me because he thought he wasn't good for me. It wasn't because he didn't want me. He was being...selfless."

"And you believe him?"

"I'm choosing to. I want to believe him. You were right. I'm still in love with him."

Tyler nodded his head.

"It's hard, because I do have feelings for you."

"I know." He leaned in and placed a soft kiss against my lips. "But you don't love me."

"I do love you. I love who you are as a person. But I'm not in love with you."

He nodded.

"I'm sorry."

"I could tell you weren't over him. If I had agreed to be your boyfriend, would things be different right now?"

I shook my head. "I don't think so."

"Tyler?" A girl's voice sounded from upstairs.

"I'll be right there!" he called back. He grabbed my hand. "It's not what you think."

Wow, Brendan was right. Tyler got me and now the chase was over. How could Brendan's awful advice actually be right? Was everything really just about sex? "So that's why you didn't ask me to come into your room? Of course. I'm sorry, I shouldn't have come here."

"Penny..."

"And that's really why you didn't want me to take you up on your offer of being my boyfriend? All you ever wanted was sex."

"No. What? No. I mean, yes I wanted to have sex with you, but I wanted more than that. I just wasn't sure I'd ever get more. I took advantage of the situation. And I'm sorry." He looked over at the stairs. "We didn't do anything. She gave me ice for my nose. We just fell asleep in my room."

"I want you to be happy too."

Tyler smiled his small, pained smile. "Well I've never been happier than I was last night. Before every possible thing went wrong."

"Thank you for trying to protect me."

"Don't put me in a good light for that. I think I did it more for my own ego than for you."

"Still." I bit my lip. "Do you think we can go back to being friends?"

"I..." Tyler shrugged. "It's going to take me some time to stop picturing you on my bed in nothing but green high heels."

"You're not easy to forget either." I looked over at him. "Actually, you're not leaving very much to the imagination right now."

Tyler laughed. "I should probably get back up there."

"Of course." I stood up quickly. I felt a little dizzy. I shook my head to help clear my head.

"Do you need me to walk you back?"

"No. I'm okay. Go back to your lady friend."

He rubbed the back of his neck. "It's Natalie."

I smiled at him. "I hope that you two can be together now. I'm sorry that I interfered so much. I'm going to go." I turned away from him and walked to the door. It hurt a little that he was able to move on so fast. But hadn't I? A selfish part of me was hoping he'd fight for me. Not literally this time. But he didn't seem hurt at all that we'd just become a one night thing. He had known what it would be the whole time. I was the only one who didn't know my feelings.

"Penny?"

I turned around. He walked over to me. He was looking at me intently. "Yes?"

"In case I never get another chance..." he grabbed both sides of my face and kissed me. I kissed him back. I wanted to remember what it was like to be with him too. When he released me, I felt a little lightheaded again.

"Feel better soon," he kissed my forehead.

"You too."

"I'll see you on Monday."

I watched him as he walked back up the stairs. When he disappeared from view, I let myself out of the frat house. That had gone better than I had ever expected. I actually felt like for the first time ever we were going to be just friends. I took a deep breath. Professor Hunter wasn't going to like that. It didn't matter. We were going to be honest with each other from here on out. And I could honestly say that I was just friends with Tyler.

The autumn sunshine felt good against my face. I crossed Main Street and began to walk toward Professor Hunter's apartment. There was a lot more I wanted to talk to him about. I was exhausted. Part of me wanted to go back to my dorm room and just talk to him tomorrow. But it needed to be now. He needed to know that I was choosing him. There were just some contingencies. I shook my head. Guys hated ultimatums. But I didn't know how else to do it.

I stopped at a bench and sat down. I felt out of breath and my head was pounding. Maybe I should call him and ask him to pick me up. I reached in my pocket and felt the envelope. I looked down at it as I pulled it out of my pocket. I ran my fingers across the top of the envelope. There was a small rip in the center of it. I gulped. This was the envelope that I had seen him with on my birthday. He had looked so distraught that night. And I had convinced myself that it had nothing to do with me. But it had everything to do with me. I pulled the envelope to my chest.

Whatever was in here had upset him. Could it be worse than him sleeping with Isabella?

I pulled it back down to my lap and stared at it. In the center of the envelope was my name. Even his handwriting was sexy. It reminded me of the note he had left me in my syllabus. I smiled. I took a deep breath as I opened up the envelope.

I pulled out the contents. On top there were two tickets. They were VIP tickets to the Macy's Thanksgiving Day Parade. *Thanksgiving? Is he asking me to meet his family?* I had watched the parade on television every Thanksgiving morning with my parents for as long as I could remember. I always wished I could go.

I quickly unfolded the note beneath the tickets. It was dated October 14th, the day before my birthday. I took a deep breath and read.

Penny,

I woke up late the first morning that classes started. I wouldn't have come into the coffee shop at that moment unless I had forgotten to set my alarm. Who knew that such a small thing could change the rest of my life? You've captivated me from the very start. You're timid, yet bold. You're humorous, yet sincere. You're young, yet wise. You're gorgeous and you don't know it. You're contradictory, and challenging, and passionate. And I love you. I love you with all I am.

These past few weeks have been the hardest of my life. Because you have captivated me, body and soul. I eat, breathe, and dream you. And when you're not beside me, I feel such loss. When I see you in class, I can no longer breathe. When I think about you, I can no longer eat. And only nightmares of losing you accompany me in slumber.

I thought I knew what love was. But I was wrong. The love I have for you is something that I have never known.

It is constant and all consuming and it terrifies me. The only thing scarier than realizing what my love for you is, is the fact that I have lost that love.

I wanted to protect you. I didn't want to drag you into my darkness. But I realize that when I am with you, I am not the man I once was. When you look at me, I can feel the way you see me, and I become something better. I want to be the man that you need. And I feel like I can be everything you want.

But you need to know that I have many flaws. And one of them is weakness. When I realized my feelings for you, I left. I left you, and I have never regretted anything so much in my life. Because without you, I am not living. Only with you am I strong. Only with you am I good. Only with you am I whole.

And I am selfish. Because I want you to be with me despite my demons. I want to kiss you every morning when you wake up in my arms. I want to whisper I love you in your ear before we fall asleep at night. I want my days to be consumed by your love. And I want you to love me back even though I am telling you that I am not good for you. Because it is your choice. I tried to stay away from you and I cannot. I am not a good man. But if you choose me I will not push you away again. I will trust your judgment. And every ounce of me hopes that you'll make a mistake and come back to me. Every fiber of my being wants you to make the wrong choice. And if you do, I promise to be the best that I can be for you.

I don't care that you lied to me. I don't care that you only just turned 20. I don't care that you are a student in my class. All I care about is you, Penny. My greatest love.

Tears were streaming down my cheeks. He opened up to me. He finally opened up to me. He had written this before my birthday. He had almost ripped it up that night because he wanted to protect me. But I was so glad that he couldn't stay away. Because I loved him too. I loved him so much. I couldn't seem to stop my tears. I wept for a long time, sitting there in the middle of Main Street.

I went to fold the paper to put it back when I realized there was another sheet behind it. I put the tickets and the note back into the envelope. I wiped my eyes so I could read what was on the last sheet of paper. It was a bunch of legal jargon. I scanned it. New York City Supreme Court. December 29th, 2014. It felt like my heart stopped beating. I looked down at the bottom. James Hunter. His signature was above his printed name. And beside it was Isabella Hunter. There was a blank line above her name. His divorce papers. She hadn't signed them, but he had. Last year, just like he had said. This was the proof that he was done. It was the proof that I needed to trust him. He was getting divorced. I quickly stood up and began walking back to his apartment. I needed to see him. I needed to tell him that I still loved him.

The street began to wobble in front of me. I slowed down and then stopped completely. My vision was blurry. The pain in my head seared. I tried to reach out for something to steady myself but there was nothing there. I gasped for breath. I reached into my pocket for my phone. *Oh God.*

"James," I mumbled as I fell to the ground.

PART 2

CHAPTER 10

Saturday

I sat up with a start and blinked hard as the room came into focus. *Where am I?* "James?"

"Shhh. Penny."

I looked up into the familiar eyes of my mother. "Mom?" My voice caught a little. It was so good to see her.

"It's okay, sweetie, I'm here."

"Where's James?" I lifted my arm but it was attached to an IV. I was in a hospital bed. I looked down at the tubes in my hand.

"Penny, who's James? Do you mean Brendan?"

"What?" My mom's eyes were red. I wasn't sure if it was because she had been crying or because she was tired. But it made me want to cry. I was so happy to see her. But where was Professor Hunter? I needed to talk to him.

"The nice young man that found you?"

"Found me?" I pulled on the IV. *Shit that hurts.*

"Penny."

I looked over at my dad. He had just stood up from a chair. He put his hand on my shoulder.

"Take it easy, Pen. You have a concussion." He looked over at my mom and then back down at me. "You need some more rest."

I looked over at my jacket. It was draped across the back of the chair my dad had been sitting in. I wanted the envelope. I wanted to read what Professor Hunter had written again. I needed to see him. "I know I have a concussion. But I'm fine. I don't need to be here. This is silly."

"Penny," my mom said.

"Really, I'm fine."

"You fainted in the middle of Main Street. You're not going anywhere." She leaned down and hugged me. I automatically relaxed and rested my head on her shoulder.

"It's so good to see both of you." I swallowed hard, trying to hold back my tears.

"Aw, Penny. We've missed you. When we got the phone call we were both so worried. If Brendan hadn't been here to tell us what happened, I would have gotten in a fist fight with that incompetent doctor."

My dad laughed.

"I'm so sorry," I mumbled into her shoulder. "I just..."

"It's okay, Pen." My dad said. "Just try to be more careful in the future. You're going to worry us to death."

I laughed and unwound from my mom's hug. I eyed my jacket on the chair again. "Can I have my jacket?"

"If you're cold we can get you some more blankets." She patted my back.

"I just need my jacket."

My dad walked over and grabbed it off the back of the chair and handed it to me. I put my hand in one empty pocket and then the other. The envelope was missing. "How long have I been here?" For a brief second I thought I had lost my mind. Maybe I had made Professor Hunter up.

"Just a few hours, sweetie."

That wasn't enough time to create such wonderful memories. I bit my lip. Or such painful ones. I hadn't made him up. There was no way. It felt like I was going insane. "Is Brendan here?"

"He's waiting outside," my dad said.

"Can I talk to him? To thank him?"

"Of course. We'll give you two a moment." My dad walked over to the door and gestured for my mom to follow. She leaned down and squeezed my arm before following my father out of the room.

I heard them talking in the hallway. A second later there was a knock on the door and Brendan walked in. A smile broke over his face.

"Well you look a million times better."

I bit my lip. "I passed out, huh?"

"You did."

"I guess it was good that you were stalking me, then."

He laughed and sat down next to me on the side of my bed. "I wouldn't say that I was stalking you."

"Then what would you call it?"

"Looking out for a friend. You weren't in great shape when we were talking." He shrugged his shoulders. "I was worried about you."

"I'm glad you were stalking me."

"Yeah, me too. Hey, move over."

"Brendan..."

"I've been sitting in an uncomfortable chair out there for hours. I want to lay down too. So scoot."

I slid over and he immediately laid down next to me on his side. He put his hand under his head and propped himself up on his elbow so that he could look down at me. "Your parents seem nice."

I laughed. "It's kind of weird that you met my parents."

"Why?"

"I don't know." I rolled onto my side to face him. "I've never introduced them to someone that I was dating. Not that we're dating, obviously. We kissed though. So it's a little strange."

He laughed. " Well, I think they like me."

"Well you did save their only child."

"I did. By the way, I feel obliged to tell you that you're showing a lot of skin." He was smiling at me.

"What?" I looked at my back. The slit on the hospital gown was revealing my backside. "Oh my God." I quickly rolled onto my back.

"It's not like I haven't seen a lot of you already. I'm starting to think your favorite pastime is flashing people."

"Hardly. Just you apparently."

"I'm not complaining." He smiled at me.

"Thanks by the way. For saving me, I mean."

"I kind of had to, or else all of my meddling in your life would have been for nothing."

"Is that right?"

"Yeah, that's right."

I took a deep breath. "What did you tell my parents?"

"You mean about why you fainted? Or about us?"

"Both."

"I told them that you were dating two guys at once and they got in a fist fight over..."

"No you didn't," I said, cutting him off. *Holy shit.*

"You're right. I didn't tell them that. I just said you had fallen the other night and still weren't recovered. So you fainted."

"Thank God."

"They didn't ask any questions at all. Apparently you're quite clumsy."

I laughed. "Yeah, I am." I looked at him curiously. "And the other thing?"

"What did I tell them about us?"

"Yeah."

"I told them that we were friends."

"And did they look confused that I was friends with someone who was so much older than me?"

"I'm not that much older than you. Besides, I assumed they wouldn't be surprised since you're dating your professor. I'm sure that was a fun conversation. They probably just thought I was one of his friends or something."

"They don't know about James."

"Oh." He had a small smile on his face. "Why?"

"I don't know." I turned to face him in the bed again, making sure my gown covered me. "He didn't want me to tell anyone about us. And then we weren't really together anymore. There wasn't anything to tell."

"And that's it?"

"No. I shouldn't be dating my professor. I don't want to tell them. I'm worried about what they'll think of me."

"Well they seemed to like me okay."

"But you're not my professor."

"Right. Plus I'm super charming. And I saved their only child."

I laughed. "You probably can't do wrong in their eyes now."

"If you say so." He leaned down and kissed me. His kiss was soft and gentle. I put my hand on his chest to stop him. He pulled back and looked at me. I could feel the tears start to fall down my cheeks.

"You're right, Penny. You shouldn't be dating your professor." He wiped my tears away with his hand.

I stared up at him. He was right. Of course he was right. I shouldn't be dating my professor. I thought about how upset my parents looked when I woke up. They'd be ashamed of me. *Am I ashamed of myself?* I should be with someone nice like Brendan. Or Tyler. But none of that mattered. Because I was in love with Professor Hunter. I loved him despite everything.

"Get some rest, Penny."

CHAPTER 11

Sunday

When I woke up I turned toward Brendan, but he was gone. In his place was my cell phone and the envelope from Professor Hunter. There was a note on top.

Penny,

I've given you my two cents. You have my number. I hope to hear from you soon.

-Brendan

I put my fingers between my eyes and squeezed to help diminish my headache. I leaned back down against my pillow and looked at his note again. Brendan was right. I knew he was right. I had always known that I shouldn't be with Professor Hunter. But I wanted to be. I needed to be. If he really still felt the same way about me, then there was no choice to make. It was always going to be him.

I glanced at the clock on the wall. It was 2 a.m. Professor Hunter would be asleep. I picked up my phone. I had two missed calls from him, but no voicemails. I clicked on his name. He had shown me his divorce papers, but his wife still hadn't signed them. Maybe we just needed to take a break until it was official. If it was love, time wouldn't matter. We could wait until it was right.

I typed out a text to him. "Are you up?"

His reply came almost immediately. "Yes."

Me: "Can we talk?"

James: "I'll come get you. Are you in your dorm?"

Me: "We can talk on the phone. Call me."

James: "I want to see you."

I bit my lip. I didn't want him to know I was in the hospital. He already felt bad enough about what had happened. He couldn't come here anyway. I was pretty sure visiting hours were over.

Me: "Let's just wait until the morning. I'm actually pretty tired."

James: "Penny, where are you?"

I swallowed hard and responded: "Please don't freak out."

James: "Where are you?"

I sighed and let my head sink back into the pillow. "I'm in the hospital."

James: "I'll be there in twenty minutes."

Me: "I think visiting hours are over."

I waited a few minutes for a response but none came. I rolled onto my side and put my phone back down on the bed. They weren't going to let him up. Just in case, I folded up the note from Brendan and slipped it into the envelope that Professor Hunter had given me.

I was just drifting asleep again when the door opened. Professor Hunter was standing there in jeans and a zip up hoodie. He wasn't wearing a shirt underneath his hoodie and I could see his muscular chest. He closed the door and made his way over to me without saying a word. He kicked off his shoes as he looked down at me.

I couldn't read his emotion. Worried. Angry maybe. Lost.

He lifted the sheet on my bed and climbed in next to me.

"James," I whispered. I tried to hold back my tears. It was so good to see him.

He wrapped his arms around me. "I shouldn't have let you leave." He kissed my forehead.

"I didn't give you much of a choice."

"No, you didn't." He kissed my forehead again. "How long have you been here?"

"We can talk in the morning." I didn't want to tell him that we needed to wait. I wanted him to hold me like this forever. Being in his arms was my favorite thing in the world.

"How long, Penny?"

"Since this afternoon I guess. Not long after I left your place. I passed out on Main Street."

"And someone found you?"

"Brendan." He pulled back from me slightly.

"I'll have to thank him."

"How did you get up here?" I didn't want to talk about Brendan with Professor Hunter. I didn't want him to get angry again.

"Having money has its advantages."

"You bribed the hospital staff?"

"I didn't say that."

I looked into his eyes. "I'm glad that you're here." I was quiet for a minute as I stared at him. "I'm sorry."

"You have nothing to be sorry for. Even though you're not nervous around me anymore, you still like to apologize for things you haven't done." He smiled at me.

"You still make me nervous."

He lowered his eyebrows slightly. "Why?"

"You're so hot and cold. I never know how you're going to react to things. It's unsettling. And confusing."

"There's nothing to be confused about anymore. I'm here and I'm not going anywhere." He placed a gentle kiss against my lips.

I wanted to cry all over again. I was so sure that I wanted to wait. The plan was to put the brakes on for awhile. But now that he was here, I couldn't think straight. He was caring, and kind, and sincere. I pulled back from his kiss. His face was shadowed in the dark room so I couldn't see his expression. But I could still make out his black eye. I could feel his heart beating underneath my hand and it was beating so fast.

"Do I make you nervous too?" I asked.

"Sometimes. I'm nervous right now."

"Why?" I rubbed my hand against the scruff on his cheek.

"You left me today because you needed time to think over things." He pulled my hand off his face and kissed my palm. "And I can't tell what you're thinking." He turned my hand over and kissed each of my knuckles. "I don't know what you've decided."

"I opened my present."

"And?"

"You've never opened up to me like that before."

"I want to be able to give you what you need, Penny."

"Why is it so hard for you to talk to me?"

"Most people look at me and judge me in one second. I'm well off. My parents are well off. They think everything has been handed to me. And when I was younger, it was. So I can't correct their opinion. I haven't met anyone who sees more than that."

"Because you refuse to open up. So what else are they supposed to see?"

"You see more."

"That's because I don't care about your money. I care about you."

"I know. I'm trying, Penny. I'm not used to this."

"This?"

"The way I feel about you."

He had written that he loved me. *Why can't he say it out loud to me?* I wanted to hear him say it. "I've never been in love before."

"I know." He ran his fingers through my hair.

"Have you?"

"I've never felt like this."

"Does love always hurt this much?"

"I'm not trying to hurt you. I don't want to ever hurt you again."

"You're not good for me."

He sighed and put his arms around me again. "No, I'm not."

"But I love you anyway." I could feel my tears falling again. "I'm sorry. Geez, I don't know why I'm so emotional today."

"It's a side effect of having a concussion."

"Oh." I laughed and wiped the tears off my cheeks. I wanted him to say he loved me back. I needed him to say it.

"You're so gorgeous."

I laughed. "I have a huge bandage on my head."

"You're still gorgeous."

I wanted to hear those three words out loud. I needed to know that it was real, that he still felt the same way. I traced the bruise around his eye with my index finger. "I love you."

He ran the tip of his nose against mine, but didn't say a word.

"I'm actually really tired now." I rolled over so that I was no longer facing him. Having a concussion really did make me emotional. But it wasn't just that. *Why won't he say it back?* Maybe this wasn't love. Maybe it was lust on hyper drive and I was just as insane as I felt.

"Hey." He leaned over and grabbed my chin in his hand. "What's wrong?"

I sat up so that his hand fell from me. "Why won't you say it?"

"Say what?"

"I've told you multiple times that I love you. You never say it back. Why won't you say it?"

"I have said it."

"No, you haven't."

"I haven't?"

"No."

He pushed the sheet off of us and straddled me, pinning me in place. "I could have sworn I said it."

"You haven't."

"My mistake." He kissed my shoulder. "I love you." He kissed my neck. "I love you." He pulled down the neckline of my hospital gown and kissed my clavicle. "I love you." He tugged on the string behind my neck and pulled the gown down even more. "I love you," he said as he kissed me between my breasts.

It was exactly what I wanted. And more. The machine I was attached to that monitored my heart rate started beeping faster.

He laughed at the machine as he kissed the bruise on my stomach. "I love you." He pushed the fabric to the side and kissed my hip bone. "I love you."

A moan escaped from my lips. I could feel him smile against my skin. My heart was racing and the beeping of the machine was a constant reminder. I could feel myself growing wet each time his lips touched my skin. I never wanted him to stop.

His breath lingered between my thighs. "I love you." He put his lips around my clit and gently sucked.

I closed my eyes and lifted my hips to meet him. He pushed my hips back down, spread my thighs with his strong hands, and placed a slow stroke against my aching pussy.

The machine was beeping so loudly I thought it might break.

He made a slow, torturous circle with his tongue and looked up at me. His eyes were filled with want. "I love you. And I want to make love to you."

I gulped. "Then do it."

He sat up between my thighs and slowly unbuttoned his jeans. I reached my hand that wasn't attached to the IV out and unzipped his hoodie. His perfectly sculpted torso seemed to glisten in the dark room. He stared down at me as he pulled down his fly. He pushed his pants and boxers down his hips. His erection was already full. He slid the rest of my hospital gown to the side and looked down at my naked body. I loved his eyes on me.

He glanced over at the monitor. "Your heart is beating so fast." He leaned down and kissed my left breast.

"Because you're torturing me."

"Am I?" he said as he took my nipple in his mouth. He swirled his tongue around it and then bit it gently with his teeth.

I turned my head and moaned into the pillow. My breathing hitched when both his hands slid to my ass. He lifted my lower back and slowly entered me. I moaned into my pillow again. He leaned into me and lowered my back down onto the bed. He kept one hand on my ass and put his other on the pillow next to my face.

I turned to look at him, and as soon as I did, he placed a kiss against my lips. I ran my fingers through his hair and grabbed the back of his neck. He squeezed my ass as he thrust himself deep inside of me. I moaned into his mouth. He bit my lip as he pulled back slightly.

"Are we going to break that thing?" he asked. The monitor was beeping relentlessly.

"I don't care." I grabbed a handful of his hair and brought his lips back down to mine. I wrapped my legs around him and let the sensation of him filling me take over. With each thrust of his hips I climbed higher and higher.

"I love you, Penny."

"I love you, Professor Hunter," I panted. I ran my hand down his chiseled abs and slipped it behind his hoodie. I ran my fingers down his muscular back and onto his ass. It tensed each time he thrust his length inside of me. I squeezed his tight ass and he moaned in response.

He moved his hand to my thigh. "I'll never get enough of you."

I groaned as he began to move faster. He knew my body so well. He knew exactly how to make me unravel.

He leaned in and whispered, "Come for me, my love." He tilted his hips down, making his erection hit me in just the right spot.

"Professor Hunter," I moaned as my toes curled. I felt myself clench around him. He silenced me with a kiss. Only he could fill me with that complete feeling of warmth and bliss.

"Penny," he groaned in my ear. He lightly bit my ear-lobe as he found his own release.

CHAPTER 12

Sunday

Someone cleared their throat. My eyelids felt heavy. I slowly opened my eyes and saw my parents standing by the door.

Oh shit. Professor Hunter had his arm around me and his eyes were still closed. *Shit!* I elbowed him in the stomach.

"Penny," he mumbled and kissed my shoulder.

I elbowed him again. I was relieved to see that my hospital gown was tied back in place. James must have done it after I had fallen asleep. "Mom, Dad, hi."

"Huh?" Professor Hunter opened his eyes.

Oh my God. I had no idea what to do. I pushed Professor Hunter again so he'd get off the bed. "James," I whispered and tilted my head toward my parents.

He slowly sat up. His hair was sticking up in that sexy way it always did after we slept together. *Oh my God, he has sex hair.* And my parents are standing there seeing him with sex hair. I ran my fingers through my hair just in case I looked anything like Professor Hunter.

Professor Hunter rubbed his eyes and looked over toward the door. "Oh." He pretended to cough as he zipped up his pants. "Oh, umm..." he quickly climbed off the bed and laughed awkwardly.

Holy fuck. Did they hear him zippering his pants?

He looked down and zipped up his hoodie to hide his naked torso.

This isn't happening.

"Wow, this is not how I expected to meet you Mr. and Mrs. Taylor." He ran his hand through his hair and looked over to me. He looked so uncomfortable and nervous. Which made him look even younger. *Thank God he looks so young.*

"Mom, Dad, this is James."

James walked over to my parents and held out his hand to my father. "I've heard so much about both of you. It's a pleasure to meet you, sir."

My dad looked at me and then back at James. He seemed pissed. "That's quite the shiner," he said dryly and shook James' hand.

"Oh." Professor Hunter touched his black eye and tried to laugh it off. "I had forgotten about that. Just a misunderstanding." He turned toward my mom. "And Mrs. Taylor." He put his hand out and she quickly shook it. She didn't look angry at all. She actually looked ecstatic.

"Excuse my outfit." Professor Hunter tugged the zipper on his hoodie all the way up to his neck. "I just rushed over as soon as I heard what happened." He leaned down, picked up his shoes off the floor, and sat down in a chair. He laced his shoes and stood back up.

"It's so nice to meet you, James," my mom said. She was smiling from ear to ear. "So how do you know Penny?"

"Oh." He smiled over at me. "We actually met at a coffee shop on Main Street at the beginning of the semester."

"Is that so?"

"And we ended up having a class together. Comm."

"Do you hate it as much she does?" my mom asked.

Professor Hunter laughed. "I actually love the class. It's my favorite this semester. Mostly because Penny's in it." He smiled at me. "You know, I didn't actually know she hated it, though. Her speeches are really good. She tends to be too hard on herself."

"That's what I always say," my mom responded.

This could not be any more awkward.

"It's so nice to get to meet Penny's new friends. We got to meet Brendan yesterday. Such a sweetheart. He stayed and waited for hours to see if she was okay. Are you friends with him too?"

A cloudy expression crossed over Professor Hunter's face. But only for a second. I was probably the only one who saw it.

"No. And actually, Penny and I aren't just friends. She's my girlfriend."

"Oh?" My mom looked even happier, if that was possible.

"Yes."

"I'm so sorry, James. Penny didn't tell us she was dating anyone. I'm so embarrassed. Penny, this is kind of a big deal isn't it? Your first boyfriend?"

Mom! "It's still new. I was going to tell you." I thought it couldn't get any weirder, but it just had. *Is she trying to mortify me?*

Professor Hunter turned back to me. It looked like he was biting the inside of his cheek to prevent himself from laughing. He seemed to be enjoying himself now.

"You know what? James was the first thing she said when she woke up. We had no idea what she was talking about. But I guess she wanted to see you. Isn't that sweet, honey?" She looked over at my dad.

"Mhm," my dad said and crossed his arms. He never got mad, but he looked so angry right now.

James seemed to sense the hostility in the air too. "Well, I don't want to interfere with your time, Mr. and Mrs. Taylor. I just spent all night with her."

What the hell?

"Sleeping," Professor Hunter quickly said.

"Excuse me?" my dad said.

Professor Hunter cleared his throat. "Not sleeping with her. I was just in bed with her. Sleeping next to her I mean. Just beside her." Professor Hunter shoved his hands into his pockets. He was usually so collected. But my father was intimidating him. It was actually pretty entertaining to watch.

My mom laughed. "Don't be ridiculous, James. We'd like to get to know you." She walked into the room and sat down in one of the chairs. My dad walked over to the only other chair and sat down. His arms were still crossed.

Professor Hunter half stood half sat on the edge of my bed. I reached over and grabbed his hand. He seemed to automatically relax. He squeezed my hand.

There was an awkward silence in the room. I was relieved when there was a knock on the door and the doctor walked in.

"You look a lot better this morning," she said. I saw her eyes flit toward Professor Hunter for a second. I couldn't help but be a little jealous.

"Do you think I can go home today?"

"Let's see." She pressed a button on the machine that had been monitoring my heartbeat. It started printing out a long chart. "Well that's strange."

"What is it?" my father asked.

"Well, it looks like there was a twenty minute period of escalated pulse."

Professor Hunter laughed and then turned it into a forced cough. He squeezed my hand and looked down at his shoes.

Oh my God. I hadn't even thought about someone monitoring the information on that stupid machine. *Who has sex in a hospital bed anyway? Didn't I have any control?*

"How are you feeling?" she asked and looked at me. "Are you struggling for breath at all? Have you noticed that your heart is racing? Or any palpitations?"

"No. Not at all. I'm fine."

She flipped a few switches on the monitor. "It could have been a computer malfunction. It seems to be working fine now, though. Strange." She leaned down and unplugged the machine and then plugged it back in.

"Maybe it was just a nightmare or something," I said quietly.

"Possibly," the doctor replied. "So the man who brought you in said you had fallen a couple nights ago and hit your head pretty bad. And then you fainted yesterday afternoon. Are you feeling lightheaded at all today?"

"No. I feel a lot better."

"Well you have a moderate concussion. You shouldn't have been walking around by yourself. Plus you had an empty stomach and you were dehydrated. It's no wonder that you fainted."

"Will she be okay now?" Professor Hunter asked.

"She needs to rest and build her strength back up."

"Can she leave today?" he asked.

"Let's keep the IV in for a few more hours to help with your dehydration. I'll be back to check on you soon.

And if everything looks good and your heart rate stays down, you can head home."

"How long should she stay at home?" my mom asked. "She has classes." She looked at my dad. "I can take tomorrow off. I just need to call in."

"I'd recommend taking it easy for a few days. Definitely no classes on Monday. And just see how you feel on Tuesday. Don't push yourself. I'll be back in a few hours to check in." The doctor nodded at my parents and walked out of the room.

"Okay, let me call the office." My mom stood up and grabbed her purse.

"She can come back to my place," Professor Hunter said. "If that's okay with both of you, of course." He looked at my parents.

"A dorm room isn't the best place to recoup from this," my dad said coolly.

"He actually lives in a nice apartment, Dad. It would be okay with me. I don't want to inconvenience you guys."

"It's never an inconvenience, Penny. Besides, James has classes. We can't ask him to miss them," my mom said.

"I can cancel them. I mean, skip them. Not a big deal at all."

"Well, if you're sure it's okay, James. And if that's really what you want to do, Penny," my mom said.

My dad lifted up his hand. "Nonsense. You'll be coming back with us, Pen." His tone was the same one he would use when I got in trouble when I was younger. It meant that it was the end of the discussion. He wasn't even giving James a fair chance. I was just about to protest when there was a knock on the door. Melissa burst into the room and ran over to me.

"Oh my God, Penny!" She threw her arms around me. "Have you been here this whole time? I thought you were okay." She turned to James. "Thanks for keeping me in the dark, James."

"I didn't know she was here either. I would have told you."

"Then where were you, Penny? I haven't heard from you since Friday night. I can't believe..." she let her voice trail off when she saw the expression on my face. "We can talk later." She squeezed my arm and walked over to my parents. "Thanks for calling me, Mrs. Taylor." She hugged both my parents at the same time.

My parents loved Melissa. Whenever they visited me at school they always took Melissa and me out to dinner. I was pretty sure they thought Melissa being my roommate freshman year was the best thing that ever happened to me. And they were probably right. Having a best friend that was outgoing and fun had definitely been good for me. And without her forcing me to go out all the time, I never would have run into James in the rain that night.

"Oh, I have someone I want you to meet." Melissa let go of her embrace and walked over to the door. "Hey guys, it's okay, you can come in."

Josh came in, followed by Tyler.

What the hell?

She grabbed Josh's hand and steered him toward my parents. "Mr. and Mrs. Taylor, this is my boyfriend, Josh." She looked up at Josh. "These are Penny's parents."

"Nice to meet you," he said and shook both of their hands.

My father didn't look nearly as cold when he shook Josh's hand. Maybe because he hadn't expected that Josh had just had sex with Melissa. And he also lacked a black eye.

"And that's our friend Tyler." Melissa pointed over at him. He was hovering by the door. Tyler still had bruises around the inside corners of his eyes.

My dad looked at Tyler's face and then glanced over at Professor Hunter's. His brow furrowed.

"Nice to meet you both." Tyler smiled at them but didn't move.

My parents started talking to Josh and I tuned them out. I looked over at Tyler. He was staring at me. It looked like he wanted to come over, but he stayed where he was.

"Thanks for coming, Tyler," I said quietly. I was more than a little surprised to see him. But we were still friends. It was nice of him to come.

He glanced at Professor Hunter and then shook his head. He walked over to me. "Yeah, well, Melissa needed a ride." He rubbed the back of his neck with his hand. "It's hard to say no to her."

"Right." I smiled at him. He didn't want to be here. "Well, thanks for bringing her." We had gone from so much to so little. "My parents can take them back. You don't have to stay if you don't want to."

"What? No, that's not what I meant. I wanted to come."

Professor Hunter was gripping my hand tighter and tighter with each word Tyler and I spoke to each other.

"How did you end up in here?" Tyler asked.

"I fainted. On Main Street."

"Penny," his voice sounded strained. "I knew I shouldn't have let you leave. You're so stubborn."

Professor Hunter loosened his grip on my hand.

Shit. I hadn't told him about going to Tyler's. But he wouldn't be upset when I did. I had gone there to call things off between us. "I'm okay, Tyler."

"That's what you said yesterday too. So I don't believe you."

Professor Hunter let go of my hand and stood up. "Does anyone want some coffee or something to eat?"

No one said anything.

"I'll be right back." He ran his hand through his hair and walked toward the door without looking back at me. My dad quickly got up and followed him out of the room. *Not good.*

"Penny?"

I looked back up at Tyler.

He gently took my hand between both of his. "It's hard for me to see you like this."

"I'm not in pain. I'm fine, really. And this time I mean it."

He crouched down by my bed. "Look, I know what I said the other day," he whispered. "But I need you to listen to me now. I don't care that you were with Professor Hunter. I forgive you for hurting me. I forgive you for everything. Please stop making the wrong choice. I need you to choose me. I need you to know the truth..."

"Tyler, stop."

"I was wrong before. I can take care of you. I want to take care of you. I want to be with you. Please stop doing this to me."

"I love him. I love him, Tyler. I don't know what else I can say."

"Okay." He let go of my hand. "Right." He stood back up. He leaned down and kissed me on the forehead. "I'll see you in class then." He gave me a forced smile.

"Wednesday probably."

"Okay." He walked away from my bed. "I'm going to get going guys. Are you staying?"

"Just a minute," Melissa said. Melissa came back over to my bed.

"I'll be waiting outside." Tyler walked out of the room. It was so hard to see him upset. And it was even worse knowing it was my fault.

"What did Tyler say to you?" she whispered.

"That he wants to be with me."

"And?"

"And nothing. I'm in love with James."

"We have a lot to talk about."

I wasn't sure what she meant by that. I sighed. "I know."

"When will you be back?"

"Tuesday."

"Okay." She squeezed my arm again. "Text me." She gave my mom a hug goodbye.

"Feel better, Penny," Josh said. The three of them left.

CHAPTER 13

Sunday

"James is very handsome." My mom sat down on the edge of my bed.

I smiled. "He is."

"And he seems very smitten with you."

I laughed. "I'm smitten with him too."

My mom smiled at me. "I couldn't help but notice that Tyler and Brendan seem to like you too."

I bit my lip. "I know."

"So that must have been a hard choice to make."

I shook my head. "I love him."

"Oh, sweetheart." She patted my foot. "Maybe one day."

"What?"

"Love is more than physical attraction."

"Mom." *Oh my God.* "I know that." I looked down at the sheets and tucked a loose strand of hair behind my ear.

"Relationships are hard work. You're so young. You're supposed to be enjoying yourself."

"I am. He makes me so happy."

"Then why didn't you tell us about him?"

I shrugged my shoulders. "We were a little on again off again at first."

"Is that why James and Tyler both have black eyes?"

I pulled my knees into my chest and wrapped my arms around them. "They got in a fight."

"Over you?"

"I've made some mistakes. I was confused about what I wanted."

"Penny. Try not to take everything so seriously. Is it love? Maybe someday. Don't try to grow up so fast. There's no rush."

I smiled at her. "I know." Professor Hunter was older than me. It was hard not to take things seriously with him. He had asked me to move in with him a few weeks ago. He had just told me he loved me.

My dad and Professor Hunter walked back into the room with the doctor. They were both talking to her, and they both looked more relaxed than they had earlier.

"Okay, Penny," the doctor said and walked over to me. She clicked a few buttons on the monitor and read the report. "Everything looks normal now. You all set to get out of here?"

"Absolutely."

I gritted my teeth as she pulled the IV out of my hand. She placed a bandage over the small hole.

"Take it easy, okay." She handed me some forms to fill out. "Release forms."

I quickly signed my name and handed the clipboard back to her.

"Nice meeting all of you." She smiled at James.

Back off.

She walked out of the room. My mom and dad were discussing something. James walked up to me and handed me my clothes. I slid off the bed, making sure to hold the back of my gown shut.

"I want to come back with you," I whispered.

"I'll see what I can do." He winked at me.

I grabbed my clothes and went into the bathroom. I glanced in the mirror as I untied the hospital gown. My hair was a disaster and my face was greasy. I quickly pulled my hair into a ponytail and splashed water on my face.

When I finished getting dressed, I walked out of the bathroom. I grabbed my envelope and cell phone off the nightstand and shoved them into my jacket pocket.

Professor Hunter walked over to me. "If you want to come back with me, you can." He put his hand on my cheek. "Whatever you want to do."

I nodded and went over to my parents. "Is it okay if I go back with him, Dad?"

"As long as you promise to take it easy, Pen." My dad leaned down and hugged me. "Don't worry us like that again."

"I'm sorry, Dad."

"Call us once in awhile, okay?"

I laughed. "I will. I love you."

"I love you too."

When he let go, it was my mom's turn to hug me.

"Don't forget what I told you, Penny," my mom said. "And when big things happen, call us. No more surprise boyfriends." She laughed. "I love you, sweetie."

"I love you too, Mom." It had been so nice to see them.

"Maybe we can come down sometime again soon and take you two out to dinner. Wouldn't that be nice?"

"Sounds wonderful," James said. "It was really nice meeting you, Mrs. Taylor." He put his hand out.

"Don't be ridiculous." My mom hugged him. James patted her back a little awkwardly.

"And Mr. Taylor." He put his hand out to my dad and my dad shook it without hesitation this time.

"Just because the Eagles season didn't start out well doesn't mean they won't beat the Giants," my dad said.

James laughed. "We'll see."

My parents waved to me and walked out of the room.

I went over to James and clasped my hands behind his neck. "You seem to have won over my dad."

"You never told me how intimidating your father is."

"I didn't know he had an intimidating bone in his body until today."

"Maybe it's because I had to zip up my pants when they came in."

"Do you think they heard that?"

"Well if they didn't, the accelerated heart rate may have tipped them off. Or my rambling about sleeping next to you."

"You were so flustered. It was cute. And mortifying, of course."

"Or I guess they could have just been surprised that you finally had a boyfriend after all these years."

"Shut up and kiss me."

He laughed and placed a kiss against my lips. "I like that I'm your first boyfriend, Penny."

"And I like that you're my first boyfriend. I feel like we're a normal couple right now. It's refreshing."

"Do normal couples usually hang out in hospitals?"

"No. Can we go back to your place now?"

"Yes." He picked me up in his arms.

I couldn't help but laugh. He seemed so happy today. I had forgotten how wonderful he could be. We had fought so much. "You don't need to carry me. My legs work fine."

"I know." He pulled me to his chest. "I want to."

I rested my head against his chest and breathed in his familiar scent. "You smell really good. Have I ever told you that?"

"No, you haven't."

I looked up at the scruff under his chin as he stepped into the elevator. He hit the button with his elbow.

"You can put me down if you need to."

"I don't need to." The elevator doors opened and he stepped out onto the main floor. He carried me out the entrance and set me down on my feet. It was pouring. "I'll pull the car up."

"I like the rain."

"Yeah, you're not getting a cold on top of everything else. I promised your parents I'd take care of you." He pulled his hood up and gave me a peck on the lips. "I'll be right back."

He ran into the rain. I watched him until he disappeared from view. I put my hands in my pockets and felt the envelope. I didn't want to think about it. Right now I just wanted to enjoy being with him. Maybe we could have a more serious conversation in a few days.

His car pulled up under the veranda. He quickly got out and opened the door for me. I walked over to him. He was completely soaked.

"You're really handsome."

"Get in the car, Penny."

"You love bossing me around."

"I like when you listen to me."

"I know." I slid into the seat and he closed the door behind me. When he got into his seat, he unzipped his wet hoodie and threw it into the backseat. His abs looked even sexier when they were wet. He turned on the heat and pointed one of the vents at me. After I buckled my seat-belt, he put the car in drive and we sped off.

When we were on the highway, he put his hand on the center console, palm up. I put my hand on top of his. He intertwined his fingers with mine.

"So you liked my parents okay?"

"Your parents are fantastic. And I appreciated that they tried to ignore the fact that we're, well...you know."

"Banging?"

"You're very eloquent with your words, Miss Taylor." He flashed me one of his smiles that made my knees weak.

"Are you going to get in trouble for canceling so many of your classes?"

"I haven't canceled that many classes."

"You cancel class all the time."

Professor Hunter laughed. "Well, no one has said anything to me yet. I doubt any students would complain about having more free time."

"True. But I really do feel better. Maybe we should both go to class tomorrow."

"The doctor specifically said to take tomorrow off."

"I know. But I've been skipping class a lot recently. And when I went I barely paid attention."

"I noticed."

I bit my lip and looked out the window. "I'm going to fail statistics. I've never failed a class in my life."

"Then why do you think you're going to fail?"

I looked back at him. "My Stat professor has a really thick accent and it's hard to understand him. I was teaching myself by reading the book but I was so unmotivated recently that I've fallen really far behind. And there's a test next week. And I don't even understand why I'm bad at it. I was great at math in high school. I took A.P. Calculus and I never had a problem."

"It's more business oriented than math oriented."

I laughed. "I guess I suck at business then. That's not great for the major I chose. Either way, I think I need to hire a tutor."

"I can tutor you."

"In Stat? You're a marketing professor."

Professor Hunter laughed. "So you really haven't read that much about me online then?"

"Not much, no. Are you secretly a statistics expert?"

He laughed again. "No, I wouldn't say that. But it is your lucky day, because you're dating a genius."

"I know that you're intelligent, but you took Stat ages ago. You're forgetting that you're an old man."

"Do you want my help or not?"

I laughed. "Yes."

"Good. You're definitely not going to fail Stat."

"That's very sweet of you to take such an interest in my education, professor."

"I have selfish motivations."

"And what are those?"

"I don't like to see you upset. And I'm pretty sure you'd be upset if you failed a class."

"Yeah, probably." I ran my fingers across the palm of his hand and up the inside of his forearm. "Any other reason?"

"If you have to retake classes you'll be in school forever."

"And that would bother you?"

"Yes, it would bother me." He pulled into the parking garage underneath his apartment building. He parked between two of his other cars and turned off the engine. "When you graduate I can finally have you all to myself."

He grabbed his sweatshirt out of the back seat and climbed out of the car. *All to himself?* When he opened the door for me, I grabbed his hand and we walked over to the elevator. After sliding his access card in the reader, the doors slid open and we both stepped on.

"Well after I graduate, I'll get a job. If anything, we'll probably have less time together."

"Maybe."

"You don't think I'll be able to find a job?"

"I didn't say that." He let go of my hand and leaned against the wall beside me.

"Then what do you mean?"

He shrugged his shoulders. "I just meant that you won't really need to work."

"Of course I will."

"Not necessarily." The elevator came to a stop and Professor Hunter swiped his other access card through the reader. He lifted me into his arms and carried me into his apartment.

"So that's your master plan for after I graduate? You want me to stay in your apartment all day while you work? I'd be bored out of my mind."

"Well, it would be our apartment, not mine."

"No it wouldn't. I wouldn't have any money to pay for my half of the rent."

He laughed as he put me down on the couch. He knelt down on the floor beside it. "I have enough money for both of us, Penny. Besides, I don't rent this apartment. I own it."

"James...I'm getting a job after I graduate. I want to be able to provide for myself. I'm not going to mooch off of you."

He lifted up my tank top and kissed me right below my belly button.

"Hey, stop trying to distract me." I cupped his chin in my hand.

He was smiling at me. He found this conversation extremely humorous for some reason.

"It's a good thing I am young. Because now I have extra time to convince you that that's a terrible idea."

"Mhm. It doesn't sound that terrible to me right now," he said.

"Certainly you'd be sick of me by then anyway."

He lifted my legs, sat down on the couch, and put my legs on his lap. "No, I don't think so." He slowly unlaced one of my sneakers, pulled it off my foot, and dropped it on the floor. Grabbing my other foot, he repeated the process with my other shoe.

It was hard to talk about the future with him. I didn't want to discuss everything right now. But he was being so nonchalant about the fact that he was still married. He couldn't commit to me in his current situation, so what was the point of talking about it?

"Are you hungry?" I asked.

"I'm guessing that means you are?"

"I'm starving."

"What would you like?"

"Can we order a pizza or something?"

"That sounds fantastic." He pulled out his phone from his jeans and looked over at me. "Where do you want it from?"

"Is Grottos okay?"

"Sure. I haven't tried their pizza yet."

"Are you serious? How can you live here and not try that?" I bit my lip. That's what Brendan had said to me when I told him I hadn't tried one of the hotdogs from the stand on Main Street.

"I'm assuming you like it?"

"It's the best."

"Grottos it is then." He put his phone up to his ear. "What kind of pizza do you like?"

"Plain."

"Is it weird that I didn't know that?" He rubbed his thumb along the inside of my ankle.

Tyler knew my favorite pizza place and that I only liked cheese pizza. I shook the thought out of my head. "We've never had pizza together before. How would you know?"

"Hey," he said into the phone. He ordered the pizza and gave them his address. When he hung up, he smiled at me. He was still caressing the inside of my ankle. "So what makes their pizza the best? Because I'm from New York, and I'm pretty sure New York pizza is supposed to be the best."

"You'll just have to wait and see."

"What else don't I know about you?"

"You know me pretty well. Although, we don't do much talking when we're together." I tried to raise my eyebrow at him but I couldn't do it.

He laughed. "I'm glad you can't give me a scolding look."

"I'm not trying to scold you. I think that being intimate is time well spent."

I pressed the sole of one of my feet against the zipper of his jeans.

He grabbed my foot in his hand. "Except you're supposed to be taking it easy. Which gives us a perfect opportunity to talk."

"Okay. Let's play a game."

"What did you have in mind?"

"Truth or dare."

Professor Hunter laughed. "Wait, really?"

"The idea of playing truth or dare with a guy I liked has always excited me. I don't know, we don't have to. You can just ask me some questions."

"No, I'll play."

I smiled at him. "Okay, truth or dare?"

"Truth."

"What do you usually do in your free time?" I looked around the empty apartment.

"I grade papers."

"That can't be all that you do."

"Recently I've been busy thinking about you." He smiled at me.

"So you grade papers and think about me? But what do you do for fun?"

"Thinking about you is fun when you're not mad at me. But I believe it's my turn now. Truth or dare?"

"Truth."

"Why didn't you tell your parents you were dating someone?"

"I thought our relationship was supposed to be secret."

"At first. But then things changed. You told Melissa."

"I didn't want to lie to them about you being a professor."

"So are you mad that I met them today?"

"No, not at all. I think they both liked you."

"Only because they don't know that I'm your professor."

"Maybe. My mom thought you were hot."

Professor Hunter laughed.

"Truth or dare?" I asked.

"Truth."

I wanted the game to be light and fun, so I switched gears. "So back to my original question. What do you do for fun?"

"You."

I kicked his leg playfully. "Seriously, James."

He shrugged. "I exercise most days."

"Obviously." I looked at his muscular physique. "What do you do for exercise?"

"There's a gym in the building. And I like to run outside."

"Do you even have a T.V.?"

"No. I can get one if you want."

"Don't you get bored? Alone in your apartment?"

"I've been toying with the idea of starting a new company. It keeps me busy."

"Another tech company?"

"Yeah. I've been working on some logistics for awhile. But it's in the beginning stages. It doesn't make sense financially to start it right now." He looked away from me.

I swallowed hard. "Do you mean, it's better to wait until after you're divorced?"

He ran his hands through his hair. "I'm not giving her half of this too."

"Truth or dare?"

"I think it's my turn, Penny."

"Truth or dare?" He was the one that brought her up. Now seemed as good a time as ever.

"Truth." He sighed.

"Why did you go to New York while we were broken up?"

"I needed to talk to her."

"About what? Why didn't you just talk to her on the phone?"

"I was hoping I could convince her to sign the papers."

"By having sex with her?"

"It wasn't like that."

"So what then? You went to talk about getting divorced and ended up sleeping with her? One step forward, two steps back."

"I missed you. I was a mess. I'm sorry, Penny."

"Do you still have feelings for her?"

"No."

"Then why did you sleep with her?"

"It's not like I made love to her. It was just sex."

"And what about the first time we had sex? Did that mean nothing too?"

Professor Hunter sighed. "No. It meant everything. It's different with you. Everything is different with you. I don't know what else I can say. I was upset. I made a mistake. End of story."

"It's not the end of the story because you're still married." I was trying to keep my voice even, but I was having trouble.

"Truth or dare?" he asked.

"Dare."

"Penny..."

"Fine, truth."

"And what about Tyler?"

"What about him?"

"You went to see him yesterday. What did you talk about?"

"I went to see him to tell him I wanted to be with you."

"After you read my letter?"

"No, before. I want to be with you. That's all that I want. But you're complicated. The situation is complicated. And I don't mean just because you're my professor. It's because you're still married. How can you sit there and talk about a future with me in this situation?"

"Because I know it's over. I'll talk to her again."

"No." I pulled my feet off his lap and hugged my knees to my chest.

"I'm not going to sleep with her again. Penny." He leaned forward and kissed my kneecap. "I'm getting divorced. I've already signed the papers."

"I know."

"So why are you still upset about it?"

"It makes me feel like a bad person. What if she never signs the papers?"

"I'll get her to sign them." He kissed my knee again. "I'm sorry about what happened. Please forgive me."

"I love you. I love you so much. There's a million reasons why I should give you up. But I can't. I don't want to. And we were broken up. So there isn't anything to forgive."

"Penny, Penny, Penny." He leaned over me and placed a kiss against my lips. "I love you."

"I love you, too." I started to cry. I pushed myself up into a seated position. "Stupid concussion." I tried to laugh as I wiped my tears away.

"Hey." He pulled the cushion away from the back of the couch and slid next to me. He wrapped his arm around my shoulder. "What's wrong?"

"If this really is love, then it won't matter if we wait." It's what I had decided before I fainted. Nothing had changed. I needed to be strong.

"Wait for what?"

"For your divorce to be final. For me to graduate. For things to be less complicated."

"Is this about Tyler? Or Brendan?"

"No. It has nothing to do with them."

His look was cold.

"I thought you didn't want me. I was a mess. I was trying to get over you. But I don't want either of them. I felt so empty when you stopped talking to me. I just didn't want to feel empty anymore." My words hung in the air for a long time.

"I felt empty too." We were silent again as we looked into each other's eyes.

"I choose you. I just want to wait till it's right."

He looked down at my legs and traced a circle around the inside of my knee. He was silent for a few minutes. "Penny, I've spent my whole life doing things I didn't want to. I don't want to wait anymore. You make me happy. To me, that's all that matters."

"Am I not worth waiting for?"

"That's not what I meant. Of course you're worth waiting for." He grabbed my hand and rubbed his thumb against my palm. "But I feel like I've been waiting my whole life already. You're young. I get that." He sighed. "But two years is a long time. I don't want to wait anymore."

"Then we can just wait until your divorce is final. What's the point of being together if we can't fully commit to one another?"

"I am committed to you. I've told you I love you. I don't take that lightly."

"But our relationship is a secret and you still have a wife. How happy do you think we can be for the next two years like this?"

"What if I disclose our relationship to the dean?"

I looked up at him. "What?"

"Is that what you want? Will that prove to you how I feel? We won't have to hide our relationship anymore."

"We'll get in trouble."

"Not necessarily. Only if someone complains."

"What about Comm?"

"I'm not sure what will happen with that."

"I don't want to have to take it again."

"So how about I quit?"

"Teaching?"

"If it's the only way."

"I thought you loved teaching. It's your fresh start."

"You're my fresh start. And I don't love teaching nearly as much as I love you."

I straddled him on the couch. His hands slipped to my waist as I leaned forward and hugged him. "I don't want any of that. I'm sorry. I just want your divorce to be official. I don't want you to have to change who you are. I love who you are." I put my forehead against his. "I don't want to wait. I just don't want to have to feel guilty about not waiting."

"There's nothing to feel guilty about. But I'll have my lawyer figure something out, okay? I'll take care of it."

"Soon?"

"Soon."

CHAPTER 14

Sunday

"Favorite soda?" he asked.

"Cherry Coke."

"I had my fridge stocked with a bunch of things when I thought you'd be staying here more often." He pulled out a Cherry Coke and handed it to me.

I took it and grabbed the fridge handle before he closed it. "Let me see." The fridge was completely full. I reached in and grabbed a packet of juice boxes. "Juice boxes? Seriously? How young do you think I am?"

"Those are actually mine." He grabbed the pack, put it back in the fridge, and closed the door.

"Why don't you just buy a bottle of apple juice if you like it so much?"

He looked embarrassed. "I was never allowed to have them when I was a kid." He shrugged.

That was probably the most personal thing he had ever confessed to me. I imagined him as a little boy demanding juice boxes and being denied. I thought it would make me laugh, but it made me feel sad. His parents sounded worse and worse every time I learned something new about them. "Okay." I handed the soda back to him. "I actually want one of those."

"You do?"

"Yes, please."

He smiled and opened the fridge back up. I took two juice boxes, he grabbed two plates, and we sat down at the kitchen counter.

I picked up a slice of pizza and took a huge bite. I was so hungry. It was only a matter of seconds before the first slice was gone.

Professor Hunter was staring at me. "I'm glad to see that you've gotten your appetite back."

"That's what your love does for me."

He smiled and took a bite. "This is pretty delicious."

"I told you." I took a sip out of the juice box. "Why is everything so much better with a straw?"

"I don't know, but it really is." He took a sip from his juice box.

I started laughing.

"What's so funny?"

"It's just...you look like a model and you're drinking from a juice box. It's like, the sexiest apple juice ad ever."

"Marketing at its finest?"

"Absolutely."

Professor Hunter laughed. "What do you want to do with our day off tomorrow?"

"It's not really a day off. I'm supposed to just recuperate, right?"

"We're both ditching class. So it's kind of a day off. We can do whatever you want."

"I think I'd like to see what a normal day is like for you. The behind the professor's facade special."

"You do like to watch a lot of T.V., huh?"

"I don't think I watch an unusual amount. You're the weird one. Who doesn't have a T.V.?"

Professor Hunter shrugged. "Sometimes I watch stuff on my computer. Speaking of which, I need to send out that email about canceling class. I'll be right back."

"It really is okay if you need to go to class."

"I don't need to." He kissed me and slid off the stool. He went over to the door I had never been through and disappeared behind it.

I grabbed another slice of pizza. I was glad we had ended up talking about everything. There was this calmness between us now. We had been surviving through tension and now we wouldn't need to. It had been a long time since I had felt so relaxed.

A few minutes later my phone vibrated. I picked it up and slid my thumb across the screen. Professor Hunter had sent the email.

"Comm 212 is canceled tomorrow morning as well. I've had some pressing personal matters that have needed my attention. But speeches will resume as planned. Everyone with last names beginning with A through M will be going Wednesday, and everyone else will go on Friday. I will have my regular office hours on Tuesday if you have any questions. Please feel free to email me as well. I'm looking forward to hearing your speeches."

-Professor J. Hunter

There were several unread text messages on my phone, but I decided not to read them. I put my phone back in my pocket and wandered to the door that Professor Hunter had disappeared through. I knocked lightly on the door, but there was no response. I slowly opened the door.

"Professor Hunter?" My voice echoed down a hallway. I had expected to find one room, not a hallway. There were several doors lining the right side. All along the left side were potted plants. It was like I had stepped out of an apartment and into a fancy office. I stood there for a moment, thinking about what to do. It seemed like snooping if I opened every door. But then I heard his voice at the end of the corridor. I walked toward the door at the end of the hallway. I was about to knock when I heard him talking again.

"Send the photos when you have them."

Silence.

"That's fine. I just need it done."

Silence.

"By the end of the week at the latest."

Silence.

"No, I'll need it delivered. I don't want a cyber footprint on this. Thanks, Max."

What the hell is he talking about? I had heard the term cyber footprint in class before. It was like the paper trail of the internet. But why was he worried about one?

I knocked on the door. "Professor Hunter?"

I heard the shuffling of papers. A drawer opened and closed. And then Professor Hunter opened the door.

"So I'm a pressing personal matter?" I smiled up at him. He was blocking my view of the room.

"Yes."

I glanced over my shoulder down the hallway. "Your apartment is a lot bigger than I realized."

"Do you want me to give you a tour?" He stepped out of the room and closed the door behind him. He grabbed my hand to lead me down the hall, but I didn't move.

"Well, what's in there?" I nodded my head at the door he had just come from.

"It's my office. Nothing fancy."

"I'd like to see that." I tried to give him my most innocent smile.

"It's kind of messy."

"Good, because the rest of your apartment is unnervingly clean." I stood up on my tiptoes and clasped my hands behind his neck. "Please?"

"It's really not much to see."

"So it doesn't matter if I see it then."

He smiled at me. "Whatever you want." He opened the door back up. I let go of him and walked past him into the room.

It was just as big as his bedroom. The room was long and wrapped back around to the front of the apartment so that there were windows overlooking Main Street to one side. All the furniture was modern and the room had kind of a sleek vibe to it. His desk was positioned near the window to get the best view. Two of the walls were covered in floor to ceiling bookcases. There was a whiteboard on the other wall, covered in some type of mathematical formulas, but nothing I knew how to decipher. He hadn't been joking. The room was clean, but there was stuff everywhere. It was a lot more like what I assumed a bachelor pad would look like. There was even a dartboard and a little basketball hoop above the trash can.

"You're kind of a hoarder," I said as I walked farther into the room.

"I'm not a hoarder," he laughed. "I actually use all this stuff."

"What on earth do you need this many computers for?" There were at least a dozen throughout the room.

He shrugged his shoulders.

"And you do have T.V.'s." There were a few mounted next to the whiteboard.

"Oh. Well, yes, but I just use them as monitors. They're hooked up to my computers."

I looked at the leather sofa in the corner. There was a pillow and a blanket on it. "So the rest of your apartment is immaculate because you spend all your time in here?"

"I spend most of my free time in here, yes."

"Well, you seemed very judgy of my wonderfully comfortable dorm room bed. Yet, you usually sleep on a leather sofa?"

"I've been finding it hard to fall asleep in my bed when you're not in it with me." He pressed his lips together.

"Oh." The way he was looking at me made me flush. He was so distracting. I walked over to his desk. "So this is where all your personal stuff is?" I lifted up a picture frame off his desk. There was a picture of him with a woman I didn't recognize and a younger man that looked a little like him. They all had similar features. Professor Hunter's hair was slightly longer in it and he was smiling brightly. He looked a little younger. They were all dressed in fancy clothes. It looked like he and the other guy were wearing tuxedos. "Are these your siblings?"

He walked over to me. "Yeah."

"What are their names?"

"Jennifer and Rob."

"When was this taken?" I had a fleeting thought that it might be from his wedding.

"At the launch party of my company."

"Is that a thing? That's rather extravagant."

"It was a P.R. nightmare."

"How old were you?"

"22."

"Hmm."

"What?" He was smiling down at me.

"You look so happy in this picture. Do you miss it?"

"Running a company?"

"Yeah."

"You'd think that being a C.E.O. would mean I didn't have to answer to anyone." He sat down on the edge of his desk. "But most of my time was spent doing things I didn't love. I do miss certain parts though."

"Is that why you're thinking about starting a new company?"

"Well, as you have so eloquently pointed out, I've had a lot of free time. I needed something to occupy myself."

I laughed and moved between his legs. I put my hands down on his thighs. "I had a question about my present."

"And what is that?"

"The tickets to the Thanksgiving Day parade. Is that an invitation to meet your family?"

He smiled down at me. "If you want it to be."

"Do you think they'll like me?"

"Jennifer and Rob will love you."

"What about your parents?"

"If you could just laugh off everything they say like they're crazy people, that would be best."

"You don't think they'll like me? Why?"

He pulled me closer to him, making my hands slide farther up his thighs. "I don't like to try to think like them."

"Maybe they'll love me."

"Isn't my love enough?"

"Yes." I moved one of my hands to the waistline of his jeans. "Speaking of which, it's a shame that I'm supposed to be taking things easy. That probably means no sex."

"I don't think that's what that means."

"I'm pretty sure." I slipped my hand slightly beneath his waistline, running my fingers through his happy trail.

"I don't consider you to be one to shy away from breaking rules, Penny."

"Me?" I unbuttoned his jeans and slowly unzipped them. "I'm a stickler for the rules, Professor Hunter."

"So you'd be mad if, for example, I did this?" He leaned forward and pushed my jacket off my shoulders. I shook it the rest of the way off.

"Furious."

"What about this?" He pulled off my tank top and unhinged my bra.

"I'm so upset with you right now." I tried not to smile.

"Hmm." He slid off the edge of his desk. "What if I did this?" He pushed my yoga pants over my ass and slowly pulled them down my thighs. When they reached my knees, he released the fabric and they fell to the floor.

I gulped. "I can barely look at you I'm so angry."

"I figured. I'll respect your wishes then." He zipped his pants back up. "I'm going to go take a shower."

What? "Professor Hunter..."

"Don't worry, I'm taking you with me." He lifted me over his shoulder and carried me out of his office.

CHAPTER 15

Monday

I slowly opened my eyes. Light was shining through the blinds. Professor Hunter's arm was wrapped around me. I turned to look at him.

He groaned quietly, but his eyes remained closed. His hair was a little curly and there was scruff along his jaw line. He was perfect in every single way. And I was the luckiest girl in the world. I moved my head so that it was pressed against his chest. Everything seemed so simple when I was with him. It was when we weren't together that all the stupid thoughts hanging above me came falling down. I liked being in our own little bubble.

He was right. There was no point in waiting. We should be happy together now. And his bed really was more comfortable than mine. Or maybe it was just that it was comforting to know he was beside me. Maybe I'd just stay here forever. I kissed his collarbone and then underneath his chin.

"Mmm," he mumbled.

"I like waking up next to you."

"I could get used to this." He ran his fingers through my hair.

I laughed. "So what does the elusive Professor Hunter usually do when he wakes up in the morning?"

"Are you a morning person?" he mumbled.

"I signed up for classes late and got stuck with all 8 a.m.'s. I've gotten used to waking up early."

"Well." He rolled over and looked at his alarm clock. "You're like clockwork then. It's 7:30."

"Is Comm the only 8 a.m. class that you teach?"

"Yes. It's funny, I didn't want to teach it at all. I kind of got stuck with it. But I'm so glad that I did."

"Me too." I kissed his collarbone again.

He yawned and sat up. "I usually go for a run before breakfast. But I just want to hang out with you today. What do you want for breakfast?"

"What do you usually have?"

"Ellen usually fixes me something. But I gave her the next few days off."

"Is that your chef?"

"She cooks and cleans and does everything that I don't know how to do. You'll like her. Come on, let's get up." He lightly slapped my ass.

I laughed and climbed out of bed. I was wearing one of his t-shirts and he was just wearing a pair of plaid pajama bottoms. He looked amazing.

"Does Ellen know about me?"

"Yes. She was the one who went grocery shopping for you. She's excited to meet you."

I followed him into the kitchen. "And she's the one who buys you juice boxes?"

"Mhm. She's a keeper." He opened up the fridge. "How about a bagel?"

"That sounds perfect."

He grabbed a bag of bagels out of the fridge and pulled two out. I watched him slice them and put them in the toaster. "Do you want some coffee?"

"Do you have any orange juice?"

"That I do." He poured us each a glass.

"So I was thinking a little about my speech. And I'm not really sure what to talk about this time. Usually I was flirting with you or losing my mind. I guess I should just do something normal for once?"

"I wouldn't worry about it too much." He winked at me.

"I haven't even thought about a topic yet, though."

"Certainly you'll get an A. You're sleeping with your professor, after all."

"What happened to no perks?"

"Well, Miss Taylor. That concept kind of flew out the window when I fell in love with you."

"Oh yeah?"

"Yeah." He grabbed our bagels and some cream cheese.

"Maybe I should give detailed instructions on how to seduce your professor."

He took a bite out of his bagel. "You didn't seduce me. I seduced you."

"No way. Short skirts, my best push up bra, uncalled for texts, and my unbelievably illicit answers in class seduced the crap out of you."

"I had you right where I wanted you."

I believed him. I may have flirted my way closer to him, but he was always one step ahead of me. He even gave me a fake grade to make me storm into his office.

"So what do you usually do after breakfast?"

"Go to class."

"What other classes do you teach?"

"I teach that grad class twice a week. And I have a few 300 and 400 level marketing courses."

"That's vague. Tell me what the 300 level ones are and I'll try to sign up for one next semester."

"You probably shouldn't take any more of my classes."

"But I like taking your classes. It means I get to stare at you the whole time."

"Which is very distracting."

"You seriously don't want me to take your marketing classes?"

"Well, I was thinking about it. And I think after this semester it really would be best if we disclosed our relationship to the dean. Maybe after winter session? That way your Comm grade won't be in jeopardy."

"Which means I can't take any more of your classes?"

"It does."

"Pros and cons."

"We can spend more time together at night that way. We won't have to worry about people seeing us together around campus. It'll be really nice."

"I'll think about it." Melissa had said other professors might see me differently if they knew. I didn't want that to be the case. "So what do you do after breakfast on the weekends?"

"Work."

"On your new company?"

"There's always something to do." He shifted in his chair. "Actually, there's something I wanted to discuss with you."

"Okay." Why does it feel like I'm in trouble?

"My brother is coming back from Costa Rica this weekend."

"That's fantastic. I can't wait to meet him. I want to get to know your family."

"I invited him here indefinitely. Earlier this month. We weren't together and..."

"James, that's fine. He's your brother. It'll be fun."

"Yeah, he's definitely fun." He took a sip of orange juice.

"Where will he stay?"

"There are guestrooms in the hallway before my office."

"Did you not want me to stay over while he's here?"

"Were you thinking about staying over more?" He looked pleased.

"Well, you were right about your bed. It's a lot more comfortable than mine."

"Is that the only reason?" He pulled me into his arms.

"I'm only in this relationship for the sleeping arrangements. Did I not make that clear when we started this?"

"No, you failed to mention that."

"Well now you know. I'm going to go brush my teeth." I pulled his hands off me and made my way back into his bedroom and into the bathroom. His toothbrush was in the holder. I opened up a few of the drawers, searching for one I could use. I shouldn't have thrown that one away from the other day. But I never imagined I'd be back here. I was so glad I was back.

There were no toothbrushes in his vanity. I bit my lip and eyed his. *Is that weird to do?* I didn't really know what the normal protocols for couples in this situation were. All of this was so new. I peered out the bathroom door. It couldn't hurt. He wouldn't even know. I quickly grabbed his toothbrush and brushed my teeth. I had this weird, excited feeling when I realized I was using Professor James Hunter's toothbrush. *This probably is weird.* I finished up in the bathroom and went back out into the kitchen. He was reading something on his phone.

"I'll be right back." He put his phone in his pocket and went into his bedroom. When he came back out he was looking at me curiously.

"What?"

"Did you use my toothbrush?"

"Maybe?"

For some reason he found that funny. "You are definitely making yourself at home. Even though you're only after me for my sweet sleeping arrangements, you can stay whenever you want. You'd move in for good if it was up to me. I only brought up Rob because I wanted to warn you that we were going to have company for awhile."

"I know. So what do you want to do now?"

"I can help you with Stat."

"All my notes are in my dorm. Besides, lame. We have a day off."

"So you want to do something more fun?"

"Yes. But I can't really go anywhere with my secret professor boyfriend and a huge bandage on my forehead."

He walked over to me and grabbed my chin. I tilted my face toward him as he slowly took off my bandage. "There, that's better." His phone buzzed and he quickly answered it. "Hunter."

Silence.

"No, I'll come get it. Thanks." He hung up and turned back to me. "You have a delivery."

"What? Here?"

"Apparently so." His expression was cloudy. He walked into his room and quickly changed into jeans and a v-neck t-shirt. He looked unbelievably sexy and brooding.

"I haven't given anyone your address, Professor Hunter."

"I know. It's rather curious." He kissed my forehead next to my stitches. "I'll be right back."

I watched him get on the elevator. I had a sinking feeling in my stomach. *What the hell?* My parents were the only ones that knew I was with him. And I didn't give them his address. I sat down on the couch in his living room to wait for him.

I just wanted today to be fun. I was finally getting to know him better. Hopefully this delivery wouldn't change his mood. Whatever it was, I didn't want it.

Oh shit. Brendan. Brendan was the only one who knew Professor Hunter's address. I got up and went into the bedroom to grab my phone. There were a few texts from Tyler and Melissa. My mom had sent one to check up on me. But there weren't any from Brendan. And why would there be? He didn't have my number. I had his. In the pocket of a pair of jeans probably on my dorm room floor.

Maybe the delivery wasn't from him. It was probably spam. Dirty spammers could find you anywhere. I went back into the living room, clutching my phone. The elevator doors dinged and opened. Professor Hunter's face was hidden by a huge bouquet. He placed the flowers down on the kitchen counter and looked over at me.

"Are these from you?" I wasn't sure why I asked the question. I could tell by the expression on his face that they were definitely not from him.

"No, Penny. I don't know who they're from." There was a small envelope attached to one of the stems.

"Probably my parents." I walked over and grabbed the envelope.

"Probably." His tone was cool.

Please be from my parents. I slid the card out of the envelope. The front said "Get well soon." I could feel Professor Hunter's eyes on me. I opened it up and read the note.

Penny,

I went to the hospital last night to check on you and you were gone. When I didn't hear from you, I figured I'd find you in the place where you always seem to go back to. FYI, you're incredibly bad at taking advice. Horrible really. I'll have to adjust my tactics. Flowers are probably a good start, wouldn't you agree?

Feel better,

-Brendan

I looked up at Professor Hunter. He wasn't trying to read the card, just my reaction. I put it back in the envelope and set it on the counter. "They're from Brendan."

"A friendship rose kind of thing?" Professor Hunter raised his eyebrow.

I sighed. I wasn't going to lie to him again. Even though a lie was a lot more tempting than the truth right now. "No. He likes me. I'll talk to him..."

"Get dressed."

"What?" That was not the reaction I was expecting at all.

"We're going out."

"Okay." I watched him as he cleared our dishes. He looked mad. I wasn't sure what to say. "James?"

He didn't answer me. It was possible he didn't hear me over the sound of the water running, but it seemed like he was ignoring me. I sighed and headed into the bedroom and then the closet full of clothes Professor Hunter had bought for me. I pulled on a pair of skinny jeans and looked in the mirror. They were probably the nicest jeans I had ever worn. I also grabbed a sweater and some brown leather riding boots. The outfit made me look more sophisticated than I usually did. I wondered where we were going.

When I walked back out, Professor Hunter slid his phone into the pocket of his jeans. He leaned against the kitchen counter. His hands were pressed against the granite countertop.

I walked up to him. "I'm sorry."

He ran his hand through his hair. "Let's go."

"James."

He gave me a sly smile. "I feel like when you call me by my first name I'm in trouble. I don't want to fight."

"I don't want to fight either."

"Good." He grabbed my hand and pulled me toward the elevator. "I need to pick up some things."

"What kind of things?" We stepped onto the elevator.

"Well, my girlfriend needs her own toothbrush."

I laughed. "Sorry, I didn't know what to do."

He pushed the button to close the door and then pulled me against him.

"I don't want to go back to reality tomorrow."

He smiled down at me. "Me either."

"Let's just run away together."

"Just name the place."

I sighed and leaned against his chest. He ran his hands down my back and stopped when they were on the small of my back.

"Let's do something fun today. I don't want to go shopping."

"Good, because we're not just going shopping."

I looked back up at him. "But you just said we were going to go buy toothbrushes."

"Yeah." He tucked a loose strand of hair behind my ear. "I lied."

The elevator doors dinged and opened. He grabbed my hand and led me toward his car.

"Wait, then what are we doing?"

"It's a surprise." His eyes twinkled. He opened up the car door for me.

I smiled and got in. He closed the door behind me. I loved how spontaneous he was. Or maybe he had intended to do whatever we were about to do this whole time.

"Am I at least dressed okay?" I asked as he put the key in the ignition.

"Not at all."

"What? Let me go change then. What should I be wearing?"

"That would kind of take away from the surprise." We drove in silence for a few minutes. Once we turned onto the highway I couldn't resist it anymore.

"Can I at least have a hint?" *Where is he taking me?*

He turned toward me. "I'm hoping to change your mind about something."

"About what?"

"I already gave you your hint."

CHAPTER 16

Monday

"Hey," Professor Hunter said softly. He rubbed his hand on my cheek.

I opened my eyes. I must have fallen asleep. He was looking at me intently with his dark brown eyes. He looked excited.

I looked out the window. "Where are we? Philly?"

Professor Hunter laughed. "No, not Philly."

I looked out the window again. "Are we in New York?"

"I don't think you've experienced it the same way that I have."

"Because I'm not rich?"

He shrugged. "I want to show you my New York."

I looked at the clock on the dashboard. It was only 10:30. "You like speeding."

"I tend to do everything efficiently."

"You mean fast." I regretted the words as soon as they came out of my mouth.

He bit his lip. "Penny," he said and grabbed my hand. "I know what I want. I want you. All of you. I know that I'm older than you. And I may be ready for something more serious than..."

"I didn't mean anything by it."

"Still."

"I'm running just as fast beside you." I squeezed his hand.

He leaned toward me until his lips were an inch from mine. "Okay," he whispered and opened up my door from the inside. He leaned back in his seat and quickly got out.

I swallowed hard and stepped out of the car. The city was loud. There wasn't anything appealing about it to me. But when I looked over at Professor Hunter smiling at me, I realized there was one thing. Him. I'd go anywhere for him. I walked over to him and clasped my hands behind his neck as I stood on my tiptoes and kissed him. "I like New York better already."

"Well you're about to like it even more." He turned toward the building closest to us. "Because Totonno's Pizzeria is *the* best pizza."

"You brought me all the way to New York to prove a point?"

"One of the reasons." He opened the door to the pizzeria.

The floor looked like a checker board and the walls were covered in frames of newspaper clippings, awards, and black and white family photos. It was quaint and not at all where I had expected to end up. But it was perfect.

"This is your favorite pizza place?"

"Yes. Grab us a seat." He walked up to the counter in the back while I sat down at a table for two by the window. I wasn't sure what I expected. There was still so much I didn't know about him. But he was trying.

"This place doesn't really seem like you," I said as he sat down across from me.

"What do you mean?"

"You tend to be kind of extravagant."

"Not always. I used to come here to eat all the time."

"What was your favorite part about living here?" I put my hand in the center of the table. He immediately grabbed it.

"There's always something to do."

"So you've been pretty bored in a college town?"

"Hardly. You're very entertaining." He flashed me a smile. He was so handsome. I noticed a few women in the restaurant staring at him.

"You know that women stare at you everywhere we go, right?"

"Is that so? I haven't noticed."

"You must have noticed. Everyone drools over you. I mean, look at you."

"I'm too busy looking at you."

I felt myself blushing. "You're out of my league."

"You're out of your mind."

I bit my lip. "Why me?"

"What do you mean?"

"If you wanted to date a student..."

"I didn't want to date a student." He lifted up my hand and kissed my knuckles. "Are you asking why I'm attracted to you? Or why I love your personality?"

"Both I guess."

"You don't have much self confidence. It's rather curious."

"Why would I? No one's ever looked at me the way that you're looking at me right now."

"I know you don't see it. But you are always the most beautiful girl in the room. I enjoy that you don't see it. It's intriguing how naive you are. You're very alluring."

"Alluring?" I laughed. Alluring was how I'd describe him. It's not how I'd describe myself.

"Yes. I find you unbelievably sexy." He stared into my eyes. "Every inch of you."

I could feel my face flush.

"Did you want more intimate details? Because I could go on for days describing the blue of your eyes with the small flecks of green in the sunshine. Or the freckles on your shoulders. Or that birthmark on the inside of your ankle. Or how your ass jiggles just the right amount when you walk. Or how your breasts fit perfectly in my hands. Or how you get a cute little wrinkle in your forehead when you frown at me. Or how it makes me feel when you bite your lip when you look at me. Or the intoxicating smell of you. And the taste of you." He swallowed hard. "And the way you're looking at me right now...it's sexy as hell."

I gulped.

"So if you refuse to see how beautiful you are, you'll just have to accept the fact that I'm attracted to you. And for things that aren't physical." He paused and kissed my knuckles again. "I love that you're down to earth. I love that you're shy. It's refreshing that you don't seem to want to be the center of attention everywhere we go. I like that you just want to be beside me instead, captivating me alone. I love that you're open to second chances and quick to forgive. Yet you're extremely stubborn as well, and I love how that challenges me. I love how intelligent you are. I love that you like experiencing new things. And I love that you're a hopeless romantic, or else we wouldn't be sitting here right now."

I stared at him. I knew my face was bright red. No one had ever said things like that to me before. He did know every inch of me. He wasn't lying. "I'm a hopeless romantic because I chose you? Why is that hopeless?"

"I told you that I wasn't good for you, yet here you are. Besides, you had plenty of other options."

"I didn't."

"Tyler and Brendan?"

"I was always going to come back to you. I can't stop thinking about you. I can't and I won't."

"See...hopeless romantic."

"I don't like that phrase. It makes it sound like we're doomed."

"I think we've already been through the hardest things."

"I hope so."

He lowered his eyebrows slightly as he looked at me. "So really, the question is why did you choose me?"

"You're joking, right?"

"I'm curious."

"It seems as though you have plenty of self confidence."

"Is that one of the things you like?"

"Yes. I like that you always seem so sure of what you want. Even if what you want scares you."

He put his other hand on top of mine, so that mine was sandwiched between his. He wanted to hear why I loved him. He needed validation too.

"You know how good looking you are. You're classically tall, dark, and handsome. When I see you I get butterflies in my stomach. And when you touch me I get chills." I suddenly felt nervous. "I've never been so attracted to someone in my life."

"That's how I feel about you."

I laughed.

"Penny. I do."

I looked into his eyes. He was being sincere. I wanted him to know how I felt too. I wasn't done telling him what I loved about him. "You're also dark and brooding and mysterious. But when you let me in, when I get to see glimpses of the real you, I fall harder and harder. Like the juice box thing."

"You like that my parents didn't let me drink apple juice out of a box?"

"No, I like that you told me that. You're cute."

His eyebrows lowered again. "I'm not cute."

"Yes you are. You're being adorable right now."

He smiled at me.

"And I love that you're..." I looked down at his hands on mine, "...domineering."

He laughed. "You mean in bed?"

I shook my head. "Yes, in bed. But in everything else too. I'm indecisive. I'm so bad at choosing things."

"You chose me."

"I did. But you saw all the stupid stuff I did along the way," I said.

"Which was my fault."

"No. It was because I'm a mess."

He smiled at me. "Do you know what I am currently enjoying most of all?"

"About me?"

"Yes about you."

I gulped. He was giving me that hungry look. The look that made me want him. I crossed my legs under the table. "What are you enjoying most?"

"How insatiable you are."

"Insatiable? How so? By wanting to spend time with you?"

"In bed, mostly."

Oh my God. "I don't think that's true."

He laughed. "If I wanted to, I could have you coming in the bathroom before our pizza arrived."

When he talked like that to me it was hard to think about anything else. I wanted him. And he knew it.

He smiled at me. "Or maybe I could do it right here. I believe I owe you an orgasm with an audience after the office blowjob incident."

I gulped. "But you liked that."

"I did. And you'd like this." His foot brushed against my leg. "Besides, I promised you I'd retaliate." He hitched his foot on a leg of my chair and he pulled it closer to the table. The chair squeaked against the floor.

"I thought you were joking." My heart rate was accelerating. Just the way he was looking at me made me wet.

"I would never joke about pleasing you." One of his hands left mine and disappeared beneath the table. A second later it was on my knee. His skilled fingers slid up my thigh. His eyes grew darker with each inch his hand moved higher.

"Professor Hunter..."

At that moment our pizza came to the table.

"James! It's so good to see you," a short woman with an Italian accent said. She placed our pizza down on the table.

Professor Hunter removed his hand from my thigh and shook her hand. "It's been ages, Marie. I was in the city for the day and this was the first place I stopped."

"We all miss you here. And who is this?" Marie turned to me.

"This is my girlfriend, Penny."

"It's a pleasure to meet you," I said. I reached out my hand to shake hers.

"No, no, the pleasure is mine." She leaned down and hugged me. "Every Monday James would come here and have lunch. Always alone. Always glum. I'm so glad he has finally met someone. You better make him happy," she said in a voice a little more serious than I expected. When Marie released me from her hug, she smiled at Professor Hunter. "It's so good to see you, James."

"You too, Marie," James said as she walked away. He put his hand back on my thigh. "Another time then. I will get you."

I smiled at him. "Why did you eat lunch alone every Monday?" I asked.

"Just a habit." He picked up a slice of pizza and put it on my plate.

"Why did she think you were single? You still wore your ring when you lived here, didn't you?"

He sighed. "No, actually."

"Why?"

"I stopped wearing my wedding ring the first time I confronted Isabella about her infidelity. I thought she'd feel threatened and stop. I thought maybe the idea of me sleeping around would bother her. It didn't."

"Did you? Sleep around?"

"No." His voice was stern.

"I'm sorry, I didn't mean to pry."

"It's okay. I want you to be able to ask me questions. But I don't want to talk about her. I just want to focus on us."

"Okay." Our lunch had taken a rather quick turn. I wanted to go back to our happy bubble. I wanted people to stop interfering. "So this is the best pizza, huh?" I held up my slice.

"Fold it before you eat it. Trust me."

I followed his instructions and took a bite. *Mmm!*

"What's the verdict?"

"It's freaking fantastic."

***

Professor Hunter pulled his car up to a tall building. A valet rushed over.

"What's this?"

"Trump International."

I looked up at the gold veranda. It said Trump International Hotel and Tower, also in gold. It was a big glass, modern building. "Why are we going to a hotel?"

"I have a surprise for you." He winked and climbed out of the car.

I loved how mysterious he was. I loved the surprises. I loved him.

Someone rushed out of the hotel to greet us. Professor Hunter handed him the car keys and then opened the door for me. He grabbed my hand and walked with me to the entrance. A man in a suit opened up the door for us.

"Good afternoon," he nodded at us. "Welcome to Trump International."

"Thank you," said Professor Hunter.

The inside of the hotel took my breath away. The floor was marble and the walls were wooden with mirrors and gold accents. Chandeliers hung from the ceiling. The counter, where a few men and women were standing, was also made of marble. Professor Hunter escorted me to one of the plush lounge chairs. I sat down and watched him go up to the counter and start talking to one of the women at the desk.

He handed her a card and leaned on the counter as he chatted with one of the men. It looked like he was completely in his element. I liked seeing him like this. The woman handed him his card back and gave him another card.

"Right this way, sir," one of the men said and stepped toward the elevator.

Professor Hunter turned around to me. I quickly joined him and grabbed his hand.

"James, is that you?"

I looked up at the man who had just stepped off the elevator. He was probably Professor Hunter's age. He was handsome and suave.

"Mason, good to see you." The two of them shook hands.

"I see that you finally took my advice." Mason looked at me. His gaze made my skin feel cold.

Professor Hunter lowered his eyebrows slightly. "No. I thought you would have heard. I'm getting divorced."

Weird response. What advice was Mason referring to?

"Oh, I'm sorry, man," Mason said. And then he started laughing. "Geez, that's a lie. I'm not sorry at all. I'm surprised it lasted as long as it did."

"You two never did get along."

"No, not at all. So, who is this then?" Mason was looking at me again.

Before I could respond, Professor Hunter said, "This is my girlfriend, Penny."

Mason smiled. "Girlfriend? You didn't wait around long. Nice to meet you, Penny." He put his hand out for me.

I shook it. "It's nice to meet you. How do you two know each other?"

"James and I grew up together. Oh, the stories I could tell you..."

"Maybe another day," Professor Hunter interjected and laughed.

"I'll have to hold you to that," I said.

"Well," Mason said and looked down at his watch. "I have a meeting I need to get to. If you ever change your mind, you have my number, James." Mason winked and walked away.

As soon as Mason was out of earshot, I said, "What was he talking about?"

"Yeah, you don't want to know. Let's go to our room."

We stepped onto the elevator with the man from the front desk. There was instrumental music playing. I had heard of elevator music, but I had never been in an elevator that actually played it. I looked up at Professor Hunter. He was smiling at me. Whatever the surprise was, he seemed so excited. I liked when he looked happy. The playful grin on his face made him look younger.

The doors dinged and opened. The man guided us down an equally ornate hallway to our room.

"If there is anything else you need, please don't hesitate to call the front desk. Turndown service is at nine. Have a good afternoon."

"You too," Professor Hunter said. He slid the access card into the reader and opened the door.

I quickly walked past him. "Oh my God." I almost ran up to the window. We had the most amazing view of the city and of Central Park. It was beautiful. I had never seen anything like it.

"I told you that I could get you to like New York." He pushed my hair to one side and kissed the back of my neck. His hands slid to my waist.

"It's beautiful."

"You should see it at night." He kissed my neck again. His fingers traced the waistline of my jeans.

I turned around to face him. "Are we spending the night?"

"I haven't decided yet."

"But I have to go back. I have classes."

"Me too." He ran his nose down the length of mine and pressed his forehead against mine. "But I don't want to go back."

I wrapped my arms around his back and placed the side of my head against his chest. "Me either." It was comforting to hear his steady breathing.

He ran his fingers through my hair.

I looked back up at him. "I know I've made mistakes. Thank you for forgiving me. Thank you for letting me back in."

"Thank you for forgiving me."

"You're different here."

"Different?"

"More relaxed, I guess."

"Well I'm not Professor Hunter here. I'm just me."

I smiled at him. "James. I still need to get used to saying that."

"You do. Because Rob will give me hell if you go around calling me Professor Hunter." He laughed.

"So, James. What would you do on a Monday after eating lunch alone?"

"I'd go back to work."

"Was your office around here?"

"Well." He looked out the window. "There." He pointed to one of the buildings in the distance. It overlooked Central Park too.

"Is your headquarters still there?"

"It is."

"Your company must do really well."

"It's not my company anymore. But yes, it does." He smiled at me.

"And what about after work?"

He unfolded his arms from around me and walked over to the bed. I hadn't noticed it before, but there was a white box on the bed with a red ribbon around it. "It would depend on my mood. Sometimes I'd grab drinks with some of the guys I worked with. Or I'd have dinner back at my place."

"Do you still have an apartment here?"

"No. Not anymore."

I could have asked him if he sold it. Or if Isabella lived there alone now. But I didn't want to. I was going to focus on us. Nothing else mattered. "What did you do after dinner?"

"It would depend on my mood." He lifted up the box. "Tonight it's your decision." He walked over to me and handed me the box.

"What are the options?"

"Open it."

I pulled the red ribbon free and lifted off the top. I picked up the red, silky dress and let the box fall to the ground. The dress was adorned with a sheer red material with small flowers embroidered in it. It was probably the most expensive piece of clothing I had ever touched. "It's beautiful."

"So, I have tickets to an art gallery opening on the Upper East Side. And you can wear that. We can go shopping for whatever else you want. I already have reservations at Eleven Madison Park."

"What is Eleven Madison Park?"

There was a twinkle in his eye from my question. "It's one of the most prestigious restaurants in the city. I want to treat you to a night as one of New York's elite."

"New York's elite?" I laughed.

He smiled at me. "Or you can wear exactly what you're wearing. And we can go to a comedy club that I love in East Village. We can walk through Central Park and we can eat at the Tavern on the Green before the show."

I folded the dress and put it back in the box. "I think I'd like to go to the comedy club."

He grabbed my waist and pulled me against him. "God I love you."

I laughed as I looked up at him. "Was that a quiz, Professor Hunter?"

"No. I would have been happy doing either thing. I've just never met anyone who'd choose option two." His eyes were suddenly smoldering. He could so easily take my breath away.

"And you're happy that I did?"

"Yes." His hands slid to my ass. "Besides, now we have more time for other things."

"You do realize that we came to a hotel with no luggage? And we're probably not staying the night."

His skilled fingers unbuttoned and unzipped my pants. He kissed the side of my neck. "Your point is?"

Do I have one? I tried not to focus on his hands. "The people at the front desk probably think we're having an affair."

He let go of my waist and sat down on the edge of the bed. He quickly hooked his index fingers in the belt loops of my jeans and pulled my waist toward him. He pushed my sweater up a few inches and kissed my stomach. "Well, if they already think so..." His breath was warm against my skin. I had the familiar pull deep down in my stomach.

He raised his left eyebrow, giving me that challenging look. I wasn't sure what he wanted me to do. He continued to stare at me as he pulled off his shirt. *Does he want me to strip for him?* I slowly pulled my sweater off. He continued to look at me without saying a word. I suddenly felt extremely shy. I slowly pushed my jeans down over my hips and let them fall down my legs. His Adam's apple rose and fell as he regarded me. Him watching me made me feel so sexy. I moved my hands to the back of my bra and unhinged it. I let it slowly fall down my arms onto the floor. My skin tingled from his gaze. I hooked my fingers under the lace of my thong. He leaned forward and pulled it down himself. His hands glided over my ass and down the back of my thighs.

I laughed as he pulled me down on top of him.

He kissed the base of my neck and rolled over on top of me. "Besides, I promised you an orgasm." He got off the bed and knelt beside it. "I'm a man of my word." He wound his hands around my knees and pulled my ass to the end of the bed.

My breathing accelerated. I wanted him. I always wanted him.

He spread my thighs wide and kissed the inside of my knee.

"Insatiable," he whispered against my thigh.

He was right. I'd never get enough of him. I propped myself up on my elbows. It was sexy watching him. He liked teasing me. He liked pleasing me more. "You're insatiable too," I panted.

"Hmm." His breath was hot between my thighs. "Is that so?" His tongue made one long, slow stroke against my wetness. I collapsed back down on the bed.

His hands left me for a second and I heard the zip of his jeans. He kissed my thigh again and then pulled me off the bed and onto his waiting erection.

I gasped from surprise. "Oh God." I tilted my head back as I let the sensation of him inside of me take over. He grabbed my hair and tilted my head the rest of the way back, leaving a trail of kisses down my neck. His hands found my hips and he moved them up and down, guiding me along his length.

I groaned.

He leaned into me and bit my lip, pulling me back up toward him. His hands squeezed my ass as he stood up. I quickly clasped my hands behind his neck and wrapped my legs around him.

"I want all of New York to know you're mine," he growled.

I didn't know what he was talking about. All I knew was how good he felt, possessing me. He pushed my back against the cool glass of the window.

My body shivered. People would be able to see us. "James..."

He thrust deep inside of me.

"James," I moaned, completely abandoning my hesitation.

He grabbed my hands and unwound them from his neck. He pushed them against the glass and held them firmly as he began to slide his cock in and out of me again.

I needed to touch him. All I wanted was to run my hands through his hair. I tried to move my hand.

He spread my arms farther apart and pushed the back of my hands more firmly against the glass. I couldn't move at all. He tilted his hips.

I moaned. The glass squeaked as my back slid against it.

He kissed me hard, silencing me. I wrapped my legs tighter around him as his tongue invaded my mouth. *Fuck this is hot.*

With each thrust of his hips the intensity grew. I couldn't move at all. He was in complete control of my body. And I loved when he was in control of my body. He knew what I liked better than I did. I clenched myself around him.

"Come for me, Penny." He kissed me again and groaned into my mouth as he found his release. The coolness of the glass and the warmth of him filling me was all I could take. I shattered around him. He released his grip on my hands. I immediately ran them down his muscular arms.

"You're so sexy," I said.

He laughed and collapsed to his knees, pulling me down with him. He held me against his chest and sighed into my hair.

CHAPTER 17

Monday

"Is he a good friend of yours?"

"Who? Mason Caldwell?"

"Mhm." We had just been seated at the Tavern on the Green. It was a beautiful fall day and we had opted to eat outside. Small lanterns hung in the tree above us. It was beautiful and romantic and perfect. The whole day had been perfect.

"We used to be really good friends." Professor Hunter shrugged. "We fell out of touch after school. Our parents are still close. And the ad agency he works for has helped me out before."

"He seems nice. I've never met any of your friends."

"You find out who your true friends are when things aren't easy anymore. Turns out I didn't have many."

"He didn't even know about your divorce. From my experience, you don't open up very easily. Maybe you're being too hard on your friends."

Professor Hunter smiled at me. "You're probably right."

I looked out toward Central Park. It really was pretty. "Do you eventually want to move back here?"

He rubbed my palm with his thumb. "Not if you don't like it."

I looked back at him. "I like it when I'm with you."

He eyed me curiously. "We can go wherever you want, you know. It doesn't matter to me. Wherever you'll be happy."

"After I graduate?"

"Yes."

"You talk so easily about our future," I said.

"That's because I already know that you're in my future."

"But there's still..."

"I will never run away from this feeling. I'm not letting you go."

I stared at him. "How many children do you want?"

He frowned. "What?"

"You want to talk about our future. So let's talk about it."

"I'm not sure I'd be a very good father."

"Why would you say that?"

"I'm..." he stopped and looked up at the waitress who had just approached our table.

"Welcome to the Tavern on the Green. I'm Lexi and I'll be your waitress this evening. Can I get you both something to drink?"

Professor Hunter looked down at the wine list and then back up at Lexi. "We're actually ready to order. We'll both have the cioppino. And could we just have two glasses of apple juice?"

She looked a little surprised. "Sure. I'll be right back."

I smiled at him. "Apple juice? You can have a drink if you want."

"I don't want one." He sighed and let go of my hand.

"We don't have to talk about kids. I'm sorry, that was such like a weird thing for me to bring up. We only just started dating. I just..."

"No. It's fine. I've just never thought much about it."

"That's okay."

"Do you want kids?"

"One day. I'd want at least two. I always wished I had a sibling growing up."

"Hmm." He sighed. "Two sounds good then."

I smiled at him. He was acting weird. It still felt like he was holding back something from me. "So is that why you think you'll be a bad father? Just because you don't want kids anytime soon?"

"No, that's not it." He grabbed my hand again. "I just haven't spent much time around children."

"I don't want them anytime soon."

"Good. I want you all to myself for as long as possible."

"So what exactly is cioppino?"

He laughed. "Trust me, you'll like it."

***

As we walked out of the Upright Citizens Brigade Theater I was still laughing. "That's so cool that Amy Poehler used to do improv here."

He smiled at me. "So you liked your choice?"

"Yes. Today was perfect." I looked up at the sky. The stars were dull in the night sky. The city was too bright. "It's weird not being able to see the stars."

"Pros and cons."

We walked slowly back toward the hotel. It was nice walking through the street holding hands like a normal couple. We'd never be able to do this on Main Street. Maybe he was right. Disclosing our relationship would be for the best. I heard music playing in the distance.

A smile spread across Professor Hunter's face. "Come with me." We jogged into Central Park until we came to a guitarist. He was strumming his guitar and singing. I laughed as Professor Hunter twirled me and then pulled me in close.

His hand was on the small of my back. It reminded me of when he had walked me home in the rain. The smell of him and the look in his eyes took my breath away.

"Do you know this song?" My voice sounded airy. I wanted to know what it was so I could find it on YouTube and remember this moment forever.

"I believe it's called hands down." He twirled me again and placed both of his hands on my waist.

"Every day I spend with you I fall harder and harder." I looked up into his eyes.

He leaned down and kissed me. When the song ended he didn't pull away. We kept swaying to the loud sounds of the city. "I should get you home."

"Does that mean going home with you? Or are you sending me back to my dorm?"

He laughed. "I'd like to bring you home with me."

"I don't want tonight to end." I put my hands in his hair and brought his lips back down to mine.

There was a quiet groan in his throat as he pulled away. "I love you, Penny."

"I love you, James."

***

I rolled over and looked at him. He looked so relaxed. This was real. I wasn't dreaming. I would do anything for this man. I liked being in his apartment. I liked that the sheets smelled like him. And I liked waking up next to him. I suddenly had an urge to make him breakfast in bed. I looked at his alarm clock. It was only 7 o'clock. There was time. I quietly climbed out of bed and went into the kitchen, closing the door behind me.

Someone cleared their throat.

I turned my head and saw someone sitting at the dining room table. I almost screamed, but then I saw who it was. She was tall and thin, and had perfectly straight brunette hair. She was just as gorgeous as the pictures I had seen of her. *Isabella.*

"How did you get in here?" I didn't mean to whisper, but my voice came out so small. I didn't know anything about her. Was she violent? Would she suddenly be because she had found me here instead of her husband? I was sleeping with her husband. *Fuck, I'm sleeping with her husband.*

"I'm his wife."

That didn't really answer my question. Had he given her a key? Did she just tell the front desk and they let her up? I was wearing one of Professor Hunter's t-shirts. I pulled the fabric down. This was the feeling I wanted to avoid. This was why we should have waited. "I..."

"Don't embarrass yourself. I know all about you, Penny. I like to keep track of who my husband is currently screwing."

I felt goose bumps rise on my skin. Had Professor Hunter talked to her about me? I looked over at the door. *Please get up.*

She pulled a manila envelope out of her purse and set it on the table. "Don't flatter yourself. James definitely didn't mention you the last time I saw him. He was occupied by other, more pressing matters."

I glared at her. The last time they had seen each other they'd had sex. *What the hell is she doing here?*

"Oh, did he not tell you? You were together at the time, weren't you? It was only a week ago." She put her elbows on the table. "I know exactly how he works. I know exactly what he wants. And clearly you can't give him what he needs. If you could satisfy him, he wouldn't have come crawling back to me."

I swallowed hard. "He did tell me."

"So let me guess," she said, ignoring my comment. "You've given him quite the chase. Or is the fact that you're a student enough?"

"What do you mean?"

"He only wants what he can't have. You must see that. As soon as you say you'll stay, he'll leave you."

I thought about everything we'd been through. Him giving up on me after my lie. Right after I told him that I loved him. All of our fights. Even him having sex with Isabella had pushed me away again. Was he purposefully sabotaging our relationship? Giving me just enough to cling onto?

"You do see it. I can see it in your eyes. You just realized that this..." she waved her hand around the apartment, "...is all a lie."

Professor Hunter wouldn't lie to me again. I wasn't going to let her convince me to not believe in him. What we had was real. She was just jealous. "I don't think you know him as well as you think."

She leaned forward and raised her eyebrow. "Is that what he told you?"

"He didn't need to."

"I've known him since we were kids. I know him better than you ever will. And if you'll excuse me, I need to talk to my husband in private." She stood up.

"I think you should go." I was surprised by my own courage. He wouldn't want her here. I felt protective of him. I didn't want her to hurt him anymore. She was cold and manipulative and horrible.

Isabella laughed. "Penny, I'm doing you a favor. Trust me, you don't want anything to do with him."

"If he's as bad as you say, then why haven't you signed the papers?"

She put her hand on top of the manila envelope. "I'm actually here to discuss that."

Thank God.

"You look relieved. You shouldn't be. I can tell that you're just as addicted to him as he is to you. That would be sweet in any other situation, but not in this one."

"What are you talking about?"

"He really hasn't told you?"

"Told me what?"

"I think you already know. You just don't want to believe it. Besides, James is bad at hiding his shortcomings."

"We love each other. That's all that matters."

"How old are you, Penny?"

I shouldn't be answering her questions. She had already made her mind up about me. I stayed quiet.

"Right. You're young. You don't know what love is. Have you ever even been in a serious relationship before? Can you even tell when someone is lying to you?"

"He's not lying to me."

"Withholding information is just as bad as lying. It's something that you should know. You did that to him, did you not?"

How the hell does she know all this? I looked over at the bedroom door. He had to have talked to her about me. *Did he do it that night? Right before they slept together?* I needed to know. "If James didn't talk to you about me..."

"He has his sources and I have mine," she said, cutting me off. "So how about you get to class. What I need to discuss with him is none of your business." Her words were icy. It felt like she had slapped me.

"It is my business."

Isabella sighed. "Remember that I tried to warn you. But fine, we'll do this your way. "James!" she called. "James, get the hell up!"

It only took a second for James to come to the door of his bedroom. He took one look at me, from head to toe. Was he looking to see if she had hurt me? Her words had been painful enough.

He turned to Isabella. "How did you get in here?" I had never heard him sound so mad before. He definitely hadn't given her a key. He walked over to me and stood in front of me. *Protecting me? Or hiding something?*

"Don't be so cold James. I'm your wife, after all."

He ran his hand through his hair. "Get out of my apartment."

She ignored him. "I see that you aren't being very discreet with your new girlfriend. She's a little young for you, don't you think?" She looked at me. "And really not your type at all."

What is his type?

James pulled his phone out of his pocket. "Get out or I'll call the cops, Isabella."

"Hmm, so now we can add threatening to the list?" She undid the tabs on the envelope and pulled out some photographs. She tossed them on the table. "On top of blackmailing?"

"Isabella..." James said and started toward her.

"I'm glad the girl that you're currently fucking is here." She said it in a disgusted way. "Now she can know what kind of man you really are."

James quickly grabbed the photographs and turned them so that they'd be face down on the table. I didn't get a chance to see what they were of.

"You didn't give me a choice. Why do you have to make everything impossible? Do you enjoy torturing me?"

"Yes." Her voice was cold.

"I just need you to sign the papers."

"What, so that you can be with her?" she scoffed. "You must be joking."

"What I do now is none of your business. Sign the papers." His voice was authoritative.

"This is ridiculous. She doesn't even know you."

"Neither do you."

"And whose fault is that?"

"You can't blame this on me."

She laughed. "You know, the press is going to have a field day when they hear about how my husband cheated on me with a student. It's so cliché, don't you think? They'll love it. The university probably won't love it as much, though."

"I'll leak the photos."

"No you won't. How do photos of me screwing another man help you in any way? All it shows is that you can't satisfy your own wife."

"No. It shows that you have a history of infidelity that makes your claim to anything that's mine invalid."

"And she doesn't do the same for you?" she pointed at me.

I felt small. I was a spectator. I shouldn't be here watching them. But I also couldn't seem to walk away.

"I don't want anything that's yours," Professor Hunter said. "Sign the papers now and you get half. Wait and get nothing."

She pulled out some more papers from the envelope. "I already did, you egotistical asshole." She threw them at him. He stepped to the side and let them flutter to the ground. He leaned over and picked one of them up.

"You signed them?" I hadn't meant to say anything.

Isabella stared at me. "He's all yours. Good luck. You're going to need it. He's fickle. He gets bored easily. He's going to eat you alive."

"Isabella! Enough!"

"What, are you afraid I'm going to let something slip that you haven't told her? Stop running, James. Stop throwing yourself into new things. Get some help. She's not the answer and you know it." She walked over to the elevator and pressed the button.

The doors opened and closed and she was gone. The apartment seemed eerily quiet. He looked down at the paper in his hands again. He set it down on the table and turned to me.

I wasn't sure what the protocol was here. *Should I go to him? Should I wait for him to come to me?* It looked like he was scared. I wasn't sure of what. He looked so young, standing there, completely uncertain.

"What am I not the answer to?" I asked.

"What did she say to you while I was in bed?"

"James."

His Adam's apple rose and fell.

"You're hiding something from me. Tell me."

"You need to get to class."

"James." I could feel the prickle of tears in my eyes. "Why won't you tell me?"

"We can discuss it tonight."

I could tell he was hurting. He was upset. Isabella had broken into his home. He was rattled. He needed time to calm down. I wanted to comfort him. I walked over to him and wrapped my arms around him. He seemed surprised. His body was tense and uninviting until he folded his arms around me.

"Are you okay?" His voice was wound tight.

"I'm okay." I kissed the scruff beneath his chin. This should have been a happy moment. He was divorced. We could be together without feeling bad.

"I need you."

"I need you too."

"No. I mean, I *need* you. Right now." He grabbed the back of my neck and kissed me hard. He moved his hands to my ass and lifted my legs around him. He carried me easily back toward his bedroom.

He needed to know that I was okay; that we were okay. I'd give him whatever validation he needed.

CHAPTER 18

Tuesday

"He's divorced." I was sitting cross-legged next to Melissa on her bed.

"That's great news. So why do you look...not great?"

"I talked to Isabella. His ex-wife."

"What, why?"

"She broke into his apartment."

"Oh my God. Psycho much?"

I laughed. "Yeah." I looked down at my lap. "But she said I didn't know him at all. He's hiding something from me. He said we could talk about it tonight. But what if...what if it's something that I can't handle?"

"Penny." She put her hand on my knee. "He's your first boyfriend. If it's something you can't handle, then so what?"

"It's not what I expected. We've gotten so serious so fast."

"I know." She sighed. "I still don't get it. What happened that night? I thought you two were done."

The fight. "I thought he had broken up with me. Apparently he hadn't."

"Which involves Tyler because you two can't keep your hands off each other?" She gave me a mischievous smile.

"Yeah. Actually we had sex."

"What?! When? During the party?"

"Right before James showed up."

"So..."

"So?"

"So...what the hell, Penny? How did you go from having sex with Tyler to getting back together with James?"

"He explained everything to me. He said he was trying to protect me. He never stopped wanting to be with me."

"He ignored you for weeks. He acted like you didn't exist. He...hurt you. Penny, I've never seen you like that before."

"I know." I closed my eyes and leaned against the wall. "I didn't mean to fall in love with my professor."

Melissa laughed.

I opened one eye, glanced at her smiling at me, and closed it again.

"Penny." She grabbed my hand and squeezed it. "You can't help who you fall in love with."

"Which is why I'm worried about tonight."

"How bad could it be? You've hung out with him so much. If it was bad you would have seen it."

"You're right." I looked at her for a minute. "Have you talked to Tyler?"

"I haven't really seen him since the hospital. He's a big boy though. He'll be fine."

I looked down at my lap.

"Hey," she said. "You have to make the choice that's right for you. So if dating your recently divorced, brooding professor is what you want, then own it."

"You're always right about everything. Except your advice about getting under someone else."

"It worked out in the end, didn't it?"

"Yeah, it did." I smiled to myself.

***

After having dinner with Melissa and catching up some more I finally got a text from Professor Hunter: "I'm outside."

"I've gotta go," I said to Melissa and slid off my bed.

"Penny. It won't be that bad. Whatever it is, you probably already know it."

I smiled at her. "See you later." I closed the door behind me. It felt like my heart was beating out of my chest. He was divorced. I should be happy right now, not nervous. I opened up the door to my dorm and saw his black Audi.

He stepped out of it and walked around to the passenger side door. Instead of opening it, he pulled me in close.

"Someone will see..."

He placed his lips on mine, silencing me. He kissed me hard and I kissed him back. It was like he hadn't kissed me in weeks, not hours. When he pulled away I was breathless. I knew my face was flushed.

"You look so beautiful."

"You look so handsome," I said. He was wearing jeans and a dress shirt. The top few buttons on his shirt were undone.

He opened up my door for me. When I got in he immediately closed it and walked around to his side. He got in and buckled his seatbelt. But he didn't put the car into drive.

"Are we going to your place?" I asked.

"It's too stifling."

"Maybe we can go for a walk?"

"We can't. Not here."

"You just kissed me outside of my dorm. It's dark. It's fine."

"Okay." He pulled the car into a parking spot and got out. I got out before he had a chance to open up my door for me. He eyed me curiously.

"I'm not used to dating a gentleman."

"I know." He smiled at me. He grabbed my hand and together we walked toward the green. The area between the dorms was filled with a manicured lawn, walkways, and benches. He held my hand as we walked on one of the brick paths. It was chilly and there were only a few other people out. Our feet crunched on the fallen leaves. When we reached a bench that seemed particularly shadowed, he gestured for me to sit down. He looked down at me for a second and then sat down next to me.

"I need to know exactly what she said to you this morning."

"She already knew about me."

"I didn't..."

"I know. She made it clear that you didn't do much talking last time you saw her." I shrugged.

He sighed. "I'm so, so sorry."

"No, it's fine. Really. I see the appeal."

He frowned at me.

"Yeah, I'm joking. She's horrible."

He put his hand on my knee. "There was a new employee at the front desk. He's been fired."

"James, it wasn't his fault."

"Yes, it was."

I wanted to argue with him. He couldn't go around getting people fired for no reason. The man at the front desk had probably asked Isabella for her I.D. Her last name was still Hunter. But I had to choose my battles with him. And tonight I only wanted to talk about what he was keeping from me.

"She said you only want things you can't have. That's why you like me. Because I'm a student."

"But I do have you."

"She made it seem like you'll get bored with me and move onto something else."

"I'm not going to do that, Penny."

"I know. You wanted to know what she said." I grabbed his hand. "She said that you're addicted to me."

"I am."

"She made it seem like that wasn't a good thing."

He squeezed my hand but didn't say anything.

"And she said you were withholding information from me. That's it. We didn't talk for that long."

He nodded. "Saying I'm addicted to you is a bad choice of words. I love you. I love spending time with you. I love being with you. I missed you today."

"I missed you too." He didn't want to talk about what I had brought up yet. So maybe I'd bring up something else. "What is your type?"

"What?"

"She said that I'm not even your type."

"I don't have a type."

"Are you sure it's not tall brunettes?" I smiled at him.

"No." He laughed uneasily. "She's definitely not my type."

"So you like redheads?"

"You're the only redhead I've ever been with. I don't have a type. You're it. I don't want to be with anyone else. Just you."

I didn't care what type of girl he usually dated. None of that mattered. "Don't you trust me? Whatever it is you need to tell me you can."

"I do trust you." He looked up into the sky.

A raindrop hit my forehead. I looked up too. The drops fell faster until it was full on raining.

He abruptly stood up. "Let's get back to the car," he said.

Not when I was this close. "James, tell me."

"You're going to get a cold."

"James, tell me!"

"I've already told you. More or less." He put his hand through his hair. He looked completely distraught. "I thought you understood."

"Understood what?" I felt so dense. "What am I not the answer to?" I stood up. "What did she mean when she said to stop running? What are you running from? Don't push me away again. Don't do what she said you would."

"I was trying to protect you. I told you that."

"But what are you trying to protect me from? Why do you think I shouldn't be with you? It can't possibly be that bad. Just tell me what it is."

"Damn it, Penny." He pulled me against his chest and kissed me. It was angry and hard and hot. His hands slid to the small of my back. He pushed my shirt up slightly so that his palm was against my skin.

"Stop." I pushed on his chest. He was so manipulative. "Stop using sex as a weapon."

"I don't..." He looked at my face and released me from his grip. He took a step back from me. "I didn't realize I was doing that."

What I had said seemed to hurt his feelings. But I couldn't dwell on it right now. That wasn't what I wanted to talk about. "Tell me what you're hiding. You told me no more secrets. Don't you want us to work? Tell me!"

"I have told you! I told you that I was drunk all of college. I told you that I've had sex with dozens of women. I told you I threw myself into my career in order to avoid my life. Everything I did was so that I didn't have to face reality. Whatever horrible thing you can think of, I've probably done it. I told you I wasn't a good man. I told you that."

I swallowed hard. The rain against my face felt soothing. I wasn't sure what to say. I did know all that. That couldn't be what he was hiding.

"I'm an addict, Penny." He looked so young and so vulnerable.

What? He didn't drink that much. He didn't seem like an addict to me at all. He usually seemed calm and collected and completely in control. And then Isabella's words came back to me. I didn't see it because he wasn't addicted to drugs or booze right now. He was addicted to me. *I'm his drug?*

"Penny? Say something."

"All this talk about forever..."

"I mean it."

"But what happens when you get bored with me? Will you go off chasing your next high?"

"No." He lowered his eyebrows. "I'm not addicted to you. It's different with you, it's not the same."

"How do you know?"

"I was trying to avoid my life. I was miserable. Every day I felt like I was suffocating. I needed an escape. But I'm happy now."

"Because of me? Or because of teaching? Or what?"

"It was my decision to come here."

"Because you walked in on Isabella..."

"Yes. But I came here for me. I'm living the way I want to live. I'm not answering to anyone else. I don't need an escape anymore."

"Isabella said you needed to get help."

"I've gotten help."

"So you're not addicted to drugs, or alcohol, or work, or...sex anymore?"

"No. I haven't been addicted to anything since I left the city. I was living a life that wasn't mine there. I was numb. Those things made me feel alive. They sustained me. They were a choice I could make for myself."

"So you chose to do them? That doesn't make you an addict, James. If you had control over your choices..."

"I couldn't stop, Penny. Whenever I was able to pull myself out of one thing, I just moved on to the next." His words hung in the air. "Don't look at me like that. I'm not addicted to you. I'm not going to move on. I need you in my life. I need you, Penny."

He needs me. All of his words now seemed to have a double meaning. But didn't I need him too? When he didn't talk to me for weeks I was a complete mess. My world had become isolated and cold. And I had hated it. I hated my life without him.

"Penny, I've made so many mistakes. But I was young and stupid."

"You're still young."

"Okay. But I'm not stupid anymore." He gave me a forced smile.

"Addicts are like...it's not something that goes away, is it?"

"No, it's not."

"So, how do you control it?" I felt stupid asking these questions. The age gap between us suddenly felt larger than before. He was an adult, with adult problems. All I was worried about was my next Stat test. And now him.

He lowered his eyebrows slightly. "My therapist helps me with that."

"You have a therapist?"

"I do." His eyes searched my face. "He doesn't think I'm addicted to you either."

"You talk about me?"

"Yes."

"He knows that you're dating a student?"

"Doctor patient confidentiality. He did advise me against it. I think he's glad that I ignored his advice though."

"Why?"

"I'm happier when we're together. Everyone can see that."

It was weird, standing in the rain so far apart. It made me feel so separate from him. I didn't like that feeling. "Why didn't you just tell me?"

"Because I liked the way you looked at me. Like I was strong and in control. It made me feel like I could be those things for you. I thought everyone could see my demons when they looked in my eyes. You never did. You just saw me. I didn't want that to change."

"I don't think any differently of you." His words made me want to cry. I didn't have much self confidence. I thought he was the opposite of me. But we were more alike than I thought. He was so broken. I didn't want him to feel that way.

"You do. You're looking at me right now like I'm weak."

"I don't think that you're weak. You're incredibly strong for overcoming something like that."

He put his hands in his pockets. We were both completely drenched. He was staring at me. The distance between us was unbearable.

"I don't want you to leave me," he said slowly. "But if this is too much..."

"No. James." I closed the distance between us. "I'll never let you go."

"I'm not addicted to you."

"You keep saying that. And all I can think about is how rude it sounds." I smiled at him.

"I don't understand how you can keep choosing me. I'm..."

"Perfect. Everything that you've been through has made you who you are. And I love the man I see in front of me. I love you so much."

It started raining harder. "I'm divorced." He almost had to yell it over the rain.

"I know."

"No more of this waiting nonsense?"

"No. My heart is yours."

He was smiling down at me. "I'm divorced!" He picked me up and twirled me around.

I laughed as he set me back down on my feet. I rubbed my palm against the scruff on his cheek. "You're all mine."

"All yours, Miss Taylor." He turned his head and kissed my palm.

CHAPTER 19

Tuesday

"I think you might still be addicted to sex." Our wet clothes were in a heap on the floor and our naked bodies were intertwined on his bed.

He laughed and kissed the top of my head. "Maybe it's just because I like using it as a weapon with you?"

"I'm sorry."

"No, you're right. You're...frustrating. Sex is the only way I can seem to control you."

"Control me?" I rolled onto my side and perched my head up on my hand. "Hmm. I could control you in bed."

"No, you couldn't. I'm stronger than you."

"I could tie you down."

"Good luck trying. It'll end up being you tied to my bed. Which doesn't sound bad at all."

"Maybe later. James, did you really blackmail her?" I thought about the phone call I had overheard the other night. He was asking someone for photos and didn't want there to be a cyber footprint.

He sighed and rolled over to face me. "That wasn't much of a segue." He stared at me for a minute. "It's the last thing I could think of to do. I know it was stupid. I wanted to be with you. I didn't want her to control my life anymore. You said you wanted to wait and I had no intention of waiting."

"I like that you're bad."

He laughed. "You do?"

"I've spent my whole life being good. It's fun being bad for a change."

"What, do you think dating a bad boy automatically makes you a bad ass?"

I laughed. "Absolutely...*Professor Hunter.*"

"Touché."

"I don't care if people think this is wrong."

He tucked a loose strand of hair behind my ear. "We should probably talk about that."

"Isabella's threat? You think she'll really reveal our relationship?"

"I think it would be best if we go to the dean in the morning."

"But..."

"It's better if he hears it from us."

"I don't want you to get fired."

"Yeah, me either. I know you're worried about what will happen. I told you it's not explicitly against the rules. And I don't think that anyone's complained."

"So you think nothing will happen?"

"I hope nothing happens. But I don't want you to worry about it." He kissed my forehead and climbed out of bed. He pulled on a pair of plaid pajama bottoms.

"Where are you going?"

"Get some sleep. I need to make a phone call."

"To who?" It was late. Who could he possibly want to call at this hour?

"My lawyer." He looked down at my naked body. "I won't let anything happen to you. We'll figure this out."

***

When I woke up the bed was empty beside me. I sat up and rubbed my eyes. It was 3 a.m. I climbed out of bed and grabbed one of his shirts out of his closet. It didn't matter what he had just told me. He was clearly different now. I didn't know if it was because of me or what, but I didn't care. He was strong. And I loved him more than ever. If it was going to be a problem, it would be something we'd get through together. Life without him was not a life I was interested in.

He wasn't in the kitchen or living room, so I made my way through the hallway toward his office. The door was open so I walked in. His hands were in his hair and he was staring down at his cell phone on his desk. All he was wearing were his plaid pajama bottoms and his glasses. He looked sexier than ever.

"James?"

He looked up at me. He looked so tired. And upset.

"Why didn't you come to bed?"

"I did," he sighed. "I couldn't sleep."

I walked over to him. "We'll figure it out. Just like you said." I leaned against his desk.

He shook his head. "I was so busy thinking about my feelings for you that I didn't think about all the repercussions..."

"You did think everything through. We talked about that on our first date."

He shook his head again. "I never thought that the dean would find out before I talked to him, though."

"Has he?"

James stood up and walked over to the window. He pulled the curtains to the side and looked down at the street.

I walked over to the window and looked down. *Shit.* There were three news trucks parked outside of the apartment building. "Maybe it's for something else?"

James shook his head. "No. The story is being printed in the Delaware Post in the morning. I've tried everything." He let go of the curtain. He put his hand through his hair again. "I fucked up, Penny. I should have thought about what Isabella would do if..."

I grabbed his arm so that his hand fell from his hair. "James, you couldn't possibly know what Isabella would do."

"I should have. It's my job to protect you."

"It isn't. I made my own choices. I knew I was breaking the rules. I kept pursuing you. I wanted to be with you. I knew there might be consequences. I can face them."

"It is my job to protect you." He wrapped his arms around me and rested his chin on top of my head.

I sighed and leaned into his chest. "The worst that can happen is that you get fired and I get expelled."

"I don't care if I get fired. I just don't want you to get expelled."

"I have good grades. I can get into a different school."

"It's a scandal, Penny. Other universities may not see your grades as valid."

That's what Melissa had said. Melissa had warned me about what would happen. But I hadn't listened. And if I had the choice, I wouldn't listen again. I loved Professor Hunter. I was happier than I had ever been.

"James," I said and leaned back so I could look up at him. "If I could go back, I'd do it all over again. Even if I knew I'd be expelled. You make me so happy. I want to be with you. That's all that matters. If anything, I should be apologizing to you. You told me to forget about you. On multiple occasions. I didn't listen..."

"Stop, Penny. I couldn't leave you alone either. And I didn't want you to leave me alone. I never meant it. I can't even imagine not being with you."

"So we'll face it together."

"Mhm." He looked down at me and smiled. "I'm not used to having a partner in crime."

"Well get used to it. You're getting me kicked out of school, so you should probably stick with me for awhile. It's the right thing to do."

He laughed and looked down at me. "You should probably call your parents." I must have made a face, because he added, "I'm sorry, Penny."

"I think I'm dreading that discussion more than talking to the dean."

"I'm sorry."

"Please stop apologizing. James." I put my hands on the side of his face. "I love you. That's all that matters."

He smiled down at me. "I love you too."

"So will you please come to bed now?"

"Mhm." He leaned down and kissed me.

CHAPTER 20

Wednesday

The alarm woke us up at 6 a.m. We had a meeting with the dean in an hour. And I had a terrible sinking feeling in my stomach. I had tried to be the positive one last night. But now I needed to call my parents. And I was terrified. I needed to do it before they saw the paper, though. I didn't know what the article said, but James had made it seem like we were screwed.

James turned off the alarm and rolled over to face me. He eyed me curiously. "You're still here."

I didn't know what he was expecting. Maybe he thought I was going to abandon him. "Of course I'm still here." I propped my head up on my hand. "I need you to promise me something," I said.

"Name it."

"No matter what happens, please don't resent me."

"Penny..."

"Promise me."

"I don't resent you. Please don't think that I'm mad at you about any of this. This is everything I ever wanted. Actually, it is tempting to just run away with you. For you, I'd leave it all. I need you to know that."

I do know. I wasn't sure if he wanted me to say the same thing back. I needed to finish school. I needed to think about my future. But he was laying there telling me that I was his future. I wanted him to be mine. "I'd leave it all for you too. But I'd be uneducated."

He laughed. "You're very intelligent. A diploma doesn't change that."

"I forgot that you just want me to be a housewife anyway."

He smiled and ran his fingers through my hair. "Well today can't go all that poorly because you just told me you want to be my wife. I'm certainly in a good mood."

"I..." I was suddenly embarrassed. I hadn't meant it in any way. We had talked about our future but we had never actually discussed getting married.

"Don't be flustered." He put his hand on my cheek. "I'm 27 years old. You're the love of my life. I know you feel the same way. You risked everything to be with me. So you must realize that I have every intention of marrying you, Penny Taylor."

I gulped. "But we..."

"Are you going to fight me on this too?" He gave me a mischievous smile.

He wanted to marry me. He wasn't proposing but he was telling me that he eventually would. It was fast and crazy and just like our whole relationship had been like. And I couldn't have been more excited. "No." My voice sounded airy.

He smiled and climbed out of bed. He disappeared into his closet. I was only 20 years old. He was my first boyfriend. But everything felt right. This is how I imagined love would feel. The rest of the day suddenly seemed easier to face. I wasn't just in love with him. I was going to marry this man. I shouldn't be ashamed of telling my parents or the dean. This was my choice. I needed to own it. Just like Melissa had told me.

I quickly brushed my teeth and washed my face. When he reappeared in the bedroom he was wearing a pair of navy blue pants and a gray dress shirt with the sleeves rolled up. He looked handsome and sophisticated.

He looked at his watch. "Ellen's already here. So unfortunately you'll need to get dressed."

I was wearing one of his shirts. I was excited to meet his chef or maid or whatever her title was. I'd just call her Ellen I guess. I went into the closet as he went into the bathroom.

I had never met the dean before. And this would probably be the only time I did. Professor Hunter was dressed in business casual clothes because that's what he usually wore. I pulled on a pair of jeans, a tank top, and a light cardigan. I slid on a pair of flats and walked out of the closet. He was standing by the window, looking out at the street below. Another news truck had arrived on the scene and there were about a dozen people standing outside. I wasn't sure if they were reporters or paparazzi or what. This situation was surreal. I didn't want to think about them. We'd know our fate soon enough.

"Do you think this is okay?"

James turned his attention to me and smiled. "I'm not sure if he's going to be paying attention to what you're wearing. But you look beautiful." He gave me a chaste kiss, grabbed my hand, and led me out to the kitchen.

A woman was standing at the stove. She had short brunette hair and looked a little older than my mother. She was wearing an apron. As soon as she heard the door open, she turned toward us. She had a huge smile on her face. I instantly liked her.

"You must be Penny. Oh dear, aren't you pretty. James didn't exaggerate."

I could feel my cheeks turning pink.

"Penny, this is Ellen," James said.

I smiled at her. "It's so nice to meet you."

"I've heard so much about you, dear."

I smiled up at James. He shrugged his shoulders. It was cute that he talked to her about me.

"And how do you prefer your eggs?" Ellen asked and turned back to the stove.

"Scrambled." This was weird. I wasn't used to someone making breakfast for me. "Do you need help with anything?"

Ellen laughed. "I like you already. But no. Sit, sit."

I sat down in a stool next to James. He put his elbow on the counter and rested his chin in his palm. He was still wearing his glasses. He was smiling at me.

"You look sexy in glasses," I whispered to him.

"Is that why you're looking at me like that?" he whispered back.

"Like what?"

He leaned forward until his lips were against my ear. "Like you want me right here, right now."

His words sent a chill down my spine.

He pecked my cheek and pulled away from me. There were two newspapers on the counter. The Wall Street Journal and the Delaware Post. I assumed he always got The Wall Street Journal, but he had asked for the local paper because of the article it contained.

"Have you read it?" he asked Ellen.

Ellen sighed. "The things people say. If they could see how happy you are, you'd think they'd leave well enough alone. My husband is ten years older than me and no one ever gave me a hard time for it. Love is love. Circumstances be damned."

James laughed. "I'm guessing it's bad then?"

"It's not good." Ellen continued cooking.

James picked up the paper and unfolded it. At the bottom of the first page there was an article titled, "University of New Castle Conceals Student, Professor Affair. See more page B9." James sighed and turned to B9. He put his hand on my knee and we both began reading.

Student-Professor Affair Uncovered at the University of New Castle

Bill Raffer, The Delaware Post 10:12 p.m. EST October 21, 2015

An investigation is underway involving adjunct professor, James Hunter, and a student from one of his classes at the University of New Castle.

Hunter, Blive Tech International founder and board member, started teaching at the university last semester. Although Hunter does not have a PhD, he was given a teaching position due to his experience starting Blive Tech International. His loose credentials have led him to a loose interpretation of the University of New Castle's code of ethics. Two months ago he began engaging in a sexual relationship with Penny Taylor, a sophomore in his communications class. Taylor, age 19, is an exemplary student on a First State scholarship. Although there have been no sexual harassment complaints as of yet, Taylor is unavailable for comment. Allegations of sexual harassment as well as other instances of sexual misconduct are imminent.

Hunter was fired from his last teaching position in New York City for physically threatening the dean of admissions, Jared Halloway. All charges were dropped in the matter, but Halloway commented that, "Hunter attacked him, completely unprovoked." Dean of students at the University of New Castle, Joseph Vespelli, hired Hunter despite known allegations of violence and Hunter's lack of credentials.

Hunter has also engaged in misconduct during his own days in college at Harvard University. He was arrested for underage drinking as well as vandalism.

The University of New Castle has never needed explicit rules against student-professor relationships. An unnamed source from the university says that their code of ethics skirts around the idea of something happening because it shouldn't have to state common morals, but that these events will make the university reevaluate the core values of the institution.

Hunter's wife, Isabella, was distraught when she found out about the affair. She filed for divorce as soon as she uncovered the truth, but their marriage had already begun to unravel before that when Hunter had sold his shares of Blive Tech International and declared he wanted to become a professor. "I should have realized his motivations," said Mrs. Hunter. "I should have warned the college. I feel like part of the blame should be on me. I can only imagine what this poor girl is going through."

Mrs. Hunter was almost in tears during her interview. The separation only became final yesterday afternoon. She went to the press and to the college immediately to request that Hunter resign from his teaching position. She believed he was doing more harm than good in the classroom, emphasizing that there needs to be a mutual trust between students and their professors.

In response to the allegations of having a sexual relationship with a student eight years younger than him, Professor James Hunter said, "Our relationship was completely consensual. There is no explicit rule that states such a relationship is against the code of ethics of this university." And when asked if he would end the relationship, he said, "I can't deny that I am in love with her. Nor do I have any intention of ending my relationship with her." In response to his wife's allegations, Hunter said, "My wife and I have been separated since last December, when I filed for divorce after I found out she was cheating on me. The documents are public and can be acquired from the New York City court." Said documents have not yet been released from the court.

The University of New Castle's dean of students, Joseph Vespelli, was contacted but declined to comment. His offices have informed us that an official statement will be released shortly.

Contact senior investigative reporter Bill Raffer at (302) 150-4527, braffer@delawarepost.com, on Facebook or Twitter @braffer

"Shit," James whispered. He folded the paper and threw it down on the counter. "I didn't think they were going to release your name."

"I'm going to lose my scholarship." Reality had just come crashing down on me. My parents were going to kill me. I needed that scholarship.

"What?"

"There were all these rules when I got it. I don't remember what they were. I'm sure being in the paper about sleeping with my professor broke at least one of them. James..."

"Don't get upset before we know, okay?"

He seemed so calm. How was he so calm? "Isn't this slander? How could they possibly print this? There isn't any proof. Can't we do something?"

"It doesn't matter. It's Isabella's word against mine. Stay here today. Let me go to the meeting alone. Let me handle this."

"No. I'm not letting you take all the blame for this. It's my fault too."

"I don't want you to get..."

"James. No. I'm coming with you."

Ellen walked over and set our plates down in front of us. She gave us a sympathetic look. When she walked away I looked back up at James. "And it does matter. Can't you sue them for printing this nonsense? They didn't even check any of their facts. It's a joke of a news report."

He sighed. "I just want this to blow over as fast as possible. A lawsuit will make it worse. It'll draw it out. I don't want to drag you into this. I'll be fine."

Drag me into it? I'm in the middle of it already. He wasn't dragging me into a fight with his ex-wife. This involved me too. I must have made a face because he squeezed my knee.

"Really, it's fine."

"I'm coming."

"Well, we need to get going soon if you insist on coming, so eat."

I wasn't hungry. I couldn't believe he wasn't mad. I was mad for him. I picked up my fork and took a bite of the eggs. They were probably the most delicious eggs I had ever eaten. "Ellen, these are fantastic."

She smiled over at us. "I'm glad that you like them. Eat, James."

I hadn't realized that James was just sitting there. "Are you okay?"

"Yeah." He smiled at me and began to eat.

The dynamic between James and Ellen was pretty clear. She was very motherly and caring. She was the mother he never had. I appreciated her even more because of that. When I finished my eggs and toast I pushed my plate away.

James stood up but hesitated. "Do you want to wear a hoodie or something? I don't want..."

"I want to be with you. No more hiding. Besides, everyone already knows."

"I'd really prefer if you let me do this by myself, Penny. There's no reason why you should be there."

"I'm going to get in trouble too. I have to be there."

He lowered his eyebrows slightly. "You won't. But if you insist, let's go do it then." He held out his hand for me and I grabbed it.

"Good luck," Ellen said to us as we stepped onto the elevator.

When the doors closed I looked up at James. "I like her. She seems really nice."

"She is."

I looked down at my shoes. "Are you nervous?"

"Not really. I have everything that I want. Teaching doesn't define me. Like I told you on our first date, I don't think we're doing anything wrong. This feels right to me."

"It feels right to me too. It's weird, you know. I never in a million years thought I'd be in this situation. I didn't even have my first kiss until last semester. And now I'm embarking on this big scandalous affair with my professor. I'm not even sure my parents will believe me."

James laughed. "You should have called them already. This is just going to get worse as the day goes on."

"I'll call them later. I need to know what the dean says first." I squeezed his hand. I was procrastinating. I was dreading that phone call. "What did you vandalize?"

He laughed again. "There was this professor I hated. I had him for an 8 a.m. The night before one of his classes my friends and I broke into the classroom and drew...vulgar things all over the chalkboard."

"With chalk?"

"Yeah."

"Is that really vandalism?"

He shrugged. "I didn't think so. And I didn't get arrested for it either. It was a harmless prank. Hilarious, but harmless."

"So another lie."

"Mhm."

"And were you arrested for underage drinking?"

"I got a warning. They had a three strikes policy like they do here. I only had two strikes, one for that and one for the chalkboard thing. I was never arrested while I was in Harvard."

In Harvard? I didn't want to press him about it right now. The doors opened and we walked over to his car. He opened up the door for me.

"Well, you're lucky I don't hate you. Or maybe I would have pulled a prank like that on you. I wonder what you would have done if you came into class and there were obscene things all over your chalkboard?"

"I probably would have thought you were giving me suggestions of what I should do to you next." He raised his eyebrow at me and then pulled the car out of the parking spot.

I laughed as we exited the parking garage. As soon as his car emerged, cameras started flashing. I held my hand up in front of my face. "So are they here because you're a rich, eligible bachelor or would this really normally be that big of a deal?"

"I don't know. I'm sure my name doesn't help the situation." He sped off down Main Street. It was early and there was barely anyone out. "I want you to let me do the talking, okay? I'm going to fix this for you. That's my top priority." He pulled into a spot outside a building I had never been in before. Luckily there weren't any news vans outside.

"I wish you had just been a student."

He laughed. "I think you love that you're dating your professor."

My stomach was in knots. "I do. Let's get this over with." I reached for the door handle.

"Hey." He grabbed my chin in his hand. "We got this, okay?" He leaned toward me and kissed me. When he began to pull away I grabbed a fistful of his hair and deepened the kiss. I needed reassurance. I wanted to believe that I wasn't throwing away my education for nothing. He was my future. This was real. It had to be.

I heard the familiar groan in his throat. "We need to stop or I won't be able to go in there. Having an erection during our meeting with the dean would probably be frowned upon."

I laughed and kissed his cheek. "I love you."

"I love you." He opened up his car door and walked around to my side. He put his hand out for me and I grabbed it. We continued to hold hands as we went into the building. It was the first time we had done something like this in public. And I was grateful for his touch, because I was so nervous.

We entered through the side door and made our way through the lobby and down the hallway. He dropped my hand when he opened a door and I walked in before him. There was a young, blonde receptionist. She immediately smiled when she saw James, but her face fell slightly when he grabbed my hand again.

"Hi, Becca. We have a meeting with Joe."

"Yes. Joe is expecting you." She picked up a phone on the desk and punched in a few numbers. "Your 7 a.m. is here." She looked over at me. "Yes, she's here too." She paused again. "Okay," she said and hung up the receiver. "He'll be right out." She looked once more at James and then her eyes drifted back to her computer screen.

James escorted me to some chairs and we sat down. It felt like time was standing still. He leaned toward me and whispered in my ear, "Penny, you're hurting me."

"Oh, geez, sorry." I stopped gripping his hand so tightly. He rubbed his thumb against my palm. The small gesture helped calm me.

He leaned toward me. "Don't worry. The dean likes me. I think everything's going to be fine," he whispered.

"Why didn't you tell me that in the first place?"

"Because I didn't want you to get your hopes up."

"And now?"

"And now I need to believe it's true too." He squeezed my hand.

An older man with salt and pepper hair came out of a room behind the front desk. He took one look at us holding hands and shook his head. He turned and walked back into his office.

James sighed and stood up. He kept his fingers intertwined with mine. We walked together into the dean's office.

The dean was sitting behind his desk. He looked up at us. "Close the door, James." He sounded tired.

James closed the door and we both sat down across the desk from the dean.

The dean sighed deeply and leaned forward in his chair. "Excuse my bluntness, but this is a fucking mess."

"Joe, it was never my intention for this to happen."

"What, you didn't intend to sleep with your students when you accepted this position? Or you didn't intend for anyone to ever find out?"

"I never intended to sleep with a student. Singular, not plural. And I was going to tell you. I didn't want you to find out this way."

"And we met before I knew he was my professor." I couldn't sit there and say nothing. "And he made it clear that we couldn't fraternize. I refused to listen. It was my fault."

James squeezed my hand hard. He was pissed at me for speaking.

"I take full responsibility for this, Joe," he said calmly.

Joe pinched the bridge of his nose and shook his head. He looked like he was in pain. "Sorry, what is your name?" he asked and looked at me.

"Penny Taylor."

"Well, Penny, this is not your fault. James is an acting professor at this university. It's his responsibility to uphold the rules." He turned back to James. "We have a code of ethics, which I know you're aware of. Although not explicitly stated, dating a student violates the core values of this institution. What the hell were you thinking? And not only did you fail to disclose this relationship to me, but I had to find out in the damn newspaper." He slammed his fist down on top of his desk where today's newspaper was sitting. "Your ex-wife has made it a point not only to disgrace you but this entire university. It's like a fucking reality T.V. show."

"Joe..."

"I don't want to hear your excuses. You should have told me, James." He sighed and leaned back in his chair. "I know all that stuff your wife said is a lie. But it's going to be hard to convince other professors as well as your students' parents otherwise. They made it seem like you molested her or something." He paused and sighed. "It's a mess. They're pulling me down with you. I've already given my okay to launch an investigation. All your students will have to be interviewed because of the press's allegations, even though no one has openly come forward. And if you're lying about it just being her...if you laid a finger on any other girl...then I recommend you just resign right now, because..."

"It's just Penny."

Joe sighed again. "Well the board has already decided to suspend you during the investigation. That decision is over my head, but I completely agree with them. We may be able to lift your suspension if everything comes back clean after that. But my recommendation is that you two terminate your relationship immediately. This can't go on if you intend to keep working here."

"We're not doing that." James voice was stern.

"Well I don't have any other ideas. We've already had dozens of calls this morning from concerned parents. I have to act or I'll probably be fired next. Stop seeing her and if the interviews with other students show no other instances of misconduct you can keep teaching at this university under a probationary period. If there are no more violations we'll lift the probationary period in six months. And continuing to screw one of your students counts as a violation. So it needs to end. Otherwise we have to let you go."

"Then I guess I resign," James said calmly. He pulled out an envelope from his pocket and put it down on top of the desk. "Here's my letter of resignation." He slid it toward the dean.

"James?" I looked up at him. *What the hell is he doing?* We hadn't discussed him doing that. When had he written that letter? I hated that he always kept me in the dark. This wasn't the plan. He was supposed to fix it for both of us.

Joe stared at him. "That makes you look guilty of everything people are saying. You'll never get another teaching job."

"I only see two possibilities. I do everything your way, except I keep seeing her in secret, or I quit. And since continuing to work here and keep seeing her seems to be out of the question, I quit."

"Is this really worth ruining your reputation over? The press is already jumping to conclusions. If you resign it'll basically be a confession that you slept with all your female students. It'll look bad on the school too. I need you to say you made a mistake and stop seeing her. Stay out of the news during the investigation. Keep quiet for your six months of probation. That's it. I need this to disappear as soon as possible. Don't screw me on this."

"I don't know what to tell you, Joe. I love her. I'm not doing that."

"You've got to be shitting me."

"I'll have an interview with the press," I interjected.

"Penny," James said. "Please let me handle this." He looked even more pissed at me.

How could he be pissed at me? He had decided to resign without telling me. If anything, I should have been mad at him. "I'll tell them that it was completely consensual. And that I love him. Everyone will calm down. Maybe they won't care if we date then. And you can still conduct the interviews with other students. Everything will come back clean. It will all blow over."

Joe eyed me again. He looked mad at me too. But I could see his mind working.

James shook his head. "No. I don't want her talking to the press. I'm not dragging this out longer than necessary."

"James, let me help you keep your job."

"Enough," he said. He stared into my eyes.

He wanted to protect me. But I needed to protect him too. He loved teaching. I didn't want to be the reason why he had to stop.

I looked at Joe. "Do you think it will help?"

"Several news stations have already called me. It'll be national news by the end of the day. I don't know if it'll matter at this point. It's just a matter of public opinion. They've already labeled him. And in my opinion the only way to change their opinion is for you to terminate your relationship."

"Can't we at least try my idea?" I asked.

"Penny and I need to talk in private for a second." James stood up.

"Nothing about your relationship is going to be private now." Joe stared at us. "Sit down, James. Let's just get this over with." Joe looked down at a paper on his desk.

James slowly sat back down. He leaned toward me. "Penny, we've already talked about this," he whispered.

"No we haven't. You never said you were going to resign..."

"I mean about waiting until you graduate. I'm not doing it. We've had this discussion. If I stay we won't be able to be together. I'm not waiting to be with you. I've already made my decision. And it was the easiest decision I've ever made. Please just let me handle this. I'm not changing my mind."

I didn't know what to say. I felt like he was reprimanding me for caring. I wasn't trying to fix it because I didn't respect his decision. I just wished that he had discussed his decision with me before coming in here. I was just trying to help.

Joe cleared his throat. "Midterm grades are due at the end of this week. You'll still need to submit those. I've already gotten other professors to cover your classes during the investigation. They can just continue doing it until the end of the semester. You two have one class together. The validity of your grades is in question, Penny. You'll have to re-present your speeches to your new professor so he can sign off on them. This way you won't have to completely retake the course. Or you can stop taking the class. That's up to you. But the drop/add window has passed, so you'll have to withdraw and pay the fee for changes in registration. It'll appear as a W on your transcript, but it won't hurt your G.P.A. You'll have to let me know by next Tuesday before the window closes.

"So I'm not being expelled?" I asked.

"No," Joe said. "I'm giving you two strikes which will go on your record. You broke the rules too, but the blame for this lies on James. It has to. The university has standards for their professors. I don't know how your relationship started and I don't want to know. Don't give me reason to make your punishment harsher."

I stayed quiet. All I got was a slap on the wrist. I had been fully prepared to get kicked out of school. It felt like a huge weight had been lifted off my shoulders. James rubbed his thumb against my palm. He promised it would be okay and it was. But it wasn't for him. He was resigning. And he was mad at me for trying to get him to change his mind. He was giving everything up to be with me.

"So I'll talk to the press today and let them know about your resignation," Joe said. "Unless there is any way I can change your mind?"

"I'm sorry, Joe," Professor Hunter said.

I felt numb. I couldn't believe this was happening. I remembered running into James at the coffee shop. I never thought I'd see him again. And now it felt like I was ruining his life. We had only known each other for two months. What were we doing here? I felt like I was going to throw up.

"I'd prefer if you didn't flaunt your relationship around the school. I know I can't tell you what to do anymore, James. But I'm asking this as a favor. Let things settle down. We're still running the investigation. The university has to come out looking like we did everything we could do. Especially now that you're resigning. It makes you look guilty. I believe that it's just her, but this is only just the start. It's going to get worse before it gets better." He grabbed the newspaper off his desk and tossed it in the trash. "And I have to ask, under the circumstances. What happened to your eye?" He looked at James' bruise. It was fading, but it was still visible.

"Just a misunderstanding."

"Good." Joe sighed. "I thought the next thing you were going to tell me is that you got in a fist fight with a student." He laughed and shook his head. "That's the last thing this school needs right now. And I didn't want to have to talk about that in the interview."

Shit!

James shifted in his chair.

"Penny, do you mind if I have a word alone with James?" Joe asked. "We need to discuss a few more things."

"No, that's fine." I wanted to get out of there. I felt young and foolish. I had ruined James' life. How was he sitting there so calmly? How could he always be so sure of everything? I felt sick to my stomach.

"Go to class," Joe said. "And be prepared for most of the student body to already know."

I looked at James. His gaze was cool. He nodded at me and let go of my hand.

I stood up. "Thank you for being so understanding, Mr. Vespelli. And I'm sorry about all of this."

"Well you really should have thought about that beforehand, shouldn't you have? One more strike and you'll be expelled. Don't let me see you in here again."

I swallowed hard. I looked once more at James. I wasn't sure what they had left to discuss. He'd tell me later. "Thanks," I said again quietly and walked out, closing the door behind me.

CHAPTER 21

Wednesday

I sat down in my usual seat. I was the first one there. The whole building had been eerily quiet. It felt like I was dreaming. James had made the decision to resign without talking to me. He already had the letter with him. I felt small. He said he would fix it, but I didn't know that's what he had meant. I should have felt happy that we could finally be together. But I didn't. All I could think about was the fact that he had made the decision without me and left me in the dark on purpose. I felt so alone. This wasn't how a relationship was supposed to be. We were supposed to work out things together. I wiped my eyes with my palms.

I wondered how many people in my class would have seen the article. Not many, surely. I didn't read the newspaper. It wasn't likely that many college students did either. But something like this would circulate fast. Even if the article hadn't released my name, it would have been easy to guess that it was me. The speeches I had given were always out of line. Especially the one where I freaked out and talked about hating marketing.

The door opened and I looked up. Tyler walked in. He quickly walked over to me and sat down at the desk beside mine.

"I was hoping you'd be here early. How are you holding up?" he asked.

"I've been better. So I'm guessing you saw the article?"

"Yeah." He looked down at his hands. "Did you know?"

"Know what?"

"That he was married?"

"Not at first."

"God, I knew he was a piece of shit. He fucks students and screws around on his wife? Why do you want to be with someone like that?"

"Not students. Just me."

"That's not what the article implied."

"The article was wrong. And he did file for divorce before he met me. That part was true."

He sighed and leaned back in his chair. "So what happens now?"

"We met with the dean this morning. They're going to interview all his students to verify that he hasn't broken any other rules. To clear his name." I looked at Tyler's broken nose. I couldn't really ask him not to say something. Their fight had happened. I didn't want him to lie for me. I wasn't even sure if it mattered at this point. James resigned. *Who cares what people say now?*

"I'm not going to say anything, Penny. I started the fight. I'd get in trouble too."

"Thanks."

"So are you going to stay with him?"

"I am."

Tyler sighed. "When I saw you at the hospital I kind of lost it. I don't like seeing you hurt. I didn't mean to put you in an awkward position..."

"It's okay." We both sat there for a moment staring at each other. I wanted to hug him. I wanted him to know that I still cared about him. But I didn't want to risk leading him on again. It felt like a long time before he spoke again.

"I can't believe we're over," he said softly.

"I'm sorry, Tyler."

He reached down and pulled a small box out of his backpack. He slid it onto my desk. "I'm withdrawing from this class. I actually just came to give you this."

It was the present he had tried to give me when James had shown up. It seemed like ages ago that we had celebrated my birthday. But it was just last Friday. I picked up the box. "You don't need to drop the class."

"It's not because of you. I can't stand looking at him. And I don't want him to grade me. All I want to do is punch him whenever I see him. And I don't want to get my nose broken again." He smiled at me.

"He won't be teaching this class anymore."

"No?"

"He resigned this morning."

"Oh. It might be best if I just take it next semester anyway."

"It's not fair that I ruined this class for you."

"You didn't ruin it. You made it better. Hell, I probably only would have shown up on presentation days if I didn't have seeing you to look forward to."

I smiled at him. "Please don't drop it. If you do I'll just drop it too. I need you."

My words hung in the air. It wasn't fair for me to say that to him. But it was true. He was one of my best friends. I needed him now more than ever.

"I'll think about it. Either way, I don't want to listen to presentations today. So open your present before I go."

I unwrapped the small box and lifted the lid. There was a keychain with a circle attached to it that said "As you wish." It was the quote that Westley always said to Buttercup in The Princess Bride. I felt my throat constrict. It looked vintage, almost as if it had been made by hand. On the opposite side it said "Love, Apologetic Tyler." And there were two small charms attached to it, one of a heart and one of a key. *The key to his heart.* I felt my eyes start to water. It was the most beautiful keychain I had ever seen. It was more like a piece of art. I looked up at him. "Did you make this?"

"Yeah, it took freaking forever." He glanced at the clock. "I'm going to go. Text me, okay?" He stood up and grabbed his backpack.

"Tyler?" I didn't care how I was supposed to act around him. He was so sweet and thoughtful. I stood up and hugged him.

"I wish I had met you first." His voice sounded tight. He rested his chin on top of my head as he wrapped his arms around me. "I'd do anything to have a little longer with you. But I'll never forget our night together. And I don't want to."

"I don't want to either." My tears were making his shirt damp.

"I have to go." He kissed my forehead and pulled away from me. He walked out of the classroom without looking back at me.

Why did it feel like every time we saw each other recently we were ending our relationship? Over and over again. And each time felt more painful. Could we ever go back to just being friends? My hand was clenched around the keychain. I opened it and looked down at the keychain on my palm. I wiped my eyes with the back of my other hand and sat down. I grabbed my clutch and slipped the keychain on next to my dorm key.

I took a few deep breaths and wiped my eyes again. People were starting to arrive to class. The girls a few rows in front of me were whispering, but I overheard their conversation. There was a brunette and a blonde. The blonde girl was talking about how she wished she was sleeping with Professor Hunter. And the brunette was busy trying to figure out why James had chosen me to bang. I could feel their eyes on me. The phrase, "She's such a slut," seemed to be their favorite thing to say.

I knew people finding out would be bad. I just needed to ignore them. I pulled out my phone to pretend to be busy. There was a text from Professor Hunter:

"I hope that you're holding up okay. Can I convince you to come back to the apartment instead of listening to speeches?"

Seeing his words made me feel a little better. He had resigned for me. It was ridiculous for me to feel alone. He was trying to protect me. He had always said that. And his priority was to fix it for me, not himself. I typed out a response. "I want to face this. Waiting will make it worse. How did the rest of your conversation with the dean go?"

"I just had to sign a few papers. Can we at least meet for lunch? We really need to talk."

We need to talk? It was a line I had heard countless times in romantic comedies. It was synonymous with "we need to break up." I swallowed hard. *What did the dean say to him?* The feeling of being alone quickly returned. "Okay," I typed out and pressed send.

I looked up from my phone. Everyone seemed to be talking in hushed voices and staring at me. I looked back down at my phone. *Text me back.* I needed to hear that he loved me. I needed to hear that we were okay. I thought about how pissed he was at me in the dean's office. Would he really break up with me because I tried to save his job? Or maybe he realized that I had just ruined his life.

"Hey, Penny," someone said. I looked up as Raymond Asher sat down on top of Tyler's desk.

"Hi," I said and looked back down at my phone. *Leave me alone.*

He leaned forward slightly. "So, what is the going rate?"

I could hear a few people snickering.

"Excuse me?"

He shrugged. "I heard you were a hooker."

Seriously? I couldn't believe he was saying that to me. There was nothing in the article about that. "I'm not." I looked back down at my phone.

"What, you just sucked his dick for good grades?"

"It wasn't like that." Get the fuck away from me. What an asshole.

"I think it was exactly like that." The desk squeaked and I could feel his shadow over me. "Unless you just love sucking cock. Maybe you could give me a taste."

"Dude, back the fuck off." I looked behind me. Tyler had walked back in the room.

"What, is she banging you too?" Raymond asked.

"I said back the fuck off."

"Whatever, man." He laughed and walked back to his seat.

Tyler sat down next to me.

"Thank you," I whispered.

"Yeah, well that piece of shit doesn't know anything about it."

I swallowed hard. Tyler still felt the need to protect me. "I thought you were leaving?"

"I heard some people talking outside. You said you needed me. I didn't want you to have to face this alone." He shrugged.

"Thank you."

"Are you okay?" Tyler put his hand on my knee. "You look really pale."

"I'm okay." I wasn't. I needed reassurance. James' text had been anything but reassuring. I felt like I was sinking. I took a few deep breaths. I felt like how I did when James had stopped talking to me for weeks. Like I was numb. He was breaking up with me. Why was he breaking up with me? The dean must have convinced him. I felt like I couldn't breathe. I couldn't lose him again. Losing him was the worst thing that had ever happened to me.

A man who was probably in his mid 30s walked into the room while looking down at his phone. He slipped it in his pocket and went to the front of the room. He looked right at me and then directed his attention to the rest of the class. He cleared his throat.

Most of the class had been whispering, but the room fell silent. All I could hear was my own heart beating.

"It seems as though most of you have heard about the newspaper article. I just wanted to address the fact that Professor Hunter will no longer be teaching this class. I'm Professor Nolan and I will be filling in for Professor Hunter for the remainder of the semester. There will be interviews conducted with each of you regarding Professor Hunter's conduct. I hope that you will all be telling the truth of your experiences in this classroom."

A girl in the front row raised her hand.

It looked like Professor Nolan wanted to ignore her, but it was hard to pretend like he didn't see her. She was basically right in front of him. "Yes?" he asked.

"What article?"

"He's sleeping with that girl in the back row," a boy in the middle of the room said.

The professor cleared his throat again.

"Wait, seriously?" someone else said.

"That's enough," Professor Nolan interjected. "I just wanted you all to know about the interviews that are going to start tomorrow. I think this is a personal matter that is none of my business or yours, and I'd rather not discuss it any further. I've been told that your presentations start today. First up is..." he looked down at a piece of paper. "Raymond Asher."

Raymond stayed seated. "Wait, we really don't get to know any more details?" He turned around and looked at me. "Maybe Penny wants to share..."

"Mr. Asher!" Professor Nolan said, cutting him off. "This is a personal matter. How many times do I need to say that? I suggest that you get up here and start your presentation. Or you'll be receiving an F." Professor Nolan grabbed the podium and placed it in the middle of the room. He made his way past all the desks and sat down in the seat in front of Tyler.

I just wanted to go back to Professor Hunter's apartment. I needed him right now. I wanted his arms around me. I rubbed my fingers across the keychain that Tyler had given me. The room felt stifling.

Tyler rubbed his hand on my back, making me jump.

"Sorry," he mouthed silently. "You okay?"

I nodded my head.

Raymond slowly got up from his seat and stood behind the podium. I watched his mouth move but none of the words seemed to make any sense. I looked at the back of Professor Nolan's head. I wished Professor Hunter was sitting there instead. A small part of me wanted to stand up and yell, "Yes, it was me, okay? I did it, and I don't care!" And then I wouldn't have to hide anymore. I suddenly felt nauseous.

When class finally ended I quickly grabbed my backpack. Professor Nolan turned around and looked at me.

"Hold on a second, Penny," he whispered.

I didn't want to schedule my speeches with him already. I still needed to get through the one on Friday.

"It's going to be okay, Penny," Tyler said as he picked up his backpack. He reached over and squeezed my arm. "Text me, okay?"

I nodded at him and gave him a weak smile.

As soon as the rest of the students were gone, Professor Nolan stood up and turned to me.

"I know I need to schedule my redo speeches with you," I said. "But can we please wait until at least next week?"

He waved his hand dismissively. "I trust James' grades. You don't need to do that. But he called me this morning. He thinks it's best if you just drop this class. I insured him that I'd look after you. But after today I think I agree with him."

"I..."

"It's just something you should think about. Your other classes are going to be hard, but not as bad as this one. You can think about it. But you have to give a speech on Friday if you choose to stay. I can't treat you any differently than the other students, regardless of the circumstances. So if you decide to drop this class, just email me."

"Okay." James was trying to make all the decisions. I needed to talk to him. I didn't want to go to my next class.

"If you decide to stay, I'll do my best to get the other students to stop harassing you. I'd recommend not coming to class early, though."

"Okay," I said again.

"Well, you better get to your next class. Good luck, Penny."

"Thanks." I allowed myself to exhale as I walked toward the door. Class was horrible. But Tyler had stood up for me. And Professor Nolan was nice and understanding. I didn't even have to redo my speeches.

As I walked through the hallway I could hear the whispers. I could feel the stares. I kept my eyes on the ground.

Someone grabbed my arm. I looked up at Professor Hunter. He pulled me into a custodial closet. When the door closed the whole room was pitch-black.

"Are you okay?" Professor Hunter's soothing voice made me burst out in tears.

"Penny?" his voice was laced in concern. He pulled my face against his chest and ran his fingers through my hair. "I don't like seeing you cry. Tell me what you need."

I didn't respond to him. I just continued to cry.

"Penny, please talk to me," he said gently.

"I told you I'd give up everything for you," I sobbed. "I said I didn't care about finishing school here. I said we could run away together. I'll do whatever you want. Please don't do this."

He put his hands on my shoulders. "Do what? What are you talking about?"

"Please. I can't lose you. I know what living is like when we aren't together. I don't want to feel that way again. I can't feel that way again." I took a deep breath of his heavenly scent.

"You're not losing me. Hey." He grabbed my chin and tilted my head up so that he could see my eyes. "I love you. Where is this coming from?"

"You're not breaking up with me?"

"No." He laughed. It felt like ages since I had heard him laugh. "Penny, no."

"Well don't say things like we need to talk then," I said through my tears. "When people say that, it means they want to break up."

"You really do watch too much T.V." He wiped my tears away with his thumbs. "Please stop crying."

I felt relieved. But I was still mad at him. "We're supposed to be a team."

"We are a team."

"No, we're not." I leaned back to look at him. "You made the decision to quit without even discussing it with me first."

"I listened to what Joe had to say. There wasn't even a decision that needed to be made. There was only one option."

"But you had already decided. You had a resignation letter with you."

"I like to be prepared..."

"You knew what you were going to do. You knew and you didn't tell me. I felt blindsided in there."

"I told you to let me go alone. I asked you to let me handle it. And it was my choice to make. Not yours."

"What? It was a decision that effects both of us. Why do you want to do everything alone? I gave up everything to be with you. Stop pushing me away." I swallowed hard. Isabella's words came back to me. He wanted what he couldn't have. And he definitely had me now. The small closet was making me feel claustrophobic. I tried to shake the thought away but it just made me cry even more.

"Please stop crying. I don't know what you want me to do. I want to give you what you need. Please just tell me what you want. Let me reassure you about how I feel." He wiped away my tears with his thumbs.

I grabbed the back of his neck and kissed him hard. He instinctively grabbed my waist and pulled me against him. His hands slid to my ass.

"Let's go back to the apartment," he said and kissed the side of my neck.

"No." I unbuttoned and unzipped his pants. This was what I needed. This was something that always worked between us. The only reassurance I needed was his dick deep inside of me. "This is what I need." I wrapped my hand around his erection.

He grabbed my thighs and lifted my legs up around him. He moved toward the wall, but tripped over a bucket. I slid down his torso and my feet hit the ground again. "Shit. Sorry, Penny."

I silenced him with another kiss. I needed him. I unbuttoned and unzipped my jeans and pushed them down my hips. He pushed his body against mine, pressing my back against the cool wall. He slid my pants the rest of the way down. I stepped out of them and my flats.

"I think this will reassure you," he said and knelt in front of me. I expected him to kiss the inside of my thigh, or lightly brush his fingers against my clit to tease me. But he thrust his tongue deep inside my wetness.

"Fuck," I groaned and leaned my head back against the wall.

He had done this to me before, but never like this. He was acting like he was starving and I was the only thing sustaining him. He thrust his tongue even deeper inside of me as he rubbed his nose against my clit.

"James," I panted.

He lifted my thighs over his shoulders so that he was supporting all my weight. He slid one of his hands underneath my tank top and pressed it against my breast to keep me in place. It felt like I was floating. All the tension, stress, and anxiety seemed to disappear. All I could think about was his tongue between my thighs. He rubbed his nose against my clit again.

The sensation was too much. I moaned as my orgasm washed over me.

"Do you feel better now?" He placed another long stroke against my wetness as he moved my thighs off his shoulders. I felt my back slide down the wall. "Because your cunt is delicious. I could do that forever." He pushed my tank top up and kissed my stomach. "I told you everything would be okay and it will be. I need you to trust me. I need you to trust my judgment."

"I do trust you." He was still kneeling in front of me.

"Then we should be celebrating today, not fighting." He sunk one of his fingers inside of me.

Oh God.

"I'm divorced." He thrust his finger deeper.

Fuck.

"I'm not your professor anymore." He slid another finger inside of me.

"James," I groaned.

He responded by slowly moving his fingers in and out of me. "We can finally be together, just like you wanted. So tell me, how else can I reassure you?" His fingers were driving me crazy.

I moaned.

He stood up and his fingers hooked, hitting me where only he could. "Do you need me to take you home and make love to you?" He kissed my neck. "Or do you want me to fuck you in this closet? Because I need my cock inside of you. I need reassurance too." He pressed his thumb against my clit.

"Fuck me. Oh God, please fuck me."

"I was hoping you'd say that," he said and bit my earlobe. My whole body tingled in response. He grabbed my thighs, lifted my legs around him and sunk his thick cock deep inside of me. He slammed my back against the shelves on the side of the closet as he moved his hips.

Yes!

Bottles toppled to the ground. A fake lemon scent filled the room. But I didn't care that we were making a mess. I ran my fingers through his unruly hair and deepened our kiss. I needed this more than I ever had before.

He began to thrust faster and harder. I tilted my hips to meet him and he groaned into my mouth. His finger tips dug into my hips.

"Harder," I moaned.

"If you want it harder, I'll give it to you harder." He carried me over to a table and pushed some of the contents to the ground. They must have been paper products, because they barely made a sound. He laid me down on the table and leaned over me. I unbuttoned his shirt so I could feel his six pack. "I'll never get enough of you," I whispered. He had said those words to me before. It was true for me too. If he wasn't addicted to me, then I was surely addicted to him. I needed him to know.

"Good. Because I'm never letting you go." He grabbed the edge of the table near my head and slid his length deep inside of me.

Fuck. I tilted my head to the side. He grabbed my chin in his hand and turned my head back toward him.

"Look at me when you orgasm, Penny. I want to see your face." He let go of my chin, wrapped his hand around my thigh, and moved his hips faster. Somehow it allowed him to go even deeper.

It was rough and intimate at the same time. He knew me. He knew exactly what I needed.

"Come for me, Penny."

As soon as I began to clench around him, I felt him fill me with his warm liquid. I closed my eyes, but he grabbed my chin again. I looked into his eyes as we both finished. I got completely lost in his eyes. No one had ever looked at me like that. I could feel his love for me. Nothing else in the world mattered when we were together.

He pulled me up to a seated position. He grabbed his pants off the ground and pulled them on. I silently watched him. I had felt so amped up and scared and worried and now all I felt was his love. I could actually feel it. There was this strange pressure in my chest. It made me want to cry again. I wrapped my arms around myself. I had been worried that this wasn't real. That was ridiculous.

He turned toward me as he buttoned up his shirt. He stopped and looked down at me. "I know that you're worried that I'm going to resent you because I had to stop teaching. But it's the complete opposite. For the first time ever, I feel like I'm exactly where I should be. Life is good here, with you. I'm in love with you." He paused. "I love you so much. I never knew what I was missing."

"I'm so in love with you, James Hunter."

He leaned forward and ran the tip of his nose down the length of mine. "Now, we're going back to the apartment. You don't need to face everyone today alone. We'll deal with this together. We'll make our decisions together. Well...except for this one. Because I really want to take you home right now."

I laughed. "I'm sorry. I just lost it today. Everyone..."

"Don't. Don't apologize. I know you needed me. That's why I was hiding in this closet in the first place." He smiled at me and pushed a strand of hair behind my ear. "I was prepared to resign today. I should have told you before we went into the meeting. I wasn't going to stop seeing you. It was out of the question."

"I know. I think you made the right choice."

"I'm right? What?" He smiled at me.

I nudged his shoulder. "So if you didn't want to break up with me, what did you want to talk to me about?"

"Nothing." He leaned down and handed me my pants. "We're okay."

"No, what was it?" I quickly got dressed.

"Honestly, I was really mad at you. I'm still mad at you. I told you to let me handle the situation this morning. You shouldn't have interfered."

"I know, but you also didn't tell me that you were planning to resign. How was I supposed to know what to do? If you don't talk to me, I can't know what you're thinking. I thought I was helping. Actually, I was mad at you too."

"I know. I'm still getting used to this." His hand drifted to my cheek. "I'm not used to having someone on my side."

"Well maybe you should get used to it. Because I love you. I'm not going to run off. I want to be with you."

"It's hard for me to believe that."

"Why?" I put my hands on the sides of his face. "Why don't you feel worthy of love? Why don't you trust me?"

"I didn't mean that. I do trust you. I'm just not used to being...I don't know how to explain it..."

"Vulnerable?" He was always prepared. He always knew what he wanted. He was always in control.

He didn't seem to like my choice of words. "Vulnerable? I'm not sure if that's the word I was looking for."

"I just mean that you don't have to be strong around me all the time. I just want you to be you."

"This is me."

"I know. I just mean, you don't have to be scared of showing me every side of you."

"The only thing I'm scared of is losing you."

"You're not going to lose me. I'm sorry. I was upset that you made the decision to quit without me. And then I thought you were going to break up with me. And it was hard being in class without you. I don't know if I can do it."

"Let's forget all the noise for right now, okay? Let's just enjoy us. We finally get to be together, Penny." He turned on the light so that I could see him.

He had that just fucked hair that I loved so much. He finished buttoning his shirt.

I looked around at the closet. It was a complete mess. "James, do you think maybe we should pick some of this up?"

"Eh, I don't work here anymore. Let's get the hell out of here before someone finds us." He grabbed my hand and opened up the door a crack. He pulled me out after him and we ran hand in hand through the hallway. Classes had started and no one was around.

A few students walking along the green turned to look at us as we ran to his car. He opened up the door for me and I quickly got in. He closed it and ran around to his side. As he turned his key in the ignition he leaned over and kissed me again.

There had been so much stress in our relationship. It finally felt like we were allowed to be happy. We were acting like two teenagers in love. And that's how I felt. When I was next to him, I felt like anything was possible.

"Truth or dare?" he asked and looked at me.

I looked into his eyes. He was giving me a challenging look. I didn't want to go back to his apartment. I didn't want to ever have to face reality. I wanted to get as far away from here as possible. "Dare."

PART 3

CHAPTER 22

Wednesday

It seemed like with every mile we drove away from the University of New Castle, James grew more and more relaxed. I couldn't pull my eyes away from his face. I was still processing the fact that he had quit his job. *For me.* Every few seconds he would turn his head to look at me and his smile would grow even brighter.

"What are you staring at?" he finally said.

"You."

He rubbed his thumb against my palm.

"What now?" I asked.

"Well, do you have a passport?"

"No. I've never needed one." I really wish I had a passport.

"You've never left the country?" He turned to me again. He seemed to think I was joking.

"I have. I've been to Canada. But I didn't need a pass-port."

"That's because going to Canada doesn't really count as leaving the country. So where have you been? I want to take you somewhere new."

I turned and looked out the window. "I haven't really been that many places." I watched the colorful autumn trees passing by us in a blur before turning back to him. "I've pretty much stayed on the east coast. Pennsylvania, Virginia, and Maryland. Oh, I've been to North and South

Carolina. And New York of course." I squeezed his hand. "And Florida a few times to go to Disneyworld."

"Disneyworld?" He smiled at me.

"Yeah, I love Disneyworld. Everyone loves Disneyworld. Don't look at me like that."

He laughed and turned his attention back to the road. "I wouldn't know. I've never been."

"You've never been to Disneyworld?"

"No."

I couldn't tell what he was thinking. "Well, maybe you should let me take you to Disneyworld."

He laughed. "This is my dare. I'm taking you somewhere. Not the other way around."

"So, where are we going then?"

Instead of saying anything, James put on his turn signal and took an exit that I was all too familiar with. It was the same exit I'd take if I was going home. I thought we'd be staying on I-95 until we got to the Philly airport.

"Aren't we going to the airport?" I asked. I had a sinking feeling in my stomach.

"We are. I just wanted to make a quick stop first."

Oh God. Not my house! "I don't know. I haven't decided if I want to make that speech on Friday yet. So we can't go anywhere that far I guess. And I forgot that I really should be studying for my Stat test. You know what? Let's just turn around. Let's spend the day in your apartment. Don't we have to get stuff ready for your brother anyway?"

"Ellen will get everything ready for Rob's visit."

"I forgot, I think I have a psychology test tomorrow too. Oh geez, we better get back."

"You chose dare, Penny. Who backs down from a dare?" He drove down Concord Pike and put his turn signal on again.

No, no, no! "You know what? I actually think I've been around here before. There's this cute little diner right down the street. I'm starving. Do you want to stop and eat?"

He lowered his eyebrows slightly. "Penny, you're a terrible liar."

"What? Psh. Professor Hunter..."

"You really should stop calling me that." He turned into Windy Park.

My neighborhood. I took a deep breath. "How do you know where I live?"

"Oh, is this your neighborhood?" He looked over at me and raised his left eyebrow.

"James, pull over."

He continued to drive down the street and stopped at the stop sign before turning onto Smith Lane.

"James!"

He turned the corner and pulled to a stop at the bottom of my street.

"Penny, you'll be lucky if your parents don't already know. It'll be better if they hear it from you. You said you'd call them..."

"And I will call them. I can't do this in person."

"You can."

"James, I can't." I dropped my head back on the headrest.

"We need to do this. Today."

The way he said we made me feel slightly better. But not better enough to tell him to drive up the street to my house.

"You don't have to do it alone. I'm going to be with you. I'll even do most of the talking if you want."

"I feel like that'll make it worse. I need some air." I opened up the car door and stepped out into the sunshine. It only took a second before he was standing beside me. He didn't say anything. He just leaned against the car and stared at the manicured lawn in front of us.

I sighed and leaned against the car too. "Who uses a dare to make their girlfriend disclose their illicit affair to her parents? You're super lame. How about you dare me to give you head at that diner I told you about a minute ago? Or maybe we can join the mile high club on an airplane?"

He pressed his lips together.

"Please don't tell me that you're already part of the mile high club."

"Stop trying to change the subject." James put his arm around my shoulder. "I'm not going to force you to tell them. If you really don't want to, that's your decision. It would make me feel a lot better about everything though."

"Unless my dad punches you in the face."

James laughed and looked down at me. His expression grew cloudy. "Wait, do you seriously think that's going to happen?"

"I have no idea. I usually don't upset my parents. Disappointing them isn't exactly something I do all the time. I'm a little out of my element. And I've never even brought a boy home."

"Luckily I have tons of practice with disappointing parents. I'm not even sure if my parents love me."

His words made me wince. "That can't possibly be true."

"I don't think it's far from the truth." He looked down at me. "I'd really prefer if your parents didn't hate me. That's probably asking too much given the situation. The sooner we tell them, the sooner they might be willing to forgive me though."

"They won't even be home for several hours," I said. His parents hadn't taken him to Disneyworld or given him juice boxes. And they had forced him to marry someone that he didn't love. They were clearly horrible. I wanted my parents to love him. I almost felt like he needed my parents' love. But I was worried once my parents found out that he was my professor, they'd hate me and him.

"Okay. How about you give me a tour of your hometown? Unlike you, I've really never been here before." He smiled at me. "And if you still don't feel like telling them in person by the time they're supposed to come home from work, we'll leave. They won't even know we were here."

"Oh, Penny! Is that you?"

Crap. I turned around and saw Sally Bennett, the neighborhood gossip, coming toward us. "Hi, Mrs. Bennett."

She gave me a hug and then looked over at James. "And you must be the new boyfriend I've heard so much about?"

James' looked taken aback. "Hi, I'm James." He put out his hand for her to shake.

"Pulling Penny away from her classes are you? Her parents won't be pleased to hear about that. But your secret is safe with me." She finally let go of James' hand.

Ditching classes with him was going to be the least of my parents' worries. I wasn't sure why Mrs. Bennett had said our secret was safe with her. No secret was ever safe with her.

"So what are you two kids doing here?" Mrs. Bennett asked.

"I was just showing James where I grew up. A little tour of town."

"Well that's fun. Your parents are going to be so thrilled that you're visiting. I think having an empty nest doesn't suit them very well. I was thinking about giving them one of my cats. I know you already have a cat, but trust me, two is better than one."

I laughed. "I'm sure they'd really appreciate that." Maybe Mrs. Bennett coming over and handing them a cat would take away some of their anger toward me.

"Did you know that I used to babysit Penny when she was a wee little thing?" Mrs. Bennett said, ignoring my statement. "The thing that stands out the most was that it was almost impossible to ever get her in the tub. She was always so feisty. I always thought it was the red hair."

What the hell, Mrs. Bennett? My face had to be completely red.

James laughed. "She's still pretty feisty."

It was Mrs. Bennett's turn to blush. "Oh my." She lightly touched James' arm. "Well I don't want to interfere with the tour. I'll let you two kids get to it."

There wasn't much of a choice now. Mrs. Bennett told everyone everything. My parents would know I was in town as soon as Mrs. Bennett got home to her phone.

James looked down at me. "Not a fan of baths, huh? I never would have guessed that. We always have so much fun in the shower."

I grabbed his car keys out of his hand and walked past him.

"Hey." He grabbed my wrist. "What are you doing?"

"You wanted a tour."

"I'll drive." He held out his hand for the keys.

"You won't be able to see anything I show you then. Can't you give up control for just a few minutes? I want to show you something." I walked around the car and opened up the driver's door. James was a lot bigger than me. I went to grab the lever to adjust the seat but there were only buttons. So fancy. I pressed one and my seat got even lower. I couldn't even see over the steering wheel.

James laughed as he sat down in the passenger's seat. "Here." He leaned over me and pressed a few buttons. As the seat rose, he placed a kiss against my lips.

I grabbed his chin. "You should probably put your seatbelt on, James."

He lowered his eyebrows slightly and sat back in his seat. As soon as his buckle clicked into place, I put my foot on the gas.

The car jolted forward. I did a very jerky u-turn as I adjusted to the sensitivity of his gas and brake pedals.

"Maybe I should drive," James said. He was gripping the armrest and looked incredibly nervous.

"I got this." I smoothly drove us out of the neighborhood and back onto Concord Pike.

"So is Wilmington one of those small towns where everyone knows each other?" James asked.

"If you haven't noticed, all of Delaware is like that."

"I have kind of noticed that. It's very different from New York."

I laughed and pulled the car into a parking lot next to a park. We easily could have walked here from my house, but I didn't want to leave his car parked outside, just in case my parents came home for lunch. "Well you should be comfortable today then. No one ever really notices me. So today we can pretend like we're in New York." I handed him his keys before stepping out of the car.

When James reached me, he wrapped his arms around me. I immediately hugged him back. We stood like that for a long time. I felt so calm when he held me like this. And I realized that he was hugging me because of what I said. This was him telling me that he noticed me. His sweet cologne mixed with the smell of the autumn leaves made me feel more at home than I had ever felt.

I took a deep breath. "Let me call my mom. I'll tell her we're here and that she should come home for lunch. You're right, the sooner the better."

He pulled back slightly and looked down at me. "Are you sure?"

I looked into his dark brown eyes. "I'm sure."

CHAPTER 23

Wednesday

"Hi, Mom," I said into my phone. My palms felt sweaty. *What if she already knows?!*

"Hi, Sweetie. Sally called me a few minutes ago. I was actually just about to call you. What are you doing home? Is everything alright? Are you feeling sick again?"

Geez, Mrs. Bennett! "Yeah, everything's great! Nothing weird or out of the ordinary going on at all." *What am I saying?*

My mom stayed silent.

"I just wanted to show James around. He was curious about where I grew up." I looked over at him. He was leaning against the railing of the small bridge, staring down at the water. We had walked hand in hand along the walking trails in the woods. If I didn't have to confess this huge secret to my parents, it would have been the most amazing fall afternoon.

"Did you two want to come over for dinner? I can make spinach quiche!"

Spinach quiche was my favorite home cooked meal. "Actually, Mom, I was hoping you and Dad could come home for lunch? James and I have to get back soon and I want to make sure I get to see both of you." I needed to tell them before someone else did.

"Well..." there was a pause. "Yeah, I think I can. I'll have to give your father a call. I'm not sure if he has any meetings today. Are you sure you don't want to stay for dinner, Penny? I'd love to get to know James better."

My stomach seemed to flip over. She was going to know all she cared to know in a few hours. "James actually needs to get back soon."

"Well, okay. How is your head feeling? Are you still getting dizzy?"

I touched my forehead. "I'm feeling a lot better. You have absolutely nothing to worry about." Health-wise that was true. But she'd have a whole mess of problems to worry about soon. Why did I just keep piling lies on top of lies?

"Are you sure everything is okay, sweetie? You don't sound quite like yourself."

"Really, Mom, I'm good. Text me about lunch, okay?"

"Okay, Pen. I'll call your father now."

"Great. See you later." I hung up before she could ask me any more questions. I forgot how easily she could read me.

"I need to get back soon, huh?"

"I didn't want to commit to dinner in case, well, everyone's freaking out."

He nodded. "Probably a good idea." He put his elbows back on the railing.

I leaned on the ledge beside him. "I used to run on these paths in high school."

"I didn't know that you liked to run."

"I don't," I laughed. "I made myself. I wanted to make sure I was in good shape for volleyball. I actually hate running."

"You played volleyball?"

"Why do you always seem surprised when I tell you about my athletic abilities? I'm an only child. I used to play stuff with my dad all the time. He never had a son." I shrugged my shoulders. "I was actually pretty awesome at volleyball."

"You're probably awesome at everything you do." He put his arm around my shoulders.

"I used to dream of having a boyfriend to walk with back here. I even used to dream about sneaking out of my house and coming over here for secret rendezvous."

"Hmm." He leaned down and kissed me. "You were always quite scandalous. The news of you dating your professor shouldn't shock your parents at all then."

I laughed uneasily. I almost said that dreams were different than reality. But that would have been a lie. Being with him was like the best dream come true.

"What were you like in high school?"

"What do you mean? Like I am now. Or, like I was before I met you, I guess. Shy and quiet. Completely invisible. I don't feel invisible anymore."

My phone buzzed and I pulled it out of my pocket. "They will both be home in an hour." I was almost disappointed. "What's the plan exactly? How do you think we should bring it up? We already told them that you were a student. And you look young, James. I feel like they're going to think I'm joking."

He pulled me against his chest. "I don't think there is any right way. Let's just try not to think about it."

"How can I possibly not think about it? I want them to love you as much as I do."

James ran his fingers through my hair. "I think it's more likely that your dad will punch me in the face than love me."

I laughed. "He's not going to do that," I said. But I didn't really know. I had no idea what to expect.

"I'd love a tour of your house. So I can plan my escape route and everything before they get there. Just in case."

"If you need to make an emergency escape, please don't leave me in the crossfire."

"I would never."

***

I felt a little nervous when I opened up the front door. I wasn't ashamed of who I was at all. But James was rich. He wasn't used to a normal colonial house in the suburbs. My house was classically homey. I stepped inside and turned on the light in the hallway.

My cat, Teddy, ran into the room meowing. I laughed and lifted him up in my arms. "This is Teddy," I said as I turned back toward James.

"I didn't realize you were a cat person."

"I wouldn't classify myself as a cat person." Melissa had always joked around with me, saying I'd be a future cat lady. I was glad that my fate seemed to have changed. I held out my cat to James.

"Oh, um, okay." He grabbed Teddy and held the cat out in front of him. He looked so uncomfortable. Teddy began to squirm in his hands. "Oh God." He tossed Teddy onto the floor, and the cat immediately darted out of the room.

I started laughing. "So, I'm guessing you aren't an animal person?"

"Was it that obvious? I just never had a pet growing up. Now cats and dogs just kind of freak me out."

I laughed and grabbed his hand. "Well, I just have the one cat. So you don't need to worry about running into any more. And I'm pretty sure Teddy is going to stay away from you the rest of the afternoon."

"I hope that's not a bad omen."

Me too. "Don't be ridiculous. Okay, well, this is the dining room." I walked through the archway into the dining room. It was simple, just a table and chairs and some pictures on the walls.

He walked over to the wall and looked at a picture of me hugging a tree with bright red leaves. I couldn't believe my mom still changed the pictures in here depending on what season it was. In a few months it would be me sitting by the Christmas tree in probably just a diaper or something super embarrassing. At least I was clothed in my tree hugging picture.

"You're so adorable."

I laughed. "I'm really glad there aren't any pictures of my awkward stage in here. I begged my mom to stop putting them all over the house. Maybe she finally listened." I looked over at the china cabinet and then snapped my head back toward him. I had spoken too soon. *Please don't go over to the china cabinet.*

As if sensing the aura of terrible images of me, James walked over to the china cabinet.

"Don't you want to see the kitchen?"

He leaned down and looked at a picture of me smiling with braces.

Kill me now.

He looked over at me and smiled. "Super adorable. I have no idea why you've never had a boyfriend before."

"Oh shut up." I grabbed his arm and pulled him away from the dining room.

"Seriously, Penny." He pushed my back against the doorframe between the kitchen and dining room. "You're beautiful."

"Not in that picture."

He placed a soft kiss against my lips. "Well you should have seen me in junior high."

"You were probably always sexy."

He laughed. "I'm sure Rob will love showing you picture evidence of how that is so not true."

"I'm excited to meet him."

"It'll be fun having him around." James released me and walked into the kitchen. "I like your house. It's...warm." He smiled at me.

That was a good way of describing it. I felt safe here. "Warm. I like that." I lead him into the family room.

"Garage and back door. Noted."

"James, you're not going to have to make an escape. It's not like you're my super old professor. You're not even that much older than me. Plus you aren't even my professor anymore. It could be so much worse. And I think they just want me to be happy. You make me so happy."

"Hmm." He gave me a small smile.

"Come on, we haven't finished the tour." I showed him the living room, the office, and bathroom. "And that's the basement," I said, pointing to a door. "And the laundry room." I pointed to a different door. "And that's it."

James looked over at the stairs. "Well, what's up there?"

"My parents room, two guest rooms, and two more bathrooms. Oh, and my room."

"I think I'd like to see that."

"You want to see my room? I'm not allowed to bring boys upstairs." My parents had never really needed to state that as a rule. No boyfriend, no boys upstairs rule needed. I tried to give him an innocent smile.

"Is that so? Maybe I can convince you to bend the rules just this once?" He raised his left eyebrow.

"How much time do we have before they come home?"

James looked at his watch. "Half an hour."

"Okay. But really quick. I do not want our discussion to start out that way. Absolutely no funny business."

James lifted his hands up to either side, acknowledging that he'd behave.

I bit my lip and turned toward the stairs. I was hoping he'd abandon his resolve. I suddenly felt young and giddy. How many times had I imagined having a boy in my room? And I wasn't just bringing up any boy. I was bringing up my sexy, brooding, rich, successful professor. Maybe my parents would just be happy. James was a catch.

I made my hips sway more than usual as I walked up the stairs. I could feel his eyes on me. I tried to remember what kind of disarray I had left my room in. Hopefully it wasn't as bad as I was picturing.

"You're kind of a slob." He laughed as he stepped over some of the clothes on my floor and walked passed me.

"I'm a lot better when I have a roommate. A lot of it was from when I was packing. It's hard to know what to bring to school when you only have so much space." I picked up some of the clothes and put them into a hamper in the corner.

James walked over to my bookshelf and looked at the titles. "Jane Eyre? Are you a fan of all the classic romances?"

I laughed. "No, actually. I read it for my senior thesis. Jane and Mr. Rochester drove me crazy. Clearly they should have been together the whole time. It made me so mad." I tossed some more clothes into my hamper. I just realized the irony of what I had said. I had told James that I had wanted to wait. Was I really as annoying as Jane Eyre?

James was smiling at me. "I couldn't agree more."

"Honestly, I think I'm done reading classics as soon as I'm done with school. I prefer reading books like Harry Potter." I hoped that didn't make me seem too young.

"I prefer books like Harry Potter too." He put his hands in his pockets.

"Really? You've read Harry Potter?"

"Why is that so surprising? I'm pretty sure that Harry Potter was actually my generation's thing, not yours. And who doesn't love the concept of magic? Besides, there was this cute little red headed girl in it that I loved reading about." He smiled at me.

"I was Ginny Weasley for Halloween last year."

"Quite the leap from Ginny to sexy Poison Ivy."

"Yeah, well I started dating this sophisticated, older gentleman. I was trying to impress him."

"You don't need to change for me. I love you just the way you are." He looked over at my bed. "Stuffed animals and all. Geez, that's a lot of stuffed animals."

I laughed. "Yeah, well, I didn't have my boyfriend's sweater to snuggle up to at night. Or the man himself."

James walked over to my bed and sat down on the edge of it. "The Beatles?" he asked, nodding his head toward a poster on my wall.

"I'm an old soul."

"You're full of surprises, Penny Taylor."

"I hope that's a good thing."

He smiled at me. He looked so out of place, sitting on my unmade bed full of teddy bears. But he looked surprisingly comfortable. He looked happy. "What is the wildest fantasy you had in this room?"

"Honestly, nothing that risqué. I just had tons of dreams about getting my first kiss."

"Was your actual first kiss everything you dreamed it would be?"

"No. The first kiss we had was much more like my dreams." I walked over to him, stopping when I was standing right in front of him.

He lightly brushed his fingertips against my thigh.

I swallowed hard.

"And why is that?"

"It was sexy and romantic." Just remembering the feel of the cold, wet steel of the car against my body made heat rise to my cheeks. "Until you told me I had to stop thinking about you, of course." I laughed as he grabbed my hand and pulled me on top of him. I quickly moved my legs so that I was straddling him on my bed.

He put his hands on my waist. "It's good that all you dreamed about was kissing. Because I want to make all your fantasies come true. And if it was something else, I'd be obliged to comply. Even though your parents are going to be home any minute."

I wouldn't have thought having Professor Hunter in my bedroom would have been sexy. But he made everything we did sexual somehow. I ran my hand along the scruff on his jaw line. "James, I'm so nervous."

"I know. I'm nervous too."

"What if they freak out?"

"We'll figure it out together."

I glanced at the window. "We should probably go downstairs."

"We probably should." But instead of getting up to go downstairs, he leaned forward and kissed me.

I let myself get lost in his kiss. I needed the distraction. I needed to think that everything was going to be okay. "You're good at distracting me."

He smiled and ran the tip of his nose down the length of mine.

I sighed and climbed off his lap. "Okay, let's go downstairs," I said and I smoothed my shirt down.

"Penny, it's going to be okay." He gave me a small smile as he stood up.

"How can you be so sure?"

"As long as I have you, everything will be okay."

That was sweet. But it was also naive. My parents were going to kill me. And him. I felt like I was going to throw up. I grabbed his hand and led him out of my room and down the stairs.

CHAPTER 24

Wednesday

"What's the game plan?" I asked. "Should I just tell them everything real quick? Just throw it all out there?"

James rubbed his thumb against my palm.

"So, slow then? Just let it all unravel?" I bit my lip.

"Take a deep breath, Penny."

I heard a car door slam outside. "Oh God." I squeezed James' hand. I felt like I was going to faint. "Try to look natural, okay?"

"Natural. Got it."

"You're dressed really professorly today by the way. I don't know whether that's a good or bad thing."

"Professorly?" James laughed. "Yeah, that's not a word."

"Now I'm making up words. How am I going to tell them that I'm dating my professor when I can't even talk?!"

"Luckily I'm not your professor anymore. Does that make it any better?" He was smiling at me.

"Not really."

"I think maybe it makes it a little better." He raised his eyebrow.

"Okay, maybe a little better." My heart beating seemed to be the only sound in the room.

"Thanks for doing this. It means a lot to me." He squeezed my hand. "More than you know."

"Sometimes it still feels like I made you up. Maybe this will make it feel more real."

"It is real."

I looked up at him. Melissa's words came back to me about owning my relationship. "I love you, James."

"I love you."

When the front door opened I felt a little less nervous. I wanted to prove to James that I wasn't embarrassed that I was dating my professor. Because I wasn't. I was the lucky one. Maybe my parents would see that. I had won the lottery. They had to see that.

"Penny?" My mom called from the hallway.

"Hi, Mom!" I went over and hugged her as soon as she walked into the kitchen.

"It's so good to see you, sweetie." My mom pulled back. "And James!" My mom put down the paper bags she was holding on the kitchen table and went and hugged him.

James always seemed surprised when people showed him affection. He patted my mom's back awkwardly and smiled over at me. "It's great to see you again, Mrs. Taylor."

"I hope sandwiches are okay. I stopped by that little French bistro on the way home that you like so much. La Patisserie."

"That sounds fantastic." I wasn't sure why I had been so worried. I forgot how much my mom seemed to like James. Or maybe she was just happy that I finally had a boyfriend.

"If I wasn't so happy to see you both, I'd reprimand you for skipping classes today. Why the sudden urge to come home?" My mom opened up the fridge.

I need to tell you something. "We both didn't have anything important going on today. I thought it might be fun to show James where I grew up."

I heard the front door open again. I took a deep breath. It was my dad that I was really worried about.

"Hey, Pen." As soon as my dad entered the kitchen he opened his arms.

I quickly gave him a hug. He still saw me as his little girl. I wasn't sure how he'd see me after I confessed I was dating my professor. I think that was what I was most afraid of. I didn't want my parents' opinion of me to change. It was funny, but I still thought of myself as a good girl, even though it was definitely no longer true.

My mom set the table and poured us each a glass of her homemade lemonade. When we sat down, James put his hand on my knee. I wasn't sure if that was a sign to start telling them, but I took it as one.

"So, what's up with you two?" I asked. "Do you have anything new and exciting going on?" I took a huge bite of my sandwich. I was already chickening out. James kept his hand on my knee.

"Just the usual. What about you two? How's Comm going?" My mom started to eat her sandwich too.

"Comm has been...interesting," I said. "Actually, the real reason that I'm here is that I have something I need to tell you." My mouth felt dry. I took a huge sip of lemonade. *This is it.* "Actually, that *we* need to tell you." I looked over at James.

"Oh my God." My mom slowly placed her sandwich down on her plate. "Oh my God, you're pregnant?!"

James choked on his lemonade.

"What?!" my dad said way louder than he usually talked.

"No. No! I'm not pregnant." I laughed awkwardly. I had not meant to word that as strangely as I did. "I couldn't possibly be..." I let my voice trail off. I wasn't here to confess to them that I was sexually active. That was a conversation that I could not imagine ever having with my parents. But was it any worse than confessing what was actually going on? *This is a disaster.*

My parents just stared at me.

I swallowed hard and glanced sideways at James. He looked completely shocked that my mom had thought I was pregnant. I knew the idea of children freaked him out. He seemed to have completely lost his cool.

"Definitely not pregnant," I added, more for James than my parents. I took a deep breath. "Actually, what I needed to tell you is that James isn't a student at the University of New Castle."

My mom started laughing and put her hand on my dad's shoulder. "That's it? You scared me half to death."

Is my news worse than a pregnancy scare? I was even more terrified than before to tell them.

"So what do you do, James?" my dad asked. "Are you in vocational school or something?"

"He's actually done school, Dad. He graduated a few years ago. Several actually. He's 27."

"Oh?" my mom said. She glanced at my father and then back at us. "Well, that's quite an age difference."

We were all silent for a second. The disapproval almost seemed palpable. It felt like I was slowly peeling off a Band-Aid when I should be ripping it off as fast as possible.

My dad was frowning. "So that brings me back to my original question. If you're no longer a student, what is it that you do for a living, James? And why on earth are you dating a teenager?"

I had never heard his voice so cold. "Dad, I just turned 20." No one acknowledged that I had spoken.

"Well." James shifted in his seat.

Thank God he's taking over.

"This is not going to sound great. But I want you both to know that I love your daughter very much." He shifted in his seat again.

Rip off the Band-Aid! I couldn't take it anymore. Just tell them!

"I actually resigned from my current position this morning," James continued. "But before that, I had a job at the University of New Castle." He paused again.

It felt like I was torturing everyone. Enough was enough. "He's my professor," I blurted out.

My parents stared at me. And then my mom burst out laughing. My dad quickly started laughing too.

I looked up at James. He shook his head. He was as confused as me. I expected cursing and maybe sobbing. Definitely not laughter.

"I don't know what you've done to Penny," my mom said between bouts of laughter. "Because she never pulls pranks on us. Well done. You both had us going."

"She can't even pull an April Fool's Day prank," my dad added. "That was hilarious!"

I never in a million years expected them to have this reaction. But it made sense that they thought I was joking. I never broke the rules. "Mom, Dad." My throat caught when I said Dad. The whole thing was so preposterous that they didn't even believe me. "We're not joking. You said it yourself, I don't know how to play pranks. It's not even April Fool's Day."

"Of course you're joking," my mom quickly said. "The age difference? Your professor? It's not even believable. It's ridiculous. It's absolutely ridiculous."

"James is my Comm professor. *Was* my Comm professor, I mean."

"You're joking. You are, right?" My mom suddenly looked pale. She looked over at James and frowned, as if seeing him for the first time.

"We met before I knew he was a professor."

"And you..." my mom's voice faded. "And he..." She closed her mouth again.

Stunned silence. I could work with stunned silence.

"Mr. and Mrs. Taylor, I know how this might sound, but..."

"She's a sophomore," my dad said calmly. "She's only a sophomore."

"I thought she was senior," James said.

"You thought she was a senior? So you only hook up with seniors, is that it?"

"Dad, it wasn't like that at all."

"I think you should probably leave, James. We need to have a conversation with Penny in private."

"I really think we should talk about this," James said calmly. "I am in love with your daughter. I'm not going anywhere."

"You're a 27 year old man. She's a sophomore," my dad said again.

"I'm 20 years old, Dad. It's not that big of an age difference."

"Seven years? You need to focus on school, Penny. You're not ready for the same things that he's ready for." He pointed at James as if he was an object instead of a person.

"I am ready for those things. I love him, Dad." What was he even referring to? Sex? How could he not realize that I was sexually active. I was dating my 27 year old professor. *Of course I'm having sex.*

"You're ready for marriage? And children? And responsibilities? You have no idea what it's like to be an adult. You don't even know how to write a check. You're just a child. He's an adult. You're too young to date him."

"I'm not even ready to get married again..." James instantly closed his mouth.

Oh no. I was hoping that could be a discussion for a different day.

"You were already married?" My mom finally broke her silence.

"I'm recently divorced, yes."

"How recently?" she asked.

"I filed for a divorce last year."

My parents just stared at him.

Oh, shit.

James cleared his throat. "It became official yesterday, but..."

"You got divorced yesterday?" my mom asked incredulously. "You started a relationship with my 20 year old daughter while you were still married?" She didn't hide the disgust in her voice.

I definitely preferred stunned silence.

"Mr. and Mrs. Taylor, please just let me explain. I would never put your daughter in a position like that. As far as I'm concerned, my relationship with my ex wife was terminated as soon as I filed..."

"You put her in a terrible situation," my dad cut in. "You're her professor. You were her married professor."

"Yes, I was Penny's communications professor. And I realize that I crossed the line. I completely understand why you're upset. But my marriage really has nothing to do with this."

"I was the one that crossed the line," I cut in. "You shouldn't be mad at him, you should be mad at me." My phone started to buzz in my pocket, but I ignored it.

"We are mad at you," my dad said. "But we will deal with you later."

This was ridiculous, I wasn't a kid anymore. They couldn't just ground me. Could they? This whole situation was so bizarre. "It was my fault. I fell in love with my professor and he told me to stay away from him. I didn't listen. You two met and fell in love in college. This isn't any different than that. You were my age when you met. You should understand better than anyone."

"Those were completely different circumstances," my dad said.

"Were they that different? Yes, you were the same age, but you were both as young as me. You have to at least accept the fact that I'm in love with him. And he resigned for me. So that we could be together."

"Did he get divorced for you too? Was he cheating on his wife with..."

"It wasn't like that," James said. "I would never cheat on someone."

"You have a very strange sense of morals, James," my dad said.

I could tell that James was trying to remain calm, but that statement clearly angered him. I could see it brewing behind his eyes. I continued to ignore my phone buzzing in my pocket.

"I would never do anything to hurt Penny," James said, as calmly as he could.

"You already have. What's going to happen when other professors find out? And students? Can't she be expelled for this?" my dad asked.

"We talked to the dean this morning when I resigned. Penny got two strikes on her record, but other than that, nothing. The news is circulating fast and I assume most of the college already knows. That's why we're here. We wanted to tell you before you found out from someone else. Despite my loose morals, I respected you both enough to want to tell you the truth in person."

My dad didn't seem at all consoled by James' speech. "And what now? You just quit your job. You're divorced. You probably have alimony to pay. And you're dating a college student. What kind of future could you possibly have? You're just going to drag her down with you."

James eyebrows lowered slightly. "I'm starting a tech company."

"A tech company?" my dad laughed. "And where are you going to get the startup money for such a venture? I was wrong about you. You're not an adult. You're just as immature as any college student."

"Dad!" My father was a nice person. I had never heard him make snap judgments about anyone in my life. What was he doing?

"He's probably here to ask us for money," my Dad huffed.

More anger was brewing behind James' eyes. "I have the necessary funds to start the company," he said calmly.

The house phone started ringing. When no one answered, it automatically switched onto the voicemail recorder.

"Hi, I'm trying to reach Penny Taylor or the parents of Penny Taylor. This is Ellen Fitzgerald with..."

I immediately stood up. *Shit! Why now?*

James grabbed my arm. "Penny, don't. It could be the media."

"It's not." Before I could walk over to the phone, my dad picked it up.

Crap!

"Hello, Ellen. This is Penny's father speaking."

"Who is it?" James whispered to me.

"She works for the First State scholarship committee." There was only one reason for her to be calling. I was going to lose my scholarship. My dad was already upset. This was going to make it so much worse.

"Allegations?" my father said. "There are no allegations..." he went silent and looked over at James and me. "The Delaware Post? I don't even know what you're referring to."

Silence.

"Penny has successfully maintained the 3.5 average."

Silence.

"I don't see how this is a behavioral issue. Her professor clearly..."

Silence.

"Ellen, I really don't see why..."

Silence

"How dare you insult my daughter?!"

Silence.

"You'll be hearing from my lawyer." My dad slammed down the phone. His face was visibly red.

"Peter?" my mom said. "Peter, take a deep breath."

"Get out of my house!" my dad yelled at James.

James quickly stood up. "Mr. Taylor, I don't know what you just heard on the phone, but..."

"There's an article in the Delaware Post about this mess? Why didn't you two start with that?!"

I had never heard my dad yell like that. "Dad, what did Mrs. Fitzgerald say?" I wasn't sure why I even asked. It was pretty clear.

"She said you lost your scholarship because you're sleeping with your professor." He pointed at James. "Didn't you think about that, Penny? Did either of you think of any of the consequences?!"

"I can get a job, Dad. I can pay the difference. I'll figure it out. Please just calm down."

"You know how we feel about you working during school. It's out of the question. You need to focus on your grades. Something that you've clearly put on the back burner recently."

I swallowed hard. It felt like he had slapped me.

"Mr. Taylor, the scholarship isn't an issue," James said. "I can pay the difference. I'd like to pay the difference."

"So you're going to start a thriving tech company and pay for my daughter's education? Do you have the necessary *funds* for all that? What, do you have a wealthy family to fall back on? Are you just some rich, entitled kid that never grew up? That goes around screwing students because you think there are never any consequences? Well, we don't want your money. We don't want anything from you. Haven't you done enough?! Get the hell out of my house!"

"Dad!" I stood up beside James. How could he say that to him? He knew nothing about James.

I could see that James' couldn't keep his cool anymore. Mentioning his wealthy family was the last straw, even though my father didn't actually know he had a wealthy family. He had unintentionally hit a nerve. Something seemed to just snap.

"Mr. Taylor, you don't know anything about me. And it does not appear that you want to. Yes, I was your daughter's professor. Yes, I got divorced yesterday. Yes, I am not ready to get married today or tomorrow. But I have every intention of marrying your daughter. And I will provide for her. I want to provide for her. You don't have anything to worry about. Her future is secure. That is all you need to know."

I wasn't sure what I was supposed to do. This couldn't be the end of the conversation. James couldn't just walk out right now. My dad was fuming.

"How could it possibly be secure?" my dad pressed. "You just ruined her education. And you ruined your own career. This is a scandal. No one's ever going to want to hire you or her."

"I don't need anyone to hire me. I told you, I'm starting my own company."

"You have no tech background. You're a communications professor."

"Working at the University of New Castle was not my career. I wanted to give back. It was never a permanent situation. I just needed a break. I needed to start over. I was doing a good thing there."

"A good thing?" my dad scoffed.

"Yes, a good thing." James' voice was louder than usual. "I founded my first tech company when I was 22 years old. Right after I graduated with honors from Harvard University. Blive Tech International. Maybe you've heard of it? It's a publically traded fortune 500 company. Well, I sold it last year for 2.8 billion dollars. I don't need to work another day in my life. Your daughter, our future children, and our grandchildren won't need to work a day in their lives if they don't want to."

2.8 billion dollars? I couldn't even conceptualize that much money.

James pushed his chair back under the table and looked down at me.

I could see the hurt on his face. The snap judgments that my father had made had stung. They had stung me too. I couldn't believe my dad had done that. I knew that losing the scholarship was a big deal. I wasn't naive. But I could work to make up the difference. I didn't mind working during school. What I did mind was that it suddenly felt like I had to choose between my parents and James. That was the hardest part of all. I didn't know how the afternoon would go. But I had never expected this. I wasn't a kid anymore. I had made the decision to be with James. And I wouldn't let my parents belittle him like this. He didn't deserve that. I took a deep breath and grabbed James' hand. "I think we should probably go."

I only saw it for a second. But it had definitely been there. A flash of relief. He hadn't expected me to choose him. I hated that he didn't believe in me. Or us. Hopefully this would be what he needed to finally understand that I wasn't just going to abandon him. He meant everything to me.

"Wait," my mom said, breaking her silence. "A break from what, James? Why did you need to start over?"

"I felt empty in New York. I needed a fresh start. Teaching helped with that. I wish that the circumstances had been different. But Penny is my fresh start. She made me feel whole again."

"I do understand," my mom said. She looked at my dad. "Penny was right. We were her age when we fell in love. I'd like to think that if the circumstances were different for us, we'd still be together. Please don't go, Penny." She paused and looked over at my dad. She gave him a pleading look. "Peter, say something."

"So that means your last name is Hunter?" my dad asked.

"Yes."

My dad sighed and sat down. "James Hunter, the founder of Blive Tech International. I didn't realize you had taken a sudden career change into teaching."

"I needed the change."

"You know, I actually own stock in your company."

"You do?"

My dad nodded. He put his hands together on the table and looked down at them for a second. "I'm sorry. It's just...Penny's our baby." My dad didn't look angry anymore. He just seemed sad. He looked older than I remembered. As if this conversation had aged him. I had never meant to hurt him.

"I know," James said. "I understand that you're just trying to protect her. And I truly am sorry about how this happened."

"You can't really understand until you've had children of your own."

They were both silent for a second. Both their apologies seemed to be enough. The tension was slowly seeping out of the room.

"So, your relationship was written about in the paper?" my mom asked.

"Yes, there was an article in the paper this morning," said James. "If you read it, you should know that it is not accurate."

"What do you mean?"

"It's mostly from my ex wife's point of view. And it implies that there will be charges of sexual misconduct from other students I've had. And from Penny. That's not the case."

"Okay." My mom took a deep breath. "What happens now?"

James ran his hand through his hair. "It's really up to Penny. I've advised her to drop Comm. Unfortunately, the way that the information was leaked about our relationship does not make it easy going forward."

"I think it'll all die down if I ignore it. I just want things to go back to normal," I said.

"This whole thing has been blown out of proportion because of my name. Under other circumstances, it would not have gotten as much press as it has already. Normalcy is a long way off."

"So you resigned because of the allegations?" my dad said.

"They gave me the option to stay if I was willing to terminate my relationship with Penny. I wasn't willing to do that. Resigning was the only option."

"That's very romantic," my mom said.

I smiled to myself. It was romantic. Everything James did was romantic. Even dragging me here to tell my parents about the situation. He did it because he cared about me. He wanted us to have a future together. And he didn't want our future to involve keeping secrets from my parents.

James squeezed my hand and then pulled my chair back out for me. I felt so relieved. My parents seemed to understand. Love was love. All the messy details didn't really matter. And I felt so relieved, like a huge weight had been lifted off my chest. I sat back down and so did James.

"And if things can't proceed as normal, what then?" my dad asked.

"Honestly, I'm not sure what the backlash is going to be like," James said. "The blame for this lies on me, not Penny. It is my understanding that the University of New Castle will make that clear. If things don't go smoothly, she can always apply for different schools next semester."

No. I didn't want to change schools. Everything was going to be okay. "Mom, Dad, it's going to be fine. I went to class this morning and it wasn't even that bad." I thought about Raymond Asher's harsh comments. If Tyler hadn't shown up to defend me, would everything have been fine? I shook away the thought. That was Comm. My other classes would be different.

"Unfortunately we both need to get to work. Are you sure we can't get you to stay for dinner?" my mom asked.

"No, we need to get back." I just wanted to be alone with James. This day couldn't be over soon enough.

"Okay." My mom looked over at my dad.

"Do you mind if we talk to Penny alone for a second?" my dad asked.

"Of course." James stood up. "I'll be outside." He put his hand on my shoulder for a second and then walked out of the kitchen.

When the front door closed, my parents still didn't say anything.

"Mom, Dad, thank you for understanding. I know that you're probably disappointed in me. And I'm so sorry that..."

My dad held up his hand to stop me from talking.

I swallowed hard. I wished James was still sitting beside me.

"We just want you to be happy, Penny," my mom said.

"I am happy. I've never been this happy."

My parents looked at each other again.

"Penny," my dad said. "If he has in any way pressured you into..."

Oh my God. "No, Dad, it wasn't like that at all. He didn't pressure me. This situation is just as much my fault as it is his. If not more."

"But if there's anything that you aren't ready for and he..."

"Dad. Please stop." I didn't want to have this conversation with my parents. "He's always a complete gentleman." I winced at my own choice of words. It was almost like I had just confessed that James was a gentle lover. *Please let this conversation be over.*

"I'm sorry. But when he mentioned sexual misconduct...I just wanted to make sure." My dad seemed to be just as uncomfortable as me.

"When he mentioned it, he said it wasn't true. And it's not. We're exclusive. He's not dating anyone else. And everything we have done has been consensual." *Consensual.* I kept choosing grosser and grosser words to describe everything.

"Okay." My dad sighed. "Well, we're glad you're not pregnant." He laughed uneasily.

I knew he was trying to break the tension. "Yeah, you guys are too young to be grandparents."

My mom smiled at me. "I really wish we didn't have to go back to work. I want to hear the whole story about how you two met." She stood up and quickly cleared the dishes. "Maybe the next time you two visit we can hear a little more about the good moments and a little less about the messy ones."

Messy moments? Gross! "That sounds great."

The three of us went outside. James was sitting on the front porch step petting Teddy.

Whenever he did normal stuff it always looked funny to me. He was the sexiest man I had ever laid my eyes on. And my mind just instantly pictured him doing whatever he was doing in T.V. commercials. It was the sexiest ad for a pet commercial I had ever seen.

"I see you two are getting along now," I said.

"Yeah, I think he actually likes me." He turned around. When he saw my parents he quickly stood up.

"I'm really sorry that you two can't stay. I hope you come visit us again soon. I promise that we're not usually this hostile." My mom leaned in and hugged him.

James looked a little less uncomfortable than he had when she had hugged him earlier. "Thank you for being so understanding."

My mom laughed. "Were we? I feel like we weren't. But I do understand. And I'm so glad that you make our daughter happy."

My mom pulled away and gave me a quick hug. "Call me with those details."

"I will."

"James." My dad stuck out his hand.

"Mr. Taylor." They quickly shook hands.

"You can call me Peter." My dad nodded at him and walked over to me. He immediately embraced me in a hug. "Don't you ever think that you've disappointed us, Pen. We love you so much." He kissed the top of my head and released me from his hug.

"Thanks, Dad." His words made me tear up slightly. It was such a relief to hear him say that. My biggest fear in life always seemed to be disappointing my parents. That was why I never took risks and always followed the rules. It was strange how quickly my outlook could change. I still never wanted to disappoint my parents. But James seemed to have taken over all my worries. I was more concerned about him now and making him happy. I'd do anything for him. I hoped he knew that.

CHAPTER 25

Wednesday

As soon as my mom and dad drove off, I sighed and turned my head toward James. "That went well, right?" We were sitting in James' car. He hadn't started it yet. He was just sitting there, staring out the windshield.

"In the end, yeah. Your dad...well, he surprised me."

"I'm sorry about what he said. I've never seen him make snap judgments like that before. He's usually really nice. He didn't mean any of that. He was just upset."

"At least he didn't try to punch me in the face." He smiled at me. "What did your parents say to you after I left?"

I wanted to lighten the mood. "They grounded me."

"Wait, what?" James lowered his eyebrows.

"I'm just kidding. They can't ground me, I'm an adult." I was really glad that my parents hadn't tried to ground me. I'm pretty sure I would have just let them. I felt like a kid around my parents. I probably always would.

"So if they didn't ground you, what did they say?"

What is the best way to phrase this? "They just wanted to make sure you didn't sexually harass me or anything."

"Oh God." He put his forehead down on the top of the steering wheel and started laughing.

I started laughing too.

He sighed and lifted his head back up. "That must have been awkward."

"Well, they didn't actually put it like that." I put my hand on his knee. "I think they phrased it by asking how rapey you were on a scale of one to Michael Jackson."

"What?!"

"Just kidding. They said something like pressuring me, or something."

He put his hand on top of mine and ran his thumb across my knuckles. "I haven't have I? Pressured you?"

"No. James, I love you. I want to be with you. I'm not sure what else I can do to make you believe me."

He lifted up my hand and kissed my palm. "I do believe you. I'm sorry that I lost it in there. It almost felt like I was lecturing your father. I didn't mean to do that."

"Well, you were a professor." I shrugged. "It kind of goes with the territory I think."

"Yeah. I just feel like I kind of threw my money in his face. And that wasn't what I meant to do at all. I feel like a dick."

"He certainly pushed enough of your buttons. James, I don't think my dad is mad at you. He seemed embarrassed about how he acted. Please don't over think this. We told them. It's over. Let's just be happy."

"Just tell me where you want to go." He smiled at me and put his key into the ignition.

"Actually, I think I just want to go home."

"Home?" He raised his eyebrow.

"Mhm."

"Penny Taylor, are you referring to my apartment as home?" He looked so happy.

"It's where I feel most comfortable. And of course, it's where you are. So, yes, I consider it home." I smiled at him.

"You know, I'll take you wherever you want to go. Well, anywhere in the U.S. We really need to get you a passport."

"All I want to do is snuggle up in your bed with you."

"Okay. Home it is."

***

When we pulled up to his apartment building, there were even more news vans parked outside. James seemed to immediately tense. People with microphones jumped out of the vans as his car turned into the parking garage. He sped up to the third floor of the parking garage and pulled his car into an empty spot.

"Maybe we should've gone somewhere else," he said.

"It's fine. They'll probably leave soon. Aren't celebrities always doing weird stuff? Kanye West and T-Swizzle will get into a knife fight or something and the paparazzi will move on. Especially if you don't give them anything good to talk about."

He laughed and stepped out of the car. He opened up my door and grabbed my hand, escorting me to the elevator. "You do know that I'm not a celebrity, right?" He smiled at me.

"Right. You're just a super sexy, eligible bachelor worth 2.8 billion dollars. You're not a celebrity at all."

We stepped into the elevator.

"Yeah, I'm not worth 2.8 billion dollars." He pressed the button for his floor.

"Oh, right." Because of the divorce. His wife had gotten half his money. Hopefully he wasn't too upset about that. 1.4 billion dollars was still way too much money for one person to have.

He looked down at me and smiled. "I'm worth way more than that." He slid his card into the reader and stepped into his apartment.

"You have more than 2.8 billion dollars? That's insane, James. What on earth are you going to do with all that..." I stopped talking when I saw a huge box in the middle of his living room floor. It was at least four feet tall and six feet wide. It was wrapped in blue wrapping paper and there was a huge bow on top. There was a small box sitting on top of it, also in blue wrapping paper with a matching blue bow.

"Oh." A smile broke over his face. "I almost forgot about that. Apparently I'm going to buy you gifts with it." He walked into his living room. But I just stood in his foyer.

"James, you already got me a birthday gift. I don't need anything."

"It's not for your birthday. Besides, it's kind of for both of us." He smiled at me.

"But..."

"Oh come on. You don't even know what it is yet. If you don't like it, I'll take it back. Just open it."

I walked over to him. "I don't want you to spend your money on me. I just want to spend time with you." I stood on my tiptoes and ran my hands through his hair.

"I know." He placed a soft kiss against my lips. He picked up the small present and tapped his hand on the large box. "Please just open it."

He looked so excited. And the way he was looking at me made me excited too. I grabbed one of the folds in the wrapping paper and pulled it down. It was actually ridiculously fun to open a present this big. I pulled the paper as I walked from one side of the present to the other, and then pushed the paper out of the way.

"Is this a T.V.?" I smiled at him. I guess I had made fun of him enough so that he decided to cave in and buy one.

"Well, after this morning I wasn't really sure if you'd want to go to classes the next few days. So if we're camped out here, I thought you'd like to have a T.V. to watch. You seem to love T.V."

I laughed. "That's incredibly sweet. But you know, I have a T.V. already. I can just bring it here. Melissa won't mind. She's always at Josh's anyway."

"Yeah, but it's tiny."

"There's nothing wrong with my T.V." I laughed.

"I was going to hang it over there," he pointed to the wall across from his sofa. "And I measured and this T.V. is the perfect size for the distance between the couch and the wall. And since Rob is coming, I wanted something to watch the Giants games on. So..."

"You're adorable. I'm definitely not going to make you take back that T.V. Clearly you want it."

"But do you like it?"

"Of course I like it. It's going to be like we're in a movie theater. Thank you."

He laughed and smiled down at me. "And there's one more thing." He held out the small box. "Now, before you start protesting, it didn't even cost me anything. It's just something that I really want you to have. And after today, I think maybe now's the best time ever." He tucked a loose strand of hair behind my ear.

My heart started beating really fast. It was a really small box. *Is that a ring sized box? No.* He said it didn't cost anything. He just said a few hours ago that he wasn't ready to get married again.

He lowered his eyebrows slightly. "Are you okay?"

"What? Yeah."

He grabbed my hand and put the box on my palm. "Open it, Penny."

I took off the bow, slowly unwrapped the box, and lifted the lid. There were two plastic cards inside. My name was on each of them and there was a metallic stripe at the bottom, but nothing else. I looked up at him.

"Welcome home."

"Are these access cards to get into your apartment?"

"Our apartment, yes."

I ran my finger along my embossed name. He just gave me keys to his place. *Our place.* I liked how that sounded.

"I find it incredibly hard to fall asleep when you're not beside me. I'd like you to move in. If that's what you want too."

I looked up at him. We had talked about this before. Before our fight. A few weeks ago I thought I'd never even step foot in his apartment again. And now he was calling it ours and asking me to stay. This was a big step. And it was definitely a step I wanted to take.

He wrapped his arms around me. "So what do you say?"

"Yes. Absolutely yes." I hugged him, pressing the side of my cheek against his chest. His heart seemed to be beating as quickly as mine. I felt so safe in his arms. It finally felt like I was exactly where I was supposed to be.

CHAPTER 26

Thursday

"Close," James said. "The standard deviation of the difference should have come out to 0.625. Let's see." He sat down next to me on the sofa and scanned the math that I had done to solve the equation. "Okay, there. You forgot to transform the random variable into a z-score."

"Oh. Oops. I knew to do that too." I still hated statistics, but it seemed a lot better when James was teaching it to me. Especially because whenever I got a question right, he kissed me. Maybe I had just needed a proper motivator. I grabbed the paper back from him. I quickly fixed the equation and handed it back to him. "How's this, Professor Hunter?"

He laughed and looked down at the sheet of paper. "Much better." He leaned down and kissed me.

His phone started buzzing again. It had been buzzing nonstop all morning.

"Are you sure you don't want to answer that?" I asked. "Maybe it would be best to just get it over with."

"Talking to them will make it worse. If I ignore them, they'll get bored and move onto the next thing." He stood up and walked back over to the T.V. mount he was screwing into the wall. It was fun watching him use tools. There was something very sexy about a man who could use a power drill.

"But you don't even know who it is. You haven't listened to any of your messages. You could always answer and hang up."

"Which means I refused to comment. Which looks bad."

"Oh."

"Besides, if it's someone I know, it'll ring."

"Speaking of people we know...I was wondering if I could hang out with Melissa tonight?" We had gone to my dorm room this morning and grabbed a few things. But Melissa had been in class. I wanted to tell her in person that I was moving in with James. And even though I had been texting her, I knew she had questions about what was going on. Besides, I missed her. We used to do everything together.

He put down the screwdriver and looked back at me. "You know that you don't have to ask me permission."

For some reason it kind of seemed like I did. He hadn't let me go to my classes today despite my nagging. I knew it was just because he was trying to protect me. "I know. I just wanted to make sure it was okay." I glanced toward the window. I was kind of nervous to leave the apartment. I didn't want to have to walk past the news reporters. I was worried they'd follow me until I talked to them. And I always said stupid stuff when I was nervous.

"Well, how about you just invite her over here?"

"Are you sure that's okay?"

"Of course." He smiled and turned back to the T.V. mount.

"Do you want my help with that?" I asked.

"I'm pretty sure I can figure it out." He picked up the direction booklet off the floor and turned the page.

It was hard to focus on my Stat practice questions. My eyes seemed to automatically gravitate to him. He was wearing a pair of faded blue jeans and a black v-neck t-shirt. I was just about to suggest we both take a break when his phone started ringing.

James turned around and looked down at his phone. "It's just the front desk." He picked it up and slid his finger across the screen. "Hunter."

Silence.

"Regarding what?"

Silence.

James looked down at me. "Do you mind putting them on the phone for a second?" He put his free hand in his pocket, turned away from me, and walked toward the kitchen. "It was my understanding that she wouldn't be included in this."

Silence.

"We've already disclosed our relationship to Joe. If you have any other questions then I'd recommend discussing them with..."

Silence.

James removed his hand from his pocket and ran his fingers through his hair. "Fine. Please put Ben back on the phone."

Silence.

"Yes, go ahead and let them up. For future visitors please tell them I am out of town until further notice." James hung up the phone and tossed it onto the kitchen counter. He didn't turn around to look at me.

I put my Stat notes down and walked up behind him. "James?" I said quietly. I could tell that he was upset.

He sighed and turned around. "Apparently the people they hired for the investigation need to talk to you."

"Why would they need to talk to me? We already told everything to the dean."

"I don't know. But it probably isn't good."

"That's not necessarily true."

"Well, I guess we'll find out."

"How do you think they knew I was here?"

"Maybe they already tried your dorm room. It doesn't exactly take a great investigator to assume you'd be here."

A dinging noise sounded through the apartment. James walked over to the elevator door and pressed a button. The doors slid open.

Two men in suits stepped out. One looked about James' age and the other was probably 20 years older or so.

The older one put his hand out to James. "James Hunter, I'm Detective Tim Reed. And this is my partner, Scott Turner.

Detectives? Were they cops? When the dean had said they'd be interviewing all the students, I thought he meant a colleague of his. Not the police.

James shook Detective Reed's hand and then Detective Turner's. "I still don't see why this is necessary. Penny has already talked to Joe."

"It's a formality really. We just have a few questions." Detective Reed peered around James' shoulder. "You must be Penny."

"Yes, hi." I walked toward them. Detective Turner still hadn't spoken a word. It felt like they were trying to intimidate me. I wasn't going to let that happen. James hadn't done anything wrong. I had told my parents about our relationship this afternoon. Two men in suits weren't going to scare me now. I felt stronger somehow. And I was sick of this. I just wanted everyone to leave us alone. "You said you have some questions for me?" I crossed my arms in front of my chest.

"Right. Well, we're actually going to need to talk to you in private, Penny." Detective Reed looked up at James.

"I really don't see why that's necessary," James said coolly.

"Something has come up in our investigation. And we need Penny to be able to talk freely about your relationship."

James' eyebrows lowered. "What has come up in the investigation?"

"We can't really discuss that with you right now. I'm sure Joe will be in contact with you shortly."

"I think that you both should leave."

"James, it's fine. I'll talk to them." The last thing we needed was for James to lose his temper and punch a detective.

"You don't have to answer their questions, Penny. Let me call my lawyer. He'll handle this."

"It's fine. I really don't mind."

James stared at me for a second. "I guess I'll be in my office then." He put his hand on my shoulder and then walked away.

I stood there awkwardly in the foyer. I didn't know what I was supposed to do. But I didn't have to decide. Both detectives walked past me toward the living room.

"If you wouldn't mind taking a seat, Penny."

Okay. I followed them into the living room and sat down on the sofa. Both of them remained standing. They were definitely trying to intimidate me. *Screw them.*

"I see that James has been buying you presents." Detective Reed looked at the T.V. It was still in its box and there was wrapping paper on the ground.

"No. He bought that for himself." I had taken a criminal justice class with Melissa my freshman year. I knew they were trying to get me to admit something without actually asking a question. I folded my arms across my chest again.

"Does he wrap everything he buys for himself? Or just expensive things?"

"I don't know. We've only been dating a few months."

A smile broke over Detective Reed's face. "You know, when people act defensive, it usually means that they have something to defend."

I glared at him. "I don't have anything to hide."

"Good. I expected as much. You're an open book, Penny. Straight As in high school. Same here except for the occasional B. You're a good girl. Respectable. A First State scholarship winner even. That must have made your parents proud."

"Yes, it did." My father's words came back to me. There wasn't anything I could do to disappoint him. He'd always be proud of me. I didn't need a scholarship to prove that.

"So the question is, what made you risk all that? What made you decide to sleep with your professor? Were you worried about losing your scholarship?"

"What? No."

"What kind of arrangement did you two have exactly?"

"I have no idea what you're talking about." I knew what he was suggesting. And it made me sick to my stomach. It was like what Raymond Asher had said. Why did everyone assume it was something terrible that brought us together? Why couldn't everyone just see that I was in love with James?

"Was it for the presents? Or maybe you weren't doing as well this semester. You have a C average in your statistics class right now. Did you do it for the grades?"

"Do what exactly?" It was hard to stay calm.

"Did he, or did he not agree to give you an A in his class if you gave him sexual favors?"

I stood up. "I think you should go."

"So it's true, is it?"

"You have no idea what you're talking about. We never did anything that we didn't both want to do. James is a good guy."

"Good professors don't sleep with their students."

"Tim." Detective Turner had finally spoken. He put his hand on Detective Reed's chest, as if holding him back. "Why don't you let me take it from here." Detective Turner gestured toward the couch.

Detective Reed nodded and sat down on the sofa. I stared at Detective Turner, who was now smiling. I was a little surprised by the sudden change. Were they seriously trying to good cop, bad cop me? I internally rolled my eyes.

"Please, Penny, take a seat," Detective Turner said. "I'm sorry about my partner's outburst."

No he wasn't. I sighed and sat down, as far away from Detective Reed as possible.

"You said you have nothing to hide," Detective Turner said.

"I don't."

"Would it surprise you, then, if James was hiding something from you?"

I swallowed hard.

He put his hands in his pockets as he studied my face. "It wouldn't, would it? I've heard that James is quite a complicated man."

"And who did you hear that from? His ex wife?"

Detective Turner smiled again. "It's not too late, you know. If you're willing to cooperate with us, we can give the First State scholarship committee a call. Maybe we can get them to reissue that scholarship of yours."

"If I cooperate?"

"Yes. You see, we are building a case against James regarding sexual misconduct."

"I'm not going to lie in order to get my scholarship back. Like you said, I'm a good girl. Besides for that fact, you have it all wrong."

"Unfortunately we don't. We do want to help you, Penny. But we don't actually need your statement. Yes, it'll help, but I think we already have everything we need."

"What do you mean?"

"Two girls have already come forward saying that James agreed to give them As for sexual favors."

What? "They're lying."

"And how sure are you of that? Because Tim and I are trained to tell if suspects are lying. These girls didn't seem like they were lying. Actually, they were both in tears. They were embarrassed and ashamed because of the position that their trusted professor put them in."

"I don't believe you."

"And their stories lined up. They both said that James lured them into his office to dispute a poor grade. And that he agreed to change it only if they agreed to have sex with him."

No. Isn't that what he did to me? No. Kind of?

"Does that sound familiar, Penny? Did he do that to you too?"

"No. It wasn't like that." *Was it?*

"How about you tell us what really happened. And we'll get that scholarship back for you. Your life will go back to normal. All of this will disappear."

All of this? All of this had already disappeared from me once before. I didn't want my old, normal life back. That emptiness. I'd never go back to that. All I wanted was for these two idiots to leave me alone. "I think this discussion is over." I stood up again.

"Don't you want your old life back? We can give you back what you lost. Stop defending him. Can't you see what he's taken from you?"

"I'm not defending him, I'm telling you the truth."

"He's not who you think he is."

"Yes he is." I could feel myself losing my temper.

"He's a predator, Penny. And you're the prey. Don't you see that? Those two other girls were his prey too. Who knows how many others didn't come forward? You're probably one of a dozen. You can't hide from the truth. He seduces students. He's not a good man."

I had thought that before. That he was the predator and I was the prey. But I was wrong. And these men were wrong. James wouldn't have done those things. *But didn't he do it to me?* "Get out of my apartment." I didn't need to stand here and listen to this. They were just as bad as the person who wrote the article about James and my relationship.

"Your apartment? Is that the deal then? The gifts, the apartment? Is that to keep you quiet?"

"You're terrible detectives," I snapped.

"We're trying to protect you."

"Protect me? I don't need your protection. I wanted this relationship just as much as he did. I love him."

"He doesn't love you."

"Yes he does." Who were they to tell me how James felt? *Arrogant assholes.*

"Do you even know anything about him? Do you know that he has a criminal record? Do you know that he's spent time in jail? This is the kind of thing he does. This is the kind of thing that a bored man with too much money and no sense of morals does."

"If you both don't leave right now, some of your detective buddies will actually have a crime to solve."

"Did you just threaten us?" Detective Reed stood up. "You do know that it's a illegal to threaten a police officer?"

"Oh, I didn't realize you were police officers. I really couldn't tell. All you're doing is throwing out accusations without any evidence."

"Consider this a warning, Miss Taylor. We will be in contact again. This is far from over."

I didn't say anything. I watched them walk over to the elevator, step in, and disappear. The apartment was eerily quiet. I suddenly felt very, very cold.

CHAPTER 27

Thursday

They were lying. They were just trying to get me to confess to something that wasn't true. And if they didn't need my statement, then they wouldn't have bothered coming. There was no way that they had any evidence.

James had said he had never been arrested while he was in Harvard. So I had already surmised that he'd been arrested at some point after that. None of that mattered. He had a troubled past. He was different now. *Isn't he?*

But how much about him did I really know? The detectives had noticed my reaction when they said he was hiding something from me. Because he had done that before. But not this. He wouldn't hide something like this. He wouldn't lie to me.

I mindlessly opened up the freezer. Whenever I was upset, I always needed ice cream. I froze when I saw two pints of Ben & Jerry's Chunky Monkey ice cream sitting in James' freezer. He had seen me eating that flavor one of the many times I had been upset. He remembered. He was a good guy. That's what good, thoughtful guys did.

I reached for one of the containers. It was also what creepy guys did. Creepy, stalker guys. I put the pint of ice cream back on the shelf. That wasn't James. If anything I was the one that stalked him. James' words suddenly came back to me, sending a chill down my spine. *I had you right where I wanted you.* He *had* lured me into his office. How had the detectives known that? *Could it really be because he did it with other students too?*

There was an untouched bottle of vodka in the back of the freezer. I grabbed it and slammed the freezer door. If he had broken the law so many times, he shouldn't be worried about serving alcohol to someone underage. I unscrewed the cap and poured some into a shot glass that I found in one of the cabinets.

The burn down my throat was a much needed distraction. I poured myself another and downed it. Two girls had come forward. *Two.* One could be justified as lying. But two separate girls, with two identical stories? And it was a story that was the same as mine.

"I see you've found the liquor."

I looked up at James as he walked into the kitchen. I was waiting for him to reprimand me. Instead, he grabbed a shot glass for himself and slid it toward me. I poured some vodka into the glass.

"You know, I could get in trouble for this," he said and held up the glass.

"Is that the only thing you're worried about getting in trouble for?"

He lowered his eyebrows slightly. "What, did they tell you what supposedly came up during their investigation?"

I shrugged. "They knew you lured me into your office so you could seduce me."

"That's not exactly how I'd put that." He downed his shot.

"Then how would you put it?"

"That I was mad at you. And I wanted to see you." He ran his hand through his hair. "I didn't want to have to share you with Tyler. I wanted more. I wanted you to want more too." He hesitated for a second. "And at the same time I didn't. I wanted to get over you. I wasn't really thinking clearly. I couldn't get you out of my head."

"But how did they know that? How did they know about the fake grade? And me going into your office?"

"I'm sure there's a logical explanation for that."

"Right. I'm waiting for the explanation. What is it?"

"I don't know. That's their job. They're the investigators. They must have pieced something together."

Pieced something together. I looked down at my empty shot glass. Vodka had been a bad idea. My mind already seemed slightly foggy. I wasn't going to be able to piece anything together like this. I just wanted to talk to him. I needed to see his reaction to the accusation. "They didn't actually know if that had happened. They just inferred it."

"Inferred it? From what?" He poured himself another shot and downed it.

"From what two other girls said during their interviews. Apparently both of them said that you lured them into your office to seduce them under that pretense of a poor grade." I had a vague desire to tell him he shouldn't be drinking. But I had seen him drink before. Besides, I was really the one that shouldn't be drinking.

"Penny, you know I didn't do that. That's ridiculous."

"Is it that ridiculous? You kind of did that to me."

"And I just told you that was different. I've said it a millions time, Penny. It's only ever been you. You know that. You know how I feel about you."

"But why would those girls lie? Why would they say you did that?"

"I don't know."

"And in the exact same way? How would they have known that if it wasn't something that you just do to tons of students?"

"Is that really what you think?"

"I don't want to think that. But..."

"But you do?"

I didn't say anything. I just stared at him.

"You think I gave my prettiest female students bad grades in hopes that they'd come to my office hours? So that I could get them alone and then what? Bargain with them to improve their grades? I didn't bargain with you, Penny. You kissed me. You asked me to punish you. I can get any girl I want. I don't need to make deals with immature college students to suck me off. I'm not desperate."

I hated when he lost his temper. I was just trying to understand. Maybe the detectives were right. A person acting defensive usually had something they were trying to defend.

"Then why are you dating me?" I asked.

"Because I love you."

"You can have any girl you want, James. Maybe you should go try to find someone a little more mature. You know, someone who isn't a college student."

"That's not what I meant." His hands were gripping the countertop and his knuckles were turning white.

"It's what you said, James."

He took a deep breath and ran his hand through his hair. "I don't understand why you believe them over me. I just need you to believe me. I need to know that you trust me."

Lots of our fights seemed to come back to the issue of trust. And I did trust him. I felt guilty. I was pushing his buttons. "I do trust you."

"Okay."

I needed to believe him. If this was going to work, we needed to be able to trust each other. "Should you really be drinking that?"

He raised his eyebrow. "Should you?"

"No, probably not." I gave him a small smile.

He leaned against the counter and looked down at me. "You shouldn't believe everything you hear. The tabloid you read that interviewed my ex wife, these detectives...they have other motives. I don't want to fight with you every time something like this happens. And it happens more than I'd like. It comes with the territory."

"The rich, successful, eligible bachelor territory?"

"Minus the eligible bachelor." He tucked a loose strand of hair behind my ear. "I'm taken."

I smiled at him. "I'm sorry. The detectives just made it seem like they were so sure that you had done it."

"I mean, if you were told you had to make up a story about your male professor doing inappropriate things, wouldn't you just automatically go to sexual favors in exchange for good grades? It's not even clever."

"Right. So they're lying. But why?"

"Maybe they hated me? I could be rather distracted in class. Sometimes I was so focused on you that I'm pretty sure I was an awful professor."

"I don't think anyone hated you. Especially in Comm. At least all the girls loved you. Oh." I looked up at him. "Maybe they're just jealous you didn't choose them. Maybe they think you'll notice them now?"

"By dragging my name through the mud? Smart."

"Well, I don't know. I'm not them." I put my hands on either side of James' face. "I'm sorry I doubted you."

He put his hands on the small of my back. "If a bunch of pricks in suits told me that you had been doing stuff behind my back, I think my reaction would have been a lot worse than yours."

"My reaction was bad with the detectives too. I'm pretty sure I threatened to kill them."

James laughed. "Wait, really? You can't threaten a cop, Penny."

"I know that now."

He laughed again. "You're full of surprises." His hands had pushed my shirt up slightly, and I could feel his fingers against my skin.

"Am I?"

"Mhm." He placed a soft kiss against my lips. His hands slowly pushed my shirt up even more.

"Would it surprise you if I told you that alcohol tends to make me incredibly horny?"

"Incredibly horny? That's quite the predicament." He grabbed my ass and lifted me up, setting me down on the kitchen counter. He put his hands on either side of the counter and looked at me. I didn't recognize the look he was giving me.

"What's wrong?" I asked.

"You defended me to the detectives even though you doubted me."

"Of course."

"But why?"

"I'll always defend you. I love you."

He lowered his eyebrows slightly. He seemed confused by my response. I remembered the relief in his eyes when I grabbed his hand at my parents' house. And when he woke up yesterday morning before the meeting with the dean. He had been surprised that I was still laying next to him. He wasn't used to someone having his back. It didn't seem like he ever had anyone that he could count on. I wanted to be that person for him. Maybe I already was more than anyone else before.

"I swear to you that I didn't do what they said. I've been completely consumed by you. All I ever do is think about you."

"I know. I've been completely consumed by you too."

His smile returned. "I can't believe how lucky I am. Now, about that predicament. I think I can probably assist you with that." He lifted off his t-shirt and dropped it onto the kitchen floor.

I'd never get tired of seeing him like this. He wasn't the lucky one; I was. I ran my fingers down the crevices in his abs. I still felt that spark of electricity run through me every time we touched. I thought it might go away once we didn't have to hide our relationship anymore. The sneaking around, the excitement, the forbidden dynamic. But it was still there. And I wasn't sure that I wanted it to ever disappear.

He leaned forward and kissed me. Softly at first and then more passionately, sending shivers of desire down my spine. I clasped my hands behind his neck as he pulled my ass to the edge of the counter.

I felt my phone vibrating in my pocket. I unwound my hands from his neck and grabbed my cell.

"Don't answer it." His lips drifted to my neck.

"But it's probably Melissa." I turned my head away from him so I could see my screen. "She's here."

"Maybe you should tell her to come back."

"James, she walked here." I put my hand on his chest.

He sighed. "Her timing is impeccable." He leaned down and grabbed his shirt as I slid off the counter.

My phone buzzed again. "She's at the front desk. They told her we weren't here."

James laughed. "Oh, right." He pulled his phone out of his pocket and called down to the front desk. "Is there a Melissa down there asking to come up?" James put his hand over the receiver. "Is her last name Monroe?"

"Yes."

"Yes, please let Melissa Monroe up. Thanks, Ben." James put his cell phone back in his pocket. "So, what can I expect today?"

"What do you mean?"

"Well," he said as he wrapped his arms around me, "every time she's seen me, she's been mad at me."

"No she hasn't."

"Yes, she has. She hates me."

"She doesn't hate you. She doesn't even know you. Maybe tonight she can finally get to know you better. I want you two to be friends too."

"I'll try to be super charming." He flashed me a smile.

"Yeah, I don't think you need to try to be charming. It comes quite naturally to you."

A dinging noise sounded through the apartment. James nodded his head toward the elevator doors and released me from his embrace. "I'm probably going to need another shot." He grabbed the bottle off the counter and poured vodka into his glass.

I laughed and went to go let Melissa in.

As soon as the doors open, she ran out of the elevator and gave me a big hug. "Where the hell have you been? How are you feeling? How's your head? I can't believe everything that's been going on..." her voice trailed off as she released me from her hug. "Oh my God. This place is amazing." She walked past me and toward the windows all along the back of the apartment. I had never really seen her awe struck before. She folded her arms across her chest as she looked out at Main Street below.

"It's pretty awesome, right?" I asked as I walked up next to her.

"I didn't even know Main Street could look this pretty." She turned toward me. "No wonder you're never at our dorm any more. This place is amaze-balls. I might never leave either."

"Amaze-balls, huh?" James said as he walked up behind us. "Hi, Melissa, how are you?"

Melissa openly rolled her eyes as she turned around. "I've been better, James."

"Oh. I'm sorry..."

"You're sorry? Yeah, you should be. You know what? You and I need to talk."

James' eyebrows lowered slightly. "About what?"

"You know what."

"Hey, Melissa." I put my hand on her arm. "Maybe you and I can talk real quick? I feel like I haven't seen you in forever."

"Yeah, which is another thing I want to talk about. But first I need to talk to your boyfriend."

Geez. I just wanted to have a fun night.

James looked over at me. But all I could do was shrug. I had no idea what Melissa was upset with him about.

"If something is bothering you..." James started.

"Bothering me? Of course something is bothering me. Don't you remember our conversation the first time we met?"

"I remember that it was rather one sided."

"Very funny. But you promised me that you wouldn't hurt her. And do you know what you did that very night? You broke up with her. So yeah, you could say that's been bothering me. You lied to me."

"I don't think you understand the circumstances."

"Oh, no, I do. Penny told me that she didn't tell you she was a sophomore. Which doesn't seem nearly as bad as having a secret wife."

"I know I messed up. But Penny has forgiven me for that. For both things. And I was just..."

"Right," Melissa said, cutting him off again. "You were trying to protect her or some crap like that? Well I don't buy it. Because this whole thing," she said pointing down to the news trucks. "That doesn't protect her at all."

"Penny and I both want this. The way people are reacting is not my fault."

"Yes it is. Of course it's your fault. You can't cheat on your crazy ex wife with a student and not expect things to blow up. You're like a celebrity."

"I'm not a celebrity."

I started laughing. I started laughing and couldn't stop. And then James started laughing at me laughing.

"What is wrong with you guys?"

We both continued to laugh.

"Oh my God. You're drunk, aren't you? That's your drunk laugh." Melissa turned toward the kitchen. The bottle of vodka was still open on the counter. "Is that what you've been doing holed up in here?"

I couldn't seem to stop laughing.

"Stop laughing at me," Melissa said.

"I'm not laughing at you. I'm sorry," I said, still giggling.

"Whatever, I can't even judge you for this whole underage drinking mess you have going on. Josh gets me alcohol all the time. One of the many perks of dating an older man. Or super old," she said and looked at James.

"I'm not super old. I'm only 27."

"27 is the new 20," I said.

"Okay. I need a drink too because you're both being ridiculous. I'm glad this is going to be fun. Because I passed on a very sexy date with Josh to hang out with you guys." Melissa walked over to the kitchen.

"See, she's always mad at me," James whispered.

"Well maybe you shouldn't have broken up with me."

"I didn't break up with you. I just said I needed some time." He smiled at me. "I really wish we were alone right now." He put his hand on my waist and let it slowly slide down to my ass.

"Oh my God, James." I grabbed his hand and moved it off my ass. "Apparently you get horny when you're drunk too?"

"No, I just always want you."

"You know, you're supposed to be charming Melissa, not me. I mean, not like that obviously. In a gentlemanly way."

James laughed. "Don't worry. The only ass I want to touch is yours." He slapped my ass and walked toward the kitchen.

I loved when he was happy and playful. And I was impressed that he was able to be despite Melissa's onslaught. He was definitely better at dealing with her than I was. I tended to always just give in. I followed him into the kitchen.

"Were you guys just drinking straight vodka? No chaser or anything?" Melissa asked.

"We both just really needed a drink," James said and sat down in one of the stools at the counter.

"Gross." Melissa opened up the fridge. She was always so comfortable everywhere she went. And she had already made herself completely at home in James' apartment. *James and my apartment.* I still needed to tell her that I was moving in with him. She poured a can of cherry coke into a glass, topped it off with some vodka, and leaned against the counter. "Why did you both need a drink so badly?"

I looked at James and then back at Melissa. "The cops showed up," I said and shrugged.

"Wait, what?"

"To interview me for that stupid investigation they're doing."

"Did they tell you how the investigation was going?"

I looked at James again.

"Apparently two of my former students said I was asking for sexual favors in exchange for giving them better grades. Or something along those lines."

"And..."

"And nothing. It isn't true. Either the girls made it up, or the detectives did to try to get information from Penny.

"You have a history of lying."

"Here." James pulled out his phone and set it on the kitchen counter. He pushed it and it slid across the counter to Melissa. "Check my phone. I'm telling the truth."

I had never looked at James' phone before. James hadn't offered his phone as evidence to me. Because I trusted him. And he needed to know that I trusted him. Melissa clearly didn't trust him though. She needed the proof.

"So I can just look at your phone? At your texts? And contacts? And emails? And pictures?"

"Suit yourself."

Melissa swiped her finger across the screen. "What's your password?"

"Oh." James laughed and ran his hand through his hair. "Actually it's Penny."

"I'm your password?" I slid into the seat next to him.

"Yeah, I happen to like thinking about you." He put his arm around me.

"I hate that I'm mad at you right now, James. Because you two really are adorable," Melissa said as she looked down at James' phone.

I leaned my head against James' shoulder. His cologne seemed to affect me even more when alcohol was coursing through me. I wished we were alone too. I put my hand on his thigh.

"Insatiable," he whispered.

I gulped.

"Who's Jennifer?" Melissa asked.

"My sister."

"Oh." She looked back down at his phone. "What about Ellen?"

"That would be my housekeeper."

"Okay, fine, there's nothing on here." She placed his phone back down on the counter. "Actually there's barely anything on here. Which is suspicious all by itself."

"Sorry to disappoint you."

"Well I'm adding myself into your phone. Because if Penny winds up in the hospital again, I want to know."

"You'll be the first person I call," James said.

"I'd better be. And her parents. Have you talked to them yet, by the way?"

"We did." I lifted my head off of James' shoulder. "It went pretty well actually. My dad was not thrilled about me losing my scholarship, but other than that...it was good."

"Oh crap, Penny. I didn't realize you lost your scholarship. What are you going to do?"

"I don't know why everyone is making such a big deal out of this. You know I have the money to pay for it," James said.

"The perks of having a loaded boyfriend." Melissa smiled. "Speaking of which, I'd love a tour."

"I will let you handle the tour, Penny. I need to get some work done." James stood up.

"But you're not a professor anymore," Melissa said.

"I'm working on some other stuff." He kissed my cheek. "I'll be in my office."

Melissa didn't say anything. She just watched James disappear. "Oh my God, this place is so cool! Show me everything!"

I laughed and slid off the stool. "Okay, so this is the kitchen." This whole part of the apartment was open. I didn't really need to say anything. "And the dining room and living room."

Melissa walked over to the big box in the living room. "New T.V.?"

"Yeah. James knows that I like to watch T.V. and he didn't have one. Plus his brother, Rob, is coming to town tomorrow. He wanted something to watch football games on with him."

"That's cute. Are you excited to meet him?"

"Yeah, and I'm really curious to see what he's like. I feel like I'll know James even better once I meet his brother."

"And you two are good? I mean, I saw all the news vans outside. It's kind of ridiculous."

"We're good. I'm just trying to ignore everything else. What was class like today? Did you hear anyone talking about it?"

Melissa shrugged. "A few people. But I wasn't in any of James' classes. I feel like your Comm class is going to be a nightmare. Have you decided whether or not you're going to drop it?"

"I mean, I'm already halfway done. There are only a few speeches left. I don't want to have to take the whole class over." But I also didn't want to have to face the other students. Especially Raymond Asher. But it was also the only class I had with Tyler. Tyler was one of my best friends. I liked getting to spend time with him. And I wasn't sure how James would feel if I hung out with him outside of class.

"I get it. So..." Melissa's voice trailed off as she looked around the living room.

"Yes?"

"James mentioned paying what your scholarship used to pay. I know that he has a lot of money. But do you have any idea how much? I remember when these places were being built. They were selling them for like a million dollars or something ridiculous."

I looked at the door that James had disappeared into. I was pretty sure anyone could look up the price he sold his company for. It didn't seem like a big deal for me to tell her. "I don't know exactly. The only thing he's told me is that he sold his company for 2.8 billion dollars before he became a professor."

Melissa started laughing. But she stopped when she saw my face. "What, are you serious? Billion with a *B*? Who the hell has that much money? That's like...well I don't even know who makes that much money. I don't even have a comparison. Are you serious?"

"Yeah, that's what he said."

"Well you should totally let him pay for your education."

I laughed. "I don't want him to do that."

"You're so weird. I mean look at this place. Clearly he can afford anything he wants. And he said he wanted to pay the difference of your scholarship."

"I don't know. I'm sure we'll talk about it again. I'd just feel weird taking his money."

"You wouldn't be taking it, he'd be giving it to you. What's in there?" she asked, pointing to James' bedroom door.

"That's his room. Come on, you've gotta see his bathroom."

Melissa laughed. "Geez, this is weird. I can't believe I'm about to walk into a professor's bedroom. I have to say, if I was to guess which one of us was more likely to sleep with their professor, I would have guessed me."

"I know. I would have too." I opened up the door to James' bedroom.

Melissa laughed and lightly pushed my arm. "Holy crap." She stepped into his room and looked around.

James' room was my favorite place in his whole apartment. Probably because of how often we had sex in his bed. The shower was one of my favorite places too. I could feel my face starting to blush.

"I've never felt sheets this soft." Melissa ran her hand along the bottom of the bed. "What side do you sleep on?"

"The right side."

Melissa jumped onto the right side of the bed and laid down. "Oh my God."

I started laughing.

"I'm never getting up. You can't make me."

"But you haven't even seen the bathroom yet."

"Fine." She sighed, slowly climbed off the bed, and followed me into the bathroom. "This is like my dream bathroom." She sat down on the edge of the tub. "I need to find a professor to sleep with."

"Melissa!"

"I'm just kidding. I'm obsessed with Josh. But seriously...you're so lucky. Is that his closet?" She peered around me, back into the bedroom.

"Yeah." I was more embarrassed now. I had forgotten about all the clothes that James had bought me. Most of them still had the tags on.

Melissa wandered past me and into the closet. "Gross."

"What?" I asked and ran in after her.

"He kept his ex's clothes. You should make him get rid of these."

"Those aren't Isabella's clothes. They're mine."

Melissa pushed a few of the hangers back, studying the shirts and jackets. "Penny, these aren't your clothes. They're actually nice."

"Hey! My clothes are nice."

"Sorry, you know what I mean. They're expensive. They're classy and trendy, and really there's some of everything in here."

"Yeah, James bought them for me."

Melissa turned around. "Seriously? All of this stuff is yours? You better let me borrow this top. This is so pretty."

"Yeah, you can borrow it. Of course."

"Wait. So you let him buy you a T.V. and tons of clothes but you won't let him pay for some of your schooling? All of these clothes probably cost a fortune."

"I don't know, it's just different. I didn't ask for any of those things. He just got them for me. He wanted me to be more comfortable here."

"Geez, what else has he bought you? No wonder you chose him over Tyler."

"Melissa, it wasn't like that. I don't care about his money."

"I know. You wouldn't even add that it was a pro when you were choosing between them. Because you're insane."

"I didn't really think it was important."

Melissa shrugged. "You're right, it shouldn't have been part of the decision. Oh, that reminds me. Last time we hung out, you were going to talk to him about something he was hiding from you? I guess it wasn't so bad if you're still here."

"Oh. Yeah." This wasn't my information to share. James was clearly embarrassed about it if he had kept it from me for so long. And so far I hadn't even seen any evidence of his addiction. He seemed fine. He had three shots of vodka earlier and then walked away from it. He could have easily had more. "You know what? You were right. It wasn't anything I can't handle."

"I knew it." She smiled. I was glad when she didn't press me about it. Apparently being right was enough closure for her. She did love being right.

"So, he did actually get me one more thing," I said.

"Oh yeah?"

I nodded. "A key to his place."

"Wow, big step."

"I know. He asked me to move in with him. I said yes."

"Wait, you're leaving me? Penny, I don't like sleeping alone. You know it creeps me out. I've spent like the past week sleeping at Josh's."

"I thought you liked sleeping at Josh's?"

Melissa shrugged. "I guess. He snores though."

I laughed.

"Well, you'll still come hang out after class and stuff right?"

"Of course."

"Okay good. And I totally get it. I'd never want to leave this place either. So is his brother super rich too?"

"Melissa!"

"I'm just kidding. Kind of."

We both laughed.

"Do you want to finish the tour?" I asked.

"Is it just his office?"

"And some guest rooms." I actually hadn't seen the guest rooms. I was excited to explore some more. Melissa followed me out of James' room and I opened the door that led to the hallway. I opened the first door in the hall that I came to. It was just a normal bedroom. Ornate and perfect, but normal.

"Oh, yes! Same sheets!" Melissa said. "I can't wait to get totally wasted one night and have to crash in this bed."

"You can definitely be my first house guest."

"Awesome."

The next door was a guest bathroom. It was a smaller version of James' bathroom, without a tub. Another almost identical bedroom was on the other side of the bathroom. There was only one more door. I opened it up. I was expecting to see just another bedroom. But instead, there was a pool table in the center of the room and a bar to one side. "Wow, this is really cool." I ran my hand along the side of the pool table.

"Have you never been in here before?"

"No."

"I guess you've been too busy doing other things to get a proper tour?"

I could feel myself blushing. "Well, today he was helping me study for my Stat test next week."

"How professor-like of him."

"Yeah." I looked up at the huge picture on one of the walls. It was of a bunch of guys smiling. It took me a second to find James. He was in the center. He looked so happy. It didn't look like he had a care in the world. I recognized his friend Mason Caldwell that I had met in New York to the left of him. Otherwise, I didn't know anyone else in the picture.

"Do you think that was from when he was in college? He looks almost exactly the same," Melissa said.

"I don't know. But yeah, that's why I never would have guessed he was my professor when we first met. He doesn't look 27."

Melissa smiled at me. "Have you met any of his friends?"

"Yeah, that one." I pointed to Mason. "It was weird though. Apparently they lost touch after he moved here. James is kind of closed off. I'd like to meet more of his friends."

"Well, it'll be fun to meet his brother. I bet you can ask him tons of questions."

"Mhm." I suddenly felt nervous about meeting Rob. James had made it clear that his parents probably wouldn't like me very much. I hoped that his brother and sister would be more accepting.

"I actually need to get going," Melissa said. "Maybe we can hang out this weekend? I know it's a little awkward, but the Sigma Pi formal is on Saturday and I could really use your help getting ready."

A while ago I had hoped that Tyler would ask me to the Sigma Pi formal. That seemed like ages ago. "No, that's not awkward at all," I said. "Actually, that sounds great. I'll probably want to give James and his brother some guy time anyway. I don't want to be third wheeling with them."

Melissa laughed. "I'm pretty sure Rob would be the third wheel in that equation. Let me say bye to James before I go."

CHAPTER 28

Thursday

"There you are." James wrapped his arms around me and kissed the back of my neck.

"When was this picture taken?" I had wandered back into the room with the pool table after Melissa had left. There was something captivating about the picture. There were no pictures hanging in any of the other rooms in his apartment. And the only other picture I knew of was a small framed one of him and his siblings on his desk. This had to be important to him.

"When I was in college." He kissed my neck again.

"You look so happy."

"I'm happier now."

I couldn't help but smile. I was glad I could make him happy. "I recognize Mason. Who are the other guys?"

"They're my frat brothers."

"You were in a frat?"

"Why do you seem so surprised?"

"I don't know. I usually consider frat guys to be immature. But maybe you were immature back in college."

"Hmm." His lips tingled the back of my neck. "Is thinking about getting laid all the time immature?"

I laughed. "Yes."

"I was definitely immature then. And I guess I'm still immature. Because all I could think about all night was fucking you."

I swallowed hard. I loved when he talked like that. His naughty words seemed to have a direct line to my groin.

He pushed me forward slightly so that my hips were pressed against the pool table. "Are you good at pool, Penny?" His fingers had dipped beneath my shirt, pushing it up the sides of my torso.

"I'm okay. I haven't really played that much."

My throat made a weird noise when his hands fell from my waist. God I wanted him.

He placed the cue ball down on the table and racked up the other balls. "Show me what you got." He handed me a pool stick.

I didn't want to play pool. I wanted his hands back on me and for him to be whispering naughty things in my ear. I tried to clear my head. "Am I stripes or solids?"

"Whichever you hit in first." He smiled at me. "And let's make things interesting." He leaned against the pool table. "Whenever one of us gets a ball in, we get to choose one thing for the other person to do."

"One thing for the other person to do?"

"Mhm. So if I get a ball in, I could say I wanted your lips around my cock."

I bit my lip. This is going to be fun.

"You're up, Penny."

I bent low and arched my back. I looked over at him. He was staring at my ass. I smiled and hit the cue ball. It slammed into the rest of the balls, but none of them went in. *Shit.*

"That's a shame. I really wanted to see what you'd make me do." He grabbed another stick off the wall and lined up his shot. "I'll be solids." He easily hit one in. "Take off your shirt, Penny. And you might as well take off your bra too." He sunk his next shot, which actually included two more balls, and looked over at me.

I didn't realize how good he was at pool. I slowly peeled my shirt off and unhooked my bra. "James, this isn't even fair."

"How about a maximum of two balls in a row?" His eyes wandered up my body and landed on my eyes. "Which means you're up."

I leaned down and tried to focus on my shot. I could feel his gaze on my breasts. When he looked at me with his hungry eyes it was almost impossible to focus. But my shot was easy. The only thing I had to do was make sure I didn't hit the cue ball in. I took a deep breath and hit my first striped ball in. *Yes!* I smiled and stood up. "I think you should take your shirt off too."

He locked eyes with me and grabbed his shirt by the nape of his collar and quickly pulled it off. My eyes drifted down his perfectly sculpted torso. *Focus.* I turned back to the table and lined up my next shot. It was another easy one.

"And, Penny," James said as he walked over to me. He put his hand on the arch I had made with my back. "I forgot to mention, if you hit the cue ball in, that results in a punishment."

Everything below my waistline clenched. "A punishment?"

"But I happen to know you like being punished." He nipped my shoulder blade.

Oh God. "James, stop trying to distract me."

His fingers fell from my back, but he stayed right next to me. I could feel the heat radiating off his body and his gaze was making me blush. I did love being punished. But

I wanted to choose what he did next. The thought was so exciting that I hit my next shot too hard, sinking a striped ball and the cue ball. *Crap.*

James grabbed my waist and lifted me onto the edge of the pool table. "If you weren't pouting, I would have thought you had done that on purpose." He lightly nipped my earlobe.

I moaned and tilted my head to the side. He kissed my neck and let his lips slowly wander across my clavicle. I was expecting him to spank me. This wasn't a punishment at all.

He began to trace his hands up the insides of my thighs. His lips continued their descent and stopped between my breasts. He took one of my nipples in his mouth and lightly tugged.

"James," I moaned. I tilted my hips, wanting him to touch me.

He responded by pushing down on my thighs, pressing my ass back down against the table. His tongue swirled around my nipple. One of his hands abandoned my thigh and he began to match the motions of his tongue with his fingers on my other nipple. I didn't even understand my body's reaction to this. *How is this turning me on so much?*

His fingers traced up my leg and along the top of my thigh. Everything he did made it more and more apparent that he wasn't touching me where I needed him to. I could feel my thong getting damp. Just when I thought I couldn't take anymore teasing, he tugged hard on my nipple.

"James, please," I panted. Now I realized what the punishment was. He wasn't going to give me what I really wanted. He was just teasing me.

He moved his face a fraction of an inch in front of mine. "I want you," he said in a low husky voice. His thumbs hooked in the waistband of my leggings.

"I want you too." I lifted my hips slightly. I needed him to touch me. I needed his hands, his tongue, his cock.

"Then you'll have to play better than that." He let my waistband slap back against my skin. He picked up his pool stick and easily hit another solid ball in. "Get on your knees, Penny."

I gulped. I wanted whatever he'd give me. I slid off the pool table and got down on my knees. He slowly unbuttoned and unzipped his jeans as he walked over to me. When he got to me, he ran his thumb along my bottom lip. "Make me cum in your mouth."

His words made me even wetter. I pulled his boxers down and let his erection spring free. I looked up at him as I wrapped my hand around his base.

His Adam's apple rose and fell.

I ran my tongue from his base to his tip and then locked eyes with him as I gently kissed his tip. I wrapped my lips around him and slowly slid down his length.

A low groan escaped from his lips, making me tighten my lips around him. I loved hearing him react to what I was doing. I began to slide his erection in and out of my mouth, slowly at first, but then picking up speed. I reached up and gently cupped his balls in my hand.

He groaned again and ran his fingers through my hair. Normally at this point he'd start guiding me. I loved when he did that. But he had asked me to make him cum. I wanted to prove to him that I could do it without his guidance. I tightened my lips even more.

"Fuck."

It sounded like he had never felt anything so amazing before. I bobbed my head up and down faster. And then I paused to breathe, swirling my tongue around his tip.

"Don't stop, baby," he groaned.

I liked when he called me that. He rarely ever did. Usually I was just Penny or sometimes Miss Taylor. But when he called me baby it made me feel like I was completely his. I quickened my pace and let his tip hit my throat. I didn't even need to suppress my gag reflex. I wanted him to cum. I removed my hand from his base, grabbed his ass, and pushed his cock all the way into the back of my throat.

His cock began to pulse in my mouth. I pulled back just in time, letting his hot semen shoot into my mouth instead of directly down my throat. It was sweet and salty at the same time. I loved the taste of him. I continued to slide my lips up and down his shaft until he finished. And then I greedily drank it all down.

When he pulled out of my mouth, he immediately zipped his pants back up. "Maybe now I can focus," he said and turned back to the table.

"You're already winning," I laughed.

He shot another solid ball perfectly into one of the corners of the pool table. "But I don't even have you naked yet." He put his hand out for me.

I grabbed it and he pulled me to my feet.

"Now take off your pants." He let go of my hand.

I wasn't sure I had ever lost so badly at anything before. But it didn't really matter. I'm pretty sure no matter who won, we'd want the same thing at the end. At least, I hoped he wanted me. I wasn't sure how much more teasing I could handle. I pushed my leggings down my thighs, stepped out of them, and threw them at him.

He smiled and caught them in his hand.

I grabbed my stick and walked around the table, trying to find the easiest shot. Before I knew it, he had walked up behind me.

He let his fingers wander down my back. "I like this," he said as he touched my lacy thong.

I looked over my shoulder at him. "Well, you should. You're the one who bought it for me."

"How about you let me help you with this shot. I'd really like to see what you want me to do next."

I swallowed hard. I wanted that too. "Okay."

He leaned forward, pressing his naked torso against my back. Every inch of me wanted to turn around and kiss him. But I wanted more than that. In order to get more, I needed to get my next shot. He put his left hand on top of mine, pressing my fingers against the felt of the pool table. He grabbed the pool stick and pulled it back. Even the wood sliding through my fingers aroused me.

"Okay," he whispered into my ear as he wrapped his right hand around mine too. He pushed me forward slightly, so that my hips were digging into the side of the pool table.

I swallowed hard.

"Let's hit the nine into the left pocket." He moved my right hand back, pulling the stick back farther, and pushed my hips even harder against the pool table.

I could feel his erection pressing against my ass.

"Gently, Penny." He kissed the side of my neck. "I can't wait to see what you want me to do." He kissed my neck again.

"I think you're just trying to distract me even more." I knew I could make this shot.

"No. I want you to make it. I haven't tasted you since yesterday."

God. There was no way I could concentrate now.

He lightly slid the pool stick forward, guiding my hands, and hit the cue ball. The nine ball went right into the left pocket. "See...gentle." He kissed my neck again.

"I want you to lick me," I blurted out.

His hands fell from mine. He grabbed my shoulders and pulled my back against his torso.

"You want me to lick you?" he whispered into my ear. His tongue found the back of my ear and he gently licked it.

It felt amazing. But it wasn't what I wanted. "Not there." My voice sounded so needy. I turned around and ran my hands down his abs.

He raised his eyebrow at me. He wanted me to say it.

Instead I looked down and then back up at him.

He grabbed the sides of my thong and slid them over my hips. "You want me to lick your pussy?"

I gulped. "Yes."

"You shouldn't be embarrassed to ask me for that." He lifted me back onto the side of the pool table and spread my legs. "You know that I love the taste of you." He knelt down in front of me and massaged the insides of my thighs. "So ask me, Penny. Tell me exactly what you want me to do."

"I want you to lick my pussy." I wasn't sure why I was so embarrassed to say it. But the way he looked at me after I did made me want to say it a thousand times.

"It's sexy when you say it." He leaned forward and placed a slow stroke against my wetness.

"Oh God." I held onto the edge of the pool table so that I wouldn't fall backwards and knock all the balls around.

He swirled his tongue around inside of me, pressing against all my walls, as his nose rubbed against my clit.

Yes! I wasn't going to last long at all. I had wanted him all night. And him teasing me earlier had already wound me up so tightly.

He pushed my thighs even farther apart and held them down firmly with his strong hands.

It felt like my whole body was trembling.

He shoved his tongue even deeper, pressing his nose firmly against my clit.

"James!" I grabbed the back of his head to hold him in place. I was so close.

He continued to swirl his tongue inside of me for a few more seconds. But then he grabbed my hand, removed it from the back of his head, and pulled away from me.

"No, James. Please don't stop."

"Baby." He kissed the inside of my thigh. "I like pleasing you." He kissed my opposite thigh. "And I like when you tell me what you want." He stood up and pulled me off the table. "But you didn't ask me to make you come. I wish you had. I love making you come with just my tongue. It's your shot, though. Get your next ball in and tell me what you want."

My legs felt like jelly. I couldn't concentrate on anything. I just needed to feel release. How was I supposed to make my next shot? I pressed my thighs together, but it didn't help at all. I focused as best I could and took my next shot. The cue ball bounced off the wall and didn't hit anything. *Crap!*

He tossed me my thong. "I believe I have to earn this. But don't bother putting it back on." He easily sunk his next ball.

I threw my thong back at him. "If I had known how good you were at this, I wouldn't have agreed to this game." I was so horny. I couldn't even stand it. Why hadn't I asked him to make me come?

"I'm not sure if that's true." He hit another solid ball easily into one of the pockets. "Besides, you must have known I wasn't terrible if I owned a pool table."

I put my hand on the edge of the table. "Well, if I had been thinking clearly, I would have just asked you to fuck me on it."

His eyebrows lowered slightly. "Unbutton my jeans, Penny."

I looked down at the bulge pressing against his jeans. "That's what you want me to do to you?" I wanted him to fuck me. I didn't want to wait anymore.

"I need to be ready when I get my next shot in." He grabbed my hand and placed it on the waistline of his jeans.

I liked the feeling of his happy trail on the back of my hand. I slowly unbuttoned and unzipped his pants. He wanted to be ready to fuck me. At least that meant he was planning on eventually pleasing me. I pushed his jeans down, put my hands on the waistband of his boxers, and looked up at him.

He nodded his head.

I liked undressing him. There was something really sexy about slowly revealing all my favorite parts of him. Especially with him watching me do it. I pushed his boxers down, freeing his erection once again. I liked fucking him even more, though. I wrapped my hand around his erection.

James cleared his throat and handed me my pool stick.

I batted my eyelashes at him. "Sorry, wrong stick." I walked back to the table and bent over again. I arched my back and spread my legs. I wanted to feel him inside of me. Maybe this would tempt him.

In a second I felt his fingers along the backs of my thighs.

I arched my back even more.

"I think maybe you should try to make your next shot like this." He slipped a finger inside of me.

Oh God.

When I didn't move, he slipped another finger inside of me. "Take your shot, Penny."

I blindly hit the cue ball. It went straight into far right pocket. *Oh shit.*

James laughed and pulled his fingers out of me.

No! I turned around. "You cheated."

He silently walked around to the other side of the table and grabbed the cue ball. I liked watching him walk around naked. He wasn't shy like I was. He seemed to be confident in everything he did. He tossed the ball up in the air and caught it as he walked back over to me.

"Put your hands on the table, Penny."

"James, you cheated. You distracted me."

His Adam's apple rose and fell. "If I recall, I also helped you with one of your shots earlier. I think it evens out. Hands on the table."

I bit my lip and followed his instructions. After placing my hands on the wooden edge of the pool table, I arched my back again. Maybe he was going to punish me by fucking me.

Instead, I felt the cool cue ball roll up the back of my right leg. It shouldn't have been sexy. But everything James did was sexy. Especially when he had been torturing me for so long. My whole body shivered with desire.

"James." My voice sounded needy. I didn't want to be playing pool. I wanted to be on my back in the middle of the table with his cock deep inside of me.

He silenced me by slapping my ass hard.

Fuck. He knew how much I liked that.

He rolled the ball over the spot he had just slapped. It almost felt like a massage. A cold, super arousing massage. I closed my eyes. I was so turned on, it almost seemed I could come like this, without him even trying.

"Penny, I'm going to give you one last shot." He moved the ball to the back of my other leg and slowly rolled it up to my ass.

"One shot won't help. You're going to win next time you have..."

He slapped my ass again.

I couldn't focus when he did that. I wasn't even sure what I had been about to say.

"I like that you're full of surprises. Surprise me, and I'll give you exactly what you want. I'll fuck you as hard as you want. For as long as you want." He kissed my neck. "I'll do whatever you want me to."

Surprise him? I couldn't even think straight. He was still massaging my ass with the cue ball. How could I possibly surprise him? I suddenly hated pool. I just wanted this game to be over. I had already made him cum. But all he had done was torture me. I smiled. I had an idea. "Give me the ball."

He tossed it over my shoulder. I moved it a little to the right. I wasn't good at pool. But I was pretty good at hitting balls in along with the cue ball. And all James had left was the eight ball. I hit the cue ball into the eight ball. Both balls went into the pocket.

James grabbed my waist. "The eight ball and the cue ball?" He pushed my back down so that my torso was against the pool table. "Ending the game and ensuring that I'd punish you even more? That'll do." He thrust deep inside of me, pressing my hip bones against the edge of the pool table.

Fuck. It was everything I wanted and more.

"Tell me what you want," he said. He continued to thrust in and out of me, faster and faster.

"Please," I panted. "Please, James." I needed to come. I couldn't stand it anymore.

"Okay." He pulled me up so that my back was pressed against his torso. "Okay." He kissed my neck gently and began to massage my clit. "You can come now."

And I shattered around him. "Professor Hunter," I moaned and collapsed back down on the table. The soft felt pressed against my cheek. Sex with him was always amazing. But all the anticipation and teasing had made my orgasm so intense. I tried to catch my breath as James pulled out of me. He hadn't cum. I hadn't felt the familiar feeling of warmth shoot through me. I turned around and looked up at him.

He grabbed my chin in his hand. "I still like when you call me that."

"Professor Hunter?"

His Adam's apple rose and fell. "Yes."

"Then why did you tell me to stop?"

"I want us to just be us. Besides, I'm not even a professor anymore."

"I like calling you Professor Hunter."

His eyebrows lowered slightly.

It was the same way he had looked at me whenever I used to say his name. Before we had ever been together. I originally thought he was mad when I called him that. But I knew what it was now. It turned him on. Whenever I called him that he had wanted to rip all my clothes off. He liked that I was his student and he was my professor. I liked it too. It was sexy and dangerous. Whenever I had talked to him and called him Professor Hunter, maybe it had made him want me a little bit more. I didn't ever want to stop calling him that. I wanted him to always look at me like this. "You'll always be Professor Hunter to me."

He grabbed my waist and set me down on the edge of the pool table. "I don't know why I find it so sexy when you call me that."

"Professor Hunter." I ran my hands down his six pack.

He leaned forward and kissed me hard. And I wanted him all over again. I grabbed his hair and pulled him back.

"I want you to fuck me in the middle of the pool table, Professor Hunter."

"Then get in the middle and spread your legs, Miss Taylor." He flashed me one of his smiles that made my knees weak.

I liked when he called me Miss Taylor, too. I didn't care if that made us weird. At least we could be weird together. I pushed balls out of my way as I scooted into the center of the table. I gulped as I watched him climb onto the table after me. He leaned over me and pushed the rest of the balls out of the way. I heard them clang together as he pressed down on the center of my chest, shoving my back onto the table.

He grabbed my thighs and thrust himself deep inside of me.

"Professor Hunter," I moaned. I had missed calling him that. I wanted to say it a million times.

He kept one hand on my thigh and grabbed the edge of the table with his other hand. "I've missed hearing you say that." He kissed me hard as he continued to slide his length in and out of me.

We were so much more than professor and student now. But he was right. This was so incredibly hot. It brought me right back to our very first time in his office. "Harder, Professor Hunter."

He grabbed both my hands and lifted them above my head, knocking more balls out of the way. "Fuck, Penny." He moved his hips faster. "I'll never get enough of you."

I wanted to run my hands through his hair and down the muscles in his back, but I couldn't move. I was completely at his mercy. "I'll never get enough of you either."

He leaned down and kissed me again.

I loved when he was rough with me.

"Say my name when you come, Penny. I want to hear you say it when you clench around my cock." He tilted his hips, going deeper still.

"Professor Hunter!" I screamed as I came again. As soon as I yelled his name I felt the familiar warmth spread up into my stomach. He continued to thrust in and out of me. When he was done, he collapsed beside me, pulling my head onto his chest.

I could feel and hear his heart beating rapidly. His cologne mixed with sweat was my favorite smell in the world. I don't think I had ever felt so relaxed and happy. I sighed and nuzzled against his chest.

"I love you, Penny. I love you more than I even knew I could." He ran his fingers through my hair.

I tilted my head and kissed his chest. "I love you." I kissed his chest again. "James." I kissed his collar bone. "Professor Hunter." I kissed the scruff under his chin. "C.E.O." I kissed his lips.

He grabbed the side of my face and deepened the kiss.

"Whatever you want to be. You're mine." I smiled down at him.

He ran his palm along my cheek. "Yours." His chest rose and fell under my arm.

Nothing else mattered. I was his and he was mine.

CHAPTER 29

Friday

I rolled over to snuggle up to James, but all I felt were empty sheets. I slowly opened my eyes and yawned. James wasn't beside me, but there was a note on his pillow. I smiled and slowly sat up.

Penny,

I went for a run. I probably won't be back before you leave. Good luck on your speech today. Although you don't need it. As long as you don't curse and stray off topic.

Text me about lunch. I can pick you up and take you somewhere off Main Street. And call me if you need to talk. Or if you decided to drop Comm, which I still hope you do, I'll see you soon.

Love,

Professor Hunter

P.S. Try not to fall in love with your new Comm professor.

I smiled and climbed out of bed. He had nothing to worry about. My speech would be fine. Today would be fine. After brushing my teeth and putting on minimal makeup, I went into the closet and found a pair of jeans and a tank top. Melissa was right. These clothes were amazing. I pulled on a leather jacket. My new clothes smelled like James. Which was really comforting. And I wasn't even that nervous about giving my speech today because he wasn't going to be the one sitting there analyzing what I said. Besides, my whole class already seemed to hate me, so who really cared if I messed up. I just needed to get it over with.

I pulled on a pair of matching brown leather boots and walked out into the kitchen. I was kind of relieved that Ellen wasn't there. She seemed really nice, but I had never been alone with her. I felt weird about the dynamic. And I wasn't sure if James had told her I was moving in with him yet or not. I grabbed a granola bar and my backpack and retreated to the elevator.

I walked out of the side exit of the parking garage that I had found before. It was the only way that I knew how to leave the apartment. And since it was a weird place to leave, there were no news vans parked outside. *So far so good.*

It was strange walking on Main Street toward the lecture hall. I was used to walking along the brick paths of the green. It was nice though. No one seemed to know who I was. And there were still fall leaves to step on. One of my favorite parts of autumn was crunching leaves. I smiled when I walked past the small coffee shop where I had first met James. It was nice that I'd get to walk by that every morning. I put my hand in my pocket and ran my fingers along the note he had left me this morning. I had brought it just in case I needed some reassuring throughout the day. Whatever happened, it was all worth it.

"Hey, Penny!"

I turned my head and saw Tyler running up to me. I stopped and waited for him to catch up. Running into him already made me feel better about the day. "Hey, Tyler." I smiled at him. He lived on a side street off Main Street. He probably walked this way to class all the time.

"I never see you on Main Street. Kind of a strange way to get to class from your dorm."

"Oh, yeah. Well, I was actually staying at James'." I didn't want this to be awkward. I really, really hoped we could be friends.

"Where does he live?"

I pointed over my shoulder. "The apartment building on the end of Main Street." I was hoping to be vague. I wanted to change the subject as fast as possible.

"Wait, you mean The Monroe? The mega expensive one?"

"Yeah."

"Sweet. That must be nice."

"It is."

"So how are you doing? How's your head?"

"I'm fine. It really wasn't a big deal at all. I don't even feel it anymore." The bruise on my stomach was almost gone and I could easily cover up the stitches on my forehead if I didn't tuck my bangs behind my ears. "What about you? How's your nose?"

He laughed. "It still freaking hurts. Professor Hunter knows how to take a swing."

"I'm so sorry."

"Geez, it's fine." He laughed and put his hand on my shoulder for a second. "At least it looks better now."

"It does." The bruising in the corners of his eyes was gone. We locked eyes for a second, but I quickly looked away.

"And how's everything else?" he asked.

"Good. Well, weird, actually. There's all these news vans outside his place. And I feel like we have to sneak around even more than before. It's just really frustrating. But things with James are good. We're in a really good place."

"Good."

We walked in awkward silence for a minute.

"How's Natalie?" I finally said.

"Good. We've just been hanging out. I don't think I'm looking for anything serious right now, you know?" He looked away from me again.

I pressed my lips together. *Because of me?* My phone buzzing in my pocket was a welcome distraction. I looked down at the screen. It was an email from Professor Nolan.

Penny,

Class is going to be canceled until further notice. You should be getting a call from Dean Vespelli soon. The investigation didn't go the way we all hoped it would. If I had any other information, I'd give it to you, but that is all the dean told me. I'll be making this announcement in class today because I only just found out a few minutes ago. But hopefully you see this before you come. I think it's best if you don't attend.
- Professor C. Nolan

I stopped in the middle of the sidewalk.

"Hey, Penny, are you okay?" Tyler turned around and walked back to me. He put his hand on my elbow. "Penny?"

"Yeah, actually, I think I'm just going to skip class today." I didn't want to talk about this with Tyler. I didn't want him to look at me like I knew he would when I told him about the two other girls. Because they were lying. I believed James. This was such a mess.

"What are you talking about? You can't skip. We have to give our speeches today. You'll get an F if you don't show."

"Yeah, well..." I let my voice trail off.

"You asked me to stay in the class with you. I wanted to drop it. I did this for you. Come on, we're both going."

"I can't."

"Penny." Tyler smiled at me. "You don't have anything to worry about. I'll be right there with you."

"No, it's not that." I didn't know what else to do. I handed Tyler my phone.

He looked down at the email from Professor Nolan. "Oh."

"Yeah, so you should probably go so you can listen to what he has to say. I'm just going to head back."

"Wait." Tyler put his hand on my elbow again. "Let's go get breakfast."

"You should probably still go to class."

"I'd rather hang out with you."

"Tyler..."

"If class really is canceled, then I'm never going to get to see you anymore. And I doubt that Professor Hunter will just let you hang out with me outside of class. We don't exactly get along."

I didn't want this to be the last time I ever saw Tyler. But what if he was right? Tyler was one of my best friends. I didn't want that to happen. "Tyler, we'll still get to hang out."

"Maybe. You're one of my best friends, Penny. I don't want to stop seeing you."

"You won't." *I hope.* I had a sinking feeling in my stomach. "But okay, yeah. I haven't eaten anyway."

He smiled. "I'm craving a bagel since we've been standing outside this bagel place." He pointed to the door. "How does that sound?"

"Fantastic." I followed him inside. I had never been there before, and I wasn't sure why. I loved bagels and it smelled amazing.

"What do you want?" he asked.

"We can just order separately."

"It's crowded, you can go find us a seat while I order."

"Umm...a cinnamon raisin bagel with cream cheese."

"And to drink?"

"Orange juice."

"Okay, go find us a seat." He walked over toward the counter. The place really was busy. I got us the last open table. It was tucked in the corner of the small restaurant, but somehow seemed kind of private.

My phone started buzzing again. It was a number I didn't recognize. I didn't want to answer it. If it was the dean it could wait. I didn't want to hear what he had to say. I didn't even understand why any of it mattered. The investigation was superficial. James had already quit. I just wanted all of this to go away.

Tyler placed two wrapped bagels down on the table along with two bottles of orange juice.

"Thanks, Tyler. Which one is yours?"

"I got the same thing as you." He grabbed one and tossed it at me.

"Thanks for skipping class for me."

"Thanks for getting class canceled indefinitely." He held up his bottle of orange juice.

I laughed and tapped mine against his.

He scratched the back of his neck. "At least there's one perk to you hooking up with our professor." He gave me a small smile and took a bite of his bagel.

I wanted to be able to laugh about all this with him. I wanted him to not look hurt when he joked around about it. But at least he was joking around. That was a good sign. I really just wanted to move past this. I wanted to go back to being friends. Despite what Melissa said, I really thought we could be just friends.

"Do you want to talk about that email?" he asked.

I shrugged.

"Have you heard anything about the investigation?"

"I was interviewed by two detectives last night. They said something about these other girls that claimed James...well, it doesn't matter. It was all nonsense. Either the detectives were lying or the girls or both."

Tyler put his bagel down. "Why would his students lie about something like that?"

That was the same question that I had. But I wasn't going to doubt James. He had asked me to trust him. So I was going to trust him. Even if it was still nagging at me. "I don't know. But they were."

"Okay." He didn't sound convinced at all.

I knew it would be weird to talk to him about this. I took a bite of my bagel. It was delicious. My phone started buzzing again.

"Are you going to answer it?"

"I don't recognize the number."

"Well, maybe it's the dean."

"That's kind of what I'm afraid of."

"Answer it. Aren't you curious about why class is canceled?"

I knew why it was canceled. Because there were two lying whores out there making up stories about my boyfriend. But I was curious. "Okay." I swiped my finger across the screen. "Hello?"

"Penny Taylor?" It was a female's voice.

"Speaking."

"This is Becca from the dean of student's office. Dean Vespelli needs to talk to you. Hold for one moment please."

There was a clicking noise. And then I heard a man clear his throat. "Is this Penny?"

"Yes."

"Penny, this is Dean Vespelli."

"How can I help you?"

He laughed. "You can't really. I'm calling to tell you that the investigation went south. Three female students came forward with similar stories regarding sexual misconduct concerning James."

Three now? Seriously? "Well, they're lying."

"Not so easy to prove. The good news is that so far all the girls have been of legal age, so no charges are being pressed. But in light of these findings, all of James' classes are being canceled for the remainder of the semester."

"Okay."

"The validity of everyone's grades in James' classes are in question, so everyone will receive As given the circumstances. The announcement will be in the paper tomorrow morning."

"Oh." Is that why the girls had lied? Had they known what would happen if the classes needed to be canceled? That had to be it. Those bitches!

"But I'm calling to tell you that this doesn't include you. You'll be receiving an incomplete. It'll show up as an I on your record."

"Wait, why can't I just withdraw?" An incomplete on my transcript was worse than a W. It made it look like I didn't hand in all my assignments or something.

"You can't withdraw from a canceled class."

"You said that the blame for this lies on James. So why do I..."

"If I recall, you confessed to me that this whole mess was just as much your fault if not more. Do you have any idea how much backlash I've had to deal with?"

"I'm sorry if..."

"But that isn't the reason why I'm giving you an incomplete in the class. Apparently you did not cooperate in the investigation. You're lucky that I'm not giving you your third strike."

"Mr. Vespelli, those detectives were just trying to pressure me into telling them something that wasn't true." I lowered my voice slightly. "James never did anything inappropriate with me. Maybe the detectives pressured those other girls too."

"James did do something inappropriate. He engaged in a sexual relationship with you. And possibly three other girls."

"He didn't." I wanted to cry. I tried to keep my voice even. "And if the detectives didn't pressure those girls, then they just lied because they saw an easy way out of taking a class. Don't you see that? They must have known they'd get As if they made up stories like that. That's clearly what they were doing."

"We can't prove that."

"Well check their grades."

"I already did. None of them were doing well in James' class. But that doesn't mean that they made it up."

"Yes it does."

"Penny, I understand that this news is upsetting in more ways than one." His voice was calmer. Almost soothing. "I know that you're probably upset that you have to retake the class. But the incomplete won't mean anything on your transcript. Recruiters won't look for that. As for the accusations, there's nothing I can do. I'm trying to stop the investigation since we've already decided to cancel classes. This should be over soon. And if you're upset about what the investigators found, maybe you should talk to James about it."

He thought James was guilty. Did everyone think James was guilty? I looked at Tyler. He was almost done with his bagel. I felt like he could hear the conversation. I turned my head to the side slightly, in hopes that he couldn't hear.

"Mr. Vespelli, I know they're lying. James and I have already talked about it."

"Then ignore it. Try not to let it bother you."

I was mad. I shouldn't have to try to not let it bother me. They should be figuring out the truth. I was sick of everyone spreading rumors about James. No wonder he was so closed off. Everyone was awful to him. "I don't want you to stop the investigation. I want you to find the truth. You can't publish this in the paper yet. I'm telling you that it isn't true."

"Penny, I'm sorry. I just want this to go away as fast as possible. The university needs it to go away."

"You're rewarding students for lying. They should be getting in trouble, not rewarded."

"I need to call James. Have a good day, Penny." The line went dead.

"You've got to be kidding me." I tossed my phone down on the table.

I could feel Tyler's eyes on me. I didn't know what to say to him. James was going to freak out when Mr. Vespelli called him. I couldn't believe the university was going to stop the investigation. If they weren't going to find the truth, what was the point of starting the investigation in the first place?

"So...what's up?" Tyler eventually asked.

I took a huge bite of my bagel to stall. I didn't want to have this conversation with Tyler. Clearly he thought that James was a bad guy. And I didn't want to hear anyone else tell me that. "Good news," I said. "You got an A."

"What?"

"Everyone in James' classes gets an A."

"Really?"

"Mhm. You're welcome."

Tyler laughed. "Thanks. But I'm pretty sure I could have gotten an A without you sleeping with our professor."

I wasn't sure what I was supposed to say to that. So I just laughed awkwardly. "Maybe."

Tyler shrugged. "So if we all get As, why do you seem so upset? It's kind of awesome."

"I don't get an A. I'm getting an incomplete."

"Why? You didn't do anything wrong."

"I did. I slept with my professor. And apparently I didn't cooperate in their investigation or something. I don't know. Those detectives were assholes. It doesn't matter anyway. I don't really care." I took another huge bite of my bagel. Cream cheese seemed to make me feel better.

"Are you okay?"

"I'm fine," I mumbled with my mouth full.

"Penny, you know you can talk to me. That's what friends are for."

I shook my head. "It's so stupid. All of this is so stupid."

Tyler just stared at me.

"I know he didn't do those things. He told me he didn't. I trust him. So I'm not sure why I feel so...so..." I put my face in my hands. *Three. Three girls?* James had slept with Isabella when he said he needed space. I thought he had broken up with me. But he told me he had never broken up with me when he finally started talking to me again. So if he hadn't broken up with me, that meant he knowingly cheated on me with her during our break. It had been in the back of my head, bothering me. James said he did it because he was trying to get over me. Which made sense. But maybe that wasn't the only thing he did to try to get over me. Maybe there were more girls. Maybe there were exactly three more girls. I didn't want to think that. I didn't want to think that it was possible. But wasn't it?

"Penny." Tyler put his hand on my arm. "Please just talk to me. I hate seeing you upset."

I lifted my face out of my hands. "What if they aren't lying, Tyler? What if he...what if he did the things they said he did?" I felt guilty as soon as I said it. It was fine to think those things. But I shouldn't have said them out loud. And especially not to Tyler.

Tyler kept his hand on my arm. "Then I'll kick his ass."

I laughed and moved my arm slightly to remove his hand. "I'm sorry, I don't know why I said that. Clearly those girls just wanted As. They weren't doing well in his classes. They're just dumb so they did another dumb thing."

"Girls can do pretty dumb things."

"Yeah." I knew he was talking about me. But I wasn't making a mistake by being with James. Tyler was amazing. And he'd be an amazing boyfriend for someone else. I looked up at him. "What did you say in your last speech? You never told me."

Tyler smiled. "It wasn't a great speech. I was really worried about you."

"Yes, I'm very dramatic."

He laughed. "I chose to major in economics because a major in business seemed like a logical choice. A safe choice. And I added on a second major of finance because it was easy to get both at the same time." He shifted in his seat. "I was upset after you stormed out of class. I kind of lost my cool during my speech too."

"You did?" I couldn't picture him doing that. He always seemed so calm and confident when he did his speeches.

"Yeah." He scratched the back of his neck with his hand. "You didn't see Professor Hunter's reaction after you left. But I was sitting right behind him. It all started to come together. I think I already realized what was going on between you two before I even saw your phone. I was really pissed. So I said I chose the majors I did so that I could eventually be rich. And have any girl I wanted fall in love with me."

"That wasn't why I fell in love with James."

Tyler laughed. "Yeah, I know you're not a gold digger, Penny. Like I said, I just snapped during my speech. I didn't understand. Hell, I still don't understand." He scratched the back of his neck again.

"So what do you really want to do after you graduate? That didn't exactly answer the question you skipped."

"I just want to be happy."

I was the one that was making him unhappy. "Do you think we can ever just be friends, Tyler? Really?"

"We are friends. We were always friends."

"I don't want to be the reason that you're unhappy."

"That's not what I meant, Penny. If all you'll give me is friendship then that's what I want. I want to be a part of your life. I want you to be happy too. And if Professor Hunter makes you happy, then I'm glad that you're with him."

Maybe I was reading into the things he said too much. He was right, we had always been friends. "So what do you think you'll be doing after you graduate that will make you happy?"

"Actually, I'm interviewing for a job next week."

"For what?"

"I think I want to be a business reporter. I love business. More than I thought I would, actually. But I think I like writing even more. And I had fun giving speeches in class."

"Tyler, that's awesome."

"Yeah, I'm really excited about it. I think it could be a perfect fit for me. I'm so nervous about my interview."

"You're going to do great." I smiled at him. "If you get it, where will you be working?"

"New York."

"You're moving to New York?"

He laughed. "Maybe. I haven't gotten the job yet. But I think it will be nice to move to the city. At least for awhile. I think a change will be good."

"I'm going to miss you. I knew you'd be graduating in the spring, but I didn't think I'd lose you to the big city."

He laughed again. "It's like a two and a half hour drive from here, tops. We can visit each other all the time. I can third wheel with you and Professor Hunter. It'll be a blast."

I smiled. "James grew up in the city. He loves it there. Maybe you two have more in common than you think. I really hope you two can eventually be friends."

"If I ever lose the urge to punch him in the face, maybe we can all hang out." Tyler smiled.

"That sounds fair."

"Are you going to your other classes today?" he asked.

"Yeah. I just want everything to go back to normal."

"I feel like I should warn you. Everyone's talking about it. I'm pretty sure it's the most scandalous thing that's happened here in ages."

"I think if I just act like everything's normal it'll just blow over."

"Maybe." Tyler leaned forward slightly. "Try not to let it bother you. If you need me you can call me, you know."

"I know."

"Let me walk you to your next class. It'll make me feel better."

He was acting weird. How bad was this going to be? "Yeah that would be great. I have psychology in Gore."

"Okay, let's get going then. My next class is pretty far from there."

I quickly finished my bagel and we walked out of the shop together. "Thanks for breakfast, Tyler."

"Of course. When have I ever not paid for one of your meals?"

"I always offer to pay, I..."

"I'm just kidding. You're going to have to learn to laugh stuff off if you're going to survive today."

"Is it really that bad? I mean, what are people saying?"

"It seems like most people really liked Professor Hunter's classes. Lots of people are blaming this whole thing on you."

"Really?" I was surprised. The things that the dean had said made it seem like people would think James was a monster. Seducing students left and right. It made me feel better that people were blaming me. It almost seemed like it would be easier to deal with. I hated when people said bad things about James.

"Yeah, I was surprised too. Professor Hunter always said the weirdest stuff in class. I thought he was an awful professor. Always talking about lust and inappropriate dreams and stuff. I get it now, though. He was flirting with you the whole time. So I guess he was just a bad professor in our class."

I could feel my face turning red.

"I really thought he was a crazy person."

I laughed awkwardly. "Yeah. We probably could have been more subtle."

Tyler shrugged. "I didn't even notice and I knew you. But looking back on it now, there were a lot of signs."

We stopped outside of Gore Hall. A lot of people stared at us as they walked by. Maybe they were just staring because my face was red. I took a deep breath. I was probably imagining it.

"Just try to laugh everything off today, okay? People are idiots."

"I'm going to be fine. I doubt anyone's going to talk to me. Especially in Psych. It's a huge lecture hall. I sit by myself."

"Oh, you don't know anyone in that class?"

"It's like 200 people or something ridiculous, but no, I don't know anyone."

"Maybe I should come with you."

I laughed. "Tyler, I'm not letting you skip another class. What will the people conducting your interview think next week if you keep doing that?"

"Psh. I have all As. They're going to think I'm awesome."

"Still. I'm fine."

"Okay. Well, I guess I'll see you later." He gave me a hug.

"See, she sleeps with everyone," some girl said as she walked by us with a group of her friends. They all laughed.

What the hell?

Tyler unwound his arms from me. "Yeah, if that was a guy I would have punched him in the face."

I stared at the girl as she entered Gore Hall.

"You sure you don't want me to stay?" Tyler asked.

"Yeah. I mean, no, you should go to your class. It's gonna be fine." I wasn't as convinced as I had been a minute ago, though.

"Okay. I'll see you later."

"Good luck on your interview, in case I don't see you beforehand."

"Thanks, Penny. Remember, laugh it off." He smiled and walked away.

I remembered the advice that Professor Nolan had given me. Getting to class early was a bad idea. So instead of entering the classroom, I went to the bathroom. I sat down in one of the stalls and pulled my phone out of my pocket. There were no new messages. I thought James might text me after his conversation with the dean. Maybe they were still talking. Or arguing.

I heard the door to the bathroom close and two sets of footsteps entering.

"I can't believe class was canceled," one of the girls said. "This is so ridiculous. He was such a good professor."

"I know. I can't believe that slut got him fired."

"He probably doesn't even like her. And even if he does, it won't last long. She ruined his career."

"And she's a home wrecker. What an awful person. I feel so bad for Professor Hunter. I'm really going to miss his class."

"You're just going to miss staring at him."

The second girl laughed. "So what? He's so dreamy. And besides, it wasn't like I was going to act on it. I'm not a whore."

I looked down at my hands. I had put James in a terrible position. I never should have flirted with him. But it always seemed like he wanted this as much as me. He even promised that he didn't resent me. I still felt guilty though. Maybe I always would. He had come to teach here because he needed a fresh start. He was finally happy. Maybe I was messing everything up. He had finally gotten to be himself. Without his parents or his wife pressuring him. And now he was stuck again. I was preventing him from teaching.

Tyler had said he wanted me to be happy. Because he cared about me. I cared about James. I cared about James so much. Maybe I was being selfish by being with him. I should just disappear. The university might even let him teach again. The only requirement was that he had to stop seeing me. *And for the investigation to come back clean.*

But there wouldn't have been an investigation if I had never been with James in the first place. If Isabella had never found out about me, then he'd still be a professor. He'd still be happy. I waited for the girls to leave before exiting the stall.

I couldn't laugh this off. I couldn't just dismiss what I had heard. It was true. *Isn't it?* I quickly washed my hands and walked through the hall toward class. The professor was already talking when I opened the door. I had never been late for a class before. The door made a loud banging noise when it closed and everyone in the huge lecture hall seemed to turn and look at me.

"Penny Taylor!" the professor called from the front of the room.

Fuck, how does she know my name? There were 200 students in this class. Her knowing my name was not a good thing.

"How nice of you to join us."

A bunch of students in the class snickered.

I found a seat near where I was standing, but when I went to go sit down, the girl put her backpack on the seat to block me.

Damn it!

"Psst, over here," a boy said who was sitting several rows ahead of where I was standing. I didn't want to sit next to a guy I didn't know. But it seemed to be the only option.

"See me after class, Penny," the professor said and turned back to the board as I sat down.

What the hell? People came late to class all the time. It shouldn't have been a big deal at all. Was she going to give me a lecture about how I was a horrible person too? Well, I didn't want to hear it. Part of me wanted to get up and leave the class right now, disrupting it for a second time.

"Geez, what did you do to set her off?" the boy next to me whispered.

"Right? People come late to this class all the time."

"Do you think it has something to do with that thing with Professor Hunter?"

Of course he knew about that. Everyone knew about that. I shrugged and tried to pay attention to what the professor was saying.

"Hey, I'm not judging you. Hell, I actually owe you a thank you. I was getting a C in strategic management. And rumor has it that you just scored me an A."

"Yeah. You're welcome." At least someone was happy with me. I wasn't even sure I was happy with myself anymore.

"I'm Eli by the way. I'm in Sigma Pi with Tyler." He stuck his hand out to me.

I shook his hand. "I'm Penny. But I guess you already know that."

"Yeah, everyone knows who you are."

He did look familiar. I had probably seen him at one of the Sigma Pi parties before. "Did Tyler tell you to look out for me or something?"

"He didn't really put it like that. He just said he knew I didn't know anyone in this class and neither did you."

"Thanks for letting me sit next to you. I'm not sure anyone else was going to let me sit next to them."

He smiled and turned back to look at the board.

***

I shoved my notebook into my backpack. "Thanks again for letting me sit with you, Eli."

"Of course. What do you think Professor Thornton wants to talk to you about?"

"I have no idea."

"I'm sure it's nothing bad."

"Hopefully. I guess I'll see you Monday?"

He smiled. "Of course. But I guess I'll actually see you this weekend at the Sigma Pi formal too."

"Oh. No. I won't be there." *Awkward.*

"You're not going with Tyler? I thought you two were like a thing?"

"No, we're just friends. I think he's going with Natalie."

"Natalie? I've never heard him mention her." Eli shrugged. "Weird. Well, I'll catch you later, Penny. Good luck with Professor Thornton."

"Thanks, Eli." I'd have to text Tyler and thank him for looking out for me yet again. It was weird that one of his frat brothers didn't even know about Natalie. I hoped he was still taking her to the formal.

I looked down at my cell phone and tried to ignore the murmurs as people walked by me. Still nothing from James. I hoped he was handling the news okay. When there were barely any people left in the room, I made my way down to the front of the classroom.

Professor Thornton didn't look up from the papers on her desk. "Your grades are slipping."

"I know. I was distracted. I'm working hard on catching back up."

"If you think I'm going to go easy on you because of what's going on, you're wrong."

"I don't expect you to, Professor Thornton."

She finally looked up at me. "I just want to make things very clear. If you're getting perks in other classes because of your relationship..."

"I'm not." What the hell?!

"Don't come late to my class again, Penny." She grabbed her satchel and stood up to leave.

"I was just trying to avoid having to listen to everyone talking about me before class. I was here early like I always am, I was just hiding in the bathroom. Where apparently, I couldn't hide from what people were saying."

She sighed and stopped in her tracks. "I'm sorry about what people are saying. I just need to make sure that we're on the same page here."

"We are. I'm going to get my grades back up. I don't need any assistance with that. You'll see."

"Well, good. Prove me wrong. I hope you do. Because I have no problem failing students. And I'm not friends with Professor Hunter." She turned and walked up the stairs toward the exit.

CHAPTER 30

Friday

I looked down at my paper and winced. C-. I was devastated when James had stopped talking to me. I had completely fallen apart. All my grades had seemed to slip. I probably still had a B average in the class. But I was used to getting As. I had worked hard to make sure I was always above the 3.5 GPA that I needed for my scholarship. It didn't matter if I let my grades slip now because I had lost my scholarship. But I didn't want to. I liked getting good grades.

"As you all know, extra credit assignments are due next Wednesday," my intro to marketing professor said. "If you weren't motivated before, maybe you will be after getting these grades. Not your best work, everyone. I expect better next time." Professor McCarty sat down at his desk.

Apparently I wasn't the only one that had been slacking recently.

"Does anyone have any questions about the assignment?"

Professor McCarty had probably mentioned the extra credit when I had skipped class on Wednesday. I silently pleaded for someone else in the class to ask about it. I couldn't have been the only one that was absent on Wednesday. But no one raised their hand. I'd just talk to him after class. I didn't want everyone to look at me.

"Okay, then. I hope you all have a great weekend. I'll see you on Monday."

I waited for everyone to leave before going up to the front of the room. "Professor McCarty?"

He looked up at me. When he did, it was as if his eyes wandered up my whole body, observing me slowly.

My skin felt cold.

"Ah, Penny Taylor. What can I do for you?"

"Hi, Professor McCarty." I didn't usually talk to professors. I always sat in the back of the room and never volunteered to answer questions. "I was absent on Wednesday, so I didn't get to hear about the extra credit assignment."

"Of course." He opened up a folder and went through the papers. "I've heard a lot about you recently."

"Umm...yeah. I guess so."

He pulled a paper out of his folder. "Come here so I can show you what you need to do." He tapped the desk next to him.

"Okay." Why was he being weird? I needed to get to my next class. I could read the assignment later. I walked around the desk next to him and leaned down slightly so I could read the paper.

"So here's the assignment," he said and put his hand on the small of my back.

I felt frozen in place. *Why is he touching me?*

"All you need to do is write about a company that you think does an excellent job marketing their products."

"Okay." My voice sounded small. I wanted to move, but my body was frozen. *He's just being nice. He's just trying to show me what I need to do.* I took a deep breath.

"Simple really," he said. His hand was still on my back.

Why couldn't I seem to move? *Get off of me.*

"But it's not that much extra credit. If you're looking for something a little more, I think we can probably think of something." His hand slid down slightly, but it was still on my back.

"Professor McCarty." My voice still sounded small. "This is enough extra credit. Thank you. I need to get to my next class."

"Hold on, Penny. I think we can arrange something that will work for both of us. How about you meet me in my office during lunch today and we can discuss it?" His hand slid down onto my ass. "You want an A, don't you?"

"Stop." I was whispering. I could feel the sting of tears coming to my eyes. Why couldn't I move? Why wasn't he listening to me? "Stop," I said again.

"I'm not going to hurt you, Penny. I'll be gentle. I think we both know that you're more than willing to do this."

I finally willed my body to react and I did the first thing I could think of. I slapped him hard across the face and stepped away from him.

He grabbed my wrist hard so I couldn't flee. "I'm just trying to help you," he said.

"Help me? I don't need your help." I tried to take a step away from him, but his grip was strong. "What are you doing? You're my professor." I realized the irony from what I had just said.

Professor McCarty smiled. "And doesn't that make this all a little more exciting?"

"Let go of me." I pulled my arm as hard as I could away from him. *What a pig.*

He dropped my wrist. "I'll make it worth your time. I've worked at this university for years. I have more of a pull with other professors than James did."

"I'm going to report you to the dean." I wiped under my eyes where my tears had started to escape.

Professor McCarty laughed. "And you think Joe will believe you? You've already slept with at least one professor. No one will believe you, Penny. Joe definitely won't trust your word over mine. I'll tell him you came on to me. I know you already have two strikes. You'll be expelled."

"Fine, get me expelled." I ran over to the door and ran out of the classroom. I continued to run as fast as I could out of the building. It didn't matter that people were staring at me. I didn't care anymore.

I ran all the way back to my dorm, up the stairs, and into my room. I let my back slide down the closed door and wrapped my arms around my legs. After a few minutes the knees of my jeans were completely soaked with tears. I wasn't sure why I had come here. Everything was better when I was with James. But I was embarrassed. I told him I could handle this. I wanted to be strong.

Besides, one phone call had made me doubt him. I wasn't sure I deserved his love. And maybe those girls in the bathroom were right. Maybe he'd be better off without my love.

I didn't doubt him, though. The feeling had been fleeting. I trusted him with everything, with every part of me. Maybe he would be better off without my love, but that didn't mean he didn't want me. And I needed him right now. I needed his arms around me. I wanted him to tell me everything was going to be okay. I pulled out my phone and texted him: "Can you come get me? I'm at my dorm."

His response came in less than a minute. "Why aren't you in Stat? Are you okay?"

I wiped away my tears. "I'm okay. Please can you come?"

My phone buzzed immediately. "I'll be right there."

I wasn't sure what I was going to tell him about today. He already had enough to deal with. I didn't want him to have to worry about me on top of everything else. Maybe it was good that I had come to my dorm and cried for awhile to get it off my chest.

My phone buzzed. "I'm here. Do you want me to come up?"

I wiped my eyes and looked down at my phone. How did he know that was what I wanted? I liked my room. It was warm and cozy. His apartment was big and cold and empty. I quickly texted him back. "I'll come let you in."

I blew my nose and then left my room. I just wanted him to hold me. I didn't want to talk about today. When I opened the door, he was standing there, concern etched on his face before he had even seen me.

He took the stairs two at a time and wrapped his arms around me. "Penny, what's wrong?"

His arms around me and his soothing voice made me burst into tears.

"It's okay," he said and kissed the top of my head. "It's okay, I'm here." He lifted me into his arms and carried me through the hallway of my dorm and up the stairs.

I felt safe in his arms. He smelled like his cologne and sweat. It was my favorite combination of things.

He opened up the door to my room, kicked it closed with his foot, and then set me down on my bed. He put his hands on the bed on either side of me.

I was momentarily distracted by the sight of him. He hadn't changed out of his workout clothes. He was wearing athletic shorts and no shirt. It looked like he had thrown on a zip up hoodie at the last second before coming to get me, but it wasn't zipped. His torso glistened with sweat. God was he sexy.

"Penny." He grabbed my chin in his hand. "Talk to me."

"I just wanted to see you. Can you hold me?"

He smiled. "I'm all sweaty."

"I like when you're sweaty."

He smiled again. "Okay, move over." He kicked off his sneakers and climbed into my bed next to me, wrapping his arms around me.

I sighed and pressed the side of my face against his chest.

"If you're upset about your conversation with Joe, I convinced him to change the incomplete to a withdrawal. It looks better on your transcript."

"But Mr. Vespelli said you couldn't withdraw from a class that was canceled."

"Yeah, well Joe was being an asshole."

"Thank you." I listened to his heart beating.

"If that isn't what's bothering you, what is it?"

"It's nothing important."

James was quiet. He ran his fingers through my hair. "Why did you come here?"

"I don't know. It's cozy."

"Okay." He tilted my head up to his and pushed a strand of hair out of my face. He seemed hurt that I hadn't come back to his apartment. *Our* apartment.

"I'm sorry. Your apartment is so big and it's always cold. And it was farther away and I was crying."

"Why were you crying?"

"It doesn't matter."

"Penny, no more secrets. Just tell me."

I put my hand under my head to prop myself up. "It's harder than I thought it would be. I don't know if I can do it James."

"Tell me what happened today."

"It wasn't just one thing. It was everything. It was awful."

"Tell me." He put his hand on my cheek. "Please tell me."

"On my way to class I got a text from Professor Nolan telling me not to come to class. And that the investigation went south or something. He said Mr. Vespelli would be calling me with details."

"Well, it's good he told you not to come. I'm sure everyone had a lot of questions. You didn't need to be there for that."

"Yeah. And I ran into Tyler. He took me to breakfast."

James made a face.

"Stop. As friends. He was being nice. He knew I was upset."

"Okay. I'm glad that he was there for you. You could have come home though. I want to be the one that's there for you."

"You are that person. That's why I asked you to come."

He pushed another strand of hair out of my face.

"And at breakfast I talked to Mr. Vespelli. He told me that there were now three girls who accused you of..."

"I know. I talked to him too. Penny, if that's why you're upset, we've talked about this. You know me. You know how I feel about you."

"It did upset me. How could it not upset me? But I know it isn't true. And it was more upsetting that Mr. Vespelli was just going to give up the investigation. I don't understand why they don't want to find the truth. They're going to put it in the paper, James. They're going to tell everyone, and then people will think it's true even though it's not."

"Penny, I want them to stop the investigation. It's fine. It'll make the news vans go away."

"But those girls lied. Clearly they just wanted to get As. Mr. Vespelli even said that they all had bad grades in your classes. It's ridiculous."

"It's fine. The sooner it's over, the sooner things will go back to normal. Isn't that what you want?"

"I'm not sure anything will ever go back to normal."

He sighed. "I know. I told you to take the rest of the semester off. You can switch schools, Penny. You can pick up where you left off somewhere new in the spring. It's okay. We can go wherever you want."

"That isn't why I don't think things can go back to normal. At breakfast, Tyler warned me that it was going to be bad. Apparently everyone loves you. Which makes sense. You're very loveable."

He lowered his eyebrows slightly.

"Everyone's mad at me. I was hiding in the bathroom before Psych and I overheard these girls talking. People are upset that your classes are canceled. And it's because of me. Because I'm a slut and a whore. I ruined your career. I ruined your life."

"You saved me. Penny, I was drowning. Don't you see that? I'm not a professor. I was never meant to be a professor. It was an escape from my life back in New York. It was just like everything else I've ever done. It was just another escape."

"But you loved teaching. You were a great professor."

"I didn't love teaching. The only thing I think I've ever truly loved is you."

"I don't want to hold you back from..."

"Stop. Please stop. I don't understand why you won't accept what I'm telling you. You're all I want. You're all I care about."

"I just feel so selfish."

He rubbed my tears away with his thumb. "You're it for me. I don't know how else I can tell you." He ran the tip of his nose down the length of mine.

It comforted me whenever he did that.

"If you're going to keep going to class, you need to ignore what other people say. Because I don't like seeing you cry."

"That wasn't it. That wasn't what made me cry. It just got worse from there."

It looked like he was in pain. He didn't like when I was hurting. But I needed to tell him everything that happened. He was right, there couldn't be any more secrets between us. Not now, when we needed each other more than ever.

"I got to Psych late because I was upset about what I heard in the bathroom. The professor called me out and asked me to talk to her after class. No one wanted me to sit with them. Luckily Tyler had called one of his frat brothers who had saved me a seat."

James didn't look upset when I mentioned Tyler this time. "I'll have to thank him for that," he said calmly.

"After class I went to talk to the professor. She told me my grades were slipping. Which I already knew. But she implied that she thought I had been getting perks in my other classes because of our relationship."

James sighed.

"I told her I had gotten to class early, but had been hiding in the bathroom because I was trying to avoid hearing what everyone was saying about me. And she basically said that she wasn't sympathetic and wasn't friends with you, so that she would have no problem failing me."

"What is your professor's name?"

"I don't want you to talk to her. I feel like that will just make it worse."

"You know that I can find out without you telling me."

Of course he could. "Professor Thornton. But please don't talk to her. I'm going to get my grades back up. When you weren't talking to me I just fell apart. But I have the rest of the semester to fix it."

"Okay. I won't talk to her. Honestly, I don't even recognize her name. I don't think I've met her. There probably isn't anything I could do anyway. I don't know that many professors outside of the business school."

Professor McCarty. James would know him. I wasn't sure what he was going to do when I told him. But I had to tell him. I couldn't go back to that class. And I couldn't go to the dean. Professor McCarty had made that very clear.

"My intro to marketing class was the worst. It's what made me cry. I didn't expect anything like this to happen. I didn't expect any professors to even talk to me. And I was already upset about everything else. I got a paper back in that class. I got a C-. So when Professor McCarty mentioned an extra credit assignment, I wanted to do it. But apparently he had already explained it in the class I missed on Wednesday. And I hate raising my hand in class. It makes me all nervous and..."

"I know." James picked up my hand and kissed my palm. "You ramble when you're nervous too. It's incredibly cute." He kissed my palm again. He looked down at my hand. "It's okay. I want you to tell me." It was like he knew that I was about to tell him something bad. He already looked upset. Or maybe he was just upset that I was nervous to tell him anything.

"So, I waited till class was over and went up to ask him what the assignment was. He pulled out the paper that it was on and asked me to come behind his desk so he could explain it to me. I had never really talked to him before. I sit in the back row. I usually get As on all my papers and tests. I never had any reason to talk to him."

James was running his thumb up and down each of my fingers.

"He put his hand on my back when I went behind his desk. I didn't know what to do. I thought he was just being nice. I felt kind of frozen. I thanked him for the extra credit assignment and told him I had another class to get to. But he said he thought we might be able to work out some kind of arrangement that would be better. And he put his hand on my ass. And I didn't know what to do. I told him to stop. I eventually slapped him. But he grabbed my wrist. He said he had more connections than you at the university, so it would be more worth my time. I told him that I was going to report him to the dean. But he said that if I told Mr. Vespelli, he'd say I had come on to him. Somehow he knew I had two strikes. He knew I'd be expelled if I got in trouble again."

James dropped my hand and sat up. "Did you want to stay here or do you want me to drop you off at the apartment?" He got off the bed and began to tie his shoes.

"What are you doing?"

"I'm going to go pay your professor a visit."

"James, I don't want you to do anything to Professor McCarty. That wasn't why I told you about it. I need to know what to do. I can't go back to that class."

"He touched you." James stood up and stared down at me. He looked so angry. I had made him mad so many times. But not like this.

"And I slapped him."

James shook his head. "I'm going to kill him."

"James!"

"He shouldn't have touched you!" His voice was loud. People in the rooms next to mine could probably hear him.

"No, he shouldn't have. But that doesn't mean you should kill him! He didn't even know that we were dating. I just want you to help me switch classes. I just don't want to see him. And I don't want to be expelled. I don't want you to hurt him. The last thing I want is for you to do something that'll get you in more trouble. I just don't know what to do."

James looked down at my left hand. "Marry me."

"What?"

"Let's get married." He ran his hand through his hair. "And move somewhere where no one knows either one of us. We can start over together."

"James, you just told my parents a few days ago that you weren't ready to get married. You just got divorced. This isn't what you really want. You're just upset."

"I don't want anyone else to touch you ever again. I don't want anyone else to flirt with you. I want everyone to know that you're mine."

"I am yours."

"Then marry me. We can go to Vegas right now."

"James, I can't just marry you. I want my parents to be there. I want my friends to be there. And what about your family? I haven't even gotten to meet any of them yet. I want them to be there too."

"I don't want a big wedding. I've already done that."

"That's not what I said. I don't care about having a big wedding. I just want a few people besides us to be there."

"So that's a definite no?" He put his hands on my knees.

Did I just reject a proposal from Professor Hunter? I hadn't even meant to do it. I wanted to marry him. But not like this. Not when he was mad. "No. I want to marry you. Just not...today. This was hardly a romantic proposal, Professor Hunter."

He looked down at my left hand again and ran his thumb along my ring finger. "Romance, got it. Next time I ask, you'll definitely say yes." He smiled at me.

"If you hadn't said we should go to Vegas right now I probably would have said yes."

He pushed some of my hair behind my ear. "I wish I hadn't mentioned Vegas then." He smiled at me.

"Maybe we should just go somewhere that no one knows us, though." I wrapped my hands around the back of his neck. "I was prepared for other students being mean. I never expected my professors to..." I let my voice trail off.

"You won't be going back to his class. We can transfer you into a different one. Or you can withdraw from that too. I'll call Joe now."

"He's not going to let me do that. He's going to expel me."

"He's not going to expel you." James moved his hand to the side of my neck. "And if that creep wasn't on tenure, I'm sure I could get him fired."

"But are you sure you even want to stay here?"

"If this is where you want to be, then yes."

"Can you wait to call Joe? Maybe we can see how we feel on Monday?"

"Okay. Penny, I'm so sorry."

"You like to apologize when you've done nothing wrong."

He laughed. "I guess you're rubbing off on me."

His phone started buzzing in his pocket. He kissed my forehead before pulling his phone out of his pocket. "It's Rob. He's here early."

"We should probably go then."

"Are you sure you're okay? Are you sure we're okay? I thought you might be mad at me. I can't believe I gave them the fuel they needed for the investigation. I never even thought about them searching my office. I can't believe how careless I was."

"Wait, what? What are you talking about?"

He lowered his eyebrows slightly. "Joe didn't tell you?"

"Tell me what?" What is he talking about? What did the detectives find in his office? He didn't actually seduce those girls, did he?

"About the paper with the bad grade on it that I gave you? The one that you crumpled up and threw at me in my office. I kept it. It was in my desk. With the cute note you left me after we had sex."

"Oh." *Oh.* That's how the detectives knew what had happened between us. *Of course.* "Why did you keep that?"

"I just...I didn't want to forget. I thought it was just going to be a one time thing. And it killed me that it had to be a one time thing. I thought it was the only thing I could hold on to."

I looked up into his eyes. "That's so sweet."

"And stupid."

"No, it's sweet. Wait, didn't they need a search warrant to go into your office?"

"I would have thought so too. But the university gave them permission. My office at the school is technically their property."

"So that's how the detectives knew?"

"I think it was easy to figure out what happened after seeing those two pieces of paper. Especially since the white out on the paper with your grade on it wasn't even well done. And if they did a black light test..."

"That's embarrassing."

James laughed. "Yeah, it is. But it all makes sense now. I think I know what happened with the other girls too. "Did the detectives promise you anything if you cooperated with them?"

"Yes, they did. They said they could get my scholarship back."

"I think the detectives did something similar with the girls they interviewed. I think they told the girls they would get As in the class if they agreed with their story. I'm not sure if the detectives knew about the school's policy or not, or maybe they were just bluffing. But I think they pressured those girls into agreeing with the story that they told them. A story they inferred from your grade and the note you left in my office. All those girls had to do was say yes."

"That makes sense. The detectives told me what had happened with the other girls and were just trying to pressure me into agreeing it was the same way you seduced me. Those assholes. We have to tell the dean."

"I already told Joe that. He just wants this to disappear, Penny. And so do I. I don't want you to keep having days like this. I want it to get better, not worse."

"Are you sure we shouldn't..."

"I'm sure."

"I'm not mad at you for saving the note I left you. It's ridiculous that you think I'd be mad about that." I smiled up at him.

"So we're okay?"

"Yes." I kissed him and slid off my bed. "I love you so much, Professor Hunter." I let my hand run down his naked torso.

He smiled. "Try to remember to call me James in front of my brother, please." He lightly slapped my ass.

"I'll see what I can do. I'm so excited to meet him. Give me a second though, I'm sure I look like a hot mess."

"Just hot."

I laughed and walked over to the mirror on the wall. I quickly wiped away the smudge marks from my mascara and added some concealer under my eyes so they wouldn't look as puffy. "I'm kind of nervous."

"You don't have anything to be nervous about. He's going to love you." He wrapped his arms back around me. But his body felt stiff. He still seemed on edge.

"Are you sure you're okay?" I asked.

"I'm fine."

"James."

"I don't know what you want me to tell you. Of course I'm upset. I'm pissed. I won't feel better until I've punched him in the face."

"Please, please don't do that."

"Penny, he touched you."

"Can we please just focus on your brother visiting? Just forget about it for now. I don't want to think about it anymore. Let's just have a fun weekend."

"I'll try."

"Okay, come on, let's go. I want to meet him!"

James laughed.

"What's he like?"

He grabbed my hand and led me out of my dorm room. "He's...fun."

"You mean like funny?"

"No, I wouldn't say funny. He likes to have a good time. I invited him to stay with me when I didn't have you. He's good at distracting me." He looked down at me as we exited the building.

I laughed. I didn't want to think about when we weren't together. Just thinking about it made my chest hurt. "Is he like you at all?"

"Like me? He looks a little like me, I guess."

"Yeah, I've seen his picture. I mean, is he like you personality wise?"

James opened up the car door for me.

I quickly got in and watched him walk around the front of the car. He seemed to be pondering the question.

"No," he said as he climbed in and buckled his seatbelt. "He's not really like me at all. He's kind of the opposite of me."

"What do you mean?"

"He's not independent."

"What does that mean exactly?"

"He lives off my parents' money. He's never held a job for more than a few weeks." James pulled out of the parking lot.

"Oh. So is he close with your parents?"

"It's funny. I felt like I was the only one of my siblings who ever listened to them. And they like me the least."

"I'm sure that isn't true."

He didn't say anything.

"Do your parents know about me? Do they know about your divorce?"

"They know I filed for divorce. I told them about it before I did it. They tried to talk me out of it."

"And what about me?"

"I haven't talked to them since I left New York."

"They haven't tried to talk to you at all? That was almost a year ago."

He glanced at me for a second before turning his attention back to the road. "I didn't say that."

"So they have tried to talk to you? And you haven't taken their calls or something? James, maybe..."

"Penny. It's better this way."

I thought about the tickets he had given me to the Macy's Thanksgiving Day Parade. They hadn't really been tickets to meet his family. He had just said that I could meet them if I wanted to because I had asked.

"I'll have to meet them eventually."

"I know. How about you meet Rob first. Then you can decide if you want to meet the rest of my family."

"I think Rob sounds great. Does he know about me?"

"No, actually. He doesn't even know that my divorce is final."

"So he thinks that it's just going to be two single rich bachelors in a college town? He's going to hate me."

James laughed. "He's not going to hate you."

"He probably thinks you're going to go out every night and pick up girls."

"I'm sure he wishes that's what we would be doing. But he knows I wouldn't have done that whether I had a girlfriend or not."

"Why wouldn't you if you were single? Wasn't that kind of the point of inviting Rob to live with you in the first place? To get over me?"

"I don't go to bars and pick up women. I like to practice self-control, Penny."

Self-control. Was he referring to his addiction problem? I looked out the window. Maybe if he had sex with one college student that he picked up at a bar he wouldn't be able to stop until he had sex with all of them.

"So what made you give into temptation with me?"

"You. I've never been so instantly attracted to someone in my life. You're different than other girls I've met. You chose option two."

I laughed. "Our day in New York was perfect. I'll always choose option two."

"I know. And I couldn't seem to control myself around you." He glanced at me again. "Not because I'm addicted to you."

"I don't care if you're addicted to me, you know. I'm addicted to you."

He pulled to a stop at a light. "That's different, Penny."

"Is it that different?"

"When I'm low I feel like I can't breathe. Even when I indulge in whatever it is I'm addicted to. It's just an escape. But with you, I feel like I can finally breathe for the first time. You're not an escape. You're a new way of living that I didn't even know was possible." His Adam's apple rose and fell.

That was a fine line. A very fine line. When he wasn't talking to me I felt like I couldn't breathe. Maybe I was the one who had an addiction problem.

"Shit."

I turned my attention to the road. The reporters were blocking the entrance to the parking garage. I had dealt with enough today. This whole thing was ridiculous. They couldn't sit out here forever in their vans. This needed to end. I unbuckled my seatbelt.

"Penny, stay in the car."

I opened the door, ignoring him.

"Damn it, Penny!"

I slammed the car door. "What do you want to know? Why are you standing out here? Don't you have anything else to report on? This isn't news."

"Penny! How do you feel about the recent findings in the investigation?" One of the news reporters approached me, quickly followed by her cameraman. "Did you know that James was..."

"He wasn't. He hasn't done anything wrong. What is wrong with you people?"

James was beside me in a second. He grabbed my arm. "Penny, get in the car now."

"Is that how this started? Him telling you what to do? Did he force you..."

James put his hand in front of the video camera lens that was in our faces.

"Penny." His voice was stern.

"He didn't force me to do anything. Haven't any of you been in love? James is kind, and caring, and wonderful."

"He cheated on his wife in order to be with you."

"He didn't. Stop standing out here harassing us and go do your job. You're just spreading rumors. This isn't news!"

"We don't have any other comments at this time," James said and stepped in front of me.

Why was he being like this? Why wouldn't he stand up for himself? I climbed back into the car. Everyone else at this school was an asshole. Girls were lying to get As. The dean was just accepting crappy detectives' opinions in order to sweep this whole mess under the rug. And these reporters had chosen us to harass? This was ridiculous.

James slammed the door when he got back in the car and laid his hand down on the horn. The reporters didn't back away until he started to slowly move the car forward. He didn't say anything as he pulled into the parking garage.

But I could tell he was mad. His hands were gripping the steering wheel so tightly that his knuckles were turning white. He pulled into his parking spot and got out of the car. I had to chase him to the elevator doors that had already opened.

"James, I'm sorry. But this needs to stop. They can't stay out there forever."

He shook his head and hit a button on the elevator. The elevator came to an abrupt stop. "What the hell is wrong with you?"

"It doesn't make any sense that they're out there. They're being relentless."

"And you just made it worse. I specifically asked you not to talk to them."

"James. Doesn't it make you mad? Why won't you defend yourself?"

"I know you've had a bad day. But I'm trying very hard to remain calm right now. I need to know that you'll listen to me when I ask you not to do something."

"If you won't defend yourself, I'll defend you. Everyone at this school already hates me. I don't care anymore."

"What you just did is going to make it worse. Not better. That's going to be all over the news tonight."

"Good. I want everyone to know that you're not a bad person. It sucks walking around campus hearing people say bad things about me. But I can deal with that. What I can't handle is people saying bad things about you."

"And I can't stand that you have to hear bad things about you. I'm used to getting my way. I don't know how to fix this. I never expected this to happen." He leaned against one of the walls in the elevator.

"I know. You're used to being in control. And I'm infuriating." I shrugged.

He gave me an exasperated laugh. "I can't think straight when I'm with you. I'm so unbelievably mad at you right now. But all I want to do is fuck you in this elevator."

I swallowed hard. "I'm sorry."

"I'm sorry too." He looked down for a second and then back up at me. "If you think it will help, I'll talk to them. It might help around campus."

"Not if you're going to take all the blame."

He closed the distance between us in the elevator, pressing my back against the cold steel. "You really are infuriating." He leaned down and kissed me hard, sending shivers of desire through my whole body. I didn't like when he was mad at me. But I liked this. I liked that it made him want me in a different way.

My fingers slipped beneath the back of his hoodie and up his muscular back.

He grabbed my hands and pushed them against the side of the elevator. "There are cameras in here. And Rob is waiting for us upstairs. I had the front desk let him up."

"Okay."

"To be continued?" He ran the tip of his nose down the length of mine.

"I kind of wish Rob hadn't come early."

James laughed and let go of my hands. "Your face is flushed." He rubbed his hand along my cheek.

"No kidding."

He smiled. "Ready to meet my little brother?"

"Absolutely."

James hit the button that had made the elevator stop. I pressed my thighs together and leaned against the side of the elevator. Making me incredibly horny before meeting his brother was an odd choice. I took a deep breath. I needed to calm down. I had already been nervous to meet Rob. Now I was going to be more awkward than usual. The doors of the elevator slowly opened.

"Finally, man!"

I turned my head to see Rob in the kitchen. He was sitting in front of a pizza box at the counter. Rob looked a lot like James. He was slightly shorter and tanner. His jaw line wasn't quite as sharp and his hair was shaggy. And he dressed a lot differently. Way more like a college student. His jeans had holes in them and he was wearing a flannel shirt over his v-neck t-shirt. I had thought that Professor Hunter was a college student when I bumped into him. If I had met his brother in the same situation, I wouldn't have had a doubt in my mind.

He tossed a piece of crust back in the box and walked over to James. I thought they were going to hug, but instead Rob wrapped his arms around James and lifted him off the floor slightly. "It's so good to see you!" he said really loudly. It looked like it made James super uncomfortable. I couldn't help but laugh. Rob's good mood was contagious.

Rob set James back down on his feet and leaned close to James. "Dude, is this seriously Ellen? You didn't tell me she was super hot. Please tell me you're tapping that?"

I was sure he had meant to whisper that. He must have just been really bad at whispering. No one talked like that. I could feel my face turning even more red.

"No." James sounded mad. "That's not Ellen. That's..."

"Shit, are you serious? I get my own housekeeper? I should have come here ages ago." He patted James on the chest and walked over to me. "I'm Rob." He put his hand out for me to shake.

"Penny." *What the hell is happening?* I shook his hand.

"So tell me about yourself, Penny." He leaned against the counter and locked eyes with me. It was so strange. His eyes were so similar to James'. It was unnerving.

"For starters, I'm not a housekeeper."

His smile got even bigger and he looked over his shoulder at James. "You're the best brother ever.

"Jesus, stop talking, Rob." James walked over and wrapped his arm around my shoulders.

"So..." Rob looked back and forth between us. "You are fucking then?"

"No, Rob. Or, well, yes actually."

Oh my God! This seemed way worse than telling my parents about our relationship.

"This is my girlfriend." James squeezed my shoulder.

"Wait, what? What about the troll?"

"We're divorced."

"Seriously?! I didn't really think you had the balls to cut that cord."

James laughed.

I was pretty sure James and his brother had the strangest relationship ever. But I liked Rob for referring to Isabella as a troll. It helped redeem his inappropriateness. I was almost positive he thought I was a hooker that James had gotten for him.

"Okay, wow. So, we should probably start over," Rob said to me.

"Yeah." I laughed and stuck my hand back out to Rob. "Let's just pretend that didn't happen."

Rob laughed. "No, actually that's a great story. I can't wait to tell people I thought my brother's new girlfriend was a prostitute. And it's a compliment really. You're hot. I'm sure you get that all the time."

"Only recently."

James tightened his grip on my arm.

Rob laughed again. "She's funny. And young. You look really young. How old are you?"

"20."

Rob stared at me for a second and then looked back up at James. "Oh shit! Don't even say it. She's your student, isn't she? Oh my God, this is golden. The perfect son is fucking one of his students? I love it. Do Mom and Dad know?"

"Okay, we need to talk for a second." James let go of my shoulder and walked toward the living room, grabbing Rob's arm on the way.

"Does he get mad at you a lot too?" Rob yelled over his shoulder. "I bet that makes things exciting in bed."

"Shut up," James said.

That was the last thing I heard. I knew that James was embarrassed. But I liked Rob. He seemed so carefree. I thought he'd be a good influence on James. And James described him really well. Fun was the perfect word.

I sat down at the counter and picked up a slice of pizza. It was well past lunchtime now and I was starving. I had finished my slice by the time they walked back into the kitchen.

"Ugh, I have to share my pizza with her too? This is the worst." Rob laughed and sat down next to me. "Just kidding. Have all the pizza that you want. James caught me up on the whole illicit student professor affair thing. So apparently now I won't say anything that will embarrass him. And I'm sorry that I thought you were a prostitute."

"It's fine," I laughed.

"Thanks for helping get the troll back under her bridge. I owe you one. I tried to get rid of her for years. But I just made fun of her all the time. She was so stuck up. She always had the craziest reactions to stuff. If I had mistaken her for a hooker, I'm pretty sure she would have had a heart attack. I always thought I'd be the one to make her run screaming. I'm sure sucking her husband's cock made it easier for you to be victorious, though."

"What did we just talk about?" James said.

"Dude, chill. I'm sure Penny and I are on the same page here."

I started laughing. James was right. Rob was like the exact opposite of him. I wasn't even sure how two people so different could be related. But they were cute together. They balanced each other out somehow. I liked seeing James out of his element. If he couldn't control me, he definitely couldn't control Rob.

"See, she thinks I'm funny." He grabbed another slice of pizza. "So what do you two usually do on a Friday night?"

"Last Friday night we went to a Halloween party. And James ended up punching one of my friends in the face." I decided to leave off the fact that I had wound up in the hospital. It was a better story without it.

James pressed his lips together.

Rob laughed. "Sounds fun. I bet we could find a good Halloween party to go to tonight."

"Or we can stay in. Penny and I have been practicing what it would be like if we were under house arrest."

"That sounds awful. Did you say you were only 20, Penny?"

"Yeah."

"So a bar is out. Crashing a college party it is." He rubbed his hands together.

"I think it's probably best if I stay away from college parties for awhile," James said.

"Oh, because of the whole rapey thing?"

James made a face. "I need to go shower. Maybe you can give him a tour, Penny?"

"Sure."

"And stop saying inappropriate stuff to my girlfriend, Rob."

Rob shrugged. "I don't think I've even said anything that inappropriate."

James kissed my cheek. At the same time he shoved Rob's shoulder.

Rob laughed as James disappeared into the bedroom.

"He really likes you," Rob said, grabbing another slice of pizza and standing up.

"Why do you say that?" I knew how much James loved me. But I was curious why his brother thought he did.

"He only gets super defensive around girls he likes. And if you're wondering, he wasn't like that with the troll."

I laughed. "I don't understand why he ever went through with marrying her if he didn't love her."

"That's because you haven't met my parents yet. James is the prodigal son. And thank God he took the bullet, because they would have forced her on me next. I'm surprised they haven't called me already, saying that she's single." I must have made a face because he added, "I'm just kidding, they're not demonic. How about that tour, Penny?"

"Right." I quickly stood up. "Are you thirsty?" I walked over to the fridge and grabbed a cherry coke.

"No, I'm good."

I could feel him staring at me as I poured the soda into a glass and added the can into the recycling bin.

"Are you living here?"

I felt my face blushing again. "Um, yeah. Kind of. He just asked me to move in. But I haven't moved all my stuff in yet."

"So I guess that makes us roomies."

"I guess so. Have you already walked around?"

"No, not really. But this is the kitchen obviously. The living room and the dining room." He pointed to the rooms that were open to the kitchen.

"Mhm. And that's James' bedroom through that door."

"Well, you room together right? Or are we sharing?" He flashed me a smile.

"Oh, yeah, our room. And if I wasn't sleeping in there, we have two guest rooms. So we wouldn't ever have to share a room. In any situation." *What am I saying?* I wished James hadn't left me alone with his brother so soon. I was so nervous.

He started laughing. "You're fun to mess with. I like you already. Okay, show me my room."

I walked past him toward the hallway. *Could I be any more awkward?* "I guess you have your choice of rooms. There's this one." I opened up the first door in the hallway.

"That bed probably isn't big enough for both of us. I really like to spread out when I sleep."

"I'm not..."

He started laughing again. "I can see why James fell for you." He walked out of the bedroom.

"That's the guest bathroom."

"Sweet," he said and poked his head into the room for a second and then turned back to me.

"And the other bedroom." I pointed to the third door.

He opened it up and looked inside. "Damn, same sized bed. I guess we just weren't meant to be." He winked at me.

"I guess not." I still heard the shower running. *Come on, James.* I was running out of rooms to show Rob, and I wasn't sure what he was going to want to talk about next. "That's a game room I guess. It has a pool table and a bar."

"Now that's my kind of room." He opened up the door and started laughing.

I walked in after him. *Oh fuck.* James and my clothes were still strewn all over the room. I hadn't even thought about cleaning them up. My face had to be scarlet.

"I'm guessing this is yours?" Rob was holding up a lacy thong on his index finger.

Oh my God. "Of course it's mine." I grabbed my thong out of his hand.

"I didn't realize how kinky my brother was."

"He's not. We were just...doing laundry." *Doing laundry? What the hell?*

"Laundry?" He laughed. "Your clothes didn't make it. There's nothing to be embarrassed about. Kinky girls are the best. How about a drink, Penny?"

"I'm good." I was still holding my glass of cherry coke.

"At least let me add to that for you."

"I probably shouldn't."

"What, because you're 20? Trust me, James had his fair share of drinks before he was 21." He walked behind the bar and opened up the small fridge. He popped the top off a beer and took a sip. "Besides, you can't tell me that a hot college chick who fucks her professor and plays strip pool doesn't also drink?" He grabbed a bottle of vodka off the shelf. "You seem to like breaking the rules." He held up the bottle and raised his left eyebrow. Just like James always did when he was challenging me.

"You don't have much of a filter, do you?"

He laughed. "Give me your glass."

I walked over to him and put my glass down on the bar. He poured way more than a shot of vodka into it.

"Cheers," he said and lifted up his glass.

"Cheers." I knocked mine against his and took a sip. I could barely taste the soda.

"So is this going to get me in trouble?" he asked.

I laughed. "No, I don't think so. Sometimes it's hard to tell what will set James off though."

"Yeah, tell me about it. He actually seems more relaxed than I've seen him in a long time. You must be good in bed."

What the fuck? He really didn't have a filter. I couldn't tell whether he was flirting with me or just completely messing with me. I laughed awkwardly.

He looked over at the clothes all over the room again. "But seriously, please tell me you have some single friends. Preferably ones who are super kinky and blush as much as you."

"I'm not sure any of my friends could handle you."

"What? I'm a nice guy. I'm just messing with you because you're dating my brother. That's what little brothers do. Are you an only child or something?"

"Yes."

"Then I guess you wouldn't understand."

Was that really what little brothers did? That sounded awful. I had always wished for a sibling. Maybe I was better off without one. "I guess not. But I don't think little brothers are supposed to flirt with their older brother's girlfriends."

"I'm not flirting with you. Okay, sorry, maybe I was a little. But usually said girlfriends aren't closer to the little brother's age and super, super hot. I've been in Costa Rica for six months. It's been a long time since I've gotten laid by an American college student."

I rolled my eyes at him.

"How serious are you guys anyway?"

"He quit his job for me. He asked me to move in." *He asked me to marry him an hour ago.*

"Right, right. So back to your friends then..." He leaned on the bar. "Or if you have a twin or something. Oh fuck, now I'm going to have dreams about threesomes. You're killing me!"

"With me and James? That's pretty weird..."

He started laughing again. "No, I'm not into devil's threesomes. Especially with my brother. I meant with you and your twin."

"I don't have a twin."

"Ah, yeah, I guess you did say that you were an only child. Just my luck." He took a long sip of his beer. "What year are you anyway?"

"I'm a sophomore."

"A sophomore? So how did you and James happen exactly?"

"I thought you said he caught you up?"

"He said that you were his student. And that he quit to be with you. And that all those news vans are out there because the school thinks he slept with tons of other students too. But I doubt that's true. Cause look at you."

I laughed. I was pretty sure he was just messing with me. James was wrong; Rob was funny. Fun and funny. "We ran into each other before I realized he was my professor. He was going into the coffee shop and I was going out. We bumped into each other and I spilled coffee all over myself. So he let me borrow his sweater. It was really sweet. I never even thought I'd see him again. But then the next day I went to my 8 a.m. class and he walked in. I was completely shocked that he was my professor."

"Very cute. But I don't get it. How did you wind up together?"

"It progressed pretty slowly. We ran into each other late one night on Main Street after I had a bad time at this frat party. And he walked me home. He gave me his number, under the premise that he was concerned about me walking home alone at night." Talking about everything made me smile. I loved him so much. "We kind of flirted in class a lot. And what really set it off was that he gave me a bad grade when I thought I deserved an A. So I stormed into his office." I could feel myself blushing again. "The rest is history."

"So you fucked in his office?"

"Um, yeah." And it was incredibly hot.

"See...you're very kinky. I think I want to become a professor. I guess they have a vacancy now, huh?"

I laughed. "Professor's aren't supposed to do that. That's why James doesn't have a job anymore. You're better off just going to that Halloween party you mentioned if you want to hook up with a college girl."

He laughed. "Yeah, I'm just kidding anyway. I could not be a professor. Besides for the hot students, it sounds incredibly boring. I'm not sure what James was even doing here. I kind of thought he'd be here for a few months and then go back to New York. I get it now though."

I wondered how much Rob knew about James. Maybe he didn't even know about James' addiction problem. But he had known that James didn't love Isabella. Maybe they were closer than I originally thought. And James had asked him to live here for awhile.

"He didn't stay because of me. We only met at the beginning of this semester. I think he just needed a change from New York."

"Yeah, me too. But Costa Rica wasn't it for me either. I'm thinking a college town is right where I belong." He gave me his dazzling smile. "So, what kind of weird stuff is James into?"

"What?"

"You know. Give me something good so I can make fun of him when he gets out of the shower."

"He's not into anything weird." He just likes being in control and spanking me when I've done something bad. I bit my lip.

"You're totally lying. Come on, tell me. This is going to be hilarious."

I heard the shower turn off. "There isn't anything weird."

"Please, Penny. All we ever do is mess with each other. It's going to be funny, I promise."

I wanted to bond with him. "I don't know. Sometimes he spanks me."

A smile spread across Rob's face. "So that's what you're into? I'll spank you right now if you want."

I folded my arms across my chest. "You're kind of ridiculous."

"Thanks. You're kind of sexy. Nah, that's a lie. You're super sexy."

James walked into the room and looked down at the clothes on the ground. "Oops," he said and wrapped his arms around me.

I looked up at him and laughed. It almost seemed like he remembered that our clothes were all over the room. Had he made me give Rob the tour on purpose? I didn't understand sibling pranks at all. James smelled so good.

"Your girlfriend and I had lots of fun while you were in the shower," Rob said.

"What was so much fun?" James said.

"Well, let's see. All sorts of stuff. I think we really hit it off. Especially after I gave her a proper spanking. Oh, and here's your girlfriend's bra back." Rob pulled my bra out from behind the bar and tossed it at James.

Oh God.

James lowered his eyebrows. "I guess you decided to keep being inappropriate?"

"Absolutely. Besides, if I recall correctly, you've stolen a few girlfriends from me."

"That was a long time ago. And you weren't in love with them."

"Love? Really?" asked Rob. "I just assumed it was about the great sex. I thought that was all you really cared about?"

James' body seemed to stiffen slightly. "That was also a long time ago."

"So Penny's bad in bed? I find that very hard to believe."

James laughed. "No. I'd be lying if I said that wasn't part of the reason I fell in love with her."

"James." I lightly pushed on his chest. This conversation was so awkward. They were talking about me like I wasn't there.

"What, it's true." He put his lips to my ear. "You're also amazing on the pool table."

I could feel my face turning red again. "You guys are super immature."

"Said the hot 20 year old." Rob put down his empty beer bottle. "Okay, come on, James. I need to get laid before I steal your girlfriend."

"I'd really rather stay in."

"You're my wingman."

"You two should go. You'll have fun." I smiled up at James.

"Yeah, I don't know." He looked down at me. I knew he was concerned about me. Professor McCarty hitting on me. Me snapping at the reporters. It hadn't exactly been a good day.

"Really. Just don't be super sleazy like your brother."

"Hey! I'm not sleazy. Horny, yes. Sleazy, no. I'll take care of your boyfriend. I won't let him do anything stupid."

"See. You're in good hands." *Kind of.* I wasn't sure how much I trusted the hands of James' sleazy, horny younger brother. But James needed to blow off some steam. And if there was anything I was sure of, it was that Rob was fun.

"If you're sure you're okay."

"I'm fine. You got me that huge T.V. I think I'll be plenty entertained."

"Awesome. Let's go," Rob said and walked past us.

As soon as Rob was out of the room, James leaned down and kissed me. "I want to stay with you."

"Yeah, me too. But I think maybe a night out with Rob will be good for you."

"I'm sorry that he's so...well, inappropriate."

"I think he's great. I mean, yes, super inappropriate. But I think he's just trying to be funny. I hope. I don't know, I like him. He's nice."

"Nice isn't exactly the word I'd use for him."

I shrugged. "So you're all about sex, huh?"

He ran his hand through his hair. "No. I mean, I told you about my past."

"Does Rob know about everything? He won't let you go...overboard?"

"Yeah, he knows."

"So you're in good hands."

"I guess." James smiled down at me. "If he's ever bothering you, just let me know. He's all talk. He's harmless."

"He's fine. I'm getting used to taking care of myself."

James frowned.

"I just mean I'm getting thicker skin. I didn't mean because you aren't taking care of me."

"Okay." He tucked a loose strand of hair behind my ear. "Tomorrow I'd like to go shopping for some stuff that will make our apartment more comfortable. Whatever you want. I want you to feel at home here."

"That sounds perfect."

He leaned down and kissed me again. "Try not to fight with the press while I'm gone."

"I'll be on my best behavior."

"Me too. Text me if you need anything." He kissed me once more and pulled away from me.

"I will." I picked up my pants off the floor and folded them.

He smiled at me on his way out the door. I heard him and Rob laughing and then it was completely quiet. I wondered if they always acted that way with each other's girlfriends. I had expected James to get super angry with Rob. But he had just thought it was funny. It was so nice seeing him laugh. I grabbed the rest of our folded clothes and walked down the hallway.

After putting our clothes in the hamper, I went back out into the living room and sat down on the couch. James had finished mounting the T.V. on the wall. I turned it on and picked up one of the many remotes. It took me awhile to figure out how to use it, but I eventually got Shark Tank on. I loved watching Kevin O'Leary make fun of everyone. This was probably my top choice for a Friday night. Although I'd prefer to be snuggled up with James while I watched it. His apartment seemed eerily quiet despite the T.V. being on. I turned up the volume. I had never been alone here before. Maybe after we picked out a few things together I'd be more comfortable.

My phone buzzed in my pocket. I pulled it out. James had sent me a picture of him and Rob sitting at a bar. Rob was giving me the middle finger. Or maybe he was giving it to James. I laughed. It was the only picture I had of James. I touched the screen. He was so handsome. He'd probably have to beat off all the drunk girls at the bar with a stick. Hopefully Rob would just give the middle finger to everyone that came up to them.

I had an unread message from Tyler. I opened it up and smiled. "I hope your day was okay. I was thinking about you. Did you meet Eli?"

"Yes, Eli saved me from having to stand in the corner of the lecture hall. Thanks for telling him to save me a seat."

I was surprised to see my phone buzz right away. I guess since we were just friends now, there was no protocol about waiting a certain amount of time to text back.

"I'm glad I could help. What are you and Professor Hunter up to tonight?"

"He's out with his brother who's visiting from out of town. I'm watching Shark Tank."

"I'm watching too. I'm waiting for Kevin to start talking about his wine club."

"I know! I love when he does that." I glanced back up at the T.V. It was such good quality that I could almost see each of Kevin's pores. Little T.V.'s had their advantages.

"It's definitely the best part of the show. I'm DVRing it. I can pause it if you want to come over."

"That's very tempting. But I've had a pretty crappy day. I think I just want to stay in. Thanks, though." I could just imagine how James would react if he came back and I was gone.

"What happened?"

I looked up at the T.V. Maybe another perspective would be good. Tyler's first reaction probably wouldn't be to punch Professor McCarty in the face. But I didn't want to talk about it. I didn't want to think about how I felt frozen. His hand lingered on my ass for close to a minute before I got the courage to slap him. Just thinking about it made me feel sick to my stomach. "I'm just not sure I can do this anymore. I think maybe I should try to change schools. All of this just seems too hard."

My phone started ringing. I guess that wasn't a sufficient answer. "Hi, Tyler," I said, putting my phone to my ear.

"Penny, really, what happened?"

"It's nothing." I could hear my voice catch in my throat.

Tyler was silent.

"It was really stupid. I don't even know why I'm upset about it. My intro to marketing professor made a pass at me. He wanted to work out an arrangement for extra credit or something. I don't know. Like I said, it was dumb." I felt so weak. I wanted to be able to believe that it wasn't a big deal. But it was. I wished James would come home.

"Penny, that's not..." he sighed into the phone. "You should be upset. Shouldn't you tell the dean about this?" Tyler had said I should tell the dean about Professor Hunter. But this was different. He wasn't saying it out of spite this time.

"He said he'd say I came onto him if I tried to tell the dean about it. I got two strikes for what happened with James. I'll be expelled if I do anything else wrong." I wiped my eyes with the back of my hand. I felt so stupid.

"Have you told James?"

"Yeah. He said he thought he could fix it. But I don't know if I even want him to try. Today was harder than I thought it would be. Everyone's so mad at me."

"I'm not mad at you. And I'm sure everyone who wasn't doing well in James' classes loves you."

I laughed. "Yeah, Eli seemed happy about it."

"See."

I sighed and leaned my head against the back of the couch. "I just don't want to be here anymore."

Tyler was silent for a few seconds. "Where would you go?"

"I don't know. I think James wants to go back to New York. Maybe I can try to enroll in NYCU or something in the spring. I want to finish school. I just don't know if I can here."

"That would be kind of awesome if you went to New York. If I get that job I'm not going to know anyone when I move there after graduation."

"Yeah, it would be nice." I thought back on my pro con list I had made between James and Tyler. One of Tyler's cons had been that I didn't know where he'd end up after graduation. It was weird that we might end up in the same place after all. "Ah, Kevin's talking about his wine club!"

"Yes!"

We were both silent as we watched Kevin O'Leary go off on a weird rant about the Confrérie des Chevaliers du Tastevin.

"I'm pretty sure those people aren't going to get a deal now," I said.

"No way. So what's Professor Hunter's brother like?"

"Like the complete opposite of James. He's not reserved at all. He says the most inappropriate stuff. But he's really funny. It was nice having him here tonight. He kind of made me forget about everything going on. I think he makes James really happy."

"Well that's good. Professor Hunter always seemed very tightly wound in class."

"Yeah. So are you excited for the formal tomorrow? Are you still going with Natalie?"

"Mhm. It should be fun." He didn't sound convincing at all.

"Melissa is really excited about it."

"Isn't Melissa always really excited about everything?"

I laughed. "Fair enough." The show had just ended. I had been right, the couple hadn't gotten a deal. "I think I might head to bed early."

"Okay. I need to get back to going through possible interview questions anyway. I was just taking a break to watch Shark Tank."

"I never thought you'd be one to stay in on a Friday night studying and watching T.V."

"I really want this job."

"Well, you should be super prepared. I really hope you get it."

"Thanks, Penny. Text me if you want to toilet paper your pervy intro to marketing professor's house or something."

I laughed. "That's actually a really good idea. I'll think about it."

"Night, Penny."

"Night, Tyler." I hung up the phone and looked back up at the T.V. I wasn't sure if I'd actually be able to fall asleep. I flipped through the channels. There were tons of scary movies on because it was getting so close to Halloween. After several minutes of searching, I turned the T.V. off. I just wanted today to be over. And I missed James. It had only been a few hours since he had left. I wanted him to have a good time tonight. He needed this.

I wasn't sure when I had become a needy girlfriend. Maybe I always had been. We fought a lot. He had been right when he said I took up a lot of his time. No wonder he didn't have any hobbies. He had said that Rob wasn't independent. I wanted to be independent. I wanted to be able to take care of myself.

I climbed into Professor Hunter's bed. *Our bed.* I loved that the sheets smelled like him. I couldn't seem to help it. I wanted to be with him all the time. Especially right now. When I closed my eyes I kept picturing myself behind Professor McCarty's desk. Maybe I should toilet paper his house. Eventually I drifted off into a fitful sleep.

***

I sat up with a start. Something had awakened me. I reached my hand out, but James still wasn't in bed. It felt like my heart was beating out of my chest. I heard the noise again. Laughter. It was just James and Rob laughing. I looked at the alarm clock. It was almost 2 a.m. I sighed and laid back down. I yawned and closed my eyes. Scary movies always freaked me out, even though I had just seen clips as I was channel surfing.

The bedroom door squeaked open. I rolled over and looked at James as he walked into the room. I could just make out him taking off his shirt from the little bit of moonlight shining through the curtains into the bedroom. He stumbled to the side slightly and started laughing again. "Shit," he mumbled as he almost fell over. He tossed his shirt into the middle of the floor.

"Are you okay?" I climbed out of bed. I could smell the alcohol on him.

"Hey, baby." His voice was deep and soothing. His smile was electric. I don't think I had ever seen him like this before. He was drunk. He was really, really drunk.

"Do you want some help?" I didn't want him to fall over and hurt himself.

"God you're beautiful." He put his hand on the side of my face. "I missed you tonight."

"I missed you."

"You're really, really beautiful, Penny."

I smiled at him. "You've already said that." He was cute when he was drunk.

He laughed and then looked past me at the bed. "Oh, shit, did I wake you up? I thought I was being really quiet."

I laughed as I unhinged his belt for him and pulled it out of his belt loops. "You weren't being quiet at all. I heard you guys laughing. You scared me. I thought someone had broken in or something."

He started to laugh again. "No. No, no, it's just me. It's just me, baby." He was looking at me in that hungry way. "I'm glad you're awake, though."

I unbuttoned and unzipped his jeans for him. "You're drunk. You should probably get some sleep."

"I don't want to sleep. I missed you. I want you. I've been waiting to have you all day." He ran his hand through his hair.

How was he so sexy when he was drunk? No one was sexy when they were drunk. I pressed my thighs together. "It's the middle of the night."

"You told my brother that I like to spank you. But you didn't tell him how much you like it. How wet you get just thinking about it. You like getting punished. And if I recall, you were very, very bad today."

And just like that, I was awake, wanting him, needing him. I was just wearing one of his t-shirts and a pair of underwear. I pulled off the t-shirt. Without a word, I turned around and placed my hands on the mattress, arching my back.

His hands were on me in less than a second, pushing my underwear down my thighs. He spanked me hard.

Fuck. He was right. He was always right. *I love this.*

"That was for going to your dorm room instead of coming to me when you were upset."

He spanked me even harder. "And for talking to the reporters."

I wanted him so badly.

He spanked me again. "And for flirting with Rob."

"I wasn't flirting with Rob."

He spanked me again. "And for talking back." His fingers slipped between my thighs, pressing against me.

I moaned.

"You're so wet. I think you like this even more than I do. And trust me, I'm enjoying myself." He leaned forward slightly, pressing his erection against my ass.

I moved my legs even farther apart, waiting for him to enter me. I needed him. "Professor Hunter, please."

"Fuck, I love when you call me that." He spanked me even harder than before. "And that was for rejecting my proposal."

"I do want to marry you." Had I hurt his feelings by saying no? "Ask me again right now. I'll say yes. A thousand times yes."

I thought he was going to spank me again. Instead, he rubbed his hand gently across my sore ass cheek. "This is mine." His gentle touch made me shiver.

"Of course."

"You said no to me." His hand was still cupping my ass. "I don't like when you say no to me." He grabbed my hips and thrust himself deep inside of me.

Yes!

He groaned and dug his fingers into my hips. "I really don't like when you say no to me," he said again.

"I'm sorry."

He grabbed my hair and pulled my head back, making me arch my back even more. "God, you're so beautiful."

I laughed. "You're so drunk."

"Fuck, that feels good."

"What?"

"When you laugh." He reached around my waist and tickled my stomach.

I started laughing again. "James, stop. I can't breathe!"

He groaned softly and pulled out of me. "I think I just found my new favorite punishment."

"No, please don't tickle me." I laughed and climbed onto the bed.

His eyes were so playful. He climbed onto the bed after me. "I never realized how ticklish you were."

I squealed and tried to move away from his hands. But he easily grabbed my ankle, holding me down as he climbed on top of me. He grabbed my hands and held them above my head.

I liked when he overpowered me. I was even more aroused than I had been before. I could feel my heart racing. "Okay, you win. I surrender."

He smiled down at me. He let go of my hands and lifted up my hips, sinking himself deep inside of me again.

"Professor Hunter," I moaned. This is what made all the bad things worth it. The way he touched me. The way he held me. The way he looked at me. The way he made me feel. I loved the way he made me feel. Like he adored me. And cherished me.

He leaned over top of me and kissed me hard. I loved when he kissed me like that. It was like he hadn't gotten to kiss me in weeks, not hours. He didn't taste like he usually did. What had he said his favorite drink was? Scotch maybe. Maybe he tasted like that. I had never had scotch before.

He moved his hips faster. "You're so beautiful."

I laughed again.

"Fuck, Penny. It's like you're trying to tease me." He grabbed my hands again, holding them in place with just one of his. "Now you're going to get it." With his free hand he began to tickle me again.

I squirmed under his grip, laughing. It somehow made me more aware of his thick cock slamming in and out of me faster and faster. The feeling of being overpowered, and laughing, and him so deep inside of me made the familiar pull in my stomach happen even faster. "Professor Hunter!" I screamed as my orgasm crashed down on me.

He groaned as he found his own release, filling my stomach with that wonderful warm feeling. He collapsed on top of me. "Please tell me that you liked that as much as me. Your heart's beating so fast."

I laughed and ran my fingers through his hair. "That's because it's hard to breathe when you're tickling me."

"Hmm." He kissed my neck.

"It felt really good, though."

"Hmm." He kissed my neck again.

"You're funny when you're drunk."

"I'm not drunk," he mumbled into my neck. He laughed. "Maybe I'm a little drunk."

"You said I'm beautiful about a million times."

"That's because you are beautiful." He leaned down and kissed my clavicle. "You're beautiful and you won't marry me." He sighed and placed his head against my chest. "It's okay. I understand."

"You understand what? I told you the reason why I said no. I just didn't want to go to Vegas." I ran my fingers through his hair again.

"No. The real reasons." He yawned. "You don't need me."

"I always need you."

He sighed. "No. You don't need me. I can't even protect you. He touched you. I let that asshole touch you."

"James." I put my hands on either side of his face. "That wasn't your fault. You weren't even there. I do need you. You're all that I need."

He shook his head out of my hands and placed his head back down on my chest. "It's not just that. You don't love me."

What? "James, I do love you. I love you so much."

He yawned again. "No. No one loves me."

"James."

I was answered by light snoring.

"James." I didn't try to stop my tears from falling. How could he think that I didn't love him? How could he think that no one loved him? He was so sweet and thoughtful and perfect. Why did he feel like he wasn't worthy of love? If that was how he felt, then I wasn't a good girlfriend. I knew he was drunk. He didn't really know what he was saying. But wasn't that when people were usually the most honest? I didn't want him to feel broken.

But I kept doing things that made it seem like I didn't love him. I ran back to my dorm today instead of going to him. And I said no to his proposal. No wonder he thought I didn't love him. I wrapped my arms around him. He always made me feel safe. I wanted him to know I wasn't going anywhere. I wanted him to know that I loved him back. I wanted him to be able to trust me.

CHAPTER 31

Saturday

When I woke up I was sweating. James' arms were wrapped tightly around me. He always seemed so confident. I didn't realize how insecure he really was. In a lot of ways we were complete opposites. But I was insecure too. And he always gave me what I needed. I had to make sure I was giving him what he needed.

"Hey," I said softly, running my fingers through his hair.

He slowly opened his eyes. He lifted his head off my chest and looked down at me. "Hey."

"How are you feeling? You were really drunk last night."

He laughed. "I'm fine. Although I don't remember much about last night." He looked down at my naked body and smiled. "I remember that."

It was strange. He didn't seem hung over at all. Maybe alcoholics didn't get hangovers? But he wasn't really an alcoholic. He wasn't addicted to anything right now. Was he?

"Do you need some Advil or something?"

"No, I'm okay." He reached up toward my face.

"Oh my God, James." I sat up and grabbed his hand. "Your hand is bleeding. Why are you bleeding?!"

"Oh, shit." He ran his hands down his face. "Fuck. I remember that too."

"What happened? James, you need to clean it. It's going to get infected or something." I grabbed his arm and pulled him toward the bathroom.

I opened up a drawer in his vanity and then another. "Do you have peroxide? Or Band-Aids or anything?" I pulled open another drawer.

"No. Penny, I'm fine. Really, it doesn't even hurt." He put his hand on my shoulder. He was smiling at me in the mirror.

"This isn't funny. We were just in the hospital. I don't want to go back. Is Ellen here? Maybe she has something?"

"She doesn't work on the weekends. Penny, it's fine. See?" He moved his hand into a fist and winced.

"Jesus, James." I turned on the water and grabbed the bar of soap. I put his hand underneath the faucet.

He gave a sharp exhale and turned away from me in the mirror.

It didn't seem like it was still bleeding. There was just tons of dried blood on the back of his hand. And it looked like he might be missing a layer of skin on his knuckles. I gently washed away the blood. I turned off the water and patted his hand with one of his fluffy hand towels. He still wasn't looking at me. He was acting guilty. Really, really guilty. I had a sinking feeling in my stomach.

"James, what did you do?"

"Thank you. I'm sorry, I didn't know I was bleeding."

"James."

He looked down at his hand and then back at me. "I wanted to fix it."

I swallowed hard. "Fix what?"

"He touched you. That asshole touched you."

"You didn't. James, you promised me that you wouldn't hurt him."

"I didn't promise you that I wouldn't hurt him. I told you exactly what I was going to do. I said I was going to punch him in the face. And that's what I did."

"You said you were going to call Joe. This wasn't the way to fix it."

"He shouldn't have touched you."

"He's probably going to the dean right now. Or calling the cops on you."

"Trust me, he's not."

"What does that mean? Can he not move or something?"

James laughed. "No. I just made it very clear that I'd visit him again."

"You threatened him?"

"You don't understand."

"Obviously. Because there was another way to handle this. So you're right, I don't understand why you got drunk and beat up another professor. Why would you do that?"

"Because I couldn't be there to protect you! Do you have any idea how that makes me feel?"

"Yes. Because you never let me protect you."

He ran his hands over his face. "That's different."

"It's not different. And I've never beat someone up because of it."

He leaned against the sink. "I did what I needed to do. He's a freaking pervert. He deserved it."

"And that's how people see you. Because you won't defend yourself. And you won't let me try to protect you. I don't want people to see you like that. I want everyone to know how wonderful you are."

"But I'm not wonderful. I'm used to people saying bad things about me. I can handle it."

"You are wonderful." I put my hands on both sides of his face. "You're so wonderful. And smart, and funny, and sexy, and perfect. Even when you get in fist fights you have good intentions."

"I didn't have good intentions. I wanted to kill him."

"You can't convince me that you're a bad person. I don't know why you keep trying to do that. I love you."

"I'm not going to apologize for what I did. I'm still mad." He looked down at his hand.

"If you're mad about what's going on, then maybe you should do something else about it."

"What else can I do?"

I just stared at him.

"What? Talk to the press? Penny, that really would just make it worse."

"Yes. Please. Please tell the real story."

"Joe's going to be mad."

"I don't care. I don't want to go here anymore anyway."

"You don't?"

"No. I want to take the rest of the semester off. And try to enroll somewhere else in the spring. I want that fresh start you talked about."

"You'd give up going here to be with me?"

"Yes. All that I care about is being with you." I needed him to know that he had become the most important thing to me. I adored and cherished him too. "I love you, James Hunter."

He was staring at me so intently. For the first time ever, it seemed like he might actually believe me.

"I love you with everything that I am."

He grabbed my waist and kissed me. "I love you." He lifted me up onto the sink. "And it's rather convenient that you're already naked."

I laughed as he pressed his lips against mine again.

***

"Good morning," I said as James and I emerged from our bedroom.

"Well, you two look like you're in a good mood," Rob said as he opened up the fridge door. "Must be all the sex." His head disappeared behind the fridge door.

I looked up at James. "Could he hear us?" I whispered.

James put his lips next to my ear. "He might have been able to hear you. You're unbelievably responsive."

I pushed on his chest.

"I'm just kidding," James whispered. "I'm sure he couldn't hear us."

"Do either of you want some scrambled eggs?" Rob asked. "I assume you're both hungry after your double header."

"I would love some, but only because it's breakfast time and I have a normal person's hunger," I said and sat down at the kitchen counter.

Rob laughed. "Don't be shy now. You know, for such a nice place, the walls are kind of thin. Don't you think, Professor Hunter?"

"Shit," James mumbled.

"You don't have to be embarrassed. Penny already told me all about how kinky she is. I would have been surprised if she wasn't screaming Professor Hunter all night and morning."

"Please stop talking," James said.

"Besides," Rob continued. "We had to go on that top secret mission last night so I didn't end up getting laid. It was nice to have something to jerk off to."

I could feel myself gaping at him. He couldn't possibly be serious.

"Damn it, Rob, we've talked about this. Stop saying stuff like that around Penny. I don't want to have to kick you out."

Rob cracked an egg. "It's fine. Penny and I are cool."

"Actually, we're not cool," I said. "Because James told me all about your secret mission. And you told me that you wouldn't let him do anything stupid. Punching a professor in the face *is* something stupid. What is wrong with you?"

"I tried to stop him."

"Not well enough."

"He's bigger than me." Rob shrugged and cracked another egg.

"You two must have been a disaster together growing up," I said.

"No, only me really. James is the perfect one. I'm a terrible influence on him." He pushed the eggs around the pan with a spatula.

"That's kind of what it seems like."

"Geez, you sound like my mom. What, you think I wanted to go kick some guy's ass last night? That was not how I saw last night going at all. That was all him." He pointed at James.

I couldn't help but laugh. This must have been how they behaved growing up. Blaming each other for everything. It was actually kind of adorable.

"So what are we doing today?" Rob asked. "Is there someone else we need to beat up?"

"Penny and I are going shopping. We need to pick up a few things for the apartment." James sat down next to me at the counter.

"I don't mind third wheeling." Rob put some of the scrambled eggs on plates and handed them out.

"Thanks, Rob, these look great," I said and took a bite. I wasn't sure why James still wanted to go shopping. I had just told him that I wanted to move.

"Actually, if it's alright, I was hoping to do something with just Penny. We'll only be gone for a few hours."

"Fine. I have some stuff I need to do too anyway."

"You do? What are you going to do? Nothing illegal I hope?" I asked.

"Very funny, Penny. No, I ordered an Xbox from this place down the street. I need to go get it and set it up."

"I can't even remember the last time I played videogames," James said.

"I know. It's going to be so much fun crushing you. I call dibs on James after your lunch date." He pointed his fork at me.

"I'm good at videogames," I said. "Maybe I can crush both of you."

Rob laughed. "I seriously doubt that."

"I played tons of N64 growing up. I can beat anyone at Mario Kart."

Rob laughed again. "Yeah, this isn't N64. Xbox is for grownups."

"I'm sure it's not that different."

"Well, I guess we'll see later. Game on, Penny. Oh, and Professor Hunter, could you please pick me up some condoms? Like a huge box? Like all the condoms they have in the store."

"Please don't call me that. And there's some in my nightstand. You can have them."

"I think the two of you are going to need those."

"Yeah, we don't use them."

Geez. Is nothing personal between these two?

"Fuck, I hate you. I hate both of you so much."

James laughed and grabbed my hand, pulling me toward the elevator.

CHAPTER 32

Saturday

"What about something like this?" James stopped next to a huge painting of the beach. There was a boardwalk that overlooked the sand and water.

"It reminds me of Rehoboth." I leaned my head against his shoulder.

"Me too. It's kind of perfect, right?" He wrapped his arm around my back.

"That's the day I fell in love with you, you know."

He kissed my temple. "You barely knew me."

"I knew enough."

He turned back to the painting. "Let's get it."

"I thought you liked the idea of moving? Why are we buying stuff for a place we might leave?"

"We can bring it with us. Where do you think you want to go?"

"I don't know. Aren't you happiest in New York?"

"I'm happiest when I'm with you." He kissed my temple again.

I smiled up at him. "Maybe I should apply to some places and see if I can get in anywhere before we choose. I'm not sure how easy it's going to be. You said people might not think my grades are valid."

"You can get in wherever you want."

"What do you mean by that?'

"I'm more than willing to make a hefty donation to any university that you choose."

I laughed. "I don't want you to do that."

"How do you think I got Joe to change your incomplete to a withdrawal?"

"James. You're exasperating. I didn't ask you to do that. And now I'm going to drop out. That was a terrible investment."

"Eh. Maybe they'll name a lecture hall after me or something. You know, when things die down."

"I kind of doubt that."

"Then choose your next university wisely so I don't have to keep wasting money. Besides, I've always wanted a building named after me."

I laughed and looked back up at the painting. "I want you to decide where we go. I'm indecisive. You're better at making decisions than me."

"I'd rather make that decision together." He squeezed my shoulder. "Until then, I definitely want this painting. You like it, right?"

"Yeah, I do."

"Okay. I'll be right back." He walked over to the art gallery manager.

I turned back to the painting. It was really fun picking out stuff together for our place. James and the manager walked back over.

The manager pulled the canvas off the wall. "Let me package it up for you. I'll be right back."

"James, could we maybe get the picture you sent me the other day printed out?"

"Of Rob giving you the middle finger? I'm sure we can get a better picture than that."

"It's the first picture you ever sent me of yourself. I like it. You look really happy. I even made it my background image." I handed him my phone. I had cropped Rob out of it so that it was zoomed up on James' face.

"You're incredibly cute." He handed me my phone back. "Can it at least be smaller than the painting we just got?"

I laughed. "Yeah, that's fine. Just like a normal sized picture would be great."

"Okay." He wrapped his arm around me again. "So what else do cozy places have?"

"James, I need to confess something."

His arm seemed to stiffen.

"It's not bad. I just..." my voice trailed off. "When I told you I went to my dorm room after I was upset because it was cozy, that wasn't the whole truth. I was embarrassed. When you described what your brother was like, you said he wasn't independent. You made it seem like that was a bad thing. And I don't want you to think of me that way. I wanted to prove to you that I could be strong and take care of myself. And I couldn't. I..."

"Penny, I want to take care of you." He kissed my forehead. "I want you to let me take care of you."

"I need you." I wanted him to know that. When he was drunk he had said that I didn't need him. I did. I needed him in every way.

He lowered his eyebrows slightly. I wasn't sure if he remembered confessing that he thought I didn't need him. But it seemed to effect him either way.

"Penny, I need you too. You shouldn't be embarrassed about that."

"I know. But I told you I could handle it. I just wanted you to think I was strong. And I was embarrassed about how wrong I was about everything. Everyone was so horrible. I just felt..."

"Hey." He cupped my chin in his hand. "I do think you're strong. I think you're perfect. You don't need to prove anything to me."

I smiled up at him.

"Does that mean my apartment is cozy enough already?"

I laughed. "It could be cozier."

"Mhm. So back to my original question. What else do we need?"

"A rug in the living room might be nice."

"Good thinking."

***

"What about L.A.?" James asked, as we pulled to a stop at an intersection.

"I think I want to stay on the east coast."

"Finally, now we're getting somewhere." He turned to me and smiled. "North or south?"

"North. I think I'd miss the snow."

"Me too." He put his foot on the gas when the light turned green. "But I don't want to go too far north. Tons of snow would be worse than no snow."

"You're probably right." I pulled my legs up onto my seat. New York seemed to be a good fit. Minus the fact that I preferred a back yard with grass and friendly neighbors. But central park had been beautiful. That whole day I had spent with him in New York had been wonderful. "If we moved to New York, where would we live?"

"If we moved to New York, I think I'd like you to give the city a try. Maybe an apartment in Manhattan?"

"Would that be weird? You know so many people in the city. I wouldn't know anyone at all. Tyler said he was going to interview for a position where he'd have to move there, but that wouldn't be until after he graduates. And he might not even get it."

James didn't even seem to react to me mentioning Tyler. Maybe he was starting to accept the fact that he was my friend.

"You'd know me. Penny, if we moved to New York, I'd still be hanging out with you all the time. I prefer spending my time with you."

I could tell that was where he wanted to be. "You said you left New York because you needed a change. If you went back, do you think you'd be unhappy again?" I couldn't help but think about his addiction problem. His brother had been here for less than 24 hours and James had already drank more than I had ever seen him drink. Maybe being around people he used to know wasn't what was best for him. But he had seemed so happy during our day trip to New York. It was his home.

"I'm not sure I could possibly be unhappy as long as I have you." He didn't turn to me and smile. He wasn't saying it to be flirtatious. He said it because he thought it was true. It was similar to what he had said to me after he hadn't spoken to me for weeks. That he couldn't possibly have a good life without me in it.

"I think we should go to New York then."

He laughed. "I thought you didn't like the city?"

"I liked it with you."

He put his hand on the center console and I quickly grabbed it. He ran his thumb across my knuckles. "Is that really what you want to do?"

"NYCU has a beautiful campus. And it's only a 15 minute subway ride from Manhattan."

He turned toward me and smiled. "You've been thinking about this for awhile?"

I shrugged. "I did a little research. And wouldn't it be easier to start a company there? With all your connections and stuff?"

"Connections and stuff?" He laughed. "I don't need investors. I can start it anywhere. I was starting it here. But yes, I probably would have had to go to New York every now and then."

"So let's just go permanently."

"Is that really what you want to do?"

"Yes." I squeezed his hand. I wanted to start my life with him.

"You're sure?"

"I'm positive."

He pulled to a stop outside his apartment building and leaned over and kissed me. "So how about we tell the reporters what really happened?"

They were already rushing over to his car.

"You don't care about making Joe mad?" I asked.

"Nope. I care about making you happy." He kissed me again before stepping out of the car.

I opened up the door to follow him.

"James! Are the allegations true? Have you seduced several students at the University of New Castle?" A woman's microphone was already waving in front of his face.

"No." He looked over at me and held out his hand.

I grabbed it and he pulled me beside him.

"Just Penny." He was talking to the reporter, but he was looking down at me.

"How did your affair start?"

"It isn't an affair. I filed for divorce last year. My ex-wife and I have been separated since then." James tucked a loose strand of hair behind my ear. We were in front of dozens of cameras, but it somehow seemed like we were alone. I loved how he made me feel like I was the only one that mattered.

"How long has this been going on?"

"We met right before classes started."

"You met outside of class?" The woman looked surprised.

I turned toward the reporter. "Yes, we met in a coffee shop. Actually, we didn't really meet so much as he bumped into me and spilled coffee all over my shirt. He was really sweet; he let me borrow his sweater so I wouldn't have to walk around campus with a big coffee stain down the front of me. I thought he was just another student. I was shocked when I went to class the next day and found out he was a professor."

The woman smiled at us.

Maybe we can win them over.

Another reporter stepped in beside her. "How many students did you have relationships with before Penny?" He was gruff and didn't seem touched at all by the story of how we met.

Maybe we can't win them over.

"None. Just Penny."

"And what about Blive Tech International? Did you make a habit of sleeping with your employees? Maybe your young interns?"

"No. All of my relationships at Blive Tech International were purely professional. I don't even think I ever met any of the interns."

"So what made you be unprofessional in your current position? What made you break the code of conduct at the University of New Castle?"

"We didn't break any rules. Student-professor relationships aren't mentioned in the handbook. Given the fact that we didn't do anything wrong, I think we've both suffered enough backlash. I'm appalled by how the university has handled this situation. And I'm greatly disturbed by how the entire campus has reacted. By harassing Penny and I instead of trying to find the truth."

"Of course there's been backlash. Because the university has found the truth. There's evidence that you've had sexual relationships with several students in addition to her."

"Which isn't true. I get it, okay? It's their word against mine. But every girl that came forward was failing or almost failing one of my classes. With their testimony, their classes were canceled and they got As. They must have known what would happen. I don't think their motive could be any more obvious. The university should be punishing them, not us. Or at least trying to get to the bottom of what happened instead of pretending lies are the truth."

"Three young, innocent women with no priors are definitely trusted over a rich bachelor who didn't even need this job. Why did you even start teaching here? Was it just so you could sleep with your students?"

"I was trying to give back to the community. And it's just one student. Just Penny. I had no idea when I accepted this job that I was going to fall in love."

"She's eight years younger than you."

"She's only seven years younger than me. You should really get your facts straight."

The reporter frowned.

"What made you pursue this relationship?" the first reporter said, pushing herself back in front of the surly one. "Even when you knew what might happen if people found out?"

"Something happened to me when I met Penny. Everything just...nothing was..." His voice trailed off. "What no one seems to understand is that we're just two normal people who fell in love. Yes, the circumstances weren't ideal. But what we have is. I don't really care what people say about me. Spread all the rumors that you want. All I care about is Penny. All I care about is what we have."

"If you aren't guilty then why did you resign?" the rude reporter asked.

"I resigned because the dean told me that I couldn't keep working here if I continued my relationship with Penny. That was never an option. Like you said, I don't need this job. But I do need her."

"Did he sexually harass you, Penny? Did he force..."

"No. Haven't you been listening at all? Absolutely not. He resigned so he could be with me. Because he loves me. James is sweet and thoughtful. He's smart and kind and charming. He's always been such a gentleman. He never forced me to do anything. I'm so in love with him. I don't understand why you're choosing to vilify him. And I agree with James completely. Make up whatever you want about us. We're not going to let you affect our relationship. We're not going to let all this toxicity hurt us. That's why I'm done here. I'm not going to finish school at a university that clearly doesn't want me."

"Are you moving? Are you transferring to a different school?" The nicer reporter asked.

"Look, you're all going to need to find a new hobby," James said. "Because we're not going to be here for much longer. We don't want to be associated with a community that is filled with hate. I expected more from the students around campus. And I definitely expected more from the other professors at this institution. Maybe that's a story you should be chasing. Penny and I are going to try our luck somewhere else."

"Where are you moving?"

"We don't have any more comments at this time." James pulled me back to the car and opened the door for me. He walked around the back of the car to avoid the reporters and climbed into the driver's side. "You were right. That was a good idea. It was nice to finally say something bad about this ridiculous university."

"Yeah. Fuck them."

James laughed. "You're right. Fuck them."

CHAPTER 33

Saturday

"Hey, guys!" Rob said as we stepped off the elevator. "Why won't you die?"

I looked over at him. He was sitting on the couch with a videogame controller in his hand. Sitting right next to him was Brendan. *God no. Why is Brendan in our apartment?* I just had the most relaxing day with James. This was surely going to set him off. *Why now?*

"Boom, suck it!" Brendan stood up and made a rude gesture toward Rob.

Rob threw his game controller at him. "Suck that."

Brendan caught it in one hand and looked over at me. "Hey, Penny." He was smirking at me.

"Hi, Brendan." Stop smirking at me.

James tightened his grip around my waist.

Damn it.

"Oh yeah, Penny, I ran into your friend in the elevator," Rob said. "If I had known he was so good at this game I never would have asked him to play, though."

"You're such a sore loser." Brendan tossed both controllers down on the couch and walked over to James and me. "Hey, man. We haven't officially met, but I've certainly heard a lot about you." He put his hand out for James. "I'm Brendan."

James let go of my waist and shook his hand. "I think I owe you a thank you for taking Penny to the hospital the other day."

"No problem."

"I'm glad to see you're still alive," Brendan said to me. "I've been waiting for your call all week." He leaned down and hugged me.

"Sorry," I said and patted his back awkwardly.

"Yeah, I'm thankful for what you did." James put his hand on Brendan's shoulder. "But I don't appreciate the fact that you made out with my girlfriend."

Brendan released me from his hug and laughed. "Oh. You know about that? Well, she wasn't exactly your girlfriend when that happened. Either time."

"Either time?" James said.

Rob laughed and ran over to us. "Seriously? You hooked up with Penny? This is just too good. Anyone want a beer?"

"What do you mean either time?" James asked.

"The second time doesn't really count I guess," Brendan said and leaned against the kitchen counter. "I kissed her, she didn't kiss me back."

"When?" James turned to me.

"In the hospital," I said. I had already told James about the first time I had kissed Brendan. I barely even remembered being in the hospital. But I remembered that now. Brendan was right. I didn't kiss him back. I had already decided to be with James.

"Don't get mad at her. I'm pretty sure she was doped up on morphine and she still pushed me off. Clearly she chose you. I didn't even get a thank you for sending her flowers. I'm not used to losing. I'll have a beer," he said to Rob.

"You got it." Rob slid a beer down the counter and Brendan picked it up.

"I do really appreciate the fact that you were there when Penny fainted," James said. "But I think it's probably best if we don't make it a habit to hang out here."

"Calm down, James. Brendan's cool. He even apologized for hooking up with your girlfriend. That's a quality guy," Rob said. "Besides, you can't blame him for trying. That's the risk of having a hot girlfriend."

"I'm not sure I'm completely comfortable having two guys here hitting on her," James said.

"I'm not hitting on Penny," Rob said. "She's the one that clearly wants me." He winked at me. "Was she a good kisser, Brendan? I bet she was a good kisser."

"A great kisser." Brendan smiled at me.

"I knew it," Rob said.

"Okay," I said. This was so ridiculous. "Will you all just stop? Stop talking about me like I'm not standing right here. James, Brendan's just a friend. I told you that. And actually, you should be thanking him because I talked to him that afternoon when I left your place confused. And he told me to choose you. He was actually really nice and helpful."

"That's true," Brendan said. "She told me you were a better lay than Tyler, so I told her she should choose you. I didn't even hit on her. Or wait. Maybe I did. I think I probably said that if she really wanted to know what a good lay was she should call me."

"I said stop talking. But yeah. See. He was just being a good friend. Despite that last part. And Rob," I said, turning to him. "I don't want to sleep with you. I'm in love with your brother. So please just stop saying super weird things to me. It's really inappropriate."

"I do like you," Rob said. "You're like a million times better than the troll. Feisty too. I like a girl that can stick up for herself."

"Oh my God. I asked you to stop."

Rob smiled at me. "Stopping." He pretended to lock his mouth and throw away the key. "And Brendan's not going to hit on Penny anymore either, right Brendan?"

I wasn't at all surprised that Rob had immediately started talking right after he had thrown away the key.

"Sure, I won't hit on her anymore," Brendan said. He took a sip of his beer.

"How about you two go hang out at Brendan's place?" James said.

"But I just set up the Xbox! Let's all play Golden Eye. We can shoot it out." Rob patted James' chest and walked back toward the living room. "Besides, Penny promised to school us."

"I doubt that," Brendan said and followed him back to the T.V.

"Of course Rob had to befriend Brendan," James whispered to me. "I don't like this at all. I want you all to myself."

I laughed. "James, they're just joking around. You do have me all to yourself."

"They're not joking around." He looked down at me and smiled. "Even three men flirting with you isn't enough to make you realize how beautiful you are."

He didn't seem as mad as I thought he would. Maybe he was finally understanding that all I wanted was him.

"You're the only man that makes me feel beautiful." I wrapped my arms around his neck.

"Hey, love birds! It's game time!" Rob called over to us.

James put his lips against my ear. "Let's take them down."

"Okay, partner." I reached down and squeezed his ass.

He laughed and grabbed my hand. "Rob is right. You are feisty. And all mine. I can't wait to move and have you all to myself again. There are so many things I'd rather be doing than playing videogames right now."

The way he was looking at me made me gulp.

He led me over to the couch and pulled me onto his lap as he sat down.

I laughed as he wrapped his arms around me.

"You guys can't seriously play like that. Come on, I need help killing Brendan." Rob handed us each a controller.

Instead of moving off of James' lap, I looked down at the controller. "Wait, why are there two joysticks?"

"This is going to be hilarious," Rob said and restarted the game.

"Wait, you have to tell me how to use this."

James kissed the side of my neck. "So, the right joystick lets you move your view up and down. And the left one lets you move your guy around."

"Why did they make it more complicated? Aren't advancements in technology supposed to make things better, not worse?"

James laughed and kissed my neck again.

After we selected our characters, the screen split into four quadrants. It took me awhile to even realize which one was me. Unfortunately, I was the one continuously running into a wall. "Crap, why is this so hard?" I slid off

James' lap and tried to focus. I was stupidly good at N64. I was a huge nerd growing up and I loved sitting on the couch after school playing videogames. And I even used to crush my boy neighbors in Golden Eye. But this wasn't anything like N64. I was currently running around in circles staring at my feet.

"Speaking of hard," Rob said. "Penny sitting on your lap got you a little excited there, James."

"What?" James looked down at his pants. "I don't have..."

Rob snuck up behind him in the game and shot him in the back of the head.

"Asshole." He shoved Rob's arm. "Game on. I'm going to kill you next."

"I have a better idea," said Brendan. "Let's see who can kill Penny first."

"No! Just give me a second to figure this out." I had just tilted my head back up when blood filled my screen.

"Gotcha!" Brendan said.

"Damn it, Brendan!"

He started laughing as my girl came back from the dead. Rob immediately shot me in the face and started laughing too.

"What is wrong with you guys? Just give me a minute to learn what to do."

James had started laughing with them.

"Hey." I nudged his shoulder.

"I thought you said you were good at videogames," he said and smiled down at me.

"I am good at videogames! I don't know what this crap is." My girl reappeared on the screen again. James' character was standing there holding a gun to my face.

"Don't you dare, James."

He immediately shot me.

"James! You're supposed to be on my team!" I started laughing too. I really was terrible at this.

"What?!" Rob yelled. "You're both supposed to be helping me kill Brendan!"

"I can't kill anyone, this game is impossible." I fired my gun at the floor.

"Maybe we should all play a different game?" Rob said. "I know you're fond of pool, Penny."

I could feel my face turning red.

"You're good at pool?" Brendan asked. "We could play that instead. It's too easy to beat everyone in this anyway." He shot Rob in the chest.

"Shit," Rob mumbled.

"No. Actually, I kind of suck at pool," I said. I had finally gotten my character to run in a straight line. I hid behind a column. Someone's character was approaching me from the other side of the column. I still wasn't sure what I was doing, but I was determined to kill whoever it was. And he didn't seem to realize he was walking into a trap.

"Yeah, I guess not," Rob said. "If you were I wouldn't have found your underwear all over the pool table. James clearly demolished you."

Brendan started laughing. "Strip pool? Now that's a fun game."

I tried to ignore them talking and focused on the character approaching my hiding spot in the game. As soon as he walked past me, I fired my gun. My first shot missed, but my second shot hit him in the side of the head. "Yes!" I screamed and stood up. "I just killed someone!"

"Shit, you just killed Brendan!" Rob said.

"Nice," James said. He held up his hand and I high-fived him.

"See, I am good at videogames!" I high-fived Rob too.

"Yeah, I kind of thought you were lying. But you just killed the master himself," Rob said. "Why *are* you so good at videogames, Penny?"

"I was a very nerdy youth." I sat back down on the couch.

James wrapped his arm around my back. "You're ridiculously cute."

"I never would have guessed you were a nerd growing up," Rob said. "That probably explains why you're so kinky now though."

"Rob, come on," James said.

"Oh. Was that inappropriate too? I thought that was just a nice compliment. I guess I don't know where the line is."

"Obviously," James replied.

"Let's play a different map. I'm demanding a rematch," Brendan said. "I refuse to accept the fact that I just got beat by a girl who's never touched an Xbox before."

"You're just mad because she's touching an Xbox instead of you," Rob said and switched to a snowy mountainside.

Brendan laughed. "Fair enough."

"I'm so sorry," James whispered in my ear.

"It's fine." I smiled up at him. I liked hanging out with the guys. I was already desensitized to Rob's comments. And James seemed to really be enjoying himself.

***

After several rounds of Golden Eye, Brendan stood up and stretched. "I think I've redeemed myself."

"Yeah, whatever," I mumbled. I had only gotten one kill since our first game. And I was pretty sure James had let me kill him on purpose because he felt bad.

"Yeah," Rob said. "Clearly Penny just got lucky before. I think I'm done playing for the night. Who wants to go out?"

"I think I'm going to stay in tonight," James said and yawned.

"Stop being lame." Rob stood up and stretched too.

"You can go," I said. "Melissa asked me if I'd come over and help her get ready for the Sigma Pi formal."

"Are you sure?" He rubbed his hand along the side of my neck.

"Yeah, go have fun."

"Actually, I do have a few things I need to get done," James said.

Rob laughed. "Crap, do we have to go beat someone else up? That was fun and all, but I have some other things in mind for tonight."

"No, nothing like that." He gave me a mischievous smile.

"Why are you smiling like that? I'm with Rob on this one. Please stop beating people up."

James laughed. "I'm not going to beat anyone up. Do you want me to drop you off at your dorm?" Rob and Brendan had already started walking toward the elevator.

"No, I think I'd like some fresh air after sitting on the couch all day."

"Okay." He tucked a loose strand of hair behind my ear.

"Try to pace yourself tonight." I couldn't help but be a little worried about him. It was my responsibility to look out for him now. And I didn't know enough about addiction to be able to really help. It made me a little nervous. The only knowledge I really had about addiction was how addicted I was to him. Rob didn't seem to have James' best interests in mind. I wanted James to be safe. At least there was a third person with him tonight that could help hold him back if he tried to assault Professor McCarty again.

"You don't need to worry about me." James winked at me.

"What on earth are you planning to do? Now I'm more worried than before."

"There's nothing to worry about tonight." He kissed my cheek and got up off the couch.

CHAPTER 34

Saturday

The leaves crunched under my feet. James had looked excited about something. And he said I didn't need to worry about him. So maybe he wasn't even planning on drinking at all. But I was worried.

Before I had left the apartment, I googled addiction. I wound up on a Wikipedia article about sexual addiction. It was all about how people couldn't control their sexual urges, thoughts, and behaviors. James had told me he couldn't stop thinking about me. He had given into his urges in his office because he thought that would make the urges go away. But it had just made him want me more. Like he couldn't quit me.

Now I was more worried than ever. There was such a fine line between addiction and what he considered love. And I was scared. I was scared that I wouldn't be able to help him if I was the one that was currently reinforcing his behavior.

I rolled my eyes at myself. I was being silly. It wasn't like I was a psychology expert. One Google search didn't mean anything. And we hadn't even covered anything about addiction in my Psych class. I knew how James felt about me because it was the same way I felt about him.

But no matter what I told myself, there was this small unsettling feeling I was holding onto. What if I moved to New York and he was addicted to me? He'd eventually move onto the next thing. Just like Isabella had said. And I wouldn't have anything else in New York. I wouldn't even know anyone else. I'd be completely alone in a city I didn't even like. But if he ever left me, I'd feel alone anyway. It didn't matter where I was. I knew what it was like to lose him. So if he was just addicted to me, I was doomed either way.

"Hey!" someone yelled behind me.

I'd recognize his voice anywhere. *Austin.* Hopefully he was trying to get someone else's attention. I picked up my pace.

"Hey, babe, wait up!"

My stomach already felt unsettled. And now it seemed to flip over. I turned around and saw Austin running up to me.

"I thought that was you," he said and stopped in front of me. "Damn, you look good. Dating a rich guy suits you."

Fuck you, Austin. I turned back around and started walking again.

"Don't be that way." He caught up to me and started walking beside me. "I'm just messing with you. Although, I didn't believe it at first. You're not really one to break the rules."

"Don't you have some girl with low self esteem to take advantage of?"

He laughed. "You're kind of putting yourself down with that comment."

"I'm not the girl you thought you knew." I felt different around Austin than I used to. He used to be able to talk me into doing anything with him. But now there were no butterflies. I finally saw him for what he was. Being with James had changed me for the better. He had made me more confident. I started walking faster. I just wanted Austin to leave me alone. This week had been bad enough. I didn't need to hear whatever he had to say.

"I know. The girl I dated never would thrown water in my face at a bar. A guy has to respect that kind of move."

"We never dated, Austin."

"Actually, we did. I just wasn't quite as committed to it as you were."

"Yeah, you don't have to tell me. I already knew that." *Why are you even talking to me right now? Go away.*

"The girl I dated also wouldn't have fucked her professor."

I stopped and turned to him. "What is your problem? Why do you always find the need to put me down? Does it make you feel good about yourself or something? You don't get to judge me anymore. We're not together."

"My opinion clearly still bothers you, though."

I glared at him. "Yes, it bothers me. Because I don't understand how someone could possibly be as immature and hateful as you. It bothers me that someone like you even exists." I started walking away.

"That's not why it bothers you. It bothers you because you still want me. You like what you can't have."

I laughed. "No, I love what I have." And I did. I loved James with every ounce of my being. Maybe it was good that I had run into Austin. It just reminded me that there was a lot I wanted to leave behind at the University of New Castle.

"Really? Because I'm pretty sure you loved me. Every time we hung out you spread your legs. You were never able to resist me."

"You're such an asshole."

"Come, on, babe. I'm having a party at my place tonight. You should come. Maybe we can pick up where we left off." He put his hand on my shoulder.

"Don't call me that." I pushed his hand away.

"You used to like when I called you babe."

"Yeah, that was before I met James. Why are you even talking to me? I'm pretty sure last time we talked, I made it very clear that I wanted nothing to do with you. So no, I'm not coming to your stupid party. Please just leave me alone."

"You should be thanking me, you know."

"Why on earth would I ever thank you?"

"For taking your v-card. For showing you how to fuck. Without me, you never would have landed your professor. Men don't like sweet, innocent girls. And you were as sweet and innocent as they come."

I stopped again. "You know what? You're right. I do need to thank you."

A smiled spread over his face.

"For being a stepping stone toward happiness." I poked him in the middle of his chest. "Because of you, I ran into James in that coffee shop the morning before classes started." I poked him again. "Because of you, I realized I was sick of dating immature assholes." I poked him once more. "And because of you, I was able to fall head over heels for a guy who's actually nice to me."

He stared at me. "Nice to you? He just likes to sleep with students. The guy is a total creep."

"He only slept with me. It makes sense that you're one of the many idiots that believes any rumor you hear. He loves me. And I love him. Something which you'll never experience because you're the creep."

He laughed. "I've missed this. We've always had such playful banter. If I remember correctly, our fights always transitioned into super hot makeup sex."

"You're disgusting. I don't know what I ever saw in you. And you know what? You're awful in bed. And your penis is tiny." *God that felt good to say.*

He frowned for a second but then laughed. "That's not what the other girls that I was fucking while we were together said."

I started walking away again.

"Hey, the party is the other way. Where are you going?"

"Wouldn't you like to know?" This time he didn't follow me. I couldn't wait to move to New York.

***

"Are you okay?" Melissa said as soon as I came into the room.

"Yeah, I'm fine."

"Penny, you don't look fine. You actually look really upset. What did James do this time?"

"What? Nothing. James has been fantastic. I ran into Austin on the way here." I kicked off my shoes and jumped onto my bed.

"Oh. Awkward."

"Yeah. I kind of just stopped thinking about him after that night at the bar. It was almost like he didn't exist. I liked it better that way."

Melissa laughed. "So what did he do tonight?"

"He was joking around about me sleeping with my professor. I don't know. He was being Austin. He was trying to get me to sleep with him again."

"That does sound like Austin. His name is basically synonymous with asshole."

"Yeah." I sighed. "It was kind of fun telling him off. I told him he had a tiny penis." I smiled to myself.

"Go you. Attacking the only thing he has to offer."

"Well it's the truth."

Melissa laughed. "So, you're okay?"

"Yeah. I'm good. It's just been a really bad week." I propped one of my pillows against the wall and leaned back on it. "I'm just so sick of all the rumors spreading around." I didn't want to talk to her about that right now. I wanted to help her get ready for the formal. "That dress looks amazing on you, Melissa."

"Are you sure it's not too revealing?" she asked and looked at her reflection in the mirror. She turned to the side to examine the deep V in the back.

"I don't think I've ever heard you ask that question before."

Melissa sighed. "I know. Why am I so nervous about tonight? It's silly. I'm kind of used to going to these things with you though."

"You'll be fine. You went to that luau thing by yourself and had a blast."

Melissa sat down on the edge of my bed. "I know. But it's not as fun without you there. Oh, I forgot to ask! What is James' brother like?"

"He's...a handful."

Melissa laughed. "Are they alike at all?"

"They have a lot of the same features. But they're very different personality wise. James is always so reserved. But Rob just says whatever comes into his head and is really open and friendly."

"So, he's super sexy too?"

I laughed. "He's good looking, yes."

"Where are they tonight?"

"I don't really know. James said they had some things to do or something. He was kind of secretive about it."

"Weird. What do you think he's doing?"

"I have no idea."

"Maybe it's something romantic."

"I don't know why he would have taken Rob and Brendan with him instead of me then."

"Wait, Brendan, Brendan? The guy you made out with while you were stalking James? Why are they hanging out? That's so awkward."

"Yeah. Rob befriended him. I thought it would be weird. But the three of them seem to get along really well."

"I think I want to start hanging out at your new place more often," Melissa said. "It's like an eligible bachelor sausage fest." She got off my bed and began to do her makeup.

I laughed. "Actually, I kind of wanted to talk to you about that."

"That sounds ominous. Are you actually here to just get the rest of your stuff?" She smiled at me.

"No. That's not it. It's just been a lot harder than I thought around campus."

"Yeah, I know." She paused in her mascara application "There are a lot of rumors going around. Whenever I hear someone say anything, I always defend you. I've started to hate girls in general."

I laughed. "Me too. But it's more than that. It's my professors too. They...well they're...it's just really hard." I didn't need anyone else beating up Professor McCarty.

"I'm sorry, Penny. I did kind of warn you that would happen though."

"I know." Melissa loved being right. But she wasn't going to like what I told her next. "But it's just too much. I think I'm going to take the rest of the semester off."

"What? But the semester's halfway over already. Last time we talked you said you were going to finish. You even said you'd finish Comm, which I thought was crazy. Lucky for you, you just get an automatic A for shagging the professor."

I laughed. "I didn't get an A. I had to withdraw from Comm."

"I thought everyone was getting an A in James' classes?"

"Everyone except for me. It was my fault too."

"Sorry, Penny. That really sucks. But you can take it again next semester. There's no reason to drop all your classes. That's insane. Why would you want to just retake all the same things next semester?"

"I'm actually not sure I want to take classes here next semester either."

Melissa put down her eyeliner. "What are you talking about?"

"I can't handle all of this..."

"Penny, you can't just drop out of college. You don't want to be a college drop out! You don't want to be one of those girls who finds her dream guy and just forgets how to have her own life. You're being ridiculous. This isn't the sixties."

"I'm not going to drop out of college. I'm just going to transfer to a different one."

Melissa looked even more upset. "You can't leave."

"I'm thinking about going to NYCU. It's only two and a half hours away. We can still visit each other all the time."

"You're moving to New York? Penny, I'm sorry, I can't just say nothing about this. You barely even know James. You can't just up and move because he wants to."

"It was my idea."

"But why? Just because a few people are saying stupid stuff? Who cares. Just ignore them. You shouldn't run away and hide from your problems."

"It's not just a few people. It's everyone. The whole campus hates me."

"That's not true. I'm sure the people who weren't doing well in James' classes love you."

"I can't go to class anymore. I just can't do it."

"Why? I don't understand. Austin made you feel like shit for months and you handled that. These people don't even know you. I know you're stronger than that. If James is pressuring you to move then..."

"It's not James, okay?! My intro to marketing professor hit on me."

"What?"

"He basically said he'd give me an A if I had sex with him. He grabbed my ass."

"So we'll get him fired. He's the one that shouldn't be allowed to come to campus anymore, not you. Have you told the dean?"

"No. My professor said if I told the dean he'd say I was the one that came onto him. Melissa, I don't want to have to deal with stuff like this for two more years. James and I need a fresh start. We need to go somewhere where people don't see us a student and a professor."

"It'll blow over. I'll report your professor myself. We can figure this out."

"I need this, Melissa. It's what I want to do."

"But I don't want you to move." She ran over to my bed and hugged me. "What am I supposed to do without you?"

"I told you, we can still hang out all the time. Every weekend if you want. And you have Josh."

"But he's graduating next semester. I don't want to be here all alone for two years. You're the only friend I've really made. You're right, everyone else here sucks." Melissa laughed. Her phone started buzzing and she released me from her hug. "You made me smudge my makeup." She lightly pushed my shoulder and grabbed her phone off the dresser. "It's James." She looked back at me.

"My James?" I looked down at my phone. I didn't have any missed calls or texts from him.

"What other James do I know? Does he know you were telling me that he's stealing you away? Is he calling to convince me that I shouldn't be mad at him?"

"I have no idea why he's calling you."

"Should I answer it?"

"Umm...yes." Why is he calling Melissa? Is something wrong?

Melissa put her cell phone to her ear. "I heard you were kidnapping my best friend and taking her to New York."

Silence.

"No, that's not how she worded it." Melissa smiled at me.

Silence.

"Yeah, she's right next to me."

Silence.

"Yeah, I guess. Hold on one sec." Melissa pulled the phone away from her ear and put her hand over the speaker. "He says he needs to talk to me in private."

"Why?" I asked.

"I don't know. He said it was important. I'm going to go out in the hall."

"Wait, what's going on?"

"I don't know." Melissa left the room, closing the door behind her.

I tapped my knee impatiently. What were they possibly talking about? It was a long time before Melissa came back into the room. She didn't say anything. She just walked to the mirror and began to finish doing her makeup.

"What was he calling about?"

"We talked about a lot of things."

"Why are you torturing me? We both know that you're going to tell me. Just spit it out."

"We actually had a very nice talk. He's starting to wear me down."

"So he just called you to chat?"

"Kind of. He told me he punched your professor in the face. Several times."

"I'm not thrilled that he did that."

"It's kind of sweet though. He was defending you. He's like your knight in shining armor. With a violent side."

"He just wanted to talk to you about my creepy professor?"

"No, not really." Melissa frowned and then turned to me. "I think you're right. Maybe a fresh start would be good. I think James really does love you. Moving seems fast and crazy, but your whole relationship has been fast and crazy."

"So you're okay with me moving?"

"I mean, I'm upset that you're abandoning me. But I want you to be happy. And after my conversation with James, I think that maybe I've been too hard on him."

"You think?"

Melissa laughed. "I've just been looking out for you. You know that. You tend to like guys that are terrible for you."

"Just Austin."

"James counts in that list too. Dating a professor wasn't exactly in your best interest. Especially when there was a super nice guy who clearly adored you. With nice abs and a great personality."

"How is Tyler doing?"

"He wanders around the frat house like a sad puppy."

I looked down at my lap.

"I'm kidding, he's fine. I've even seen him make out with that Natalie girl he hangs out with. Like I told you before, he's a big boy, he'll be okay. Besides, he definitely needs to move on now since you're fleeing to New York with James."

"But I still don't get it. Seriously, why did James call you?"

"Because we're friends. Geez, not everything is about you. Stop being conceited. I thought you wanted us to get along."

"I do." She was definitely hiding something from me. "Do you know where he was?"

"He didn't say. You said he was with Rob and Brendan though, right?" Melissa suddenly looked worried. And it worried me that she looked worried.

"Yeah. Why?"

"I don't know." She turned away from me.

"Melissa, you're scaring me. What's going on?"

"I don't know. It was kind of weird. At first we were having a really nice conversation. But after a few minutes it didn't really seem like he had a reason for calling. He didn't really have anything to say in particular. And I was trying to avoid the subject because I didn't want to worry you. But he didn't sound like himself, Penny. It seemed like maybe he had too much to drink or something? He seemed off. Like maybe he had just drunk dialed me or something?"

I had a sinking feeling in my stomach. He told me he wasn't going to drink too much. He told me I didn't have to worry.

"Does he do that a lot?" Melissa asked.

"What? No." I tried to clear away my nagging thoughts. "Was there lots of music? Maybe he was at a bar or something?"

"No, I just heard a few people. Maybe it was Rob and Brendan? If they're with him, I'm sure he's fine. I'm sorry, I don't know why I said anything. I'm just being silly. Just pretend I didn't say anything."

"Do you think I should call him? Maybe he needs me to pick him up or something?"

"I'm sure he's fine. I really don't know him that well. Maybe I'm just misreading the situation. And you don't want to be that girl."

"What girl?"

"You know...*that* girl. The one that nags her boyfriend all the time. You have to trust him."

"Yeah, you're right. I do trust him. I'm sure he's fine." But I wasn't sure. I didn't want him to do something stupid again tonight. I was surprised that Professor McCarty hadn't gone to the cops. Next time James might not be so lucky.

"Speaking of the time, I need to get going."

"I didn't mention the time."

"I know, but I really am going to be late. Are you sure this is okay?" she asked, gesturing to her dress. "It's formal enough?"

"Very formal yet very sexy. It's classy. You look absolutely beautiful."

Melissa gave me a big hug. "Seriously, don't worry about James. I'm sorry I even said anything."

"Okay."

She laughed and released me from her hug. "I'm really bummed that you're not coming tonight. But you look kind of tired. Maybe you should just call it a night and go to sleep early?"

"Okay, now you're just being mean."

She laughed. "I just meant so you don't have to worry all night. I'm sure James is fine."

"Mhm."

"Bye!" she said and blew me a kiss as she left me alone in the dorm room.

I immediately pulled out my phone and called James. I didn't care if I was *that* girl. If he was drunk wandering the streets I needed to go pick him up before he did something stupid.

"Hey, hot stuff."

"Umm...James?" Geez, he really was hammered.

I heard laughter on the other end of the phone.

"James?"

"No, it's Rob. Do we sound the same on the phone?"

"Yes, you do."

"Damn it! I should have convinced you to have phone sex or something. Can we rewind a couple seconds? Hey, Penny, it's Professor Hunter."

"Gross. Rob, can you please put your brother on the phone?"

"Sorry, love, can't do that."

"And why is that?"

"You're going to be mad at me."

"What are you guys doing?"

"We ran a few errands and then I finally convinced my tightly wound brother to go to a bar. But, we both know how he is..."

"Can you please just bring him home?"

"In a bit."

"Rob, I'm serious. Bring him home right now."

"Don't be such a party pooper, Penny. We're having fun! If he's too drunk to fuck you when we get home, I'll be happy to stand in. Don't you worry."

"Stop being gross. Just bring him home safely, okay?"

"You have my word, sugar tits."

"You're drunk too, aren't you?"

"Mhm."

"You're impossible."

"You're impossible!"

"And you're seriously not going to let me talk to James?"

"Professor Hunter is currently unavailable. Please leave a message at the beep." Rob made a farting noise and the line went dead.

CHAPTER 35

Sunday

"Penny."

I immediately opened my eyes. James face was a few inches away from mine. "You're okay?" I reached my hand out and ran it along the scruff on his jaw line. "Thank God you're okay." *Ow.* I had fallen asleep on the couch waiting for him and my back ached.

"Of course I'm okay." He had a huge smile on his face.

I looked down and saw that he was on one knee by the side of the couch. *Oh my God. Oh my God!* I sat up.

"Penny, I love you so much."

He's proposing! My heart was beating out of my chest. I hadn't missed my chance. He was asking me again.

"Why are you looking at me like that? Oh, you thought..." He laughed. "No." He laughed again. "I just dropped my cell phone." He picked it up off the ground and stood up. "I said it would be romantic. This is hardly romantic."

"Oh, no, I didn't think you were proposing." I had thought he was proposing. For a brief moment when I was talking to Melissa last night I had come to that conclusion. I thought he may have called Melissa to ask her for my ring size or something. But then it seemed like he was just out getting drunk. I had been so worried about him. But when I woke up and saw him on one knee I thought maybe he really was just planning on proposing. I could feel my face turning red. I was so embarrassed.

"I was going to go get breakfast. I just wanted to see if there was something in particular that you wanted."

"I was worried about you."

"I know, I'm sorry. I should have called."

"And you shouldn't have let Rob answer your phone."

"Things got a little out of hand last night." He tucked a loose strand of hair behind my ear. "I'm sorry that I worried you, Penny."

I didn't want to fight with him. I was just glad that he was home safe. Maybe we could talk more about it later. I wasn't sure if him going out with Rob every night was a good idea. I wanted for him to be happy. But not if he was putting himself in danger. "What time is it?"

"7:30."

I was still tired. But I wanted to hang out with him. Now that his brother was living with us, we didn't seem to have nearly as much time together. "Can I come with you?"

"If you want."

I yawned and got up off the couch. "Just give me a minute." I quickly got ready and met him in the kitchen.

He wrapped his arms around me. "I missed you last night."

"I missed you too. What did you guys end up doing?" I already knew the answer. He got completely wasted.

"We went all over the place. Thanks for convincing me to go out. It's a lot of fun hanging out with Rob. And Brendan's actually alright."

"Why do you never seem like you're hung over?"

"I have a high tolerance to alcohol."

I bit my lip. I had convinced him to go out. So I couldn't be upset with him for having a good time. It wasn't fair that I had been worried when I was the one who kept telling him it was okay. I had thought he was going on another weird secret mission. But he wasn't acting mysterious at all this morning. He just seemed like his normal, perfect self. Whatever it was that he had done last night must have been normal after all. Just a bar and too much alcohol. I had a tendency to read too much into things. "When did you get home last night? I never heard you come in."

He grabbed my hand and led me over to the elevator. "I only just got in. Which is why I so badly need some coffee."

"Or some sleep?"

"We got a hotel in New York. I'm not that tired. I just need some caffeine." He smiled at me.

"Wait, you went to New York? Why?"

"I had some secret stuff to do."

I laughed. "Yeah, I got that." I looked up at him. "I like you when you're like this."

"Like what?"

"Playful. I think that maybe Rob is a good influence on you."

"I've always thought he was a bad influence on me."

"Well, in a lot of ways he is. He drinks too much and he says awful stuff. Really, you do drink too much when you're with him."

"It won't happen again." He rubbed his thumb against my palm. The way he was looking at me made it easy to believe him.

"But you're happy when he's here. So in that way, he's the best possible influence." I looked down at the floor for a second and then back up at him. "Are you sure you want to move? Rob just got here and I don't want to make you leave if..."

"Penny. I was just thinking that I can't wait to move." He smiled at me. He held my hand as we stepped off the elevator and led me toward the side exit of the parking garage. "And actually, I wanted to talk to you about that. The reason I went to New York was to talk to the dean at NYCU."

"About what?"

He rubbed his thumb against my palm again. "About you, of course."

"But I didn't even apply yet."

"I know. But I told her all about what happened. She seemed sympathetic. And impressed with your transcript. If you still want to go, you're in."

"Really?"

"Really. So, what do you say?"

I hadn't even realized that we were walking hand in hand on Main Street. There was no one around. It was the weekend before Halloween and it wasn't even 8 a.m. on a Sunday. No one would be up for hours. This is what I wanted. I wanted for us to be able to be us. That was only going to happen super early on the weekends if we stayed here. But New York was different. In New York we could be whatever we wanted to be. It was our fresh start. And I wanted that with him.

"Did you bribe her with lots of money?"

He laughed. "I didn't need to."

"So you didn't donate any money to the school?"

"I didn't say that either." He gave me an innocent smile.

"You're infuriating."

"No, that's you." He squeezed my hand. "So, what do you say?"

"I say we should start packing."

"I was hoping that would be your answer. Maybe we can go back up in the next few days to look at apartments? Something cozy of course."

"That sounds perfect."

"I guess there's just one last thing I need to do here." James stopped outside the coffee shop where we had first met.

"What, get a cup of coffee?"

He smiled at me and walked into the coffee shop, holding the door open for me.

When I walked in, I froze. There were rose petals all over the floor and there had to be at least a hundred candles. The whole shop was empty except for us.

"Penny." He grabbed my hand again.

I turned around and he was on one knee. *Oh my God.*

"This wasn't just where I first met you. This is where I fell in love with you. You took my breath away when you bumped into me. It was something that I've never experienced before. I've never been so attracted to someone in my life. It's very distracting when you blush."

His words made me blush even more.

He looked down for a second and then back up with me. "You made me realize that I hadn't been living. Really living. Because life without this feeling, the feeling that you give me, isn't a life that I'm interested in at all. You chose me even though I told you I wasn't good for you. You've always seen the good in me, which was something that I couldn't see in myself. You made me realize that it doesn't matter who I was before. It's about who I've become. Because of you."

"Yes."

He smiled up at me. "I have more to say."

"If you're asking me to marry you, the answer is yes."

He laughed and kissed each of my knuckles. "I'm yours, Penny. I've always been yours. I love you with all that I am. And I don't want to go another day without knowing that you're mine. Not just for today and tomorrow and the next. I want you by my side forever and always. Penny Taylor, you are the love of my life." He let go of my hand and pulled out a small box from his pocket. "You asked me if I was a believer in fate. I am now. I don't know how I ended up as a professor in Delaware. But I know why I did. Because you were here. And my life would always be meaningless if I had never met you. Because without you, I'm not whole. Penny." He grabbed my hand again. "Will you marry me?"

"Yes." I threw my arms around him.

He laughed and pulled me down into his arms.

"James, I love you so much." I put my hands on both sides of his face and kissed him. This is what I had wanted to do the morning we first met. But everything we had been through, all the ups and downs, had led us to this moment. And this moment was perfect. I wouldn't have wanted to change a thing even if I could.

"Don't you want to see your ring?"

"How did you do all this?" I turned and looked at the candles and rose petals. "How did you know no one would be here this morning?"

"It's closed today."

"I've been here on Sundays before."

"It's closed today because I bought it and I closed it." He smiled at me.

"You bought it?"

"I don't want anything to ever change about this place. I want to be able to come back here when we're old and gray and talk about how this is where we first met." He put his hand on the side of my face. "This place changed my life."

"So last night...you weren't out drinking?"

"No. I didn't even have one drink."

"But Melissa said..."

"What I told her to say. I knew you'd be totally consumed thinking that I was out getting wasted and never suspect that I was planning to propose. I told her to say she thought I was drunk if you started to get suspicious. Which I guess you did."

"You're such a jerk." Even as I said it I was smiling. He knew me so well. He actually realized how much I cared about him. And I was so relieved. He finally realized how much I loved him. I felt closer to him than ever.

"I am sorry that I worried you. That wasn't my intention. I just really wanted to surprise you."

"You did surprise me. But wait, Rob was definitely drunk when I talked to him last night, though."

"No. Rob is great at pretending to be drunk. I had to make it seem like the story Melissa fed you was true. And Rob was definitely up to the challenge."

I laughed. "So you went to New York last night and got me into a new school. And bought a coffee shop. You've been busy." I couldn't stop smiling.

"And I went and talked to your parents."

"You did?"

"I wanted your father's blessing."

"Did you get it?"

He smiled at me. "Yes, I did. Although I still would have proposed without it."

"I love you so much."

"I also bought you a ring. Don't you want to see it?" He was still holding the box in his hand. I had attacked him before he had gotten a chance to show it to me.

"Yes."

He opened up the box.

"James." It was the most beautiful ring I had ever seen. The diamond was huge, but it didn't look tacky. It was classy and elegant. And perfect.

"Do you like it?"

"It's beautiful."

He took the ring out of the box, grabbed my hand, and slid it onto my ring finger. "Now you're mine."

"I've always been yours." I looked back down at my hand. *I'm engaged to my professor.* I smiled up at him. "So why did you call Melissa?"

"I wanted her help deciding what kind of ring you might like. And I wanted to run the proposal by her. She knows you best."

"You know me best."

He flashed me the smile that had made me fall in love with him in the first place. "I'm excited to introduce you to everyone as my fiancée." He ran the tip of his nose down the length of mine.

"I'm excited to introduce you to everyone as my fiancé."

"Hmm." He kissed the side of my neck and placed his lips next to my ear. "I still prefer when you call me Professor Hunter."

"You'll always be Professor Hunter to me."

PROFESSOR HUNTER

Want to know what Professor Hunter was thinking when he first met Penny?

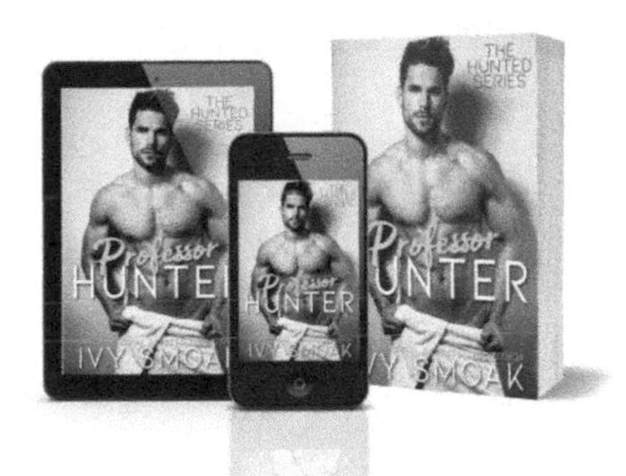

Find out in *Professor Hunter - Temptation* from James' point-of-view!

To get your free copy of *Professor Hunter*, go to:

www.ivysmoak.com/addiction-pb

WHAT'S NEXT?

Will James and Penny make it to the altar?

Find out in book 3 of the The Hunted Series, *Eruption*...available now!

A NOTE FROM IVY

Whenever I hear the word addiction, I think of the lyrics "I'm a dick, I'm addicted to you," from Addicted by Simple Plan. Probably because that song makes me smile. And if I let myself truly think about addiction my smile goes away. I've been a bystander to addiction. No, I haven't experienced the problem myself. But that doesn't mean I haven't suffered.

This is a problem that is close to my heart. But I don't want to talk about the negatives. I like to think that I'm a positive person and I like to believe that I know how to live in the present. James is strong. And my wish is that everyone with addiction problems can have his strength.

Penny and James will always hold a special piece of my heart. They are the reason I started writing. I had a story to tell, and I came alive with these characters. They changed me. They made me better. And I hope they keep me strong.

Ivy Smoak

Ivy Smoak
Wilmington, DE
www.ivysmoak.com

ABOUT THE AUTHOR

Ivy Smoak is the international bestselling author of *The Hunted Series*. Her books have sold over 1 million copies worldwide, and her latest release, *Empire High Betrayal*, hit #4 in the entire Kindle store.

When she's not writing, you can find Ivy binge watching too many TV shows, taking long walks, playing outside, and generally refusing to act like an adult. She lives with her husband in Delaware.

Facebook: IvySmoakAuthor
Instagram: @IvySmoakAuthor
Goodreads: IvySmoak

Recommend *Addiction* for your next book club!

Book club questions available at:
www.ivysmoak.com/bookclub

Lightning Source UK Ltd.
Milton Keynes UK
UKHW010743260422
402079UK00003B/491

9 781942 381310